THE DO

"ENTHRALLING!"
> —*West Coast Review of Books*

Lavender Gilbert—Iowa's sensitive dreamer, New York's hottest model. With her sensuous face on the cover of every major magazine, she suddenly had more work than she could stand. The only thing that made the day bearable was cocaine—breakfast, lunch and dinner . . .

Cat Powers—A raven-haired, sapphire-eyed beauty; an inspired performer on film—and in bed. For thirty years she had toyed with excess. Now she was getting serious . . .

"RICH, RAUNCHY, AND A RIPPING GOOD READ—I LOVED IT!"
> —Kitty Kelley, author of *His Way: The Unauthorized Biography of Frank Sinatra*

Roger Cooper—The devastatingly handsome doctor moved women's hearts while his hands healed their bodies. He wanted badly to be a family man, but his obsession with his work had already scared off two fiancées . . .

Jackie Lyell—Her husband Adrian was Roger's partner. When Adrian mysteriously left town, Jackie stepped into his administrative duties. She was poised, classy, a woman who could handle anything. But close contact with Roger turned her world upside-down . . .

THE DOLL HOSPITAL

PETER MENEGAS

ST. MARTIN'S PRESS/NEW YORK

All the characters in this novel are fictitious, and any similarity to people living or dead is purely coincidental. Tanglewood and the town of Stonebridge are products of my imagination, but medical treatments described in the following pages are based on research from a wide range of detoxification programs, rehabilitation clinics, and self-help groups. I cannot, however, assume responsibility for results and I urge no one to attempt any cures described without seeking proper medical assistance. Likewise, I do not condone or encourage the misuse of drink and drugs, and I disclaim all responsibility for any damages whatsoever argued to be a result of actions described in the following pages.

—P.M.

THE DOLL HOSPITAL

Copyright © 1986, 1988 by Peter Menegas.

Library of Congress Catalog Card Number: 87-28531

ISBN: 0-312-91529-2   Can. ISBN: 0-312-91530-6

Printed in the United States of America

St. Martin's Press hardcover edition published 1988
First St. Martin's Press mass market edition/June 1989

10 9 8 7 6 5 4 3 2 1

I wish to thank Tony McCord for the help he gave me throughout the writing of *The Doll Hospital*, for his suggestions in the early stages of development, for the hours spent—and miles covered—gathering information and pursuing interviews, for a keen editorial eye on the many stages of the manuscript. Because of those valuable contributions and, of course, because of his friendship, I dedicate to him the book we so guardedly referred to in progress as *The DH*.

No drug, no morphine or cocaine and no vice in the world gets such a hold as work and success.

Vicki Baum, *Grand Hotel*

THE DOLL HOSPITAL

PROLOGUE

NEW YORK CITY—SUNDAY

NEW YORK CITY'S BALMY OCTOBER TEMPERA-
TURES ADDED TO THE SUNDAY AFTERNOON
traffic snarl in Times Square. Yellow taxicabs and NYPD
squad cars sat gridlocked with drivers from Brooklyn and
Queens and New Jersey out for a leisurely visit to Manhattan. The bumper-to-bumper crush was aggravated by zig-
zagging cyclists, weaving rollerskaters plugged into
headphones, runners getting into shape for next weekend's
marathon.

A sleek black limousine inched its way down Broadway
in the honking congestion. At a green light on West 46th
Street, the chauffeur aggressively nosed the long car through
the flow of pedestrians and accelerated toward a small doorway marked STAGE DOOR on the south side of the shabby
one-way street.

Two men flanked a woman in the limousine's rear seat.
The older, more conservatively dressed man spied a group
of photographers lingering on the steps of the stage entrance. Lowering the glass partition between the front and
rear seats, he told the chauffeur, "Jim, don't stop here. Keep
right on going and swing round to the front of the theater."

The chauffeur gunned the engine and sped eastward toward the Avenue of the Americas.

As the limousine raced down the empty side street, the
woman turned on the seat, muttering at the photographers
through the tinted rear window "Dirty . . . *vultures!*"

The conservatively dressed man eased her back. "Easy, babe. They're only doing their job."

"Bullshit." She retreated into her hooded sable coat. "They want to see if this morning's critics drew blood from me."

"You're okay," he insisted, wrapping an arm protectively around her shoulders. "You're not going to let a couple of bad reviews get you down."

The second man pronounced, "Critics are all cunts."

The woman lowered her head against the first man's shoulder, saying plaintively "I can't go on stage tonight, Tommy. I can't do it."

"Sure you can," assured Tom Hudson, the heavily-jowled president of Red Tag Food Stores.

Gene Stone, M.D., the second man, was younger, more casually dressed. "You feeling your doll medicine yet, sugar?" he asked.

Tom Hudson frowned at the mention of the "doll medicine" that Stone had administered to the woman a short while ago at the Sherry Netherland Hotel. Hudson was engaged to marry her and disapproved of her drug dependency—and of her needle-happy personal physician from Los Angeles.

The woman did not answer the doctor's question. Her mind was chasing an obsession fueled by the injection of Demerol and Valium thinly laced with Methedrine. Looking at her secretary seated in front with the chauffeur, she fumbled to lower the glass partition, mumbling to nobody in particular "I've got to talk to Linda. I've got to tell Linda I'm not doing tonight's show. Linda's got to prepare an announcement—"

Hudson grabbed her wrist, gently insisting "You're doing your show tonight."

"I can't." She turned to him, the lenses of her dark glasses looking like two frozen black pools inside the sable hood.

"Do the show for me." Hudson pulled her against his chest to calm her hysterics. "Do it for us." He spoke more like a father than the man soon to marry her. "Remember? Isn't that why we left the hotel early? To give you plenty of time to get ready for tonight's show?"

Her lower lip trembled. In another abrupt mood swing, her voice quavering, she asked, "Why'd the papers make fun of me, Tommy? Why's everybody laughing at me?"

"You're laughing, too . . ." Stone quipped from her other side. "All the way to the bank."

The limousine crossed the Avenue of the Americas, turned south onto Fifth Avenue, took another right onto West 45th Street, and sped west to catch the green light at the Avenue of the Americas again, heading toward the theater marquees concentrated around Broadway and the backup of traffic feeding into Times Square.

As they crossed the avenue, Tom Hudson spotted activity in front of the Hunt Theater on the north side of West 45th Street; a crowd was gathering around a television crew assembling lights and cameras on the sidewalk. Above them, the marquee announced: CATHARINE POWERS . . . starring in . . . Tennessee Williams' . . . A STREETCAR NAMED DESIRE.

The glass partition hummed down again between the front and back seats as Linda, the secretary, turned to report, "Fred Stein must be going ahead with that CBS documentary he wanted to do on you, Miss Powers."

Catharine Powers sprang forward on the backseat. "I told Stein not to do that show on me," she snapped. "I told him. I *told* him."

Tom Hudson grabbed his fiancée, easing her back into the seat as he ordered the chauffeur, "Stop the car, Jim. Right here behind this garbage truck."

Halfway down the block from the Hunt, the limousine slowed, pulling behind a city sanitation truck parked at the curb.

Hudson turned to Catharine Powers. "Cat, take off your coat."

Alarmed, the actress looked from Hudson to her secretary to the gargantuan truck parked in front of them. "This is some kind of plot, isn't it?" she demanded. "Some kind of plot to tell me everything's all over? The show's closing."

"This is no plot." Hudson reached toward her fur hood to slide off the dark glasses. As he passed them to the secretary, he repeated, "Take off your coat and give it to Linda. You and I are getting out of the car here and walking."

"*Walking?*" Cat Powers's pale-blue eyes became glassy circles.

"That's what I said." Hudson hated the way the chemicals affected Cat, changing her from an intelligent, fun-loving woman into a neurotic bundle of nerves.

He grabbed the door handle. "Linda's going to put on your coat and glasses and pretend she's you," he explained.

"Hey, man," said Stone, "you sure you know what you're doing?"

One foot out of the limousine door, Hudson answered, "I know you think I'm nothing but some ignorant son-of-a-bitch grocer from Chicago, but give me a break on this one. Okay?"

"I don't think that," insisted Stone. "I love Safeways."

Hudson did not reply. Why bother correcting the L.A. doctor yet again that his chain wasn't Safeway?

He looked at his fiancée. "Take off your coat, sweetheart, and let's try my idea," he said gently.

Cat Powers obediently slipped out of the hooded sable, wadded it into a cumbersome bundle, and stuffed it through the partition to her secretary. As she did so, a half-pint whiskey bottle wrapped in a brown paper bag slipped from the coat's pocket and clanked down on the limousine's carpet.

Cat stared at the bottle, squeaking "Oh!" with pretend surprise.

Hudson shook his head. Booze along with the drugs. What had happened to Cat since she had become involved with this new show? Was the stress making her want to kill herself, damn it? But this was neither the time nor the place to scold her for packing around booze like some skidrow bum. Hudson kicked the small bottle behind the jump seat and told Stone, "When Jim stops in front of the theater, you help Linda out of the car. Try to make people think she's Cat arriving to do tonight's show. Take your time about it. Give Cat and me time to slip in the front door."

"Shouldn't I move to the backseat?" Linda asked.

"No. Let's not attract too much attention to the car down here," Hudson stated. "Just make sure you give us time to slip in through the lobby."

"I can't do it," Cat protested, one arm across her breasts as if she were naked, the other hand patting frantically at her bloated pink face, crooked fingers clawing anxiously at her unkempt hair. Voice snappish, she said, "What if they see me?"

"See you?" Hudson laughed, humoring her. "For Christ's sake, honey. You get up on stage every night in front of hundreds of people."

"Yes, but—"

He took her hand, asking honestly "Honey, do you truly think I'd let something bad happen to you?"

"Do you really love me?" Cat spoke as if they had all the time in the world to sit there talking. "Really, really, *really* love me? From the top of my head down to the tips of my toes?"

"You let me prove how much I love you." Holding her hand, he added, "As soon as you're ready, we'll go."

A few moments later the stretch limousine swung out from behind the sanitation truck, continuing toward the crowd gathering in front of the Hunt Theater. Down the block, Tom Hudson hurried Cat Powers along in the shadow of the buildings, escorting her toward the theater's glass doors; the actress's spike heels rapidly tap-tap-tapped against the pavement as she insisted, "Tommy, I don't feel good . . . Tommy, I think I'm going to be sick . . ."

Tom Hudson kept his stride, hoping Cat was exaggerating.

Ahead of them, the limousine was slowing in front of the

television cameras, the curious crowd pushing to see who was going to emerge from the gleaming black Cadillac Fleetwood.

On the sidewalk, Cat's fleshy buttocks chewed side to side beneath her wrinkled blue silk dress as she hurried to keep pace with Hudson. She whispered like a distressed child, "Tommy, I'm going to be sick . . . Tommy, it's that last shot Gene gave me back at the hotel . . . Tommy, I can't breathe . . . I can't breathe, Tommy . . . I can't get my breath . . ."

Listening to her, Hudson thought again about how much she had changed since he had first met her. It wasn't the extra weight she had put on that bothered him. It was the change in personality. Her loss of confidence.

A full year had not yet passed since he had met her at the charity gala last January in Dallas.

Tom Hudson was not a social butterfly, but he supported the international youth charity Hands Around the World and happened to be in Dallas on business at the time of its annual benefit ball.

Hudson had not recognized Cat Powers when she had been introduced to him at the ball simply as "Miss Powers." But hearing her rich voice, seeing a beguiling smile light up her face, he realized that the buxom woman in the dazzling gray silk dress was one of the last of the Hollywood legends created by the old studio star system—Catharine "Cat" Powers.

Cat shook Hudson's hand warmly, holding onto it a little too long before releasing it, then edging him away from the group to ask if he could please nab her a glass of ginger ale from a passing waiter.

Hudson remembered the press stories about Cat's recent cure at a New England drink-and-drug clinic, but he didn't think she was trying to win his pity. To the contrary. She obviously wanted to get better acquainted with him; there was some kind of instant charge between them, and she recognized it, too.

Cat sipped at her ginger ale and began talking in a matter-of-fact manner about Texas, comparing it to California and New York, laughing about how her late father had long ago made her give up a Broadway career to move west to Hollywood. Hudson was impressed that this glittering celebrity could be so straightforward and spontaneous.

"Have you acted in any plays since then?" he asked.

"Only in England," she answered. She looked at him steadily, her pale-blue eyes large and alive.

"Not here in the States? On Broadway?"

"Heavens, no. I don't have my dear, pushy old papa to protect me. To give me all the confidence I'd need to perform in front of a live audience."

"You look like the kind of lady who can survive on her own," Hudson said, forgetting he was speaking to the legendary Cat Powers.

She laughed. "I do when I have to, but every year it's getting to be more and more of a slog."

Hudson was charmed by her self-deprecating humor. Who would guess that this same woman had been married to some of Hollywood's most famous names and had turned down proposals from half of Europe's most eligible bachelors?

He asked, "What about having a man besides your father to stand by your side when you do a stage show?"

"You must be joking!" Her laugh became a healthy guffaw. "The men I meet all want to lean on *me!*"

She added with a wicked grin, "But if *you* know somebody I can lean on, Mr. Hudson, tell him to give me a call."

Hudson felt equally flirtatious. "How can I do that if I don't have your number?"

Hudson telephoned Cat twice a day from his headquarters in Chicago for the next two weeks. He flew to Los Angeles at the end of January to escort her to the Night of the Silver Stars Fund at the Mark Taper Forum. They spent the weekend together at his suite in the Bel-Air Hotel, dividing their time between the outdoor terrace with its Jacuzzi surrounded by lush ferns and the king-size bed.

In February Cat had surprised him during a Chicago snowstorm with a hot lunch catered to his office. Hudson's secretary buzzed the inner office, announcing "Mr. Hudson, waiters are here from Monsieur Jacques'." Before Hudson had time to ask why waiters from the exclusive Near North restaurant were in his office, the double doors burst open and Cat led three trolleys into the room, saying gaily "The weatherman said a snowstorm was headed this way and I didn't want my boy locked up at work with nothing to eat." After whisking off her white fox coat, Cat tied a red-checkered apron over her ivory Chanel suit and lifted the cover from a silver tureen of steaming chicken soup.

In March they flew to Puerto Vallarta. The two magical weeks they spent in a beach house there convinced Hudson that Cat was the woman he had been waiting so long to meet. She was interested in the smallest details of his national business and confided in him about problems she was having with agents and directors and keeping her weight down. Cat was as happy staying home having a simple salad and bread for supper as she was going out to party all night in the clubs and private homes that made the Mexican resort such a popular spot with the international set. The only important thing for her was to be with Hudson.

"Who would ever guess Cat Powers would lock herself away with a grocer?" he asked with a smile.

She wrapped both arms around him. "Somebody who knew my grocer's got that . . . individual touch with the girls."

"Only for you, baby," he said, nuzzling her ear. "Only for my special lady."

On April 1, Hudson proposed marriage to Cat in a long-distance call from Toronto. He added, "I warn you, sunshine, you might be an April Fool to accept."

Cat leapt at the offer. Then it was her idea for them to meet in New Orleans for Easter and celebrate the announcement of their engagement. Although she was not a Roman Catholic, one of her favorite charities was the Carmelite Convent in the French Quarter, and she wanted to say a prayer for their future with Hudson in the convent's chapel.

In May Cat signed to do *A Streetcar Named Desire* on Broadway. Hudson remembered from their first meeting how nervous she was about going onto the stage, and he promised to be at her side for the first week of the run. She subsequently arranged for her private physician, Dr. Gene Stone, to fly out from Los Angeles to be with her, too.

Cat had not used drugs, and had hardly touched alcohol, since Hudson had met her. But since the rehearsals for *Streetcar* had begun, she had become increasingly dependent on both. Hudson could not tell whether it was the strain of the production, or the influence of Gene Stone, that had led Cat down the slope.

Guiding her toward the Hunt Theater's row of doors, Hudson wondered what he should do if Cat wasn't crying wolf and couldn't make it through tonight's performance. Should he telephone that clinic in Connecticut where she had dried out before? Could they help her get back on the track to being the dynamic lady he had fallen in love with?

ANTIGUA—SATURDAY NIGHT, SUNDAY MORNING

"HOLD IT. . . . GOOD, LAVENDER. . . . NOW GIVE ME ARROGANCE—LOTS OF DROP-DEAD ARRO-gance. You're the most beautiful woman in the world and you know it. . . . That's it, keep coming toward me like that. Keep coming . . . come . . . come . . . come . . ."

Georgie Amerigo backed down the white sandy beach, his Nikon whirring as his favorite model, Lavender Gilbert, moved toward him with an easy grace. Her slender body was clad only in a matte black bikini that clung to her small, firm breasts and showed her long, lithesome legs to their best advantage; a white linen square tied around her swanlike neck billowed in the Caribbean breeze. It would make a stunning spread in the January *Vogue*.

"Enough," said the photographer with sudden finality, handing the camera to his shaggy-haired male assistant. Amerigo glanced out to the sea and then checked overhead to gauge the position of the midday sun.

"Let's do one more Star Lady set," he decided.

Lavender groaned, drooping her thin shoulders forward and sticking out her tongue. Gone was the cool sophistica-tion of a high fashion model; now she was any other ex-hausted twenty-one-year-old. They had begun shooting shortly after dawn this morning; now it was past noon and Lavender needed a rest.

Amerigo ignored Lavender's grimace and waved to the group of people waiting under a cluster of nearby palm trees.

"Set up Star Lady thirty-seven," he called. "Then we break for lunch."

Activity surrounded Lavender: a woman held up a beach towel as three stylists began stripping off the black swimsuit and adjusting scarlet-red number thirty-seven. Alongside Lavender, Juan, the Cuban hairdresser, frantically combed at her long blond hair as Maureen, the makeup girl, gobbed more cream onto her back, arms, and legs.

As preparations proceeded, the photographer's shaggy-haired assistant hopped across the hot white sand in his bare feet with a silver vial in one hand. The buzz of activity around Lavender ceased momentarily as the assistant held the vial under her nose, coaxing her to take a hit of the white powder in one nostril, then the other.

From a spot farther down the beach, Bev Jordan observed all this. Bev was one of six models from San Trop Agency in New York whom the fashion designer Chatwyn had sent down to the West Indies to shoot twelve pages for *Vogue*. Bev and the other girls had completed their location work, all except for Lavender Gilbert, the spread's principal model.

Bev and Lavender were roommates on the upper West Side of New York. Blond like Lavender, Bev was also five years older than the pretty girl from Iowa, and not as tall or winsome. Bev maturely accepted the fact that Lavender was more desirable—more marked for success—than herself. She was level-headed enough, too, to recognize that the so-called glamorous fashion world of New York could be cruel, selfish, and highly destructive. But in the past few months she had become increasingly concerned about Lavender's involvement in the suffocating fashion scene.

Apart from being the lead model for all of Chatwyn's current magazine spreads, Lavender was also the star of his national campaign for the new perfume he was launching—Star Lady. Lavender's schedule was grueling, doing print work, television spots, and personal appearances. Like most young models, however, Lavender wanted to make the most of this career break, and she was working beyond the call of duty. When Bev tried to convince Lavender to take it easy, Lavender shrugged her off. Bev could see she was letting Chatwyn and photographers like Georgie Amerigo drive her until she was ready to collapse from exhaustion, then fill her up with drugs to wring out a few more hours of work from her.

It was no secret that designers and photographers freely distributed drugs to their models, especially cocaine and uppers. Bev knew that Chatwyn budgeted for drugs on all his shoots, but of course the cost was buried under other expenses, such as "Public Relations" or "Travel."

Hysterical laughter cut into Bev's thoughts. Glancing toward the ocean, she watched Lavender prance into the surf, the cocaine giving her a renewed burst of energy.

"You're the Star Lady," Amerigo called to Lavender as he snapped a new roll of 35mm film. "You're the Star Lady and everybody wants to be just like you."

Bev sighed. She turned back to the article on drug rehabilitation she had been reading in *Time* magazine.

That evening, Antigua's temperature cooled as soon as the blazing orange disk of the sun sank behind the purple horizon. In the distance, beyond the lush compound of the Smuggler's Cove Inn, the island's low hills became a dark outline against a sky pinpointed with stars. As the hours passed closer to midnight, the rhythm of a steel band drifted toward the small bungalow that Bev shared with Lavender.

As she packed to return to New York in the morning, Bev listened to the calypso beat. The farewell party was in full swing on the hotel's louvered veranda. She had been too worried about Lavender all evening to leave the bungalow and join in the fun.

A supper tray sat untouched next to Lavender's bed. Lying facedown on her pillows, she had not moved since collapsing there when she had returned that afternoon from the photography session.

"Eat something," Bev urged as she turned from her open suitcase.

Lavender groaned into the pillow.

"Lavender, you can't go on like this," Bev said.

Lavender shook her head against the pillow. "Work's over."

"Here, maybe," said Bev. She admired Lavender for trying to act strong but knew that she was being unrealistic. "There's plenty more waiting for you in New York."

"Just this week."

"Ha! Don't fool yourself, kiddo." Bev sank to her bed next to Lavender's and studied the young woman's profile silhouetted against the white pillow—the perfect nose, the high cheekbones, the thick blond hair veiled around that incredibly long neck. Like so many pretty girls who came to New York to pursue a modeling career, Lavender had the burning desire to make it. But also like so many girls—especially the young ones—Lavender was surprisingly naive despite her worldly-wise looks and sophisticated demeanor.

"First of all," Bev continued, "Chatwyn's not going to be satisfied with all the location shots. Is he ever? He'll tell Amerigo to shoot more in the studio. Then there's the Star Lady party this Friday at the Waldorf. Press calls. The buyers' receptions. Your work is just starting—and a lot more than I bet's in your contract."

Lavender rolled to face the white wall, gripping a pillow to her face, pleading, "I've got to do it. This is my big break."

" 'Break' is the right word for it," Bev answered, "because that's exactly what's going to happen to you, Lavender, if you don't slow down. *You're* the one who's going to break."

Bev sat forward on the bed. "Honey, look at yourself. You can't get up. You can't eat. Who knows if you'll even have the energy to fly back to New York?" She looked at the travel alarm on the bedside table. "We leave the hotel in seven hours."

"I can take an upper." Lavender sniffed. "That's how I got down here."

"You can't live on pills."

"Iowa girls are strong," Lavender retorted weakly.

"Iowa girls are pretty stupid sometimes, too," Bev said. "You know what I think you should do when you get back to New York? I think you should stand up to Chatwyn. I think you should tell him you don't want any more of his drugs. Tell him you'll give him an honest day's work but that's it. Don't let him pump you full of those black beauties and toots of coke when he wants to stretch you to your limits. It's not fair and it's definitely not safe."

Lavender held onto the pillow, shaking her head, moaning "I waited so long for this break. Why is everything going wrong?"

Seeing her friend beginning to quake with tears, Bev sank to the floor alongside the bed. "Hey, don't cry. Everything's going to be all right. You just have to be a little bit stronger. Watch out for yourself because nobody else is going to. Chatwyn's the kind of monster who chews up pretty girls like you for breakfast."

"I need help," whispered Lavender, quivering under the thin sheet as if she had a fever. "I can't go on like this. But I don't know what to do."

Bev glanced to the copy of *Time* magazine she had been reading earlier this afternoon. She remembered the article on drug rehabilitation.

The focus of the article had been on a private clinic named Tanglewood. The cover story had said that Tanglewood's medical director was making the clinic into the country's leading drug cure center with a growing reputation among people from show business, fashion, and the arts.

Tanglewood was located in Connecticut, Bev remembered. She had left her car parked at Kennedy Airport and she could drive to Connecticut in a few hours. The Antigua

flight would be arriving in New York shortly after midday.
She could have Lavender at the clinic the same afternoon.

The big question was: Did Lavender really want help?
And was she willing to risk her career to save her own life?

PART ONE

SUNDAY

STONEBRIDGE, CONNECTICUT

1 AT THREE FORTY-FIVE SUNDAY AFTER-
NOON, DR. ROGER COOPER KISSED THE
young woman in the camel hair coat good-bye on the station
platform at Stonebridge, Connecticut, and waved as she
boarded the New Haven Line train, promising "I'll give you
a call when I get down to New York."

He waved one last time as the train pulled away from the
white clapboard station, then he stuffed both hands into the
pockets of his brown corduroy jeans and ambled slowly
across the parking lot to his four-wheel-drive Mercedes
Benz.

As he pulled onto the highway, Roger slumped his athletic frame against the Mercedes' padded leather door, one
hand resting on the steering wheel. With Vivaldi spinning
on the tape deck, he headed east from Stonebridge.

The Connecticut countryside was brilliant with color in
mid-October, elms, oaks, hawthorns turning gold, red, and
purple, the shining white spire of the Stonebridge Community Church silhouetted against a cloudless blue sky.

Gaining speed on the stretch through Swift's apple orchard, Roger remembered his weekend date. Her name was
Annie Cross. She was a vice president at a Wall Street investment firm. Would he see her again? Maybe. She was good
company and, he had to admit, he enjoyed going to bed with
her. Also, she had not asked prying questions about his
work—his patients.

Roger Cooper was medical director and co-owner of Tanglewood, the private clinic located ten miles outside of Stonebridge. Living in a converted coach house on the clinic's grounds, he tried to be as careful as possible about the women he asked to spend weekends with him. It was no secret that Tanglewood treated more than a fair share of newsworthy patients. Last week's *Time* magazine cover story on Tanglewood would only increase the general public's curiosity. He could not risk a snooper.

But the clinic created more serious problems for Roger in his relationships. Three years ago his fiancée, Crista, had broken off their engagement, claiming he was more devoted to work than he could ever be to a wife.

"I don't want to wake up middle-aged and complaining that my husband does nothing but work," Crista had told him honestly. "I can see your priorities already, Roger, and so let's call it quits before I start hating you for being a work freak."

Roger shifted down to second, slowing when he saw two freckle-faced kids in football jerseys selling apples from bushel baskets alongside the road.

As he thumped the horn at the neighbor boys Roger thought, with a pang of regret, of the family he had once planned with Crista. Then the telephone buzzed inside the car, interrupting his reverie.

Turning down *The Four Seasons*, he lifted the receiver from its cradle between the bucket seats.

A woman's voice spoke. "Sorry to bother you, darling."

Roger recognized the plummy British accent of Jackie Lyell, the wife of his partner, Adrian Lyell, who was pinch-hitting in Administration ever since Adrian had unexpectedly left three days ago for a quick trip to Los Angeles.

Roger liked Jackie Lyell despite the fact that she was too dramatic sometimes, too free with the "darlings." But she was always friendly and well meaning. Nevertheless, he was unable to dismiss the fear that the forty-year-old woman was ill equipped to handle Administration, even for the few days her husband was in California. He suspected she knew it, too.

"Got a problem, Jackie?' he asked.

"I'm afraid so, darling. Peabo Washington's causing a bit of trouble here."

"How serious?"

"His nurse called two attendants for help. She couldn't administer his Thorazine."

If two-hundred-pound Peabo Washington was becoming uncontrollable he would need propranolol. Two milligrams. Intravenously.

Roger's heart sank. World Heavyweight boxing champion Peabo Washington had come to Tanglewood because of a dependency on Methedrine—"speed." Roger had wanted to remove him from all drugs.

His foot heavy on the accelerator, he said into the phone, "I'm reaching the gates now."

"Sorry to bother you like this, darling," Jackie apologized, "but I know you have a special interest in Peabo."

Roger had a special interest in all his patients. That was one of the advantages of keeping the clinic small, no more than thirty-five patients.

Roger replaced the receiver and slowed down as he approached a pair of fieldstone pillars to the right of the road, inset with brass plaques inscribed TANGLEWOOD.

2 THE HOUSE STOOD AT THE END OF A LONG WOODED DRIVE, A STATELY AP-
proach stretching from the gatehouse to the honey-color
mansion built in the mid-nineteenth century by a New England textile merchant. Set in a twenty-eight-acre park, the
walled estate now included rambling lawns, a formal rose
garden, a fruit orchard, a helipad, two swimming pools,
tennis and badminton courts, and a dense patch of vine-
covered evergreens for which Tanglewood had been named.

The oak-lined approach divided in front of the four-story
main house, one fork circling round to the white-columned
entrance, the second leading to a porte cochère extending
from the left of the house.

As Roger Cooper sped toward the porte cochère, he noticed a red sports car parked near the front pillars. It had not
been there when he'd left to take Annie to the station.

Seeing a woman helping another woman from the passenger seat of the classic little red MG TD, Roger remembered
that Little Milly Wheeler, the country and western singer,
was scheduled to arrive tomorrow from Nashville. Had Little Milly and her mother come a day early?

Roger pulled the Mercedes to a halt under the porte co-
chére, threw open the door, and ran up the steps of the side
entrance.

Jackie Lyell waited inside the double doors, auburn hair
swept back from her face into a neat bun, large gold hoops
on her ears.

After glancing anxiously over her shoulder as the doorbell

chimed behind her in the main hallway, she turned back to Roger. "Peabo's in his room."

"I'm on my way." Roger hurried across the Kilims spread over glistening walnut floors.

The doorbell chimed a second time.

"Jackie," he called, "two women have arrived in a car."

Jackie Lyell nodded. "I know, darling. Everything's happening at once. The gatehouse rang just after I talked to you. It's Lavender Gilbert."

"Who?"

"Lavender Gilbert. The *Vogue* model." Jackie's large, liquid-brown eyes rounded. "She wants to check in for a cure."

"A cure for what?"

Jackie faltered. "Her friend said she'd explain everything when she got here."

"Is she here on her doctor's recommendation?"

Jackie's face reddened as she confessed, "Darling, I don't know yet."

The front door bell chimed a third time.

"Talk to her and get some details. But remember, we're filled to capacity as usual."

Roger turned toward the archway, fuming, but not at Jackie. He was angry with Adrian Lyell for leaving him in the lurch like this. Adrian knew how to deal with emergency cases, whom to accept, whom to turn way.

Why in hell had Adrian gone off to Los Angeles on the spur of the moment, leaving his wife to work in Administration for him? The nagging question fueled Roger's temper and, soon, even the mental image of Adrian began to annoy him.

A forty-seven-year-old Londoner transplanted to the United States, Adrian always looked dapper in Savile Row suits and was socially graceful with everyone from duchesses to pop stars.

Compared with Adrian, Roger knew, he himself was rough.

Not yet forty, Roger stood a brawny six foot one. His usual outfit was corduroy jeans, boots or moccasins, sometimes a tweed sports jacket, seldom a necktie. From high-school football days to Sunday afternoon baseball games in med school, Roger had developed a camaraderie with men who hunted deer rather than played polo, drove RV campers to Canada rather than dropping anchor at St. Tropez or Mykonos. A thatch of sandy hair and soft blue eyes kept him from looking macho; an easygoing manner kept his deep-chested voice from sounding aggressive or threatening.

As Roger hurried down the corridor to Peabo Washington's suite, he grew angrier when he remembered that Adrian had not given him an exact date when he would return.

There was only one thing to do: get on the phone to Los Angeles and demand some answers from Adrian.

3 WHEN ROGER COOPER AND ADRIAN LYELL HAD PURCHASED TANGLEWOOD five years earlier, they realized they would need more space than the mansion's fifty rooms. Commissioning a Boston firm of architects, they asked for two additions that would be light and cheery yet would maintain the stately atmosphere of the main house. They were pleased with the results—new stone-and-glass annexes that housed laboratories, therapy centers, guest rooms for visitors, and suites with observation panels for patients who required close surveillance.

Roger took long strides down the carpeted passageway toward one of the two new wings, the Garden Pavilion. Pushing Adrian out of his mind, he concentrated instead on Peabo Washington.

Unlike many black boxers, Peabo had not been raised in a ghetto. Born in Philadelphia, he was the son of Charles Washington, a prominent corporate lawyer, and had been educated at private schools. Peabo had turned down a football scholarship to Notre Dame and accepted a scholastic grant to Penn State, where he had taken up boxing in his freshman year. His history could be seen as a success story in reverse.

After entering Peabo's room through a small foyer, Roger found two white-coated attendants restraining the six-foot-two prizefighter.

Peabo's blue velour track suit hung like a sack from his shoulders. The sheen had gone from his cocoa-brown complexion. His movements were quick and staccato; his eyes large and wild, like a cornered animal.

"Come on, man," he taunted Roger. "Give me that needle, man. That's what you're here for, isn't it? To poke me with some needle? To make me curl up and *die?*"

Roger noticed that Peabo had reverted to a slow drawl, using expressions of a Harlem street kid. He was certain that the corner-boy manner was not part of the playfulness Peabo was famous for. Probably the tough pose gave Peabo a sense of security he did not get from the educated diction and polite manners of his own upper-middle-class background.

Keeping his own tone calm, Roger reassured him, "I don't have a needle, Peabo. We want to get you off all medication. Remember?"

"I want *this* off." Peabo jerked at the attendants' hands. Roger nodded for the men to release him.

Standing free, Peabo rearranged his blue athletic jacket, smoothing the velour sleeve, readjusting the knitted cuff.

"Peabo, what happened between you and Ellen a few

minutes ago?" Roger asked and nodded at the registered nurse, Ellen Grant, standing across the room.

Peabo brushed at imaginary lint on his sleeve. "Nothing happened, man. Everything's cool."

Roger glanced back to the nurse. "Ellen?"

The nurse stepped forward. Her complexion was darker than Peabo's, her black hair corn-rowed and beaded. She held her head high as she explained, "Peabo mistook me for his old lady."

Roger turned back to Peabo. "You thought Ellen was your wife?"

Peabo pulled up his sleeve and scratched his forearm. "I got a little messed up, man."

Roger cocked his head. "Please repeat that, Peabo. You're slurring your words. I didn't understand you."

Peabo kept scratching his arm as he repeated louder, "I said I got a little messed up, man."

Roger had not seen Peabo scratching at his skin like this for twelve days. Coupled with the renewed obsession with tidiness, he worried that the prizefighter's recovery was regressing. Amphetamines affected the central nervous system. Long-term use led to many forms of psychotic behavior, traits that appeared, disappeared, reappeared—hysterical orderliness, confusion, delusion, and scratching.

He looked back at Ellen. "How exactly did Peabo mistake you for his wife? Did he call you Karen? Did he ask about the children? What did he say?"

Ellen answered. "He accused me of stepping out on him."

"Being unfaithful?"

"You got it."

"Is that all he said?"

"He called me a whore. He demanded to know who I was balling. I told him it was none of his business and to go take a flying fuck. That's when he grabbed me and I buzzed for some muscle." She nodded at the white-jacketed attendants.

Peabo interrupted. "You didn't have to call these goons, woman. I wasn't going to rape you, you ugly black bitch."

"You bet you weren't," she shot back at him. "You couldn't. You can't get up the meat, junkie."

"What do you know about dick, woman? I know a bull dyke when I see one. How much pussy you eat today, bitch? How long you been swinging on that dildo?"

Roger inwardly cringed at the way Peabo's habit—or the withdrawal from it—had changed him from a happy-go-lucky man into a mean-mouthed bastard. But he let the heated exchange soar. A recovering patient had to say what he felt. Tanglewood also chose nurses who knew how to dish verbal abuse back to the patients.

Peabo turned to Roger. "This mean dyke and my old lady are birds of a feather, man. They both got the same hot-shit attitude."

Keeping his eyes on Roger, he said, "You know, don't you, man, she locked me up in here? My hot-shot bitch locked me up in this funny farm. So she can run around Philly. Spending my money. Looking for dick."

Roger heard wild claims from all amphetamine patients. It was part of their pattern. The drug first gave a rush, making a user "speed," his pupils dilate, his heart pound. A new user felt on top of the world. But he had to increase the dosage to continue speeding, and then, as tolerance to the drug developed, there inevitably followed depression, insomnia, paranoia, general confusion about reality.

Roger corrected him. "Your wife didn't bring you here, Peabo. Your manager did. You and your manager decided you should commit yourself for treatment."

Peabo ignored the facts. He pointed at Ellen accusingly. "I warned that bitch about locking me away, man. I warned her about stepping out on me."

"She's not your wife, Peabo. She's a nurse here. This is Ellen Grant. You've been seeing her here for two weeks."

Peabo ignored Roger. His voice rose higher as he stabbed his finger at the nurse. "She locked me up in here, man. She locked me away and I told her, I told her—"

He lunged at Ellen.

The attendants grabbed Peabo halfway across the room.
The struggle was brief; Peabo soon submitted to their grasp.

The six-foot-two prizefighter looked helplessly from
Ellen to Roger, blinking with surprise, his mouth hanging
open.

Watching the short scuffle, Roger considered how drasti-
cally Peabo's appearance and behavior had changed in the
four years since he had first seen him on television. Peabo
Washington had been on the United States Boxing Team in
the Summer Olympics. Roger had watched him knock out
the Italian, Luigi Luchese, in the third round and go on to
win a gold medal. He had next seen Peabo a year later in a
fight televised from Miami. Peabo had turned professional
and was challenging the Heavyweight champion of the
world, Sonny Moss. But the show had started long before
the fight. Peabo had given the world the first taste of his zany
showmanship when he weighed in at the press conference.
Whacking a toy voodoo doll with a bright-red plastic mallet,
he joked with reporters that he had Moss already "pinned"
to the ropes. His clowning was an immediate hit with the
press; television cameras followed him around Miami as he
drove a big black hearse with a coffin inside, the name
"Sonny Moss" painted on it in Day-Glo lettering. But the
joking stopped at the first clang of the bell; Peabo proved he
wasn't all laughs. His fluid moves tied Sonny Moss into
knots. Landing punch after punch, he defeated Moss with a
technical knockout in round two, winning the Heavyweight
title.

Dropping his head, Peabo mumbled to Roger, "I'm
messed up, man. Leave me alone. I'm all messed up inside
my head."

Roger nodded to the attendants.

As the men released Peabo this time, he slumped to the
carpet, lowering his head to his hands.

Roger waved the attendants to leave the suite; he motioned Ellen Grant to bring the tray with the Thorazine,

along with the vitamin B₃, to absorb lingering impurities in the blood, and a container of yogurt for calcium loss.

He moved toward Peabo. "You okay, Peabo?"

He saw the boxer was crying.

Roger sank to one knee alongside him, repeating "You okay?" Again he thought of Peabo's graceful dancing and weaving inside the ring, how much it differed from the awkwardness of his present jerky movements.

Peabo gulped back his tears.

"How about us keeping this the last week of Thorazine?" Roger asked. "Like we planned?"

Peabo wiped the corners of both eyes with a knuckle.

Roger fished for a flicker of Peabo's old humor. "Also, what do you say about doing something new this week? Some of that vintage showing-off you do?"

Hoarsely, Peabo insisted, "I'm messed up, man. I don't know what I can do."

Roger proposed his idea more seriously. "You asked me yesterday about rap groups, Peabo. Do you still think you can handle one?"

Peabo repeated, "I don't know what I can do."

Roger didn't know either. Peabo was able to dish out abuse. But could he listen to it for hours on end in one of the clinic's encounter groups without buckling under or becoming violent? Was he still too confused, too paranoiac to join a group? Less than a few moments ago he had mistaken a nurse for his wife.

A thought then occurred to Roger.

He would telephone Karen Washington in Philadelphia. Spouses often helped a patient make the first step back into everyday life. He would ask Peabo's wife to come to Tanglewood. He would call her tonight.

4 LAVENDER GILBERT WAS ONE OF THE
MOST BEAUTIFUL YOUNG WOMEN JACKIE
Lyell had ever seen. She had a peaches-and-cream complexion, shoulder-length blond hair, and the startling eyes that
had obviously given Lavender her name.

The young model sat, with her friend Bev Jordan, across
from Jackie on a leather chesterfield in Administration, as
Jackie explained to them the normal procedure of admissions
to Tanglewood, the often weeks-long wait for a place in the
clinic.

Bev spoke for Lavender. "This is an emergency situation,
Mrs. Lyell. Lavender's really in trouble."

Jackie looked from Bev to Lavender sitting quietly beside
her on the couch. She guessed from the model's silence that
either she was very shy or truly in dire straits from a dependency on some kind of drug.

"What's Lavender's problem?" Jackie asked.

"Cocaine." Bev looked with concern at Lavender. "Pills,
too. Amphetamines. She got hooked on coke and speed
because she's working so hard. Last week it all came to a
head when we were photographing down in Antigua. We
were all working hard. But especially Lavender."

Bev told Jackie about Lavender's meteoric career, explaining how, in a few months, she had become the most sought-after model for high-fashion spreads, working from eight to
twelve hours a day, most of the time kept going by cocaine
and uppers.

Jackie's sympathy began to mount as she listened to Bev's story. Lavender looked little better than a zombie, albeit a highly attractive, elegant one. The more Jackie listened, the more she realized that the young woman definitely needed attention.

"I'd like our medical director to interview Lavender," Jackie said.

"When would that be?"

Jackie glanced at the brass carriage clock on the bookshelf. "I'll try my best to arrange it for within the hour. If he decides that Lavender should stay here, we'd find her a room straightaway—without putting her on a waiting list."

"Then what happens?" Bev asked.

"She wouldn't have her first tests until tomorrow morning at the earliest. Blood. Urine. Liver. Also there'd be interviews with our psychiatrist and nutritionist. We'd begin developing a recovery profile."

Bev bit her lower lip. "As Lavender's in the state she's in now, Mrs. Lyell, you don't mind if I ask *you* a few more questions, do you?"

"Definitely not," Jackie said, touched by the friend's concern. She had gathered that Bev was also a model; as she wasn't as elegant or graceful as Lavender, she probably wasn't as successful in the world of high fashion.

Fleetingly, Jackie wondered about the image she herself projected. She knew she appeared efficient, even commanding in a bossy sort of way. But she felt ill at ease conducting this interview.

Tall but not lanky, Jackie filled out an American size ten dress in all the right places. She had an extrovert style, which her close friends back in London called "camp" (though Adrian, in his snider moments, had called it "ball-breaking"). However, Jackie was not as threatening as she looked. She only wished she were a little more aggressive, but she was weighted down with insecurities. Adrian knew this, too, and treated her little better than a general go-fer around the clinic, permitting her to arrange flowers, drive to the post office in Stonebridge, find new butchers, printers, and dry cleaners when they were needed. Seldom was she allowed into the inner sanctum of Administration; never in this capacity of admitting new patients. It was just beginning to puzzle Jackie why Adrian had suddenly granted her this great privilege. Was his mystery trip to California so important?

Bev began. "To be honest, Mrs. Lyell, I had never heard about Tanglewood until last week when I read a story in *Time* magazine."

Jackie nodded. Reactions from the *Time* cover story had already begun. "I've read about other clinics in the past. What their patients have to do in a cure . . ." Hesitating, Bev asked sheepishly, "Will Lavender have to scrub floors here?"

Jackie smiled. "Darling, I know some clinics believe a recovering patients should set to and muck out. But at Tanglewood we work for a cure that patients can continue when they leave here." Recrossing her shapely legs, she added, "Few of the people who come to Tanglewood go home and make their own beds—let alone scrub floors."

"What about electric shock treatment?" Bev asked.

"Here? Good heavens, no." Jackie laughed. "Roger doesn't believe in shock treatment, electroconvulsive or otherwise."

Bev looked blank. "Roger?"

"Oh, I'm sorry," Jackie apologized. "Roger Cooper's our medical director. At Tanglewood everybody uses first names."

Nodding her approval, Bev said, "That must make everything more relaxed."

"Exactly our intention," Jackie said. "Also, you won't see any doctors or nurses wearing uniforms at Tanglewood. Only the attendants and dining-room staff."

Bev turned to Lavender. "How does all this sound to you? Is it still what you want to do?"

Lavender seemed to be miles away from the conversation.

"Lavender, do you have any questions?" Bev asked more loudly.

The question penetrated Lavender's cloud; she looked from Bev to Jackie. But all she could say in response, as if by rote, was "I don't feel good. . . . Can you please help me . . . ? Please do something."

Jackie's heart broke for the young woman. "We'll certainly try," she said.

In a low voice, Bev confided, "You see what another world she's in. She hardly knows what's happening, does she?"

Jackie admitted, "I definitely think Roger Cooper should see her."

"Should I hang around until he does?" Bev asked.

Jackie considered the question. She knew Roger's evening schedule was tight. He might not find time to examine Lavender immediately. Also, she remembered Bev saying that both of them had flown all the way back from the West Indies that day. They had to be exhausted from the trip.

She decided to take a chance that a bed would be available for Lavender at Tanglewood, at least for the night. To Bev she said, "Why don't you leave Lavender here. You drive back to New York and get a good night's rest. We can speak in the morning."

Bev looked relieved by the suggestion.

Jackie handed the pad she had been using for notes to Bev. "Write down your telephone number, darling. I'll give you a ring as soon as I know something myself."

Bev nodded. "Fine."

Jackie added, "Perhaps you can also jot down the name and telephone number of Lavender's physician. Just so we have it on file."

Bev scribbled on the pad. "I'll give you our model agency's number, too. We're both at San Trop. They always know where to find me."

"That might be useful." Then Jackie hesitated. "Now, about money. . . . If we can fit Lavender in someplace, I'm going to have to ask her for a deposit. We don't take credit cards, I'm afraid, and—"

Bev smiled. "Money's no problem. Lavender's been under exclusive contract to Chatwyn for the past year."

"How nice." Jackie had heard of the American designer; she owned a piece of Chatwyn luggage.

Rising from her chair, she went to the desk and picked up the receiver of an ivory telephone. After touching four numbers, she said, "Margie? Jackie Lyell here. Can you please come to Administration? There's a young lady here whom I'd like you to take upstairs for Roger to examine when he has time."

She put down the receiver and turned to Bev. "I also need Lavender to sign a few things for me if she's going to spend even a night here."

Bev huddled alongside Lavender on the chesterfield, guiding her in filling out the short documents; in a few moments Jackie turned to answer the knock on the office door.

Jackie introduced the frizzy-haired young woman in a yellow trouser suit. "This is Margie Clark. She's a nurse here. Margie's going to take Lavender upstairs to an examination room and then later to where she'll be spending the night."

Margie Clark greeted both girls and turned to collect Lavender's suitcase as Bev kissed Lavender good-bye on the cheek. Lavender was still in a daze.

"Take care," said Bev.

Lavender nodded blankly.

A frosty nip was chilling the late afternoon as Bev Jordan stood on the steps of the main house. "Mrs. Lyell . . . there's one more thing I think you should know about Lavender," she said.

Jackie's heart sank at the ominous-sounding words.

"Chatwyn doesn't have a clue about any of this," Bev explained nervously.

Remembering that Bev had said Lavender was under an

exclusive contract to the designer, Jackie asked, "What doesn't he know, dear?"

"That I brought Lavender here. He's not going to be very happy when he finds out."

"I should have thought everyone would want Lavender to get better. Especially someone who depends on her appearance."

Bev shook her head. "Not Chatwyn. Anyway, not this week."

"What's so special about this week?"

Bev took a deep breath. "Chatwyn's launching a new perfume. It's called Star Lady. The entire campaign centers around Lavender. She's the Star Lady, and he's throwing a big press party this Friday at the Waldorf."

"Friday?" Jackie pulled back her head. "But Lavender can't *hope* to be cured by Friday even if we can make room for her here."

"Of course not. But I thought you should know as you're being so thoughtful."

Jackie's head filled with a thousand questions. "Didn't Chatwyn know Lavender was in this condition when he signed her to represent his new perfume?"

"That was six months ago."

"Didn't he see her getting worse?"

"Who sees when they're designing next season's collection?" Bev looked into Jackie's eyes. "Lavender's just one more cog in Chatwyn's many enterprises. It's awful to say but it's true. That's why she shouldn't have any qualms about coming here. Isn't somebody's life more important than a bottle of perfume?"

"Of course, darling. But . . ."

Bev said, "Also, Mrs. Lyell, Chatwyn is not entirely blameless for Lavender's condition. I won't elaborate on the subject but let's just say that it probably won't come as a shock to Chatwyn when he hears that one of his models is addicted to cocaine."

As Jackie watched Bev Jordan's red MG disappear up the

avenue of century-old oaks, she wondered if she had done the right thing by persuading Bev to leave Lavender Gilbert at Tanglewood. She hoped her first admission was not going to be a complete fiasco.

5 ACROSS THE HALL FROM ADMINISTRA-TION, BRASS WALL SCONCES GLOWED dimly against the mahogany paneling in the medical director's office. Roger Cooper sat on the edge of his desk, the phone to his ear. "This is Dr. Roger Cooper calling from Tanglewood for Mrs. Karen Washington. . . . Hello, Mrs. Washington."

He launched into the reason for his call, telling Karen about her husband's relapse, suggesting that she visit the clinic and perhaps spend two or three hours each day with Peabo to ease him into encounter groups. These groups were the first step toward taking him back into the outside world.

"Dr. Cooper," Karen replied, her pleasant voice growing suddenly sharper, "the only thing that could get me to Connecticut are divorce papers."

The announcement took Roger by surprise. He paused.

At the other end of the line, Karen demanded, "Do you really think I would drive three hundred miles to hold the hand of a man I wouldn't cross the street to see?"

Roger changed the receiver to his other ear. "I'm sorry, Mrs. Washington. I had no idea there was this kind of hostility between you and your husband."

"You don't have to apologize, Dr. Cooper," she answered.

"You're only doing your job. But living with a speed freak's not easy. When he's not on a rocket to the moon, he's sleeping in the middle of the day, screaming at the kids to be quiet at three o'clock in the afternoon. Three o'clock in the afternoon! I mean, give us a break."

Roger tried to halt her. "Mrs. Washington, I'm sorry. I'm only trying to—"

"Dr. Cooper," she went on, "I'm sure you've heard my story a thousand times before. So let's just drop it. Some marriages work out. Mine didn't."

Not pleased with the turn the conversation was taking, Roger moved from the desk's edge to his buttoned leather chair. "I understand, Mrs. Washington. But—"

"Do you? Do you understand, Doctor? Let me give you a few facts so you really understand."

She drew a breath and proceeded. "We have two beautiful kids. They drive me crazy sometimes but they're healthy and gorgeous and I thank the good Lord above for my blessings. But, Doctor, I have also got to start thinking about me. I've got my life to live, too."

Roger was impressed by the sincerity in her voice. He groped for some way to appeal to her. "Isn't divorce a little drastic, Mrs. Washington? At least at this point of your husband's problems?"

"Let me ask you a personal question, Dr. Cooper."

"Fire away."

"Are you married?"

"No."

Karen continued. "You tell me about divorce when you get married, Dr. Cooper. You telephone me and we'll talk about divorce when your spouse strikes it rich. I mean strikes it really big time. The giant big time. The cover of *Sports Illustrated. Newsweek.* Television commercials."

Her voice grew higher. "Sugar Ray Leonard? Mohammed Ali? Forget them. Peabo Washington's passed them both—in money and popularity. He's a national pinup boy. An athletic Michael Jackson. Look in your shopping

mall. There's more posters of him for sale than Snoopy. The
Japanese want to put him in Kung Fu films.

"But reality goes out the door, Doctor, when your dearly
beloved discovers the needle. Starts shooting amphetamines.
Becomes a speed freak. So when those things happen to the
person *you* marry, Dr. Cooper, you call me up and then I'll
listen to what *you* have to say about divorce."

Karen Washington was a tough cookie, but Roger liked
her style. He wondered how he could get her to channel
some of her strength into Peabo.

He tried again. "Mrs. Washington, let me ask you this.
Can the divorce wait until Peabo gets on his feet?"

She did not miss a beat. "Can we talk dates?"

"I could lie and say six weeks. But what if I said a year,
Mrs. Washington?"

There was a long silence.

"Please, Mrs. Washington. Before you slap your husband
with divorce papers, help me try to help him back on his
feet."

"Do you think such a thing is possible, Dr. Cooper?" Her
voice wavered ever so slightly. "Do you think Peabo can
ever be straight? Get back to being the sweet, warm, funny
man he used to be?"

"Excuse me for answering your question with a question,
Mrs. Washington, but can you spare your husband a few
days to find out?"

"You missed your calling as a lawyer, Dr. Cooper."

Roger pushed on. "I also believe it would be a good idea
if you brought your children with you to Tanglewood. Your
husband talks a lot about Tamara and Tyler."

Karen paused. "He does?"

"Yes, he does. Mrs. Washington," he went on more
gently, "I know this call has caught you unawares. You
don't have to make up your mind now. I can phone back—"

"No, no, no. Let's settle it now and get it over with." She
took a deep breath and said, "At the back of my mind, I guess
I knew this was coming. I just hadn't prepared myself to deal

with it. You're making a very valid request and—" She hesitated, while Roger held his breath.

"Now, I don't want you to think I'm a pushover," she continued. "Nor that I'm calling off the divorce. Because I'm not. But there are the kids to consider. So let's say that I'm giving them the time."

"You'll come?"

"Yes. Just let me think out loud for a few seconds."

Roger felt relief flood through his body as Karen Washington began a string of verbal notes.

"Peabo's sister is staying with us. She can drive up to Connecticut with me. If we get up early tomorrow morning, we could probably be with you by lunch."

Roger offered, "Mrs. Washington, I'll put your name down for two adjoining rooms here at Tanglewood."

"In the clinic?"

"That's right," he said enthusiastically. "I'll save two guest rooms by our pool. Your kids'll enjoy that. We've got a lifeguard to look after them, too."

"Wait a second, Doctor. Thanks but no thanks. I'd rather stay nearby in a little hotel or someplace. This isn't going to be easy, believe me. That man's going to tear me to pieces. You don't know that druggie like I do. I'm going to need a referee to ring a bell and say 'round one' is over and Karen Washington can go back to her corner and stick her head in a bucket of ice water."

Roger grinned. "Mrs. Washington, you sound like a champ to me."

"Let's see what happens this week."

The phone went dead in his ear.

Roger stepped out of his office as one of the clinic's four senior doctors, Dunstan Bell, was entering his own office halfway down the corridor. Farther along, an attendant, Loren Garvey, was walking Jennifer Morrisey, an alcohol recovery patient, back to her room from physical therapy; the Detroit socialite was wearing one of the clinic's long white terry-cloth robes trimmed with green cording, Tanglewood's crest stitched on the upper pocket.

Hearing the front door open behind him, Roger turned and was surprised to see Jackie Lyell coming in from outside.

Jackie was startled, too, to see Roger. "I thought you'd still be with Peabo."

"I've been on the phone to his wife. She's coming tomorrow and is going to need a couple of rooms in a hotel nearby. But we can talk about that later. What about that young model? Did you get any details?"

"I hope I did the right thing." Jackie sighed. "The girl's in a dreadful state. I sent her upstairs with Margie, counting on your having time to examine her. On top of everything else, she's exhausted from a flight from the West Indies. I thought she could sleep in room thirty-seven, at least for the night." Jackie gestured toward the Administration office. "Can you come inside and see the notes I made?"

Roger stood in Administration reading Jackie's notes about Lavender Gilbert as she moved noiselessly around the high-ceilinged room, turning on lamps, emptying ashtrays, closing the brocade curtains.

She came to stand alongside Roger. "There's something I learned a few minutes ago, too, that's not in there."

He raised his eyes.

"Her girl friend told me she has a contract with the designer, Chatwyn, to represent his new perfume. The launching party's this Friday."

"And she walked out?"

Jackie said, "I don't think she has much of a choice."

"She must be pretty bad off to walk out on a big break like that. It sounds like the chance of a lifetime."

"You look at her, Roger. See what you think. I personally think she needs help. Badly."

Roger glanced back to the pad, flipping to the attached forms Lavender had signed. "So her boss, this Chatwyn guy, doesn't know she's here."

"From what I understand from her friend, he doesn't. Nor is he going to be too pleased when he does find out."

Roger thought for a few moments. "Jackie, it might be a good idea to call our lawyers and see where we'd stand in a tug-of-war over the model."

The statement surprised Jackie. "Would somebody actually do such a thing, Roger? Pull someone out of medical care?"

"In this business, I've seen people do everything."

Jackie moved toward the desk. "I'll call our lawyer first thing tomorrow morning."

Scribbling a note to herself, she asked, "Roger?"

He paused halfway to the door.

"Darling, when you finish upstairs with Lavender, why don't you come back here? We'll have a little nightcap together. Try to end today on a more pleasant note."

Roger was surprised. This was the first time in five years that Jackie had invited him for a drink. Alone. Despite her gregarious manner, he always felt that Jackie Lyell was slightly apprehensive in his company. He guessed that she had heard the stories about why he had had to sell his California medical practice eight years ago and move East to work in private clinics. Jackie Lyell probably believed the rumors that Roger had tried to rape a woman in his consulting room.

He smiled as he opened the door. "I accept."

"Fabulous."

He called over his shoulder, "But I won't be able to stay long. I want to give Adrian a call tonight in L.A."

Jackie stared at the closed door, thinking about her husband. Although he had left last Thursday, he had not called her yet.

Jackie was trying not to think that Adrian might have gone elsewhere to find what he could not enjoy in his own bed at home.

6 LICENSED PRACTICAL NURSE MARGIE CLARK LED LAVENDER GILBERT UP THE carpeted stairs from Administration, down a wide hallway past an orderly pushing a trolley of vitamin jars and Perrier bottles, and stopped in front of a door marked EXAMINATION ROOM 3.

Inside, she set down Lavender's belongings and pointed to a leather-and-steel Barcelona chair. "Why don't you sit here, honey, and answer a few questions for me while we wait for Roger."

Lavender brushed a strand of blond hair from her face. "Do I have to?"

Margie looked closer at the model. "Don't you feel good?"

Lavender ran a finger under her nose. "I don't know how I feel."

Margie understood. New patients were usually nervous, especially the young ones. This girl was scarcely older than Margie's two high-school daughters. She thought about the drug worries she had with her kids.

"Sit quietly, dear," she said warmly. "There's other work I can do till Roger gets here."

As Margie busied herself pulling forms from filing drawers and stapling together prep sheets, Lavender sat in the chair, beginning to realize what was happening to her. She was in a drug clinic. It did not fit in at all with the plans she had made for her life.

* * *

Ever since she could remember, Lavender had dreamt of moving to New York City and becoming a top model—a world far away from Des Moines, Iowa.

Lavender's parents lived in Sunset Estates, a suburban development of split-level homes. Lavender remembered the house as middle-class and quiet on the outside, but a battleground on the inside. Her parents never stopped fighting with one another.

"Why do we never have enough money?" screamed her mother, an attractive woman who had long ago forgotten her hopes of becoming a Las Vegas dancer.

Lavender's father was an insurance salesman who had wanted to play professional football in his younger days. From his chair in front of the television, he shouted back to the kitchen, "Maybe we'd have a few dollars if you didn't try to live like somebody you aren't or can never be."

"For your information, wise guy," retorted the mother. "I might have been somebody if I hadn't married a slob like you and let you drag me down to your level."

"You were already down there. With your legs wide open."

To escape the tense, suffocating atmosphere of her home, Lavender threw herself into activities at school. She became known as the prettiest girl in school, the best dresser, and the best dancer. Excelling in drama, she planned to use a modeling career as a springboard into acting, maybe someday winning an Academy Award.

Lavender's steady boyfriend was Denny Straker, the school's star football player. In their junior year they were voted "Dream Couple" at the prom. Lavender and Denny had gone all the way in their lovemaking by the time they were seventeen, but Lavender made it clear to Denny that she was not going to marry him—or anyone else—after graduation. She wasn't sure exactly how, but she knew she was going to get out of Des Moines and make something of herself. She didn't need marriage and a family to tie her down.

In their senior year, Denny was suspended from the football team on drug charges. His family grounded him and cut off his allowance. Denny's biggest disappointment was that he wouldn't have money to buy cocaine. The drug was popular among the high school's "in" crowd; Lavender and Denny had progressed to it from marijuana.

"This might be our last toot for a while, babe," Denny announced as he laid two short lines on the glass-topped table in his parents' living room. His mother and father had gone to Chicago for a dentists' convention and left Denny house-sitting with their cocker spaniel, Rags.

Rolling a dollar bill into a tube, he said, "I don't know how long Dad's going to hold back my allowance."

"Maybe it's good we stop," Lavender said. She had always worried that she'd become addicted to drugs like the down-and-out people she saw on television documentaries and news reports.

"I can handle it," Denny announced. "You've got a good head on you, too, babe."

Lavender flicked her long blond hair over one shoulder and lowered the rolled note to the table. She closed her eyes as she inhaled the coke, enjoying the burn behind her forehead. Although Lavender was just a casual drug user, she realized that it was going to be difficult to live without this fantastic feeling.

Cocaine made Lavender feel as if she had everything in the world going for her. Coke made her buzz with excitement. It increased her self-esteem. High on coke, Lavender liked to imagine the career she would have in New York—as an actress, maybe, or a model.

What turned Denny on were the physical changes cocaine made in Lavender. He watched as her nipples hardened into taut rosy strawberries. As he reached for her breasts, he murmured, "I'll think of something to keep our supply coming."

Lavender let his hand play across her fluffy pink sweater, wondering if people recognized the point when they were on the verge of becoming addicted to a drug. She was terrified of being dependent on something she couldn't control. "Denny, maybe we better take this as a sign to go easy on coke for a while."

Denny's fingers kept working. "Leave everything to me, babe."

The next night eighteen-year-old Denny Straker was arrested

at Finnegan's All-Nite Liquor Store with a .38 handgun he had taken from his father's desk drawer. Lavender knew Denny had attempted the robbery to get money to buy coke. She wanted to visit him in jail but her parents intervened, forbidding her to have anything more to do with the boy they now called a drug addict and hoodlum.

When Denny Straker was sentenced to ten years in Iowa State Penitentiary for armed robbery, Lavender was staying with her grandparents in Mason City. She was deeply troubled by Denny's arrest. Could she have prevented it? Her grandparents saw her uneasiness and promised to pay for her college tuition next fall so she could meet new friends and make the first step toward some kind of career.

The following September Lavender enrolled as a freshman at Iowa State. She longed to be in New York City, making the rounds to model agencies with photographs of herself. But where would she get the money to pursue those dreams?

At college, she quickly discovered she had little in common with the girls in the sorority house. Their ambitions centered on boyfriends, frivolous clothes, organizing campus socials. No one had dreams about glamorous careers in Hollywood and Manhattan. Lavender moved out of the sorority house and began dating older students who seemed to have a broader, more mature grasp on their future.

Among Lavender's dates was a graduate student from Denver enrolled in a creative writing workshop taught by thirty-one-year-old novelist Larry Bernstein, from New York City. Bernstein invited students to his off-campus apartment for rap sessions enlivened by wine, grass, and cocaine. After Lavender's first few visits there, she began seeing Bernstein alone. Despite the divorced novelist's thinning hair and paunch belly, she was attracted to his seemingly worldwise ways, and soon they were making love on a regular basis. Lavender found Larry Bernstein much more sophisticated than her younger boyfriends; she also welcomed the cocaine he shared with her. It seemed to fortify her drive and hopes for the future. Gradually, now that she was able to talk about a career with someone who actually came from New

York City and could discuss the fabulous life there, she forgot about her high-school sweetheart.

Bernstein's latest novel, The Blue Canoe, *had recently sold to a paperback house, giving him money to buy the coke he willingly shared with Lavender. Amused by her dreams of becoming a high fashion model and film star, he said one weekend, "If you want to live in the fast lane, sweetheart, you've got to learn how to free-base."*

Media stories about the comedian Richard Pryor setting himself aflame had become legend on American campuses, and Lavender asked, "Isn't free-basing dangerous?"

"You've just got to know how to do it."

Like a Svengali of the drug world, Bernstein taught Lavender how to cook cocaine in a mixture of sodium hydroxide and ether, letting it dry down to crystals. After putting the crystals in the glass bowl of a water pipe, he heated it with a butane lighter and showed Lavender how to suck the vapors into her lungs.

Because cooking reduced a gram of coke by half, free-basing doubled the price of a high, although its rush was gone in two minutes. Bernstein's paperback advance quickly disappeared in $1,000 binges, and, by Easter vacation, he had stopped sending child-support checks to his ex-wife in New York.

Marilyn Bernstein, a short woman with a poodle haircut and an aggressive manner, flew out to Iowa to confront her ex-husband about the abrupt halt in money. She found Lavender living with him in the dingy off-campus apartment. Drug paraphernalia was scattered on the living-room floor.

Repelled by the filthy state of Bernstein's cramped quarters, Marilyn Bernstein turned her spleen on Lavender. "I can deal with Larry trashing himself with the campus Lolita in this pigsty," she sneered. "But when I find the two of you depriving my children of food, I lose control."

Lavender looked pretty and defenseless but she could fight for herself when necessary. Standing up to the shrill New Yorker, she argued back, "Larry's no longer your husband."

"A fact for which I get down on bended knee and thank the Lord daily," retorted Marilyn Bernstein. "But my kids are

unfortunate enough to have the schmuck for a father. So if you don't get your ass off this campus, you teenage sleaze-bag, watch me go to the Dean of Students and have you expelled for drugs, and lover-boy there fired from his job as Ernest Fucking Hemingway-in-Residence."

Larry Bernstein did not want to endanger his well-paid position at Iowa State. He remained silent as Marilyn proceeded to throw Lavender's belonging's into a Hefty garbage bag and onto the sidewalk.

By now Lavender was disillusioned with college. She plotted how she could escape. The last place she wanted to go was back home to Des Moines. Life there seemed like a pool of quicksand, threatening to pull her down into a dull, boring world where she would wake up some day and be just like her parents.

Knowing that her parents would never permit her to move to New York and look for a job, she fibbed to them, saying that her drama teacher had told her she was wasting her time in college, that a girl of her talent and appearance should be in New York studying theater with the professionals.

With money from her grandparents, she sublet a furnished studio apartment on Manhattan's Upper East Side and immediately began calling the telephone numbers she'd gotten from Larry Bernstein.

Bernstein's friends worked mainly in the media, mostly television, advertising, and publishing; they all invited Lavender round to their apartments for a drink or a smoke. For the first weeks in New York, Lavender was ecstatic about being in the city of her dreams and meeting people who were actually making money by doing creative jobs of their choice.

One of the people on Bernstein's list was a photographer, Doug Curtis. Impressed with the lavender-eyed, creamy-complexioned girl from the Midwest, Curtis used her for a fall layout he was shooting for Cosmopolitan.

By the following spring, Lavender had signed with a small modeling agency, Highlights, and her face began appearing in the glossy fashion magazines. Glamour. Harpers. Seventeen. Editors as well as photographers liked her looks, the range she had

between an innocent sweet sixteen and a sophisticated femme
*fatale. But it was eight pages of Lavender wearing Chatwyn
evening gowns—photographed in Tunisia for* Vogue*—that
gave her her biggest break.*

*Chatwyn loved the color spread and invited her to test for the
campaign for his new perfume, Star Lady.*

*Along with Chatwyn's attention came Lavender's first taste
of the success she had always dreamed about. The leading modeling agency, San Trop, asked to represent her. She moved in with
another San Trop model, Bev Jordan, on Columbus Avenue. She
began to be invited to all the right parties with a mixture of
fashion people, artists, glamorous millionaires, and a smattering
of European titles.*

But there were also drawbacks to Lavender's new success.

*Chatwyn's contract curtailed many areas of her private life.
The Star Lady contract forbade her to work for anybody else for
two years. She couldn't buy or wear any other designer perfume.
She had to be home in bed before midnight. She couldn't get
married for the duration of her contract. She couldn't date married men. It was taboo to go out in public wearing jeans or
sloppy clothes. She couldn't be seen in a coffee shop or at a lunch
counter. She was forbidden by the contract to do anything unfit-
ting for a "Star Lady." The only area that the contract did not
cover was drugs, and Lavender soon discovered the reason.*

*As Lavender's workload grew heavier, stylists and photogra-
phers gave her speed to keep her alert for the extended fashion
shoots. They also supplied cocaine—more coke than Lavender
had ever seen.*

*But Lavender no longer felt the same old euphoria from coke.
The highs did not last as long. She began to feel jittery between
hits. She felt less like a young woman whose dream was coming
true, more like somebody who had less and less control of their
life. As Lavender's restlessness increased, her temper grew
sharper. When the old fear returned about becoming hooked on
drugs, there was another job to do, another deadline to make.
Lavender told herself that she was strong, that she could go cold
turkey whenever she wanted. Every week she planned to stop*

taking drugs after the next job. But her schedule became more hectic, and the assignments came in faster. Then came the trip to Antigua, the overload of the Vogue *fashion spread and the Star Lady shoot rolled into one assignment.*

Lavender could barely remember what had happened in Antigua. She remembered being on a plane—she wasn't even sure if it was coming or going. And she remembered being on a beach. Then feeling hot, and feeling very tired . . . the rest of it was a blur. Suddenly she realized the nurse had left her and there was another person in the room.

"Hi." Roger Cooper set down his clipboard on the desk. "Jackie tells me you're a model."

Lavender jerked her head, still a little frightened by the realization that she was sitting inside a drug clinic.

"I'm Roger Cooper," he introduced. "I'm the medical director here."

Lavender managed a weak smile.

Studying the model's oval face, Roger saw that she was pretty. In fact, beautiful. Exactly as Jackie had told him. But she definitely appeared to be disoriented.

Professional concern in his voice, Roger asked, "Lavender, do you want to talk about any chemical dependencies?"

Lavender's mind fluctuated between the thought of being in a clinic and her contract with Chatwyn. Trying to muster strength in her voice, she answered, "Who says I have any dependencies?"

"Nobody's forcing you to check into Tanglewood, Lavender," Roger said. "Staying here is your own free choice. You must *want* to do this."

Lavender nodded, lowering her eyes. "I've also got my career to think about."

"How closely is your career involved with drugs, Lavender?"

"Can we maybe talk about all this tomorrow?" she murmured. "I'm tired."

"Of course," Roger answered. "Jackie said you flew from the West Indies this morning. You must be bushed."

"I am," Lavender replied, thinking that the flight seemed as if it had happened days—weeks—ago. She had no idea how long she had been here.

"I'd like to run some tests on you tomorrow, too," Roger said.

"I just want to sleep now." She turned her blue eyes on him. "Can I go sleep?"

Roger considered administering a sedative to make certain Lavender slept a full night and would be fresh tomorrow. But he dismissed the idea. The problem with treating cocaine abuse was that, like amphetamines, coke affected the nervous system. Also, street coke could be cut with anything from anesthetics, like benzocaine and procaine, to amphetamines themselves. He would need to wait until he had her test results to know exactly what he was dealing with.

Lavender's eyes became alive and nervous. "I can leave here whenever I want, can't I? I can check myself out of here whenever I decide it's time to go back to New York?"

"Of course," Roger said. "It's your life. You can decide what you want to stop—whenever you want to stop it."

"Stop?" She looked at him quizzically. "What do you mean?"

Roger's voice remained even. "Your career or a drug dependency. It's up to you what you want to put an end to. Everything's in your control—at least at this point."

7 "WHO'S HERE TONIGHT, MARGIE?" INGRID MATTHISON, R.N., SET DOWN HER PURSE and a copy of the *National Enquirer* on the desk in the third-floor checkpoint, a cubicle at the end of the third-floor hallway in the main house.

"I just finished settling a new girl in room thirty-seven." Margie slotted the blue plastic computerized cardkey into the filebox. "The rest is the usual bunch. You shouldn't have any trouble from any of them."

Tonight was the first time for Ingrid to work checkpoint during the night shift. Sandy-haired, with a snub nose dusted with freckles, twenty-eight-year-old Ingrid had been "floating" during her first two months employment at Tanglewood, gradually working her way through the four floors of the main building and two annexes.

"If you pour us some coffee," Margie suggested, "I'll give you a quick who's who while I try to pull this face together. As usual, I look like hell at the end of my shift."

"You've got a deal." Ingrid turned toward the Mister Coffee on the counter behind them in the small area.

Margie opened a drawer next to the stainless steel sink. After rummaging until she found a zipped plastic cosmetic bag she kept there for "emergencies," she turned to the mirror.

A wild woman stared back at her. Wiry brown hair. Shiny red nose. Eyes like a panda. Before she began the repair work, she reached for the tweezers to pull out two hairs sprouting between her eyebrows.

"Cream and sugar?" Ingrid asked.

"Half a Sweet 'n' Low."

Leaning closer to the mirror, Margie began, "Room thirty-one is Mary Kay Hatch. Atlantic City dancer turned drug pusher. Remember reading about her? That gal who supposedly put the needle in the arm of the rich Harvard kid who o.d.'ed at the Boston Ritz? Word has it she struck a plea bargain with the state. They're drying her out here on taxpayer's money before putting her on the stand."

Margie reached for the blue-and-green mug. Taking a long sip, she closed her eyes. "Mmm. Just what I need."

Turning back to the mirror, she continued, "Room thirty-three is Lesley Charles. You're probably too young to remember her. My dad had all her LPs. Lesley Charles was *the* leading black female singer back in the sixties. 'Road to San Jose.' 'Rocks In My Whiskey,' the sexiest version of 'Misty' you've ever heard. She's here to kick a bad crack habit."

Margie grimaced as she pulled out the second hair and then faced the mirror to concentrate on her eyes.

"Room thirty"—she opened the Maybelline liquid eye shadow—"Joe Parker. Senior vice president of Sundial Steel. Barbiturates and liquor. Steel company pays his bill. Ditto thirty-two. Paul Sabrinski. Banker from Minneapolis. His bank picks up the tab. You probably learned since you've been here, hon, that more and more big companies are setting up schemes to rehabilitate executives who turn to drugs under pressure. In fact, it's getting to be so common that the young employees here have come up with a nickname for them: 'CJs'—corporate junkies."

She blinked into the mirror to examine the work on her left eye. "Thirty-eight is Lillian Weiss. Sweet lady. But about three hundred or so pounds overweight. Addicted to diet pills. If you want to know anything, ask Lillian Weiss. She will tell you and probably a lot more. She adores gossip.

But I wish somebody would tell her to wash her pussy."

Behind Margie, Ingrid spat her coffee into the sink, laughing.

"Really!" Margie leaned toward the mirror. "She smells awful. But because she's so nice to everybody, nobody has the nerve to say, 'Lillian, dear, you smell like an old fish.'"

Moving to her right eye, she continued, "Room thirty-four is Crandall Benedict, the writer. He also loves a good gossip. But mostly about people we never heard of. Anyway me. Society people. Jet set. He visits that young preppy kid, Skip Ryan, down on Two. You know, Jimmy Ryan's son who got busted for angel dust in Chinatown. Benedict's very chummy with the whole Ryan family. Very fancy-schmancy."

She exchanged her eye makeup for a tube of lipstick, took a long swallow of coffee, and confided, "All in all, Ingrid, the third floor's no big sweat. Most patients here are in the last stages of treatment. Their days are filled with exercise, therapy, and lectures. At night they're usually dish rags after their encounter groups. Most of them aren't even on sedation."

As Margie pulled the top off the lipstick tube and turned back to the mirror, Ingrid began washing the two mugs in the small sink. She asked, "What's the deal with this new patient you just checked in tonight?"

"Lavender Gilbert? She's a fashion model, I understand. But she's not officially admitted yet. One more of those pretty girls who stuck their nose too long in the coke barrel and don't know what to do about it."

Ingrid shook water from her hands into the sink. "What about Dr. Cooper? Is he on duty all night?"

"No. Roger should be going off about now."

"What's the story on him?"

"Love life?"

"Yeah."

"You know Carol Ann Rice?" Margie worked her lips, rubbing the lipstick.

"Carol Ann Rice of *The Carol Ann Rice Show?* Is she here, too?" asked Ingrid, impressed.

"She was. About a year go." Margie searched the cosmetic bag for her gloss.

Ingrid was intrigued. "I read that Carol Ann Rice had a drinking problem after her daughter got killed in that motorcycle accident. But I didn't know she had been a patient at Tanglewood."

"Mmm-hm. Around the time her series was cancelled. While she was here, she and Roger got ver-r-r-y chummy indeed."

"Really?"

"Absolutely. But you know Roger. Mr. Proper. He waited until she checked out and they met in the city."

"Was Roger Cooper ever married?"

"No. But he came close to it a couple times, I understand. The last candidate was called Crista. She left him about the time I got here."

Turning from the mirror, Margie stuffed everything back into the white daisy bag, adding "Roger's got nobody steady these days. He's back to playing the field, I guess."

Ingrid took her place at the counter, flipping through the patient lists. Idly she asked, "Got a date tonight, Margie?"

Margie turned to the mirror for the last time, hairbrush in hand. "Just going home, after I check Garden Pavilion for Ellen. She left early and asked me to make the rounds for her."

Moving toward the door, she called, "Night, hon. Thanks for the coffee."

"Night, Margie. Get home safe."

Margie hurried along the hall; her sneakers padded down the wide mahogany staircase.

At the foot of the stairs, she saw light flooding out from under Administration's door. Jackie Lyell must be working late tonight. Where had her husband gone?

As she moved toward the side foyer, she thought of the

rounds she had to make. The first was Ray Esposito, a patient in the Garden Pavilion. Heroin recovery.

Margie opened the wall cabinet under the archway in the Garden Pavilion and withdrew Ellen's clipboard and six green computerized card keys to the annex's six suites.

The Garden Pavilion accommodated patients requiring closer surveillance than other patients in the main house. Among them were the prizefighter, Peabo Washington, and Ray Esposito.

Margie inserted card G4 into the lock of Esposito's suite. After it clicked, she pushed the door and entered a small, glossy white vestibule. In front of her stood a second door leading into the sitting room.

The vestibule's fluorescent ceiling flickered as she pushed the switch and moved along the shiny white wall to her left. She felt for the button low on the molding and pressed the computerized code noted on Ellen's instructions.

The white wall lit, darkened, quickly activating into an observation panel called a See-Wall.

Standing in front of the See-Wall, Margie looked into the suite's bedroom and saw Ray Esposito lying on a bed. Olive-skinned, with curly black hair, Esposito was naked on the sheets as his hand moved up and down on his penis.

Feeling a blush brighten her face, Margie made a note on the clipboard about Esposito's masturbation. She remembered what Ellen had briefed her about the patient in G4.

Ray Esposito was a construction worker on skyscraper sites. Ellen had told Margie that a surprisingly large number of hardhats across the country were addicted to heroin. It was the toll skyscraper workers paid for going up twenty, thirty, forty floors above ground level to weld iron beams and ride girders.

Esposito, emerging from his first week of heroin withdrawal, was experiencing an insatiable sexual drive—the Priapus syndrome.

During the Priapus syndrome, Roger Cooper suggested that a narcotic patient's spouse or lover be nearby. If not, there was no alternative but frequent masturbation—often ten times a day was normal.

Esposito had no family. At least none that Ellen had told Margie about. The only thing she knew about the thirty-one-year-old man was that he was a charity patient. It had been Roger Cooper's idea that Tanglewood should always accommodate a few patients unable to afford the clinic's high fees. At the moment there were two, Esposito and Father Wayne Hawkes, a Catholic diocesan priest recovering from alcoholism, who was due to leave the next day.

Margie pushed the button. The See-Wall flickered, dimmed, blanked to whiteness.

As Margie turned toward the outer door, she hoped that Esposito had a wife or girl friend who would arrive soon to help him through the last stages of his heroin withdrawal.

8 ROGER TOOK TIME BEFORE DRINKS WITH JACKIE LYELL TO POP INTO THE HUB FOR a firsthand report from the floor nurse about anything he might have missed in the past thirty-six hours. Whenever he had a weekend date, Roger tried to be available only for emergency calls or if junior doctors or the weekend senior-in-house needed backup.

Located down the corridor from Roger's office, the Hub was the nerve center of Tanglewood, the computer room, the dispatch desk, the one place in the otherwise serene clinic where bells rang, lights flashed, calls were bleeped to staff members' Weatherhead call-packs. Roger liked the noises and the activity of the Hub; they were the closest thing to a general hospital.

A large room with an illuminated white ceiling, the Hub served, too, as a staff room. It was furnished with couches and chairs, with pinewood tables where employees could enjoy a quick snack from a buffet stocked with fresh coffee, tea, juices, and salads as well as an assortment of croissants and quiches easily heated in the microwave oven. More complete meals could be brought from the kitchen, and all food was free of charge to employees.

Sunday night's floor nurse, Carmen Pennington, a youthful, carrot-topped grandmother with tinted blue glasses, turned from her computer desk as Roger entered through the swinging doors. She greeted him warmly. "Sent your little lady back to wicked New York already, Roger?"

"She left a long time ago," he replied. As co-director of the clinic, he knew some gossip about his private life was inevitable, but he tried to keep it to a minimum.

Sitting sideways on the low countertop, he glanced at the stack of red plastic trays alongside him. Seeing that the tray marked "Cooper" was empty, he asked, "Anything exciting happening around here I might have missed?"

Nurse Pennington looked at the farthest of the six computer screens blinking in front of her operator's chair. "New patient on three."

"I know. I just came from her." Roger reached for the duty sheet in the top tray, still concerned about Lavender Gilbert's hesitation about pursuing treatment for a chemical dependency. The model definitely had a problem. That much was clear even without tests. "You won't see her name on your screen. She hasn't decided if she's going to stay here."

Roger's eyes moved down the list of night staff. Tonight's senior-in-house doctor was Dunstan Bell. Also on duty were two junior doctors, nine nurses, and fifteen attendants.

He asked, "Anything else going on around the place?"

Carmen took another casual glance at her screens. "You know about patient resistance in G-three."

"Mmm. Peabo Washington." Roger replaced the duty sheet and looked at Suzie French, who was working behind Carmen.

Her back to the room, pig-tailed Suzie wore a headset that connected her to the clinic's main switchboard in Communications. As it was now suppertime in the clinic, Suzie's fingers were busily flipping switches on the console in front of her as she spoke through her mouthpiece, dispatching nurses with mealtime medication, buzzing waiters for room service, locating attendants to escort patients wishing to eat in the dining room, paging physical therapists, placing calls to tonight's medical staff. Dispatch was the command center for Tanglewood's manpower, centrally situated to orchestrate activity between the checkpoint computers, the floor nurse, and Communications, between the main house and both annexes, and the medical and therapy departments.

Carmen Pennington brought Roger's attention back to the Hub. Nodding at a chubby man in a tweed suit crouched over a yellow pad in the far corner, she said, "Lonny had an emergency earlier today. Mrs. Morrisey thought he had given her Emetine to make her vomit if she drank alcohol."

Roger shook his head. Many clinics injected patients with the amoebic dysentery drug for alcohol treatment. It irritated a patient's stomach, causing vomiting when alcohol was consumed. But Roger disapproved of any form of shock treatment to the system. He wondered how Detroit socialite, Jennifer Morrisey—an alcohol recovery patient—had gotten alcohol to drink in the first place.

Carmen explained. "Mrs. Morrisey grabbed a whiskey from a room service trolley. She swigged it down and immediately started vomiting. Jane Nelson answered the call and rang Dr. Bell. But Mrs. Morrisey refused to talk to anybody but Lonny Lamb. He's been treating her since she's been here. Fortunately he was at home and around in a few minutes."

Listening to the report, Roger studied the cherubic-looking doctor of internal medicine who was absorbed in his work at the corner table. Impressed by Lamb's industry, he said, "It looks like Lonny is preparing a report on it at this very moment. I should hear all about it tomorrow."

Remembering his date with Jackie Lyell in Administration, Roger rose from the counter. "See you in the morning, Carmen."

"Not here you won't," she informed him merrily. "I've got the day off. Lois Bannerman sits here and plays God tomorrow."

"Enjoy your day of rest, then."

"When does Adrian Lyell get back from California?" Carmen called after Roger.

"Sometime this week." Roger continued toward the door, deciding not to add: I hope.

Behind him, a voice crackled through a speaker over the dispatcher's console: "Dr. Bell . . . Dr. Dunstan Bell . . ."

Roger stepped aside in time to avoid being hit by a lanky man wearing a gray flannel suit and a pair of round silver glasses perched on his nose.

"Evening, Dunstan," he said as the man hurried past him.

"Can't talk now," said the pathologist as he rushed into the Hub. "See you in tomorrow's Huddle."

Roger smiled to himself as he was left in the doctor's wake; a casual observer might easily mistake the brusque autocratic Dunstan Bell—and not himself—for the medical director of Tanglewood.

Bell stopped in front of Carmen Pennington's station, demanding sharply, "Why does my patient on three, Miss Hatch, not show a change to pentazocine?"

Carmen turned to her keyboard, tapped the code for administered medications, and read a few moments before answering. "No medication change has been punched in for Mary Kay Hatch from propoxyphene napsylate."

"Rubbish. I entered it myself this afternoon."

Leaning back on her chair, Carmen held out one hand to the screen. "Be my guest," she said.

Moving round the counter, Dunstan Bell peered through his silver glasses at the computer screen. Grimacing at the green letters, he muttered, "Infernal machines. If I had my way, they'd all be thrown out the front door."

From the stack of red trays, he grabbed a handful of notes from the compartment marked BELL, stuffed them into the pocket of his jacket, and rushed back through the swinging doors.

In a cubbyhole office one floor above the Hub, Nutritionist Sarah Longman finished the last of the menus for the coming week and began studying Roger Cooper's notes on the obesity patient, Lillian Weiss.

Tanglewood did not accept patients who were merely trying to lose weight. Obesity was treated there only when patients were dependent on diet pills or other weight-loss drugs.

Lillian Weiss had finished her third week in treatment. She'd been weaned off the phendimetrazine diet bars to which she had been addicted and put on a physical therapy program to strengthen her ankles so she could carry her 535-pound body. Sarah had also developed a low-calorie diet for the Park Avenue widow. But so far Lillian Weiss's chart showed no reduction in weight. Sarah made a note to check on the patient's latest lab tests first thing tomorrow morning, before organizing a new diet for the woman.

Around the corner from the nutritionist's office on the second floor in the main house, psychotherapist Betty Lassiter sat facing Skip Ryan, a nineteen-year-old Brown University student, in his room, talking him down from an anxiety bout. During the past week Skip had joined Betty's advanced encounter group, which was known to staff and the group's members as "the Sweat Room."

Skip was recovering from abuse of phencyclidine—better

known as PCP or angel dust—but Betty also knew that young Ryan suffered from the emotional as well as social pressures that came with being one of the children of the controversial politician and scion of the powerful Ryan family, Jimmy Ryan.

A big woman who wore blue jeans and sloppy lumberjack shirts, Betty's voice was surprisingly soft as she encouraged the boy to talk about his habit.

"Think of the times you couldn't score, Skip. Remember how shitty you felt. How scared. How helpless."

"I know all that," Ryan said impatiently, "but you don't think about it when you need something. You think of the highs."

"Try to remember the bummers. The scares you had. The way you had no control over yourself. How dust kicked your ass. You couldn't stop doing its bidding, Skip. You were its slave. Now you're in control. You're on top of things. You can say no."

"It's easy for you to say all that but . . ." His voice trailed off.

"What about your journal?" Betty asked. "Are you making your daily entries?" She urged her patients to keep a day-to-day journal of their anxieties, illnesses, thoughts.

He shrugged. "Yes and no."

"You shouldn't ignore it, Skip. Apart from straightening out your head, it's good practice for you. I've read all the entries you left for me to read and I think you're a good writer. Damned good."

"They're shit."

"What are?"

"Those pages. I used to want to write. Do journalism. Write profiles and—" He dropped his eyes to his hands clasped on the lap of his track suit. "My journal's not good enough to show anybody."

"Maybe you're the wrong person to decide that."

He insisted, "Naw, it's no good."

Betty continued appealing to the troubled youth, trying

to forget that she was due home in a half hour for a supper party. Betty hoped that her roommate could entertain the eight guests until she got there. But past experience told her that she would probably be late. Betty sometimes said that her job description as chief psychotherapist at Tanglewood was 75 percent "handholding."

9 IN ADMINISTRATION, JACKIE HANDED ROGER A WHISKEY AND WATER AS SHE admitted, "Adrian hasn't called me since he left on Thursday."

Roger was seated on the leather chesterfield across from Jackie. One boot resting on the knee of his corduroy jeans, he asked, "Do you have a better idea than I do of when he might be back?"

"I'm afraid not. But certainly he can't be away *too* long." She waved nervously at the large desk across the room. "There's so much work to do here."

Sipping at his whiskey, Roger saw that his question was making Jackie uncomfortable. Obviously she knew no more about Adrian's movements than he did.

Ever since Adrian had left on Thursday, Roger had tried to be as positive as possible about Jackie working in Administration. But the arrangement still worried him. Whenever Adrian had been away from Tanglewood previously, a secretary had done his work in this office. Why had he called in Jackie this time?

Jackie glanced back to the big desk in front of the windows and said, "I've made a note to ring our lawyers first thing tomorrow morning about possible trouble with Chatwyn over Lavender Gilbert. Also, I've got the release forms ready for Father Hawkes to sign when he checks out tomorrow."

She looked back to Roger. "Oh, yes. Another thing. I found a note on Adrian's desk diary about insurance. It wasn't specific about what kind of insurance. Just 'insurance.' Who do I check with about that?"

"Call Accounts. Renee Newby can pull out the policies."

"Right." She reached for the note pad resting on the table.

Roger reflected that Jackie's eagerness to succeed in Adrian's job ironically made her less aggressive, not so much the self-assured, chic butterfly that he had always perceived her to be. He also was detecting an apologetic tone in her voice. She obviously knew that Adrian's unexpected disappearance had left the clinic in the lurch and it embarrassed her. But the question remained whether Jackie would be able to do the work. This week would be the test.

Abandoning his questions about Adrian, Roger concentrated on Tanglewood's day-to-day problems, telling Jackie that he wanted her to make reservations at a nearby inn or hotel for Karen Washington, her two children, and her sister-in-law; he reminded her that Little Milly Wheeler and her mother were arriving tomorrow evening from Nashville; he told her to double-check with housekeeping about the rooms reserved for the Wheelers in the Garden Pavilion.

When he finished his drink, Roger stressed one more time that Jackie should take all calls from the press but sidestep any questions about patients. As they shook hands good night at the office door, he assured her that he felt she could do the job but told her not to work too late that night. She would need a good night's rest for tomorrow.

The temperature outside had dropped ten degrees since Roger had driven back from Stonebridge Station. He hurried across the front lawn to his Mercedes under the porte cochère, the grass hard with frost beneath his feet.

Seeing light glowing around Administration's drawn curtains as he passed the window, he recalled Jackie's embarrassment about Adrian not telephoning.

What kind of marriage did they have? he wondered. Was it so sophisticated and lax that Adrian could leave home without contacting his wife? Roger could not imagine being involved in such a casual arrangement.

Although Roger had seen Adrian and Jackie practically every day of his professional life for the past five years, he realized he knew very little about the Lyells' private life. The more he thought about them, the more he realized that they were no longer the close-knit couple he had first understood them to be. But, then, Adrian had changed in his relationship with Roger, too.

As he put the key into the ignition, Roger thought back to one specific incident that had first told him how much Adrian was changing these days.

It had been a late Friday afternoon little over a year ago. Adrian had buzzed Roger in his office and invited him to drop around to Administration when he had a spare moment. Roger had taken ten minutes and stepped across the hallway to see what he wanted.

Adrian still looked impeccably groomed at the end of the day, wearing a herringbone suit, with a red foulard tucked into his chest pocket. Standing behind his oversize desk, he pointed proudly to a set of blueprints spread in front of him and said, "Here's something I'd like you to see."

Roger saw that the prints were obviously an architect's conceptual drawing. Glancing back to Adrian, he said, "Looks impressive—what is it?"

Adrian's mood was expansive. "The new Tanglewood." He'd beckoned Roger to step closer. "See. This is where the golf course will be. We can offer Clem Swift a price he can't refuse for his orchard. We'll leave a few trees to give the condominiums a countrified atmosphere. That's why people come to the country, isn't it? Trees. Rolling lawns. Tinkling brooks."

"Hold it just a minute," Roger said. "What condominiums? What golf course? What tinkling brooks?"

"Think about it," Adrian replied. "We have to reinvest profits. Why not like this?" He'd gestured to the blueprints. "We must keep moving forward, and I think this is the direction we should take."

Roger was horrified by the idea of building condominiums and a golf course at Tanglewood. He said, "But these are plans for a pleasure center, not a medical clinic."

"Correction—it's going to be a pioneering combination of both. People are going to have more time for leisure in the future. We've got to move with the times."

Roger could not believe he was having this conversation with his partner. "But Tanglewood is a rehabilitation center. Not . . . summer camp!"

Seeing Adrian's face redden, Roger thought that perhaps he had spoken too harshly. Not wanting to offend his partner, he continued more diplomatically, "Adrian, I'm very impressed with your foresight. I agree with you that we must plan ahead, and as usual, you've done a very thorough job. Very professional. But you must admit, this is a little off course from our original conception of Tanglewood."

Adrian looked down at the plans on the desk. For a moment he stood, saying nothing, twisting the gold signet ring on his little finger. Then he brusquely rolled up the blueprints. As he did so, he said, almost under his breath, "I'm certain that I could find some intelligent investors who would be more receptive than you."

That conversation had taken place a little over a year ago. Adrian had not mentioned his ideas about a totally new Tanglewood again until last week. Barging into Roger's office with the latest copy of *Time* magazine, he snarled, "You could have told me they were going to turn this into a PR piece on you, Roger."

Only minutes earlier had Roger finished reading the extensive article. It had tagged Tanglewood as America's leading private drug clinic, praising it as a "state of the art retreat for detoxification and rehabilitation." Much to Roger's embarrassment, not only had the magazine put his picture on the cover, it had also called him Tanglewood's "driving force." Roger believed in teamwork; he wanted no part of the limelight for himself or any other one person on the staff. He was actually beginning to wonder if it had been a mistake to have given the prestigious news magazine access to Tanglewood.

Adrian's finger trembled with rage as he pointed to one page, saying "You actually state here that you foresee our future having more charity patients."

Roger did not like being put on the defensive. He answered as calmly as possible, "If you reread that section, Adrian, you'll see I'm talking about an ideal clinic—that I'm answering a question."

"Don't deny it," Adrian shouted. "You are talking about the future."

"Adrian, you're angry," Roger said, wondering if his partner could possibly be jealous that *Time* had given Roger so much space rather than being upset by the content.

"Correction, Roger," Adrian snapped. "I'm furious. At least I was gentleman enough to come to you privately with *my* proposal for the future."

"What proposal?"

Adrian pulled back his head with sudden indignation. "What proposal? Why, Roger, I spent thousands of dollars—out of my own pocket—on architectural designs and you stand there and blithely dismiss it by asking 'What proposal?' Doesn't my opinion count around here any more?"

Adrian stepped closer to Roger's desk, his aristocratic-looking face mottled with fury, his voice barely louder than a hiss. "Well, let me tell you something, *Doctor* Cooper. Don't expect me to keep playing the gentleman. I resent being stabbed in the back like this. I'm sick and tired of being shoved into the corner and dismissed as some kind of office manager."

Slapping the copy of *Time* down on Roger's desk, he said, "Here. You can have my copy, too. I've read enough of your crusading schemes for the future."

A telephone's buzz disturbed Roger's memories. After unlocking the door to his apartment upstairs in the estate's converted carriage house, he crossed a Navajo carpet and picked up the receiver. "Roger Cooper here."

A deep voice asked at the other end of the line, "Dr. Cooper?"

"Speaking."

The man said, "My name's Hudson. Tom Hudson. You don't know me, Dr. Cooper, but I'm calling about a former patient of yours—Cat Powers. She's having a pretty tough time of it at her play tonight here on Broadway. The intermission's coming up in a couple of minutes. I was wondering if I might bundle Cat into my car and bring her up to Tanglewood."

10 THE FIRST-ACT CURTAIN FELL TO TU-
MULTUOUS APPLAUSE THAT SHOOK the baroque rafters of the Hunt Theater.

Cat Powers, costumed in the faded finery of Tennessee Williams' tragic heroine Blanche Dubois, weaved unsteadily stage right. The actress's hands were shaking; mascara ran in dark rivulets down her cheeks; she pulled at the ruffled chiffon blouse restraining her ample bosom, as if she were suffocating.

Cat Powers was not acting.

The stage manager, a short black man named Tyrone Willard, hurried past the flats of Elysian Fields No. 3 as the applause continued.

Willard was thankful that the show's star had made it through the first act. He had thought for a while that she was going to collapse.

Moving stage right, he called, "Costume change, Miss Powers. Let's make that costume—"

He stopped, seeing Cat Powers sprawled across the arms of her fiancé, Tom Hudson, while another man tore at her clothes.

Hudson was holding Cat to his chest as Dr. Gene Stone pulled up her skirt and ripped down her tights, moving a hypodermic needle toward her white buttocks.

Cat lay slumped forward in Hudson's arms, head sideways, pale-blue eyes staring blankly at the stage manager, her cupid lips twisted and smudged with lipstick, as an overhead spotlight glinted on the needle.

After Stone withdrew the syringe, Hudson jerked up Cat's tights and rearranged her skirt.

Steadying Cat between them, the two men walked her toward the stage door.

"Where do you think you're going?" Willard demanded.

"The lady's sick," Hudson called over his shoulder. "She needs attention. Medical attention."

Willard saw that there would be no stopping Hudson. He also believed that the man was probably doing the right thing. But Willard also knew that something else had to be done quickly. There was a theater full of ticket holders and no star to go on with the show. The understudy would have to step in.

Neither the show's producers nor its director were in the Sunday night house to make the announcement. The next person in authority was himself, the stage manager.

Taking a deep breath, he stepped toward the curtain,

hurriedly preparing a footlights speech that would be tomorrow morning's tabloid headline: CAT COLLAPSES BACKSTAGE.

The long black Cadillac pulled soundlessly away in the
night from the Hunt's stage door. Catching the green light
at the corner of 46th and the Avenue of the Americas, the
stretch limousine moved into the flow of uptown traffic.

The Cadillac passed a double line of limousines waiting
outside Radio City Music Hall and stayed in the left lane,
slowing to turn west on 57th Street. The usual cluster of
yellow cabs congested the front of the Russian Tea Room.
The Cadillac swerved, accelerating past Carnegie Hall,
heading toward the West Side Highway.

Tom Hudson sat in the limousine's backseat, one arm
protectively around Cat Powers. "You were beautiful tonight, puss. You were wonderful," he reassured her.

Limp as a rag doll, Cat buried her face in Hudson's chest,
shivering against him as if she could draw warmth from his
body.

Gene Stone asked from the darkness of the opposite corner, "You sure you're doing the right thing?"

"Damn right I'm sure."

"When Mel and Irving find out you yanked Cat out of
their show, they're going to scream their heads off."

"Fuck Mel. Fuck Irving. Cat's a basket case. Look at her."

Hudson cradled his fiancée with one arm, brushing back
her blue-black curls with his other hand.

He looked back at Stone. "What kind of dope did you put
in that last shot back there at the theater?"

Stone stared blankly through the dark tinted window at
the flickering lights of New Jersey beyond the highway.
"The usual."

Hudson's voice was a growl. "When we get her settled in
Tanglewood, you and me're going to sit down and have a
serious talk about the future, pal. Understand?"

Stone's eyes remained on the window. "You planning to
stay up there at the clinic?"

Apart from telephoning Tanglewood, Hudson had sent Cat's secretary, Linda Lawrence, back to the hotel to pack suitcases for him and Cat. He had told Linda to stay on at the Sherry Netherland and handle press stories, producers, and agents. Against Hudson's better judgment, he was bringing Gene Stone to Tanglewood, knowing Cat would go crazier than ever without her personal doctor from Los Angeles at her side.

Hudson answered, "I'll stay with her a couple days. Until I know she's going to get a clean bill of health. Cooper said he'll find room for all of us."

Stone jerked his head. "You talked to . . . Roger Cooper?"

"Who else? He runs the place. I found his number. Cat had it."

Stone faltered. "What did Cooper say when you mentioned my name?"

"Why should I mention your name, for Christ's sake?" Hudson looked down at Cat's matted hair. "Cooper said they've got a full house but to come on up. Cat's been a patient there before so he's going to juggle around some rooms for us."

Cat began to stir, moving against Hudson's chest.

He patted the back of her head consolingly. "Shhh, puss."

She slurred, "Tommy? Is that you, Tommy?"

"It's me, Miss Puss."

"We on the way back to the hotel, Tommy?"

"We're going to another place," he told her, pulling her close. "I'm staying right along with you."

She seemed undisturbed by the announcement. "You love me, Tommy? Really, truly love me?"

"Course I really love you. What kind of question is that?"

"Did I look pretty tonight, Tommy?"

"Pretty? You looked gorgeous."

"Beautiful?"

"Better than beautiful."

"Sexy? Was I sexy?"

"Every guy in that place tonight wanted you, puss."

She pulled at his red silk tie. "Even you?"

Hudson glanced at Stone. "These shots are driving her nuts. No wonder she's having these crackups. It's because of those damned shots you give her."

Stone was unperturbed. "It quieted her, didn't it?"

"Yeah. But how long?"

Cat tugged harder at Hudson's tie. "Am I sexy?"

"Baby, you're a knockout."

She pulled Hudson's head down toward her mouth and whispered into his ear.

Listening, he frowned and shook his head. "Not now, baby. This isn't the time or place for that kind of stuff."

She clenched her hand into a pudgy fist, beating his chest as her mood again changed abruptly. "You think I'm fat," she accused him. "You think I'm ugly. You think I'm fat and ugly and over the hill—"

"Whoa, baby. Whoa." Hudson pulled her tightly against his chest. Again she whispered her request; Hudson silently cursed Gene Stone and all the damned chemical junk he pumped into her that made Cat so crazy. What had happened to the woman he had known in the first days of their courtship? Those nights when they had curled up in front of a late show with nothing stronger than anchovy pizza and a couple of Heinekens?

"Okay," he relented. "Let me see what I can do about it."

Pushing a button on the arm rest, he lowered the glass divider between the rear seat and the chauffeur, calling "Stop the car, Jim."

As the limousine moved right on the expressway, Hudson turned to Stone. "Get out and get in front."

"In front?" Stone looked at the limousine slowing on the expressway's shoulder. "For God's sake, Tom. I've been Cat's doctor and best buddy for—"

"I don't give a shit what you've been, pal. This is my car. If I say in front, you get in front. Savvy?"

Reluctantly Stone stepped out onto the asphalt and moved into the front seat with the chauffeur.

The limousine continued north on Interstate 95, the smoked glass panel raised to its original position. In the backseat, Hudson sat with both legs spread apart. Cat knelt on the floor, her head between his legs. She began to suck his penis, pausing to talk to it in girlish whispers.

"Look at your big dick," she said to the enlargening penis. "Look what I get to suck . . . chew . . . rub all over my face . . ."

Hudson did not particularly enjoy hearing Cat speak this way, but he knew that dirty talk—or drugs—was the only way to quiet her mind. Dirty talk was safer.

PART TWO

MONDAY

11 TANGLEWOOD CAME TO LIFE LONG BEFORE DAWN BEGAN BLEACHING THE sky beyond the snarled forest on the estate's southeastern boundary. While patients still slept in the Tudor-style mansion and the stone-and-glass pavilions, the clinic commenced performing as a hotel, restaurant, laundry, as well as therapy center, gymnasium, and secretarial service.

The cedar-roofed gatehouse was manned twenty-four hours a day. During the night and early morning, floodlights lit the fieldstone wall fronting the secondary highway.

At 4:30 A.M. Monday, security guard Keith Wendell spotted a pair of headlights drawing closer down the highway and flipped the switch for the arc lamp over the front gate. He knew the approaching high beams belonged to Rita Zambetti's Subaru.

Rita stopped in front of the iron gates. She rolled down the window and held out a copy of the *Stonebridge Herald.* "Morning, Keith."

Wendell opened the gates, answering over his shoulder, "Newspaper boys get cuter every year."

The two chatted for a few minutes about next Sunday's marathon in New York before Rita continued down the driveway. Keith locked the gates behind the car; the morning paper was now rolled into the back trouser pocket of his beige uniform.

Rita left her Subaru in the staff parking lot adjoining the

main house and hurried across the frosty lawn with a heavy load of newspapers. After letting herself in the front door, she crossed the main hallway, passing Administration to a door marked COMMUNICATIONS.

Inside the small office, she flipped the light switch and set up the coffeemaker before taking off her blue watch cap and duffle coat. Next she checked the Telex for correspondence and listened for messages on the Ansaphone. By the time she had poured a second cup of coffee, she was typing reminders for the phone calls and Telexes to be answered, as well as any urgent letters left on a tape recorder.

It was usually five-thirty or six o'clock when Rita finished those chores. Her next task was to begin leafing through the stack of out-of-town newspapers she had collected this morning from Stonebridge Station on her way to work.

The New York Times. New York Journal. Christian Science Monitor. Wall Street Journal. Boston Globe. Washington Post. Los Angeles Times and *Herald Examiner*. There were also copies of the previous day's editions of London's *The Times*, *Financial Times*, *Morning Horn*, and *The Guardian*.

Rita read the papers for stories about current patients at Tanglewood. If she found a mention of somebody currently at the clinic, or gossip about Tanglewood itself, she removed the page, section, or, if the article was extensive, the entire copy from the stack.

At seven o'clock, nineteen-year-old Sylvia Lundquist would join Rita in Communications. Both girls were students. It had been Roger Cooper's idea to recruit part-time employees from neighboring colleges and universities, young people needing to defray educational expenses.

It was 4:50 A.M. Rita Zambetti was playing the Ansaphone in Communications when a light began blinking on the switchboard.

Answering the call, she was not surprised to hear a woman asking to speak to Miss Catharine Powers or Dr. Gene

Stone. Five similar messages on the Ansaphone had begun shortly after midnight.

Roger Cooper had warned the clinic staff about the press using devious ploys to learn if a newsworthy person had checked into Tanglewood, claiming to be patients' family, employees, dear, dear friends.

She replied, "I'm sorry, ma'am, but neither of those names is on my list. I suggest you call back later at eight-thirty when Administration opens."

Grudgingly, the caller agreed to telephone later.

Rita made a note to check all newspapers closely for any mention of Cat Powers. She remembered that the actress had been a patient there twice before. Perhaps she had come back—or was due to check in soon—for another cure. If so, it would be well publicized.

The switchboard lit up again. It was going to be a very busy day, Rita could already tell. Inquiries about last week's *Time* magazine piece would add to the telephone load.

At five o'clock the cleaning staff began tackling Tanglewood with brooms, mops, vacuum cleaners, waxes and powders and bleaches. Their first target was the public areas: Oriental carpets. Parquet floors. Leaded windows. Beveled mirrors. Brass door handles and fittings and umbrella stands.

The cleaning teams moved into the offices and examination rooms while specialized cleaners worked in the laboratories, dispensary, physical treatment areas. A third cleaning battery formed the day crew to attend the patients' rooms.

In the Hub, the late-night floor nurse, Lois Baxter, heard the voices of the cleaning women come down the back hallway in the main house as she sat in front of the computer screens.

Nurse Baxter folded back the corner of the Tolkien novel she was reading and turned to the computer keyboard. After tapping out the code for the Orchard Pavilion, she read on the screen that the late-night arrivals had not stirred—not opened the computerized doors—from their adjoining suites, 06 and 07. No name would be entered for the occupants of these rooms until Administration officially accepted them as guests.

Nurse Baxter next punched the third floor in the main building. She saw that Ingrid Matthison, the night checkpoint nurse, had not changed the status on the new arrival in room 37. All must be quiet. Patient sleeping.

Satisfied, the nurse checked the time—5:11:32—and went back to the adventures of Middle Earth.

Behind her, Dr. Wayne Piciska, the junior doctor who had worked a quiet night shift, sat hunched over a crossword puzzle in front of the dispatch console. The dull metal mass of buttons, switches, and wires lay quiet, like a benign, dozing animal.

At the end of the corridor from the Hub, Amy Zimmerman, the bread-and-pastry cook, arrived for work.

After turning on the kitchen's long strips of overhead lighting, she hung up her Peruvian shawl on the coat rack and replaced her Roman sandals with the pair of black cotton Chinese slippers she carried in a shoulder basket. Braids tied into her hair net, white apron wrapped around long batik skirt, she set about preparing batches of bran, wholewheat, rye, and pumpernickel bread as well as a variety of rolls. When the dough was rising and pans greased, she began making fruit tarts and cream pastries. Working alone in the kitchen was the perfect time for twenty-eight-year-old Amy, an aspiring singer, to practice her repertoire of Carole King and Joan Baez songs.

Tanglewood's three cooks and four kitchen assistants did not begin arriving until an hour after Amy Zimmerman. Ex-serviceman Buck O'Reilly, the salad chef, checked the menus nutritionist Sarah Longman prepared the day before. O'Reilly was also in charge of the Arboretum, the mansion's former breakfast room, now a bright, airy nook serving weight-watcher's salads, diet plates, and other light fares from noon through suppertime.

Deliveries to Tanglewood began shortly after the kitchen staff arrived. Most deliveries came to the Supplies room adjoining the kitchen—everything from meat, fish, and dairy products to fresh flowers and the daily assortment of Godiva chocolates. The clinic's largest standing order was for mineral water. Tanglewood consumed eight cases of Perrier a day. But there were always those patients who preferred San Pelligrino or Malvern water.

At 7:30 A.M., Jay Pope drove his battered red Volkswagen bug into the parking lot. He found the door open to the Orchard Pavilion, but used his own key to let himself into the dispensary in the lower level.

Twenty-four-year-old Pope had received his B.S.c in Pharmacology at the University of Connecticut. He lectured at the university and worked five mornings a week at Tanglewood. His clinic duties included filling prescription slips or, if the required medication was not in stock, contacting nearby pharmaceutical suppliers. He would be on duty alone in the dispensary only until his part-time assistant, student Sherry Williams, came to work at eleven o'clock.

By 8:45 A.M. the Monday morning rush had begun.

Lab technician Simone Charbonneau wanted to speak urgently to Sarah Longman about Mrs. Weiss's urine sample, but the nutritionist had not yet arrived in her office. Psychotherapist Betty Lassiter was suffering a bad hangover from her party the previous night and shouted angrily down the telephone for the coffee and sweet rolls she had ordered for her morning encounter group being held outdoors in the gazebo. Licensed practical nurse Juanita Alvarez buzzed the Hub from the third floor checkpoint, requesting information on the new occupant of room 37. Dr. Bell dialed Dr. Lamb for notes on Jennifer Morrisey to discuss with his junior, baby-faced Dr. Christopher Quine. The steady *bleep*, *bleep*, *bleep* of a call-pack broke the conversation between two other junior doctors outside the Hub. Paul Van Marten

and John Petersen had been discussing their dates for this
Friday's Boston Wharf Festival.

Classes and treatments and seminars were also commenc-
ing at this hour.

"*Strrreettch those legs. . . . Strrreetttch those legs and touuuuch
those toes. . . . Keep the feet flaaat. . . .*"

Howard Jefferson's morning stretch class had begun in
the Orchard Pavilion: banker Paul Sabrinski, corporate lawyer Eileen Dunphy, and society novelist Crandall Benedict
were groaning, stretching their limbs, agonizing over sore
muscles, remembering that a few brief hours ago they had
been lying in bed, wondering how they were going to make
it through the day without Chivas Regal, cocaine, a handful
of red-and-blue Tuinals.

In the lower level of the pavilion, teakwood doors lined
the carpeted hall. From behind the door marked MASSAGE
came the muffled sounds of *pat-slap . . . pat-slap . . . pattaty,
pattaty, slap, slap.*

Masseur Louis Mishiyama's small frame belied the
strength in his hands. Dressed in a white T-shirt, baggy
white cotton trousers, and wooden clogs, the Japanese masseur stood by the table, authoritatively kneeding the cocoa
skin of another early riser, singer Lesley Charles.

In the adjoining room, masseuse Doris Spears telephoned
Skip Ryan, reminding him that he was late for his eight-
thirty appointment.

Down the hallway, the licensed chiropractor, Mat Holders, relieved pressure from the spine of Klaus Rhinehart, a
German commercial airline pilot who had drunkenly fallen
down some steps in a New York East Side orgy club.

Physical therapist Olga Turner slowly escorted her nine-
o'clock patient, advertising director Harris Hotchkiss, from
his room. Heroin addiction caused severe constipation, and
Olga performed high colonics at Tanglewood.

The lower level also housed white-tiled chambers for
other forms of physical therapy.

A glacier of shaved ice flowed from a stainless steel

freezer, heaping chips around the squat body of alcoholic publisher Gibson Hopkins, who sat cross-legged in a sunken tub, gasping at the cold shock to his body.

Pine-scented mud oozed from a wooden spigot into a vibrating redwood pit. A Valium withdrawal patient, Westchester housewife Marianne Turnbull hesitated on the tub's edge, eyes watering from the pine essence, upper lip curled in revulsion at the sight of the quivering primal slime.

Some treatments had not yet been booked for early Monday morning. The milk-and-aloe immersion steamed at 75-degrees Fahrenheit in a transparent vat. Herbal therapist Ellen Kim was still preparing layers of seaweed and gauze for the salt extraction packs. The eucalyptus vaporizer warmed for Red Sweeney's nine-o'clock appointment.

Roger Cooper, as medical director of Tanglewood, received constant criticism from figures in the drug treatment field about Tanglewood's use of aloe baths, icy immersions, and mud shakes. But Roger sided with the psychologists and physiotherapists who agreed that physical therapy awakened senses dulled by drugs and alcohol. His motto was: *All's fair in detoxification and rehabilitation.*

In the main house, more cerebral activities were proceeding at 8:45 A.M.

"I don't want to frighten you. I'm not turning into a religious nut," said television personality Jill Howard to the seven people gathered round her in the paneled library. "But like many people, I'm fascinated with the Bible. In Matthew 27:34, we read that Christ on the cross is offered 'vinegar mixed with gall.' It's interesting to note that Hebrew scholars say that 'gall' is the drug from which we get heroin: opium."

Jill Howard's fees were high. The newswoman charged Tanglewood the same rate she was paid for public speaking engagements. But her familiar face—and soft, lisping voice—soothed patients whose nerves were frayed from grueling sessions in the clinic's encounter groups.

In a small art-nouveau sitting room adjoining the library, psychiatrist Philip Pringle sat in a club chair facing Peabo Washington. Pringle's clear blue eyes were fixed on the prizefighter. "Perhaps you think your wife is getting off more lightly than you, Peabo. That Karen is as much to blame as you for your amphetamine problem but doesn't have to suffer the consequences."

Between eight-thirty and nine o'clock, too, patients began drifting toward the dining room. Women wore caftans, track suits, dressing gowns as well as long white terry-cloth Tanglewood robes piped in green; men also wore jogging suits or Tanglewood robes over their pajamas to breakfast; one or two dressed in conservative business suits.

A large, imposing room with beamed ceilings and tall windows, the dining room was dotted with white damask-covered tables set with sparkling Waterford crystal, Spode breakfast ware, and colorful arrangements of fresh autumn flowers.

Because a dependency on alcohol and drugs destroyed the appetite, Roger Cooper insisted that all meals at Tanglewood should not only taste delicious but look tempting.

The breakfast buffet stretched in front of the tall leaded windows facing the back gardens, offering a colorful array of cut-glass bowls, Georgian silver chafing dishes and compotes, antique china platters, all interspersed with flowers and fruit. From the kitchen, waiters and waitresses carried baskets of fresh croissants, brioche, cinnamon rolls, toast, bagels, along with coffee, tea, and the clinic's most popular morning beverage—a jug of hot water to dilute freshly squeezed lemon juice.

As a rule, Jackie Lyell acted as hostess in the dining room, greeting patients at the French doors, handing them their favorite newspaper.

This Monday morning, however, Jackie was at work early in Administration. Her husband Adrian still had not returned from his mystery visit to California.

* * *

Across the lawn from the dining room's back windows stood the pool house. British politician Nigel Burden moved to the edge of the indoor Olympic-size pool. With a smooth dive, he cut neatly into the glimmering blue surface.

Although the water was a few degrees too warm for the fifty-seven-year-old Conservative former Member of Parliament, he began his thirty laps, starting with the crawl and relaxing into the breast stroke.

Moving up and down the length of the rectangular pool, head bobbing, arms spreading, legs frog-kicking, Burden felt alive. He enjoyed being the only swimmer in a pool, not having to worry about dodging others as he did at London's Royal Automobile Club on Pall Mall.

With his mind free to wander as he proceeded through his laps, he realized how much stronger he felt now compared to when he had arrived here from London three short weeks ago.

Burden had stopped drinking. His shakes, wild heartbeats, delirium tremens, were finished. He had done it with phenobarbital, a crash course of vitamin B, a full schedule of ice burials, strenuous massage, twice-daily counseling sessions, grueling encounter groups—and willpower.

Halting at the deep end of the pool, he grasped onto the blue tiling, wondering how he was going to face the big problem waiting for him when he left Tanglewood.

A voice cut the stillness of the pool house.

"Morning!"

Burden raised his eyes and saw the grossly overweight American woman smiling down at him.

Lillian Weiss, wearing a lime-green caftan and green combs in her corn-yellow hair, beamed cheerfully at Burden, her eyes brightly painted, cheeks dramatically shaded with rouge.

"Getting your morning exercise?" Lillian smiled widely.

Burden scraped one hand back through his wet hair. "Beginning," he replied, not wanting to stop his laps for polite conversation.

Lillian's wrists were stacked with gold bracelets, making her short arms look even more disproportionate to the enormity of the pendulous breasts beneath the caftan.

Making a boo-hoo face, she said, "Your son and daughter-in-law are coming to take you away from us soon."

"Yes." Burden did not recall telling her that Cyril and Trisha were arriving tomorrow from London.

Then, with a smile, she added, "I see you got new neighbors last night."

He looked up at her, puzzled. "Neighbors?"

She nodded. "You moved from the main house to the Garden Pavilion, right?"

"Yes." He had changed rooms to be closer to the pool. But how did this bloody woman know that?

A note of aggression crept into Lillian's voice. "What's the matter? Don't you look out your window? You know you can see from your room straight across to the Orchard Pavilion."

Bloody hell, thought Burden. This Wagnerian-size snoop not only knew what room he had moved to, but wanted him to find out who'd checked into the room opposite. That's how Lillian Weiss knew everything. She asked. She pried.

Burden pushed away from the pool's edge, remarking over his shoulder "As I always say, dear lady: 'Honor thy neighbor's privacy.'"

Lillian Weiss was not the nice, jolly fat lady she pretended to be.

Standing by the edge of the pool, she watched the silver-haired Englishman disappear toward the opposite end and muttered to herself, "Well, screw you, putz."

Three weeks ago, when the Park Avenue widow had first spotted Nigel Burden at Tanglewood, she had thought he was a highly attractive, very interesting-looking man—a real classy number. I wonder what he's like in bed, she thought.

Lillian Weiss had an active sex life, although not as active as she would have liked it to be. Sex was a secret preoccupation of hers, and she considered herself an authority on a wide range of erotic subjects. That Englishmen were kinky she knew from past experiences. Often perverse in their sexual habits, especially the upper classes. Many of them had a penchant for "Turkish Delight"—making love to a fat woman.

Waddling away from the pool house, Lillian Weiss regretted that Burden had turned out to be such a deadbeat. Not only had he not made any sexual advances to her, he had proved useless in giving her any information. Nigel Burden was a loser, she told herself. Remembering why he had come to Tanglewood, she thought: Alcoholics are all losers.

Outside the pool house, the air was fresh; a little nippy for a morning stroll, Lillian reflected, but she would try to walk as far as the forest's edge and back to the dining room before she had her skimpy little diet breakfast.

Swaying from side to side as she moved across the dewy lawn, she approached the white trellised gazebo and saw a small group of patients sitting around a table, having coffee and talking animatedly among themselves.

At the sight of the encounter group, Lillian veered to the left. She definitely did not want to get mixed up with those jerks.

Encounter groups and rap sessions secretly terrified her, and she refused to attend them as part of the treatment she was undergoing for her dependency on diet bars. The idea of people sitting around, openly criticizing one another, filled her with dread. She told herself, "Who needs to pay good money to listen to what some junkie thinks about you? It's stupid. Just plain stupid."

Thoughts of criticism always took her mind back to her childhood, to her younger, beautiful sisters, Esther and Ruth. Early in life, Lillian had realized she was never going to be as pretty as they were, never going to be able to wear tight-fitting toreador pants and halter tops. While Esther and Ruth got all the compliments and dates, Lillian got sympathy.

But, gradually, she had begun to realize that getting sympathy was better than not receiving any attention at all. She had discovered that the more she ate and the fatter she grew, the more sympathy she received.

And then tubby young Lillian discovered the magic ingredient: Put on a happy face.

People felt sorry for fat girls; but if the fat girl was sweet and always had something cheery to say, then people *took an interest in you.* They got you jobs. They loaned you money. Some poor suckers—as she had discovered—even asked you to marry them.

Reaching into the pocket of her lime-green caftan, she withdrew one of what she called her "energy pills": Snickers candy bars. They were her secret replacement for the sweet-tasting phendimetrazine diet bars, Nu-You, to which she had been addicted.

Approaching the edge of the back lawn, she pierced her long red fingernail into the Snickers wrapper. She rationalized that the glucose in Snickers was good for her and that it wasn't anybody's business if she ate them. She further rationalized that, as she was not eating regular-size Snickers, just the midget ones she bought by the bagful, the candy could not interfere with the new diet she was on.

Popping the baby Snickers into her mouth, Lillian glanced around her as she pierced her long fingernail into a second one. She enjoyed it more than the first; quickly she peeled the paper from two more little Snickers and gobbled them down. Then she balled the wrappers together, moved a few more feet toward the forest, and tossed the paper into the ferns.

As she turned to face the main house across the lawn, Lillian looked at the Cartier Santos watch nestled between her bracelets, checking to see how much time she had to make it back to the dining room for breakfast.

As she did so, she asked herself the question she asked every Monday morning:

Am I going to get laid this week?

* * *

In the basement of the main house, Tanglewood's chief of security, Leo Kemp, played a row of black knobs as he studied a television screen image of Lillian Weiss waddling away from the forest's edge. Her body temperature had activated a heat sensor alarm, setting off an alert in Security.

Kemp held his eyes on the small blue screen, remarking "The regulator's set too high, or else she's got as much body heat as a pig-iron furnace."

His assistant, Calvin Curtis, teased, "How'd you like to curl up with something like that on a cold winter night, Leo?"

Kemp ignored the joke as he worked to adjust the alarm's keening sound. Security at Tanglewood was his responsibility and no laughing matter.

12 ROGER COOPER'S MONDAY BEGAN ON A SOUR NOTE. THE LAST PERSON IN THE world he had ever expected to see at Tanglewood was Dr. Gene Stone. In his surprise last night at Tom Hudson telephoning him from the Hunt Theater on Broadway, he had not asked the name of the doctor traveling with Cat Powers. He had assumed it would be the actress's New York physician; had he known she was bringing Stone from Los Angeles, he would not have offered Cat a place.

Pushing aside the patient's form Stone had delivered from the actress's suite in the Orchard Pavilion, Roger tried to hide his irritation. "I'll need more facts than these, Gene," he said brusquely.

"What do you want, man? A biopsy?"

Roger ignored Stone's sarcasm. "For one thing, I need to know what drugs you've been prescribing for Cat."

Gene Stone had aged considerably since Roger had last seen him. The deep suntan, the careful grooming and expensive facelift, the trendy designer clothes, did little to hide Stone's weary, almost predatory appearance.

According to reliable sources, Stone's Los Angeles practice was made up of Hollywood film stars, Las Vegas headliners, and alimony-rich divorcees. Roger had also heard on the medical grapevine that Stone flitted around the world with his illustrious patients and could be found anywhere but in his Rodeo Drive office—except when it was being photographed for *Architectural Digest*.

Stone lounged in the chair across the desk from Roger, toying with his gold Rolex. "Cat's been here before, Rog. Dig out her file."

Roger tapped a buff folder on his desk. "I was studying Cat's records when you came in. I saw that her last visit was exactly two years ago. I need to know what you've treated her for in the meantime."

Stone leaned forward. "Come on, Rog. You know what the lady's into."

"I don't conduct treatment on two-year-old information." Roger was becoming increasingly impatient at having to spend time with this Beverly Hills "Dr. Feelgood" when he could be doing more worthwhile jobs.

Stone smiled. "You didn't help Cat much when she was here two years ago, did you, Roger? Or she wouldn't be back."

"We do have refresher visits, Gene, for people who can't join outpatient programs when they leave here. We mail reminders well in advance when those visits are due. But we haven't seen hide nor hair of Cat till last night."

Annoyed to be defending his procedure to somebody he

considered unqualified to judge him, Roger added, "You aren't the one who suggested that Tom Hudson bring Cat back to Tanglewood, are you, Gene?"

Stone toyed with the gold watch band. "You saying I have something against you?"

"And do you?"

"We don't have a squeaky clean history, Rog. I won't deny it. You and I've had our hiccups. But what's important is that you're proving to be one hell of a good man." A glint in his eye, Stone added ". . . even if you don't bat a thousand in treatment here at Tanglewood."

Neither Stone nor Roger needed to mention the incident that stood between them. Their history went back to a San Diego hospital; Stone had been a young resident at California Health when Roger had done his internship there. Later in Roger's career, when the female patient in Santa Barbara had sued him for allegedly making sexual advances toward her in his office, Stone had supplied an affidavit to her lawyer claiming that Roger had been romantically indiscreet while he was an intern.

Roger did not want to get into past history now. "If you have doubts about my performance at Tanglewood, Gene, why didn't you stop Hudson from bringing Cat here?"

"Cat and Hudson are engaged to be married." Stone shook his head. "I'll believe they'll go through with it when I dance at their wedding. But that's another kettle of enchiladas. All I know is that when Hudson up and announced backstage last night that he was bringing Cat here to get her shit together, I told him, 'Tom, hey, you're going for the best there is.'"

Roger kept his voice calm. "If you believe in us so much, Gene, then why are you being so goddamned uncooperative?" He gestured toward the incomplete form on his desk.

Stone sat bolt upright. "You want to talk about that measly little card? Okay. Let's talk. The lady boozes. She takes pills. What else do you want to know, man?"

Roger reached for a pen. "What have you been prescribing?"

Stone settled back into the chair. "Downers. Sedatives. The usual and the not so usual. She's got pressures. Try being a megastar yourself sometime, pal. Take my word for it. It's *Snakepit.*"

Roger dropped the pen. He was ashamed of himself. Why had he thought for a moment that this Rodeo Drive phony was going to give him any information? He would wait for the lab results.

Stone added, as if reading Roger's mind, "Another thing, Rog. I don't want Cat doing tests. Not at the moment. She's not up to it."

Roger's jaw clenched. Stone might be a poor physician, but he was not stupid. He reminded himself that he must never forget that fact for one minute when dealing with this snake.

Roger decided that the best thing to do was to get Stone out of the office before he lost his temper with him. He reached out and took a stack of papers from his IN tray, saying "I'll drop by Cat's room after lunch. If you'll excuse me now, Gene, I've got a lot to do this morning."

Stone did not budge from his chair. Hands folded across his silk shirt, he sat studying Roger, nodding his head approvingly. "Yeah, man," he said. "I've got to hand it to you. You pulled off the big one."

Roger did not understand. "Excuse me, Gene?"

"Here." Stone raised both hands to the slick marble and leather office. "You've done it. You've grabbed the gold ring on the merry-go-round ride this time around, pal."

"Sorry, I'm not following you."

"This clinic, pal. Tanglewood. It's a great success, isn't it? But why? What's your edge over all the other places?"

Roger answered cautiously. "Different clinics fill different needs, Gene."

"And you?"

Roger wished Stone would leave, but even now he

couldn't restrain himself when it came to talking about his clinic. "For one thing, Gene, Tanglewood offers detoxification as well as rehabilitation. In many clinics, patients first have to check into a hospital to go through detox. Only then can they start the hard work of learning how to stay off alcohol or drugs. But here we offer complete attention."

"Barrington offers both, too," Stone said. "They've also been in business for twenty years. Why do your patients come here and not go there?"

For the first time this morning Stone seemed serious, and Roger answered less guardedly. "For one thing, Barrington uses Pavlovian-type methods. Physical *and* emotional shock treatments. We depend on supportive therapy. Use only nonshock drugs."

"Also," Stone pressed on, "I get the feeling there's not one poor man in this place. Your fees are too steep for John Average."

"Our fees have to be high to cover the services we offer. We've got an overall ratio of five staff to every patient—that includes everything from medical to kitchen.

"But Tanglewood's not just for people with money," Roger added. "I personally insist that we have one gratis patient in the clinic at all times. All fees waived. Sometimes we have as many as three."

"Hey, I'm impressed." Stone nodded his head. "Mother Teresa as well as the Pied Piper to super-rich junkies."

The words stung Roger. He had put years of effort into Tanglewood, and he wasn't going to swallow snide remarks about it from Stone. He felt an urge to leap across the desk, grab Stone by the throat, and beat his head against the wall.

Instead, he bit back his rage, unwilling to let Stone see him lose his cool. "First of all, I never think of any patient as a junkie," he said stiffly.

"Sure. Of course not. But face it, you do have a houseful of A-Group celebrity dolls here."

"Sorry, Gene." Roger rose from his chair. "Tanglewood's a clinic. Not a doll hospital."

Stone laughed mockingly. "Not how I see it. Whatever the reason your patients choose Tanglewood, fellow, they're just a very elite bunch of boozey, drugged-up, freaked-out celebrity dolls . . . rich and famous dolls . . . movie-star dolls. A couple of freebie patients doesn't change that."

Roger was near exploding. But he kept his voice calm as he asked, "Gene, why are you trying to fuck me around like this?"

Stone looked up at him from his chair, blinking. "What're you so sensitive about? I'm complimenting you."

"Bullshit." Roger moved toward the door. "But I want you to remember one fact."

He pointed a forefinger at Stone. "Tanglewood has not signed or accepted any admittance form for Cat. We have no professional obligation to you or to Cat Powers—whether you call her your 'patient,' your 'celebrity doll,' or your latest meal ticket. Just remember, buster, you're on thin ice here. You play by our rules or you're gone. Get the picture?"

Opening the door, Roger jabbed his thumb toward the corridor. "Now get out of here and let me get some work done."

Stone rose slowly from his chair and ambled toward the door, patting one side of Roger's face as he passed. "Lighten up, man. Kick back and trust me. We're going to have a fine collaboration in the days to come. I like your space here. It has the kind of class I can relate to."

He proceeded through the outer office, waving to the secretary at the typewriter, and continued into the corridor.

Roger stood in the doorway of his office. The knuckles of his hand, holding the doorknob, were white.

Looking from Caroline to the door, he shook his head, saying in bewilderment "Why are some guys so damned pleased with themselves?"

He turned back into the office and closed the door. He thought back to the first time he had met Stone in San

Diego—how long ago? Even then Roger had pegged him as an obnoxious loudmouth.

It had been in the bygone days even before Roger had met Crista. He was just beginning his internship at California Health Hospital, and his lover at the time had been Deborah Hurley.

Roger and Deborah had moved from Berkeley to San Diego in July. They had not even unpacked their belongings when they went to meet California Health's twenty-two other new interns at a get-acquainted party hosted in the general hospital's staff lounge. The party was for the incoming interns to relax with the residents who would guide them through the next twelve months, the residency known as "the fifth year of med school." Roger was assigned to a beefy midwesterner, Dr. Tim Lambert.

Back home at the duplex Roger and Deborah had rented on O'Farrel Street, around the corner from California Health, they discussed the party as they sat cross-legged on the kitchen floor, eating Chinese takeout and unpacking a few more pots, pans, and dishes they had moved down from Berkeley in Roger's VW van. For the past three years, during Roger's University of California med school studies, they had been living together as husband and wife—in every way except for the marriage certificate. Deborah had abandoned her prelaw studies at Berkeley in her junior year, insisting that she didn't want a career that might conflict with Roger's. Despite his protestations that she should not sacrifice a career for him, she was holding steadfast to her decision.

On the kitchen floor of their new apartment, Deborah carefully removed newspaper from an heirloom Blue Willow soup tureen, saying "Roger, I think you should make friends with that young Dr. Kildare–looking resident we met tonight at the hospital. What's his name—Gene Stone? He strikes me as somebody who knows his way around the place and can probably show you the ropes."

"That guy in cowboy boots?"

Deborah placed the lid on the soup tureen. "You wear boots, too."

"Two-tone lizard?"

"Don't be so critical of other people, Roger. Not before you get to know them."

"Who's being critical? I'm just stating a fact. That guy's a phony. Mark my word. Did you see how he spent the whole evening sucking up to all the big brass there?"

"You just got your nose out of joint because he ignored you."

"I'm grateful he ignored me," *Roger replied.* "I like the looks of Tim Lambert. I get the feeling he doesn't waste time on Mickey Mouse details. He's a meat-and-potato man."

Deborah said, "Don't forget, you'll need all the help you can get this coming year. Interns are way down the hospital totem pole. I think Gene Stone is somebody to latch onto."

Deborah did not have to tell Roger about the lowness of interns in hospital hierarchy. From the first day of his twelve months at California Health, he found that patients did not trust interns, residents made them do all the work, visiting doctors ignored them, and the take-home pay for a 120-hour week was next to zilch. But Roger kept reminding himself that he was after experience, not popularity, not approbation, not getting rich quick.

Interns moved in dog packs around California Health, dividing their time between the hospital's four major divisions, medicine, surgery, obstetrics, and pediatrics, plus a short stint in emergency. As soon as Roger became comfortable in one division, he was whisked to the next.

The transfer from surgery to pediatrics was a welcome escape. Roger liked children. He hoped someday to have at least four of his own.

It was a sunny November morning in California Health's new children's wing when Gene Stone approached Roger in the corridor, grabbing his lapel to read aloud the tag, ROGER COOPER, M.D. Intern Staff.

Stone nodded. "Cooper. That's right." He released the lapel. Roger had seen little of Stone around the hospital in past

*weeks. He had not taken Deborah's advice to pursue a friendship
with the slick young resident.*

"Bet you're glad you're here," Stone said.

"Here?" Roger pointed to the corridor floor. "Pediatrics?"

"California Health." Stone winked. "Best nurses you've seen
in a long time, eh?"

Roger could not resist. "I think you met my lady on our first
night here."

Stone reconsidered. "That's right. You're married to—wasn't
she the redhead? Raquel Welch type?"

"A blonde," said Roger. "And we're not married. Not yet."

Stone leaned forward, lowering his voice. "I wouldn't broadcast that around the place if I were you, Cooper," he advised.

"Broadcast what?"

"That you're not married to your chick."

"Why?"

*Looking cautiously around the hall as if there might be eaves-
droppers close by,* Stone said in a low voice, "This place is run
by a pack of right-wingers. It's verrrrry conservative around
here."

"Anybody can look in my file and see I'm not married."

"Okay, man. It's your postmortem."

Resuming a conversational tone, Stone asked, "So where're
you from?"

"Berkeley," *Roger replied, still puzzled about the warning to
keep his and Deborah's living arrangements hush-hush.*

"Folks live in Berkeley, too?"

"No. My mom just passed away and Dad's bought himself a
place up in Santa Barbara."

"Santa Barbara?" Stone brightened. "Hey, one of those big
houses overlooking the Pacific?"

"Dad's got a good view and too much room, if that's what you
mean." *Roger was unaware at the time of Gene Stone's keen
interest in expensive houses, good addresses, and smart neighbor-
hoods.*

Stone wrapped an arm around Roger's shoulder. "Why don't
we break bread some night this week?" he suggested. "You and

your little lady, and I'll see if I can dig up a pair of long legs."

Deborah had not complained yet about Roger's late hours at the hospital, but he knew she desperately wanted a night out. Remembering how impressed she had been with suave Gene Stone, he accepted the invitation for dinner.

Stone chose Luigi's Seafood Grotto on a pier, and for his date brought a blond travel agent with sandals that laced to the knees and a gold crochet dress.

The dinner was disastrous. The food was inedible and conversation was hopeless. Roger had nothing to say to Gene Stone; Stone had little to say to Roger, and less to Deborah. Deborah felt inferior next to the travel agent who talked about places that Deborah had never heard of or had been mispronouncing all her life—Ibiza, Sri Lanka, the Camargue.

Against Roger's better judgment, Deborah invited Gene and his date to supper at their apartment the following week, promising to make her grandmother's recipe for chicken pot pie.

"I'll give you a call this week," Stone promised, but he never telephoned. At the hospital he avoided Roger. And Deborah started asking Roger if they were becoming a pair of boring old sticks-in-the-mud, if exciting, glamorous people like Gene Stone wanted to have nothing to do with them.

Then, during the week after Christmas, Roger heard in California Health's staff room that Gene Stone had left the hospital to join a private medical practice in Los Angeles. He mistakenly thought that Stone would no longer figure in his life.

13 THAT MONDAY MORNING, JACKIE LYELL WAS HAVING NO LUCK FINDING rooms near Tanglewood for Peabo Washington's wife and family.

On her sixth call, she explained to the woman who answered the phone at the Country Mouse Inn that she required two double rooms, preferably adjoining, with private baths.

The woman replied, "I have a cancellation on a double adjoining a single. But the single's big enough to accommodate a folding bed."

The Country Mouse Inn and Tea Rooms was a beautifully restored eighteenth-century house and converted barn. Very picturesque, very New England, Jackie remembered, and less than thirty minutes away from the clinic.

The woman quoted the price, saying she could hold the rooms only until five o'clock without a deposit.

Jackie said, "I'll take them. Book them in Tanglewood's name."

She put down the telephone and ticked off "find hotel" on her list.

Jackie had spent most of the morning on the telephone. First she had called the New York lawyers to inquire about the risk of Tanglewood becoming involved in a legal dispute between model Lavender Gilbert and designer Chatwyn. Tanglewood's attorney was in court but his secretary assured Jackie that he'd return the call as soon as he arrived at the Madison Avenue offices.

After the lawyers, Jackie had felt brave enough to try a little detective work. She had telephoned the Waldorf Astoria and the hotel's press office had readily assured her that, yes, Chatwyn was scheduled to launch his new perfume, Star Lady, there on Friday. Appropriately, the designer had booked the Starlight Room.

Jackie had also received a spate of calls. Magazine editors. Concerned physicians. The routine inquiry from the Drug Enforcement Agency. A thank you from Al-Anon.

But everything had not gone so smoothly. Jackie had irritated Renee Newby in Accounts by asking her to check on Adrian's desk diary scribble concerning insurance, but she didn't want to be responsible for any policies lapsing. Her fear was intensified by blunders she had made on paperwork she had tried to do throughout the morning.

The release form she had prepared for the outgoing gratis patient, Father Hawkes, turned out to be a readmission for fee patients. She had lost the written reservation for Little Milly Wheeler, the country and western singer, and had to call the Hub to pull the confirmation out of the computer. Later she had forgotten to enclose three payment slips with endorsed checks in an envelope.

From that point on, a landslide of chaos had begun for her.

She gave a social worker's name to a lawyer who had asked for it instead of the name of a patient's parole officer. Halfway through a long-distance conversation with an Alcoholics Anonymous official she realized she should be talking to *Cocaine* Anonymous. She kept a Tucson bank manager on a hold line for twenty minutes.

The press calls concerning Cat Powers drove her crazy. The journalists refused to take no for an answer, insisting that they knew Cat Powers was at Tanglewood, demanding details of arrival, cure expectancy, names of her entourage. Finally Jackie had had to tell the switchboard to hold all press calls.

The surprise call of the morning had been one from Carol Ann Rice, the television star, in New York. "I'm in town forming a production company and might get off a few hours to drive up for lunch. How does Thursday sound?"

"Super," said Jackie, relieved to be hearing a voice that was not making demands or asking questions to which she had no clue to what the answers were. She also suspected that lunch with the pretty, perky actress would be the only high spot in a very difficult week—although Carol Ann was probably coming to Connecticut not to see her but to ask about Roger. They'd become romantically involved after her rehabilitation at Tanglewood.

After talking to Carol Ann, Jackie looked at the desk clock. Ten-thirty. The actress's call had revitalized her spirits, putting her in a more aggressive mood. She decided to telephone Adrian at his Los Angeles hotel and find out exactly when he was coming home.

The Beverly Wilshire answered the first ring. It was not until the hotel switchboard began buzzing Adrian's room that Jackie wondered if she was doing the right thing. She remembered how Adrian hated her calling him when he was away from home, accusing her of checking on him or trying to track him down.

A woman's voice answered the phone.

Jackie was caught unawares. With sudden inspiration she affected her driest British accent, announcing "London, England, calling for Adrian Lyell."

The woman hesitated. "Let me see if he's out of the shower."

Jackie's heart beat faster. Would a room maid answer the phone and proceed to say she would speak to the guest . . . in the shower? Certainly not, Jackie decided. Not even in permissive California.

The woman's voice returned. "He wants to know who's calling."

"Is that the maid?" Jackie asked.

The voice laughed. "For what I pay mine, I'm tempted to be a maid."

"I'm sorry," Jackie lied. "This is an appalling line. I can't hear you. Let me try ringing you back."

Slamming down the phone, she sat rigidly behind the desk. The swine. He has another woman. He's having an affair. Probably with someone *more* compatible in bed. Someone who likes Adrian's "games."

She closed her eyes, remembering the "games" Adrian liked to play. Striking her on the face, bruising her thigh, commanding her to worship him.

A buzz disturbed Jackie's hideous memories.

Girding herself, she lifted the receiver, trying to steady her voice as she announced, "Administration . . . Jackie Lyell speaking . . ."

"Renee here in Accounts, Jackie. I checked all the insurance policies like you asked, Jackie, and no payment's due. The only thing I can suggest is perhaps Adrian's note pertains to one of your personal insurance policies. Why don't you do what I suggested? Ask him about it when he checks in with you."

"You're absolutely right. I'll do that."

Renee was not finished. Her voice was definitely frosty as she said, "I won't kid you, Jackie. Pulling out all those files really cut into my morning."

"I'm so sorry, Renee. Truly I am. But I just wanted to make certain—"

"You owe me a big one." Renee clicked off.

Jackie sat holding the phone, wishing she could dig a deep hole and crawl into it.

Two hours later, in Los Angeles, at 9:30 A.M., Adrian Lyell met three investors in the board room at Doheny Insurance. The offices were located on the top floor of a granite-and-glass building on Beverly Drive.

Adrian looked dapper in a gray suit and club tie as he spoke to the three other men seated at the conference table.

"I've instructed my New York attorney to submit the formal purchase offer to Roger Cooper this week," Adrian said in his crisp Oxbridge accent. "By Friday, gentlemen, the four of us should be able to put our signature on the dotted line to catapult Tanglewood into the twenty-first century."

Sam Nolan, president of Doheny Insurance, toyed with the corner of his bushy ginger moustache. There was uncertainty in his voice as he said, "Adrian, I still think we should invite Cooper to sit in on a few meetings with us. Let him hear what we have in mind for Tanglewood rather than springing this takeover on him."

Adrian was prepared for such last-minute caution. "Sam, as you well know, we're offering Roger a chance to stay at Tanglewood as medical director. In a much less visible capacity than he enjoys now, of course. Or he can take his money and run. Now what can be fairer than that?"

George Demetrious, owner of Omega Catering, supported Adrian's opinion. "Adrian's right. Why risk trouble from Roger Cooper before we firm up our own agreement?"

At the head of the board table, Sam Nolan worked his moustache, scrutinizing Adrian from beneath his thick eyebrows. "Let's not rule out the possibility, Adrian, that Roger might top *your* offer. Your contract gives him that privilege."

Demetrious spoke again. "The contract allows Adrian the privilege to ante-up Roger's counteroffer. Come on, Sam. Where's a sawbones going to find that kind of bread?" The Greek caterer folded his hirsute arms across the belly of his Hawaiian sport shirt, grinning victoriously.

"Who knows?" replied Nolan, still not satisfied. "That *Time* article last week might bring investors out of the woodwork, ready to bankroll Cooper."

Demetrious glanced back to Adrian. "That happen yet? Cooper talk about investors calling him?"

Adrian shook his head. "If investors do materialize, Roger will be too busy to talk to them. He's obsessed with his work.

That's been his problem with me, hasn't it? Lack of communication."

The discussion continued; Adrian answered each question carefully and professionally, giving affirmation where it was needed, assurance when necessary. He knew he was in top form. And he should be. This week would see him seizing total control of Tanglewood.

It had been two years since Adrian had first spotted an opportunity to gain the upper hand at Tanglewood. The chance had begun with the chief accountant telling him that the time had come for him and Roger Cooper to consider reinvesting profits back into the clinic. As Roger preferred to concentrate on medical matters, leaving financial details to Adrian, Adrian had not passed on the accountant's advice. Instead, he had privately begun weighing alternatives for the future.

Tanglewood could grow in two ways, Adrian had seen. One direction would be to become a larger, more important medical center; Roger's status as medical director would increase if such a course were chosen. An alternative route would be for Tanglewood to diversify into recreational and real estate areas. If that choice were made, Adrian could become the more influential partner at Tanglewood.

Adrian had quietly pursued the plan by which his own status would be increased. He had met with architects; he had contacted potential investors; he had gathered facts and figures on how Tanglewood could be transformed from a medical center into a health spa and real estate development.

A year passed before Adrian tested his idea on Roger. Calling him into his office, he showed him the blueprints for a new Tanglewood complete with golf course and condominiums.

Roger's reaction was negative; he dismissed the concept as a "summer camp."

Smarting from Roger's instant dismissal of the blueprints, Adrian rallied his spirits and reminded himself that he had never expected Roger to go along with his plan. Had not their ideas always been poles apart? Wasn't that the reason he had developed the blueprints in secret?

Throughout the five years of their partnership, Adrian had become more and more convinced that Roger lived in an ivory tower, absorbing himself in the esoteric side of the clinic, ignoring the business matters that financed its very existence. Frequently, too, Adrian felt that Roger considered himself to be superior; Roger acted as if the medical director were on a loftier plane than the administrator.

Gradually Adrian realized that he secretly disliked Roger. He resented Roger's superior attitude; he was jealous, too, of all the attention Roger got as Tanglewood's "young genius." Never did Roger remind observers that Tanglewood was a two-man show, that it took cash to run the clinic, and that Adrian Lyell was the man responsible for raising and managing that money.

A year ago, when Roger had abruptly dismissed Adrian's plan for Tanglewood's future, Adrian had told himself not to be upset. He would go on making his own plans for Tanglewood, and when they were ready, he would find some investors and take the whole package right over Roger's head to the Board of Management.

Then came the *Time* magazine story. As Adrian read it, his bitterness mounted. The *Time* researcher had interviewed both him and Roger for three hours, together and separately. But it was Roger's words, and Roger's picture, that found their way into the article. Except for a couple of passing references to "Money Man Adrian Lyell," Adrian's role in Tanglewood was virtually ignored. That was when Adrian decided he had had enough of playing second fiddle to do-gooder Doctor Cooper.

Paul Huttner's voice broke into Adrian's thoughts. From the other side of the board table, Huttner said, "The only worry I have at the moment, Adrian, concerns access to the land adjoining Tanglewood to the west."

Adrian welcomed the technical inquiry. He had prepared himself well for this meeting.

Reaching into his portfolio, he produced an impressive sheaf of papers. He passed them to Huttner one by one. "Water rights . . . drainage . . . roadway . . ."

At 10:30 A.M., a maid carried a coffee tray into the board room; Demetrious, Huttner, and Nolan checked their watches. Adrian was pleased to see that the three men were also ready to conclude the meeting. He wanted to get back to his hotel suite where Evelyn Palmer was waiting for him. He had spent the night, and much of the previous day, in bed with her. His desire stirred as he remembered it. Her hunger to explore the realms of sexual domination and submission matched his own. Evelyn was as kinky as he was.

From Evelyn Palmer, his thoughts jumped to the long-distance telephone call she had taken for him this morning when he had been in the shower.

Who had telephoned him from London? Perhaps his contact at the *Economist* magazine.

The memory of Roger Cooper's face on the cover of *Time* magazine still rankled. Adrian was waiting for a magazine to interview him and print *his* views. The time had come to get a taste of the limelight.

14 AT TANGLEWOOD, THE MONDAY-MORNING MACHINE GAINED MOMENtum—slowly, surely.

Nutritionist Sarah Longman found a note from the lab technician, Simone Charbonneau, in the memo box outside her office door when she arrived late for work, at 10:30 A.M. She telephoned the Orchard Pavilion lab at once. "I intended to call you first thing this morning, Simone. But last night at supper I broke a cap on my tooth and my dentist fit me in right away this morning."

Unbuttoning her green loden coat as she held the telephone to one ear, Sarah nodded as she listened. "Lillian Weiss *is* terribly overweight," she agreed. "I wanted to talk to you about her."

She fell silent for a moment as Simone gave her the news from the lab. "No . . . I understand that, Simone. Not from any diet I gave her. . . . Have you told Roger Cooper yet? . . . Good. I'll leave it up to you to tell him."

In the head nurse's office, adjoining the Hub, there were problems regarding staff relations.

Head nurse Shirley Higgins sat behind her spacious white metal desk, facing Delia Pomeroy, a licensed practical nurse.

"Start at the beginning," Shirley ordered.

A small young woman with mousy brown hair, Delia Pomeroy meekly explained her complaint. "I was working with Dr. Bell a little more than an hour ago. Around nine, nine-thirty, on two. Checkpoint had called Dr. Bell to twenty-five—Ruth Fox's room. Hallucinogen recovery. MDA. She woke up screaming this morning. Thought the Virgin Mary was chasing her with an ice pick. Dr. Bell asked for chlorpromazine. I suggested it might be more comforting for the patient if we tried talking her down before injecting her with a tranquilizer. I said I remembered how gentle conversation had helped me when I . . . was at Bellevue. Dr. Bell turned real nasty and asked, 'So why haven't you said anything before today about Bellevue, young lady?'"

Shirley Higgins calmly inquired, "And have you been in Bellevue, my dear? For treatment of a controlled substance?"

"One night," Delia blurted. "I had a bad trip on acid. It was years ago and not like I was some . . . junkie."

Sitting upright behind her desk, Shirley said gently, "Of

course not. But you must realize, dear, that Tanglewood doesn't ask such questions on our applications to test anyone. Or trick them. It merely helps us to know what nurses have had drug experiences. A way to know who can give us special help in dealing with special patients, as indeed you tried this morning." As she spoke, the only thing Shirley could remember about the young nurse's application was that she had been referred personally by the administrator, Adrian Lyell.

"Why did Dr. Bell treat me like I was some kind of liar?" Delia persisted. "Oh, he was just awful to me. Just awful." She raised both hands to her face.

Shirley opened a desk door, snapped up a Kleenex, and rose from her chair. Rounding the desk, she handed the tissue to the young nurse. "Why don't you go to the Hub? Have a nice cup of tea. Calm down while I have a word with Dr. Bell."

Delia blew her nose. "I want to go home."

"You've got a full day's work ahead of you," reminded Shirley.

"I want to go home," Delia insisted. "I already talked to Margie Clark. She's on float this week. She said she'll fill in for me this afternoon in the pavilion."

After Delia had left her office, Shirley considered the situation. The young nurse had been wrong not to have mentioned the Bellevue record on her application form if she had been a patient there. But Dr. Bell's handling of the affair this morning had been entirely unacceptable. But was Bell's manner ever anything but curt, rude, and insulting?

Shirley Higgins disliked the politics involved in her job as Tanglewood's head nurse. Accepting it as an inevitable facet of her position, though, she decided that it would be best, politically, to challenge Dr. Bell on the matter of his conduct at tomorrow's meeting of department heads.

It was 10:45 A.M., and down the corridor from the Hub, Dunstan Bell was busy in his office with his own political maneuvering.

Round silver glasses perched on his forehead, he creaked back in his swivel chair as he explained into the telephone, "As you're chairman of the ethics committee, Ephram, I want to put a flea in your ear. Quite frankly, Roger Cooper has a lot on his plate here this week, so I thought I should be the one to mention this little fact."

In a conspiratorial tone, Bell proceeded to confide in his crony—Dr. Ephram Tweed, chairman of the ethics committee that served as a watchdog over Tanglewood.

At the same time, outside the main house, gardener Luther Brown stood, wire rake in hand, watching the plum-red Rolls-Royce stop in the circular driveway. The car's front doors opened and two black women stepped out onto the drive. The driver was a classy-looking lady who held open her door for two small children—a spirited little boy and pretty girl—to scamper out from the back seat.

Watching the children race straight for the piles of dried leaves he had been raking all morning, the seventy-eight-year-old gardener laughed as the pretty lady called, "Tyler! Tamara! Don't ruin the man's hard work!"

Tipping his wool cap at the lady, Luther Brown called, "No problem, ma'am. My little great-grandkiddies at home love doing the same prank."

Chuckling to himself, he bent over his rake, wondering about the pretty lady in the fancy big car.

Who was she? Who'd she come here to see?

Luther decided that she'd come to see her husband. She was traveling with kids and another woman. She had no man with her. Ever since he had begun working as one of Tanglewood's seven gardeners, Luther had learned to fit puzzles together by watching people and cars come and go up the driveway. To him, each car told a story. He had learned, too, that stories about all these rich people were as sad as stories about poor folks, or maybe sadder. Money bought nothing but a whole lot of trouble.

15 AT 11:15 A.M., ROGER COOPER STOOD NEXT TO KAREN WASHINGTON IN THE foyer of suite 3G in the Garden Pavilion. Through the transparent See-Wall they silently observed Peabo Washington curled in a fetal position on the sitting-room floor.

Roger broke the hush. "We'll try later this afternoon, Mrs. Washington."

He tapped the button, and the view of the heavyweight boxer flickered, then quickly faded into nothingness.

"Let's walk," he said.

Karen Washington was a tall, handsome woman in her mid-twenties, and she looked surprisingly fresh after driving three hundred miles from Philadelphia. She was dressed in gray flannel trousers and a Fair Isle sweater tied around the shoulders of her white cotton blouse, her black hair pulled back from her cinnamon complexion, falling in soft curls over her shoulders.

She and Roger stopped in front of the dining room's French doors; Roger checked his watch. 11:20. "We're too late for breakfast and too early for lunch. But there should be some coffee around."

Karen did not reply. She had not said a word since they had left the Garden Pavilion five minutes ago.

"When can we try again?" she asked finally, turning her large brown eyes on Roger.

"Why don't you settle your children into the hotel?" he

suggested. "Have lunch. Then call me in my office and we'll make an appointment."

He added, "You see now, Mrs. Washington, this week isn't going to be easy."

Karen pressed her thin lips together, nodding.

Roger had expected Karen Washington to be more assertive, as outspoken as she had been on the telephone last night. Instead, she was subdued, gentle, every inch a lady.

Concerned for her peace of mind, he asked, "Mrs. Washington, do you think this is going to be too much for you to handle?"

Her eyes flickered. "How do you mean, Dr. Cooper?"

"The chemicals your husband has been injecting into his system have left him paranoiac and extremely confused. He feels bitter and betrayed. You must tell me if you think that's going to be too much for you to handle."

Karen settled both arms across her breasts. "I thought he'd be farther along than he is now."

"Physical withdrawals can last up to three months," Roger replied. "Mental adjustments can take longer."

She looked at him. "Is there something you're not telling me, Doctor?"

"No. But I spoke to the psychiatrist who met with Peabo this morning. Dr. Pringle believes there's a great deal of resentment toward you. Peabo considers you to be the main reason for his problem."

"Me?" Her nostrils flared.

"I'm telling you this to prepare you, Mrs. Washington."

An edge to her voice, Karen asked, "Did you tell Peabo I was coming today?"

Roger nodded. "I wanted to prepare him, too. So far, Mrs. Washington, you're causing the most serious problems in his mind."

"What about making friends?" she asked. "Does he talk to people here?"

"Very seldom. When he does, it's mostly to argue with them."

"None of his old horseplay? Kidding around?"

Roger shook his head. "Chemicals can change people for very long periods."

Karen began to speak but then hesitated. She waved her hand in resignation. "I'm here so I'll stay out the week. He's got a problem and it has to be worked out. For his sake and the kids' sake."

"Apart from his old sense of humor being gone, Mrs. Washington, his tongue's gotten quite wicked."

Karen did not look surprised.

"Some of the things he's saying about you are pretty raw."

Karen smiled, a slight, pretty smile, making her cheekbones more prominent. "I've been married to him for six years, Dr. Cooper. We grew up together. I know what I'm dealing with. But believe it or not, you're the first person to show me any concern during this whole awful nightmare. I appreciate it. Thanks."

Glancing at the French doors, she added more brightly, "I'd like that cup of coffee now. And a few minutes alone. Collect my thoughts before I track down my sister-in-law and the kids."

"No problem."

Roger led Karen Washington into the empty dining room, settling her at a table overlooking the garden before he disappeared to find someone to bring her coffee and fresh rolls.

The time was eleven twenty-five. In five minutes Roger was due to meet with his juniors.

Part of Roger's privileges as medical director included having two juniors to assist him, Dr. John Petersen and Dr. Wayne Piciska, instead of one medical assistant as the other doctors had. He found the two waiting in his outer office when he came back from meeting with Mrs. Washington. He beckoned them into his inner office, then waved them toward the couch against the wall as he grabbed for a buzzing phone on his desk.

"Good day, Dr. Tweed," he said into the mouthpiece. "What a pleasant surprise."

Sitting on the edge of his buttoned leather chair, he flipped through his desk calendar. "Of course you'll see me next week. Have I missed an ethics meeting yet?"

Roger spent a few more minutes in polite conversation with Tweed, before again assuring him about the meeting; then he hung up the phone.

Buzzing his secretary, he said, "Caroline, don't let me forget the ethics meeting next Thursday. Tweed wouldn't be calling me if there wasn't something afoot."

Caroline's voice came back over the intercom. "Remember you have the board of management meeting tomorrow night, too."

Roger paused. He had completely forgotten about it. "Thanks."

Then he turned to his juniors. "Okay, team. How goes it?"

"You tell us, coach," said Petersen, a brawny Swedish-American quarterback who had graduated from Johns Hopkins. Roger had great hopes for the internist at Tanglewood.

Roger looked from Petersen to Wayne Piciska. Harvard Med School. Taller and lankier than Petersen, Piciska was a serious-minded pathologist; Roger was guiding him toward research.

"Any new patients?" asked Piciska.

Roger nodded. "One's a young lady named Lavender Gilbert. She can't decide if she wants to stay with us or not. I spent a couple of minutes with her this morning, trying to talk her into giving herself a chance."

Opening their notebooks, the two juniors listened as Roger sketched the outlines of the young fashion model's case.

In Administration, Jackie counted to five before she picked up another ringing telephone.

"Administration," she announced; listening, she asked, "Who am I speaking to, please?"

The man's voice at the other end of the line replied, "I'm from Harmon Gilbert's office. Harmon's Peabo Washington's manager. Harmon told me I could get hold of Peabo—or Karen—Washington at this number."

Jackie remembered Roger's warning about not giving out details on patients. Remembering the reservation she had made for Karen Washington at a local hotel, she tried to shift the subject from Tanglewood. "Why don't you try contacting Mrs. Washington at the Country Mouse Inn?"

"The Country Mouse?" said the man on the phone. "Hey, isn't that near you?"

"Are you in the neighborhood?"

"I came up from New York on the off chance of talking to Peabo. . . . The Country Mouse. Okay. I'll check there."

The line went dead as another telephone began ringing on the desk.

16 LAVENDER GILBERT SAT IN FRONT OF THE VANITY TABLE IN ROOM 37, dressed in a pink track suit. She had slept badly last night and now, at midday, she was still disturbed from the interview she had had that morning with Roger Cooper. Their conversation was making her wonder if her worst fears had come true—was she hooked on something she couldn't control?

"Why did you come to Tanglewood, Lavender?" Roger had asked her. They were meeting in the same examination room where he had seen her last night.

"It wasn't my idea to come here," Lavender answered

defensively as she shifted in the chair alongside the desk. "It was my girl friend's idea."

"Was your girl friend concerned about your health?"

Lavender flipped her long blond hair over one shoulder. "Bev worries too much about everything. Me. Living in New York. Her career. Sometimes I think Bev hates being a model. Who knows? Maybe that's why she doesn't get more work than she does." An air of defiance was building in her attitude.

"Do *you* like your work?" Roger asked.

"I love it. The people are interesting. I get to travel. The money—" She laughed. "The money can be unbelievable."

In a more arrogant tone, she added, "But modeling's not the end-all for me, Doctor. I know there's more important things to do in life."

"Like what?" Roger asked.

"Ever since I was a little girl I thought that modeling would be a steppingstone toward an acting career."

"Tell me about the fashion world," Roger said. "How does it influence your lifestyle?"

The question surprised her. "Influence me?"

"Drugs, for instance, I know that many fashion people become involved with drugs. How does that affect you?"

"Drugs are no big deal." Lavender flipped her hair. "Not if people can handle them."

"Can *you* handle drugs?"

She answered as if she had said the line many times before. "I don't do any drugs I can't control. I hate the feeling of being out of control. I never trip. I never drop acid. I never—" She hesitated, repeating "I never do drugs I can't control."

"What about cocaine? Crack?"

"Crack?" She answered quickly. "Never. I'm not crazy. I know how quick you can get hooked on that stuff."

"But you do do coke."

She nodded.

Roger held his eyes on her. "How do you feel this morning, Lavender? Are you as tired as you were last night?"

Defensive again, Lavender said, "I was tired from a long flight from Antigua yesterday."

"Plus being exhausted from a tough work week, as I understand," Roger said compassionately.

"Very."

Reaching into the top desk drawer, Roger pulled a tissue from a box. He handed it to Lavender. "You're perspiring."

Watching Lavender dab the moisture from her forehead, he asked, "Why don't you give yourself a week here? Let us run a few tests on you?"

Crumpling the tissue, Lavender said more forcibly, "I'm afraid that's impossible, Doctor. I've got to be in New York on Friday."

"Then how about just a couple days?"

Lavender shook her head. She said with conviction, "No. Absolutely not. I've got a crazy week ahead of me in New York. Fashion shots. Press calls. The Star Lady launch."

"That does sound like a very busy schedule." Roger recrossed one leg over the other knee. "Tell me, how does it work when you've got such a busy week? Do they give you something to help you along?"

"What do you mean?" Lavender's pale eyes flickered. Again she seemed surprised.

"A line of coke? A few uppers? Do your employers or the photographers give you a little something to keep you alert?"

She lowered her eyes. "Sometimes."

"Most of the time?"

"When we're busy."

Roger sat forward in his chair, his voice filled with concern. "If you can't spare yourself a week, Lavender, think about staying here a few days to gauge exactly where you are in a drug habit."

Lavender sat alone in her bedroom, considering Roger

Cooper's suggestion. Although he had thrown her with a few surprise questions, she thought he was a sincere man. He wasn't trying to trap her or to drum up business for Tanglewood. But was he right? Might she be more dependent on coke than she cared to admit? Were Chatwyn and all his photographers making her habit worse? Should she tell them to go take a flying leap while she stayed here and got herself together?

Feeling confused and lost about what she should do, Lavender cursed Bev Jordan for bringing her there. This was all Bev's fault. Bev had taken advantage of her when she had been tired and overworked and out of it.

Lavender wished she had a hit of cocaine. Coke helped her see a situation more clearly.

Realizing that she was actually *wishing* for coke, Lavender suddenly felt frightened. She had to be strong. She had to get herself together. She could live without cocaine without being confined to a clinic.

As she talked to herself, tears began to well in her eyes; her hands started to shake as she tried to wipe away the tears.

God! What is happening to me? she wondered. I didn't plan my life to go this way. I'm supposed to be enjoying success. Making the most of my breaks. Not falling apart in some . . . drug clinic.

17

ELEVEN HUNDRED MILES SOUTHWEST OF CONNECTICUT, THE TENNESSEE sky was a cloudless blue. But despite the clear day, a cold

October wind blew across the Cumberland River, chilling the downtown district of Nashville.

Judge William Abernathy stood in a window of the Metro Courthouse, looking down at the people hunched against the bitter wind as they made their way toward the State Capitol Building on Charlotte Avenue. Winter was only a month or so away, he thought, as he turned from the window to see if the woman on the far side of his desk had finished reading the court order.

Gladys Wheeler was an old friend of Judge Abernathy, a petite, well-dressed woman in her late fifties. She looked up from the document and, removing the rhinestone glasses from the bridge of her nose, confessed in a soft, Tennessee drawl, "Judge, I can't make head or tail of all this rigmarole. If you say the court's granted me legal guardianship over my baby girl then I'm going to have to take your word for it."

Judge Abernathy was a man of medium height, his stomach protruding over the Navajo turquoise belt buckle he wore with his western-cut suit.

After taking the document from Gladys Wheeler's hand, Abernathy sat on the edge of his desk and explained, "Although your daughter is legally an adult, Gladys, her recent dependency on—" He flipped to the first page of the document to find the precise legal term.

Gladys Wheeler supplied, "Pills and liquor."

Judge Abernathy nodded. "Because of Little Milly's dependency on pills and liquor, she has been pronounced medically unfit to look after her own affairs. The court has therefore granted you and your husband, Donny Wheeler, legal guardianship over your daughter as if she were a child. Attached to the document is a restraining order that'll stop Stu Travis—despite the fact that he's still Milly's lawfully wedded husband—from troubling her any more."

Gladys Wheeler closed her eyes and clasped both hands together. "Praise the Lord."

Abernathy set the document on the desk. "I know Milly's troubles have been hard on you and Donny," he said gently.

Gladys opened her handbag and removed the petit-point case for her glasses. "Living hell."

"So now that the court's appointed you guardianship over Little Milly, are you going ahead with your plans to take her to that sanatorium place up north?"

Gladys rested both hands on the handbag. "Being optimists, Judge, Donny and me counted on the court's ruling in our favor. Donny's Learjet is waiting at the airport. Little Milly and me fly out this afternoon. A car meets us in Hartford and drives us straight to that home. I'm taking my knitting along and plan on staying there right beside Little Milly. I'm not bringing her back to Nashville till she's her old self again."

Abernathy valued his friendship with the singer Donny Wheeler. He had known Wheeler long before Wheeler's daughter, Little Milly, had begun her own career.

"What's Little Milly's daddy going to do with you two girls away?" he asked.

Gladys chuckled. "Work. What else? Harrah's Club extended Donny's engagement for another two weeks. From Tahoe, he flies up to Portland, Spokane, Seattle, then on to Vancouver, British Columbia. Folks in the Pacific Northwest love Donny Wheeler."

The smile disappeared from her face and she lowered her voice. "Course, nobody knows better than you, Judge, that Donny's had his own fight against pills and liquor. He knows what our baby's going through every minute of the day. Every hurt Milly has, hurts her daddy too."

Judge Abernathy tapped the document. "You call Donny out in Nevada, you hear? You tell Donny how the court ruled this morning in your favor. Donny Wheeler and me go way back. I want him to rest easy knowing we all worked our tails off getting his little girl out of the clutches of Stu Travis."

He leaned forward, adding "If Travis tries to stir up more troubles for Little Milly, you just pick up the phone at your sanatorium place and call me down here in Nashville. Understand?"

Gladys smiled. "Judge, I thank you for your kind offer. It's most generous and thoughtful. But Donny and me's not expecting no more trouble out of Stu Travis. We got a team of hotshot lawyers going over all the contracts Little Milly's ever made with—or through—Stu Travis. He might *think* he can raise a stink when he hears we've been appointed Milly's legal guardians. But we're ready for him. Oh, are we ready."

Abernathy stood up from the desk. Gripping both hands behind his back, he began pacing his broadloom carpet. "Gladys, there used to be a time when I thought it was good for a husband to manage his wife's career. Especially when the little lady tours the country with a show as much as Little Milly does. That's how married folks do things here in Nashville. But for some reason it didn't pan out for Milly and Stu."

Gladys Wheeler's voice took on a sharp edge. "The reason is as plain as the nose on my face: money. Money and all that high living got to be too much for Stu Travis. He's just a dumb country boy who couldn't handle all those dollars rolling in. All that cash from Little Milly's hit albums and her network prime-time TV specials and her moving picture sound tracks. Stu went haywire with all that money and started buying pot and Jim Beam and throwing those swinger parties of his up at the lake cabin. Stu Travis is no-good trash through and through. He tried to drag our Little Milly right down along with him into his cesspool of filth and degradation.

"But that's all behind us now, Judge. We got divorce papers in the pipeline to get Little Milly away from Stu Travis once and for all."

Abernathy paused in front of the window. "You just make sure she gets cured," he said. "She's got lots of fans out there across America."

Gladys sat upright in her chair, holding her folded hands

primly on her handbag. "I'm planning a few changes for Little Milly's career," she announced proudly. "For one thing, there's going to be less television and more road tours. Despite what folks say, the people out there love seeing their favorite stars in the flesh—"

She stopped. "Goodness me, I almost forgot."

Reaching alongside the chair, she lifted her knitting basket from the floor. "I brought you Little Milly's new album. Hot off the presses."

Judge Abernathy studied the cover's color photograph of the singing star. Red-haired and snub-nosed, Little Milly was dressed in fringed white leather trousers and top that hugged her small but shapely figure.

Setting down the album behind him on the desk, Abernathy said, "Gladys, you must be the hardest-working little lady in Nashville. You keep two careers going. Little Milly's *and* Donny's."

Beaming with pride, Gladys Wheeler rose from the chair. "Judge, that's the way I was made," she answered. "I'm nothing but an old workhorse. I've been around long before all this 'country and western' fad started sweeping the country. I was a little bit of a thing when my own daddy played fiddle at the Grand Ol' Opry. I mean the *real* Opry over in Ryman Hall. Not that carnival show they got up there now in Opryland."

Moving toward the office door, she went on. "I remember when folks called country music hillbilly music. The good old days when everybody gathered round like one big happy family over at Radio WSM. Roy Acuff. Hank Williams. Minnie Pearl. Molly O'Day. Those were the days when country music *was* the Grand Ol' Opry and the Grand Ol' Opry was America.

"We all worked hard in those days, Judge. We struggled to get food on the table and a dollar's worth of gasoline in the old Chevy pickup so Daddy could drive a hundred miles to play fiddle in some roadside tavern. So, you see, Judge, work comes natural to me. I don't know no different. That's how I was raised by my own mama and daddy. And that's how I tried to raise Little Milly."

Judge Abernathy held both of Gladys's hands as they stood in front of his office door. "By the way," he asked, "what's the name of that rest home you're taking Milly to up north?"

She smiled at the question. "Well, you know me, Judge. I want nothing but the best for Little Milly. So I asked around until I found the Cadillac—the Cadillac Coupe de Ville Fleetwood deluxe—of drying-out clinics. And I found it. It's called Tanglewood."

18 THE PLUM-RED ROLLS-ROYCE COR-NICHE MOVED SILENTLY ALONG CON-necticut's Highway 61 as Karen Washington followed the directions Jackie Lyell had given her to the Country Mouse Inn.

Alongside Karen in the front seat sat her sister-in-law, Desiree Washington. In the backseat, five-year-old Tamara Washington squatted on the floor, using the dove-gray seat as a desk for her coloring book; four-year-old Tyler Washington zoomed a miniature dune buggy over the seat's edge, up the arm rest, and along the back window.

"Karen, you're upset about something." Desiree looked idly out of the side window, bored with the scenery of quaint barns and ivy-covered bridges. "You haven't said a word since we left Tanglewood."

Karen held her eyes on the road, thinking about the old days when she and Peabo had first got married.

"Is it Peabo?"

"I didn't see Peabo," said Karen. "Not to speak."

Smaller than Karen, Desiree Washington had coffee-color skin and wore her black hair clipped closely to her head, large hoop earrings emphasizing an aggressive no-nonsense manner. She was a political science major at Lincoln University.

"You want to talk about him?" she asked.

"No." Karen's tone was emphatic. "I'm going back to the clinic later this afternoon. Maybe tonight I'll be able to explain what's happening."

As she spoke, Karen wished she knew what was happening herself. In her mind she saw Peabo as he used to be: a big grinning man, both hands held behind his back, making her choose what hand she wanted. When she did choose, she found an old sweat sock in one hand, a paper towel in the other. As she playfully beat on his chest for teasing her, he wrapped her in his arms. Nuzzling her ear, her neck, her hair, he told her, "Hey, baby. I'm just keeping you in training. Someday's there's going to be keys to a new Rolls-Royce in one hand, a big forty-carat diamond in the other. I want you to be able to handle it."

Desiree's voice broke into Karen's memories. "Sometimes it's good to get things off your chest."

"No—"

Karen slowed the car, pointing at a white sign to the left of the road. "Does that say 'Country Mouse'?"

Desiree looked at the wooden sign swinging from a wrought-iron cross arm. " 'Country Mouse'? Jeeezzzuzzz! Where are you taking me? Snow White's magic forest?"

Karen smiled, thankful for her sister-in-law's sense of humor. "Come on, girl. This is New England. Go with it."

Pulling off the highway into a gravel parking lot, she added, "I think it's very pretty. I won't mind spending a few days here."

A butter-yellow, two-story wooden house, the Country Mouse Inn had pristine white shutters and a row of dormer windows along its weathered cedar-shake roof. The hotel sat back from the highway, and to the left of its parking lot stood a small restaurant fronted with bow windows and a sign: TEA ROOMS—OPEN YEAR ROUND.

Tamara and Tyler stood in the backseat, peering over their mother's shoulder.

"Is this where we're going to sleep tonight, Mommy?" Tamara asked.

"I want my own room," Tyler announced.

Tamara added, "Can I sleep with you, Mommy?"

"I want my own room," Tyler repeated.

"Hey!" Karen waved her hand for order. "Sit down until the aircraft comes to a complete stop. All ten of you."

"Ten?" Tamara giggled. "You're teasing us again, Mommy. There's only *two* of us." The little girl pointed at her younger brother. "He's one. And I'm two."

Tyler screamed, "I am not one! I'm four!"

Stopping the car, Karen turned round to grab her sweater and Hermés handbag as she ordered, "You two stay here and take care of Auntie Re, okay? Mama's going inside to register and see if I can get somebody to help us with our suitcases."

" 'The Country Mouse.' " Desiree shook her head in mock disbelief. "What kind of odds do you want to lay me that the bellhop's got a long tail and eats Swiss cheese?"

Karen checked her makeup in the mirror. "A lot of help you are, dear." She had an easy relationship with Desiree, although at times she considered her sister-in-law a little too abrasive. Or was it militant?

Moving up the front steps toward the hotel's red lacquered doors, Karen paused when a woman with an eggshell-white complexion and lank brown hair emerged to face her.

Standing on the top step of the entrance, the woman

looked down at Karen, asking, without a trace of welcome, "May I help you?"

Karen was exhausted. She had packed the kids into the car at five o'clock that morning. The six-hour drive from Philadelphia to Stonebridge had not been strenuous but the short time she had spent at Tanglewood, and the shocking sight of Peabo, had drained her last bit of energy. All she wanted to do at the moment was soak in a hot tub. But she forced herself to smile at the sour-faced woman. "I believe you're holding a reservation in the name of Lyell. Mrs. Jackie Lyell. From Tanglewood. A double and adjoining single."

The woman's face showed surprise; she glanced from Karen to the plum-red Rolls-Royce.

Raising one eyebrow, she repeated, "Reservation?"

Warning bells immediately began to clang inside Karen's head. She hoped there wasn't going to be some kind of ugly scene.

Politely but firmly, she persisted. "You told Mrs. Lyell on the telephone this morning that you'd be kind enough to hold two adjoining rooms until five o'clock." She glanced at her watch to emphasize the fact they were well ahead of the deadline.

"Impossible." The woman shook her head, jabbing both hands into the pockets of her houndstooth hacking jacket. "We're totally booked."

"But Mrs. Lyell spoke to you only this morning."

The woman's voice hardened. "Lady, don't you understand English? I said there's no vacancy."

The sharp tone, the rude words stung Karen. She forced down her own temper. "One of us is obviously making a mistake. Perhaps we can clear up the misunderstanding by going inside and telephoning Mrs. Lyell at Tanglewood."

"I don't need to clear up anything, lady. I own this hotel. I assure you I know what's happening here. But if *you* want to make a telephone call, by all means do. There's a gas station down the highway. If you've got the right change, I'm sure they'll let you use their pay phone."

Desiree opened the car door. "Trouble, Karen?" she called.

Karen held her eyes on the woman. "This . . . lady here says she doesn't have a reservation for us."

Karen saw with discomfort that a couple seated at a window table in the restaurant were watching the scene. And a man standing next to a car in the parking lot was looking at them with interest.

Desiree moved toward the steps. "Perhaps Mrs. Lyell made the reservations under the clinic's name."

The woman moved down one step, both hands clenched inside the jacket's pockets. "I said there's no reservation for you people. We've been booked solid for weeks. So just go away. Leave us alone. Don't cause trouble."

Desiree looked from the angry woman to Karen, quickly guessing the true problem. She took another step forward and said, "Lady, maybe you better have another look at your reservation sheet. Before we make a few telephone calls you might regret."

The woman's face flushed with anger. "Don't you threaten me, young woman. Don't you dare come here and threaten me with your Martin Luther King rabble-rousing innuendo."

Karen also noticed the man in the parking lot had moved closer; now he could certainly hear the conversation. Under her breath she said, "Re, let's just get into the car and get out of here. Please."

Ignoring Karen's plea, Desiree challenged the woman. "Why do you mention Reverend King, lady? It's not because of color, is it?"

"Color? What color?" The white woman's laugh was nervous. "I don't know what you mean."

Karen put her hand on Desiree's arm. "Re, please. Don't make a scene. Not now. I can't take it."

Desiree sloughed off Karen's hand. "Why are you so hostile, lady? We know we have a reservation here. It's only for a few nights. We don't want to move in and take over the neighborhood."

The woman pointed at the road. "Leave. That's what you can do. Leave. Go back to Tanglewood. Go home. Go anyplace. Just get off my property and leave me alone."

Angling her head, Desiree studied the innkeeper with cold, dispassionate eyes. "Don't you even want to know who you're turning away? Maybe you saw this lady here on television?" She paused. "You *do* have television up here, don't you?"

"Of course we have television," the woman snapped. "Don't be ridiculous."

"Good. Then maybe you saw this woman and her husband—he happens to be Peabo Washington, the Heavyweight boxing champion of the world. Maybe you saw them being entertained at the White House. Seated next to the President of the United States and the First Lady. Now, you can't get more white than the White House . . . can you?"

Karen pulled Desiree's forearm. "That's enough. Come on. We're leaving."

Moving back toward the car with Karen, Desiree threatened over her shoulder, "You'll be hearing from us again, lady. You can bet on that. You're not getting off this easy."

The man in the parking lot stepped toward the Rolls-Royce; as Karen opened the door and slid behind the wheel, he leaned forward, saying "Excuse me, ma'am. But aren't you Karen Washington? Aren't you married to Peabo Washington?"

Karen shook her head. "Please. I can't talk now."

He persisted, "I drove up here to talk to your husband. I write for the *New York Journal.* I called the clinic where I heard he was staying—"

"Call my husband's manager," Karen said to the journalist and slammed the door shut.

Leaning across the seat, she opened the other door. "Desiree, get in here and shut your mouth. Shut your mouth, Desiree."

* * *

The Hi-Way Motel stood alongside the western city limits of Stonebridge, Connecticut. It was a double-story concrete building fronted with balconies trimmed with lime-green fiberglass that had cracked from summer's heat and winter's cold since the motel had been built in the 1950s, now adding to its air of general deterioration.

Karen threw down the room key on the chipped Formica table and glanced from the chenille-covered bed to the stained couch that the manager had assured her opened into a double bed.

Desiree followed her into the room with two heavy suitcases. "I think you should call Tanglewood immediately, Karen, and tell them exactly what happened."

"Desiree, can't you get it through your head?" Karen was near tears; her voice cracking. "I don't want to stay someplace where we're not wanted. Why pay for bad atmosphere?"

Desiree appraised the motel room's peeling paint, sagging Venetian blinds, scuffed linoleum tiles. "This atmosphere is good?"

Behind them trailed Tamara and Tyler, each carrying a small suitcase. Tamara curled her upper lip with distaste as she looked at the room. "Mommy, I don't like this place," she whined. "It's dirty."

Karen moved toward the bathroom. "Be patient, angel. We'll find a new place tomorrow. Mama just couldn't drive any more today. I'm beat. I need a bath."

The children followed Karen into the bathroom. Tamara asked, "Why didn't we stay at the other place, Mommy?"

Karen frowned at the yellow-stained tub. "Because they had mice."

Tamara squealed. "Mice?"

Tyler laughed. "Where's the mice, Mommy? Where's the mice?"

Desiree called behind them, "Didn't you see it? A big white rat. Standing on the front steps."

Karen poked her head out of the bathroom doorway. "Desiree, please. These are children."

There was a knock on the door.

Karen looked beseechingly at her sister-in-law. "That's the manager. He's come to tell us where to park someplace safe. Could you please take care of it? The key's in my bag."

"No sweat." Desiree opened the door, facing a plump, florid-faced man in a porkpie hat.

Holding both hands behind his back, he asked politely, "Excuse me, but could I please speak to Mrs. Peabo Washington?"

Not recognizing him, Desiree asked, "Is it about the car?"

He smiled. "Mrs. Washington's here?"

Desiree shouted from the open door. "Karen, the guy wants to talk to you."

Karen moved to the bathroom doorway, the children following her with their little suitcases. She instantly recognized the *New York Journal* reporter who had tried to talk to her in the inn's parking lot.

She glared at him as she strode toward the door. "Mister, I said to call my husband's manager. Now just leave us alone, okay?"

The reporter asked bluntly, "Mrs. Washington, is your husband at Tanglewood for a drug cure?"

Karen grabbed at the children to pull them behind her. "I said please, just leave us alone—"

Before she could shut the door, the man raised a camera from behind his back and flashed a picture of Karen flanked by Tamara and Tyler clutching their small suitcases as they stared wide-eyed at the camera.

19

BY THREE O'CLOCK THAT AFTERNOON, KAREN WASHINGTON HAD NOT YET telephoned Tanglewood to set up an appointment to see Peabo. Roger was not surprised he hadn't heard from her. She'd probably eaten lunch at the Country Mouse and, after getting the kids settled for a nap, dozed off herself. He was secretly grateful she had not called back yet. The time he had spent that morning with Dr. Gene Stone had put him more than an hour behind schedule. By three o'clock, he still had not eaten lunch. The dining room had stopped serving but, passing the French doors, he saw a few people lingering at their tables. It was a good time to try to get a bowl of soup and a salad.

Lillian Weiss was alone at her usual table in a far corner. When he saw her, he remembered Simone Charbonneau's telephone call that morning about Weiss's lab results. He decided to get a thankless job over with.

Bracing himself, he moved past the empty tables. "Mind if I join you?"

Lillian smiled flirtatiously. "I thought you'd never ask."

He sat down across from her. "What'd you have today?"

"Baked potato. Too much." She pushed the half-eaten potato away from her on the plate.

Roger had noticed in past weeks that Lillian Weiss never finished her meals. Despite her obesity, she ate like a bird in the dining room, and this had confused him. Until this morning.

"What do you do now, Lillian?" he asked, playing a hunch. "Go back to your room and stuff your face with candy?"

She jerked her head. "What did you say?"

Roger leaned farther across the table, keeping his voice low as he repeated, "What do you do now? Go back to the room and eat candy?"

"What candy?"

"The candy you keep in your room."

Lowering her eyes guiltily, she replied, "That's the maid's candy."

"Does the maid pee for you, too, Lillian?"

She glowered at him. "Did you come here to insult me?"

Roger rested both arms on the table. "Lillian, I had your new lab results this morning. There's too much sugar in your urine, and"—he nodded at her plate—"you're not getting it from baked potato."

She moved her head in quick, nervous jerks, small red lips twitching nervously.

Roger hated making the woman uncomfortable, especially as she always seemed so jolly. But if she kept on with her behavior, her treatment would go nowhere. Compassion in his voice, he asked, "Lillian, why are you wasting your money at Tanglewood?"

"It's not *my* money. My late husband's lawyers pay the bills." She grabbed the fork and sank it into the remainder of the potato, splitting it in half and popping the larger piece into her mouth.

Roger nodded. "Fine. So money means nothing to you. But you're wasting your time as well as ours if you say you 'just nibble' but actually gorge yourself on sweets when you go back to your room."

Ladylike, she dabbed the corners of her mouth and asked petulantly, "Is it a waste of time that your exercises have helped me to walk?"

"Lillian, I'm not Jesus Christ. I don't help the lame walk

and the blind see. I help people who want to help themselves."

Setting down the napkin alongside her plate, she asked, "Exactly what are you saying to me?"

"That I'm surprised and disappointed."

"So now you're going to kick me out." She sat in the chair, both hands resting on the edge of the table.

"No, Lillian, I'm not going to ask you to leave. I'm giving you one more chance. I'm putting you into group therapy. Betty Lassiter's advance group. The Sweat Room."

Her eyes bulged. "Never!"

"Lillian, you have some very serious problems. Far more serious than you're willing to admit. But perhaps you can start facing them in therapy. Your other choice is to go back to New York and find a good analyst."

"I don't believe in analysis and I think group therapy is stupid."

Roger raised both hands. "I'm sorry, Lillian. It's the Sweat Room or leave."

Tossing up her head, she announced, "If you will excuse me, Dr. Cooper, I haven't finished my luncheon."

"Sorry." Roger pushed back his chair.

As he walked toward the kitchen he heard Lillian Weiss mutter, *"Schmuck."*

Alone in the dining room after Roger Cooper had disappeared through the swinging doors into the kitchen, Lillian wondered why all the dishy men she ever met turned out to be such deadbeats.

The only men who were ever halfway civil to her were either married or faggots or eunuchs.

She finished the baked potato with a gulp and belched. Her thoughts turned from Roger Cooper to the loser she had been married to:

Sam Weiss, a New York real estate broker with a wreath of black hair encircling his bald head, nervously faced his bride on their wedding night. "I think you forgot our agreement, Lillian," he said.

"Agreement?" Lillian lay curled on the white-and-gold bed, wiggling her chubby fingers to grab Sam standing in his pajamas alongside the night table. She had known him for three months but had still not seen his putz.

He reminded her politely, "We agreed we wouldn't make love."

Patting the white satin bridal sheets her mother had sent her from Florida for her wedding night, Lillian coaxed, "Come to bed, Sam. We're not kids. I'm not going to rape you." Sam Weiss was sixty-four years old; Lillian, forty-three. Neither of them had been married before.

"No, Lillian," insisted Sam, travel alarm clock in one hand, favorite pillow in the other. "I'm sleeping in the guest room."

"Guest room? But this is our wedding night, Sam. You're my husband. Not my . . . guest."

"I know, Lillian. I know. But I told you. I'm not the romantic type."

Losing her patience, Lillian asked, "You're not a pansy, are you, Sam?"

"No, Lillian. I don't do it one way or the other. I don't go to bed with anybody. I'm sixty-four years old and still, you know, as they say—" he laughed uneasily. "—'Never been kissed.' "

"You don't know what you're missing, kid." Provocatively, she traced the tip of her tongue around her tiny mouth.

"Don't try to tempt me, Lillian. It won't work. I'm sleeping in the guest room."

She asked angrily, "So why did you marry me?"

"As I told you, Lillian. We have good times together, you and me. We have laughs."

"Why didn't you marry a clown?"

A true gentleman, Sam Weiss ignored his obese bride's barbed comment and leaned forward to kiss her forehead. "Sweet dreams, dear," he murmured.

This sleeping arrangement continued for three years, Lillian occupying the Park Avenue apartment's master bedroom while Sam Weiss slept in the guest room, until the day when Lillian received a telephone call from Sam's bookkeeper, Lou Goldberger. From Sam's lower Broadway office, Goldberger announced, "Brace yourself, Lillian. I've got some very bad news. Sam died in the washroom."

Lillian was left a rich widow, inheriting all of Sam's industrial and residential holdings in New York and New Jersey. Her mother, Bella Rosenquist, flew up to New York from Miami for the funeral. Later, at the apartment, Bella warned, "You may not be much to look at, Lillian, but fortune-hunters are going to be coming out of the woodwork to get their hands on you."

"Thanks for the compliment, Ma," Lillian said with a pout, popping another Snickers into her mouth.

"I'm serious," Bella insisted. "With the weight you're carrying around, honey, your heart's going to give out sooner than most women's. You're the ideal catch for a fortune-hunter."

"Why are you always ready with the good news, Ma?" asked Lillian, opening a box of cream-filled chocolates.

Bella suggested, "Make more girl friends. That's what you've got to do. I know it's hard for a girl your size to get around town. So invite girls here to the apartment. Have open house. Throw bridge parties. You've got a faaabulous place here for entertaining."

"Don't worry about me, Ma. I decided to open a business."

"Business?" The announcement stunned Bella. "What in God's name can you do, Lillian?"

"In the Yellow Pages I found the name of a school that teaches flower arranging. I'm going to be a florist, Ma."

Bella pulled a face. "Oh, Lillian . . ."

"Ma, for once have some faith in me."

Dried weeds. Silk rags tied onto bamboo sticks. Wire

bedsprings sprayed Day-Glo pink, green, orange. The instructor at Beryl Sanderson's School of Floral Arrangements on West 57th Street was horrified at Lillian Weiss's creations. But the young men in Lillian's class loved her outrageous sense of color, the bizarre shapes and textures she mixed together, the way she used cement blocks, covered with exotic animal pelts, for vases. Watching Lillian, the young men hurriedly copied her work and sold their imitations in East Side boutiques and Christopher Street gift shops.

Disillusioned by gay boys stealing her ideas, Lillian abandoned her plans for becoming a florist and decided to embark on becoming a socialite. Studying the gossip columns in all the New York dailies as well as the giveaway newspapers, she guessed that the easiest way to crash the New York social scene was through the art world.

"What do you know about art?" asked Lillian's Sister Number One, Ruth, over lunch at Reginette's in the Delmonico.

Lillian told a half truth. "I decided art is a good investment."

Ruth patted Lillian's pudgy hand. "Honey, let me ask you a question. Name me a rich artist."

"Picasso."

"A live one."

"Louise Nevelson."

"A man."

"Larry Rivers."

"Somebody who'll marry you."

Lillian had no answer.

Ruth proceeded, "Forget art, Lillian. Artists don't have a pot to piss in. Travel. That's the way you'll meet a rich man who might marry you."

"I have enough money," argued Lillian.

Coyly, Ruth reminded her older sister, "Lillian, you know what that little pillow on my telephone bench says: A girl is

*never too rich or"—She dropped her eyes to Lillian's
muu-muu. "—too thin."*

*Ignoring Ruth's advice, Lillian began buying canvases and
sculptures. She was soon frequenting galleries up and down
Madison Avenue and in SoHo. Her patronage quickly led to
invitations to artists' lofts. Through parties and socializing,
the bohemian group she fell in with also introduced her to
marijuana, cocaine, pills. Of all the drugs, though, she
preferred amphetamines, especially the phendimetrazine in the
diet bars, Nu-You, because they tasted like
Snickers—especially when she ate them with a handful of
peanuts.*

*In Lillian's newly discovered world, she was also getting
laid. There were the art groupies who went to bed with her
because they were "chubby chasers"—attracted to fat
women—or wanted to be included in her entourage. Many
were out-of-towners also hoping to be part of the New York
art scene.*

*"How would you like to be in a movie, Lillian?" asked
Esmeraldo Juaquin, the sculptor and avant-garde filmmaker,
one night at his lower East Side loft.*

"Little me?" she asked coyly. "A movie queen?"

*In past months, ever since Lillian had been getting laid,
she had become more tolerant of homosexuals, learning that
artistic gays loved her size, her outrageous taste in clothes, the
shattering entrances she made at discos, parties, restaurants.*

*Esmeraldo explained, "The movie will have two stars. You
and a Cuban upholsterer who made some cushions for me. He
has a dick of death and will fuck you all through the credits
to the moment you roll over with 'The End' stenciled on
your ass."*

*Lillian's enthusiasm plummeted. "You want me to do . . .
a blue movie?"*

*Esmeraldo laughed and refilled her champagne tulip. "You
pay for it, dear, and you can have any color you want."*

*Lillian realized the filmmaker was only putting the touch
on her to finance a sleazy porno flick. She threw the*

champagne in his face, shouting "You mother-fucker. I'm a lady!"

Disillusioned with the art world, Lillian began spending more and more time alone at home, sending her maid out to do all her shopping, to take her cats to the vet, to pick up her Nu-You bars.

Snacking on deli food all day long, she devoured endless boxes of diet bars. The phendimetrazine gave her energy, keeping her up late at night, as she talked on the telephone to friends around the country, running up three, four, five thousand dollar-a-month phone bills.

Lillian's Sister Number Two, Esther, was horrified by the mess she found in the Park Avenue apartment.

"Lillian," she ordered, "the first thing you have to do is fire your maid."

"She quit."

"Find a new one."

"Nobody will work for me."

"Then you've got to pull yourself together. You've living like a pig." Esther shook her head. "But then you've always been a mess."

From her bed, Lillian asked, "Why do I feel like Cinderella with two ugly sisters?"

Esther retorted, "If I were you, I'd feel more like the pumpkin."

Fat jokes. Lillian had heard them all her life. Finally she could take no more. Tired of living in a pigsty, isolated from the world, listening to her mother and sisters complaining about her, one night she called one of her favorite telephone mates, gossip columnist Myra B.

"Where can I go to lose weight?" Lillian asked.

"There's hundreds of places to go. So let's narrow them down. Where do you want to be? North? South? East? Or west?"

Air travel was difficult for Lillian. She always had to ask the stewardess to bring her an extension for the seat belt. People kept passing in the aisle to look at her.

She answered, "Someplace I can go in a limo."

"That narrows it down."

Myra B thought, then asked, "What do you want besides losing weight? Sunshine? Meeting a few eligible men? Mixing with famous people? Bridge parties?"

"Mixing with famous people."

"The place you want is Tanglewood. But one problem. They only take patients addicted to drugs."

Lillian paused. She didn't want to discuss her dependency on Nu-Yous with the biggest blabbermouth in New York. "I think I can take care of that," she said.

Sitting alone in Tanglewood's dining room, Lillian decided she had to abandon yet another start at a new life. All because of her weakness for sweeties. She didn't know why she craved chocolate and sugar and crunchy nuts, but she wasn't going to join any psychotherapy group to find out. She had heard enough people make fun of her all her life. She didn't have to pay for more fat jokes.

20 THREE SLICES OF CHEDDAR CHEESE AND A HANDFUL OF LETTUCE ON A croissant, along with a glass of orange juice, served as Roger's lunch. He gobbled it in one corner of the kitchen as he sat on a stool by the telephone and buzzed his junior, Wayne Piciska, to learn how Bunny Duncan's treatment was progressing. Piciska was trying the Texas department store heiress on phenobarbitol. Then Roger buzzed his office.

His secretary, Caroline, reported that Karen Washington still had not telephoned from the Country Mouse Inn. Caroline also gave him two other messages. Father Hawkes, the gratis patient, was checking out this afternoon and wanted a last-minute interview with Roger. Also, she had found fifteen minutes free in Roger's busy schedule to fit in an afternoon appointment with the model, Lavender Gilbert. That appointment was the first on his list.

As he jotted notes across the yellow legal pad attached to his clipboard, Roger saw earlier memos he had made to himself.

Little Milly Wheeler and her mother would be arriving from Nashville later this afternoon or early evening. He remembered they were checked into Father Hawkes's Garden Pavilion suite. He hoped Jackie was taking care of the late-day room preparation.

At the bottom of the yellow page, Roger saw the initials CP—PM.

He drew a momentary blank on this note.

Then he remembered. CP: Cat Powers. PM: afternoon. He had told Gene Stone he would drop by to see Cat Powers this afternoon after lunch.

Finishing the orange juice in one gulp, he decided he would see Cat Powers after he spoke to Lavender Gilbert.

The clipboard tucked under one arm, Roger walked across the stainless-steel kitchen, approaching the swinging doors to the dining room before he remembered Lillian Weiss.

Peering into the dining room, he saw her table was empty. Had she gone to her room to pack? Roger paused to make another note for later today or early evening: "ppm."

As he jotted "Weiss" under "telephone," he saw the name "Annie." For a moment he couldn't think who it was. Then he remembered. Last weekend's date.

How close did he want to get to Annie Cross? Should he

encourage a relationship? Tucking the clipboard back under his arm, he told himself that if he had to ask himself such a question, he already had the answer.

Nurse Juanita Alvarez escorted Lavender Gilbert to Roger's office; Roger met them at the door and told the nurse to return in fifteen minutes to collect the model. Standing back for Lavender to pass in front of him into the inner office, he said, "Thank you for giving me a few minutes."

"I decided I have to go back to work," Lavender said as she moved past him into the office. "I'm catching the evening train to New York."

"We can talk later about that." Roger gestured for her to take a chair facing a small white lucite square built into a metal console. "There're some pictures I'd like you to see first."

As Lavender seated herself in front of the small screen, Roger switched on the machine. "Some of these faces you'll recognize," he explained. A head shot of a raven-haired woman flashed on the white square.

Lavender sat forward. "That's Dorothy Lovell, the actress."

Roger pressed the control bulb. The actress's face reappeared, but this time there were deep lines and dark blotches devastating her features. As Lavender stared in silence at the grotesque change in the actress's face, Roger said, "We've been given permission to use these pictures by the victims' estates."

He clicked for the next shot, a young blond woman beaming a bright white smile.

"Candee Allen," Lavender said immediately.

"Did you know her?" Roger asked.

"Pretty well. We worked together on a spread for *Seventeen*." Lavender hesitated and looked at Roger. "Was Candee at Tanglewood, too?"

"She was scheduled to check in here. But she cancelled at

the last moment. Three weeks later her body was found in the Dakota."

Roger clicked the control bulb. The next photograph showed a young man with strong Italian features. "Nick Colonna," he explained. "The Chicago Bears."

He clicked again; a pretty black girl smiled out at them.

"Lorna Vondel." Another *click*, and a grainy black-and-white photo showed the girl being loaded into an ambulance. He added, "She didn't live to see her first soul album released."

Click. "Debbie Chung. The Olympic gymnast." *Click.*

Click. "Streeter Hall. Youngest brother of the Las Vegas magic act, the Hall Brothers." *Click.*

Click. "Kilo Rodriquez. Comedian." *Click.*

A telephone buzzed on the desk behind them. Handing the control bulb to Lavender, Roger turned to answer the phone. "I'll be right out," he said into the receiver. Turning to Lavender, he said, "Excuse me for a couple of minutes. I've got to step outside."

Alone in front of the console, Lavender held the control bulb limply in one hand as she stared at the face on the screen. Kilo Rodriquez. She remembered the young Latino comedian. Rodriquez had starred in his own television situation comedy and went on to make feature films. His cocaine tragedy had ended a brilliant career.

Squeezing the control bulb, Lavender next saw a head shot of a red-haired young woman with dramatic eye makeup. Another drug victim, English pop singer Duchess of Style.

Lavender squeezed again and stared a few seconds at the photograph of the balding man before she recognized him, Paul Rhine, the actor who had appeared in so many television commercials for yogurt; Rhine had also died from a cocaine dependency.

Again and again, Lavender squeezed the control bulb, recognizing many of the faces that flashed across the screen, remembering how their lives and careers had come to an abrupt end because of drugs. Some stories she had read about in magazines and newspapers, others she had heard about from friends.

After switching off the machine, Lavender rose from the chair, her uncertainty returning. Earlier today she had decided to go back to New York, to return to work and trust her own willpower to cut down on the drugs that Chatwyn, his stylists, and photographers gave her to get through the frantic week, and probably the next week, and the week after that one. But could she really resist the temptation? Was she as strong as she thought? What was more important, her career or her life?

Roger stood in his outer office, instructing Juanita Alvarez, "Leave her alone in my office a few more minutes. Then when you go in and get her, tell her I was called away on an emergency."

"What if she still wants to leave Tanglewood?" the nurse asked.

"We can't stop her but . . ." Roger shook his head. ". . . but I bet she stays. The girl's not stupid."

21 SOMETIMES A LONG SHOT PROVED TO BE SUCCESSFUL. SOMETIMES IT DIDN'T. Roger would have to wait and see what decision Lavender made about leaving Tanglewood. Getting on with his afternoon work, he went to the Orchard Pavilion—Cat Powers's suite.

As soon as he entered the bedroom and saw Cat Powers lying motionless on the bed—eyes closed, mouth open, undisturbed by activity in the room—he knew she had been heavily sedated.

Moving alongside the licensed practical nurse, Margie Clark, at the foot of the bed, he asked, "When was Dr. Stone last here?"

Margie checked her watch. "He left about an hour ago. He said he was going to his room next door—the phrase he used for it was 'to crash.' "

Once more Roger was furious with Stone. The Hollywood doctor had administered a strong sedative, a barbiturate or benzodiazepine, to the actress. Roger was sure of it. Whether he had given her a pill or an injection, Roger didn't know, but he was certain that Stone had done it to prevent him from proceeding with a physical examination.

A third person stood in the bedroom, a ruddy-faced man wearing dark trousers, blue shirt, no jacket or tie. The man kept to the far corner, and Roger was too angry to notice his presence as he concentrated on Cat Powers.

The actress's oval face was fuller than when Roger had seen her two years ago; she was overweight and looked older than her fifty-two years. Her dark hair was untidy around her puffy face. The slides he had shown Lavender Gilbert a few minutes earlier flashed through Roger's mind. But he was brought back to the the present problem by thinking that Gene Stone might be trying to sabotage his work.

He asked, "Margie, when did you first arrive here?"

Margie thought for a few moments. "I'm floating this week so I don't arrive at work until ten. I checked in at the Hub and saw Delia Pomeroy. She was taking sick leave and asked me to cover for her here with Miss Powers."

"Did you see Dr. Stone inject this woman or give her any pills?"

"Dr. Stone came in, shooed me out, and locked the door. That must have been about twelve-thirty."

She nodded toward the man in the corner. "I came back from lunch a little after Mr. Hudson."

Turning toward Hudson, Roger held out his hand and apologized, "I'm sorry. I didn't mean to ignore you. My name's Cooper. We spoke on the phone last night."

Shaking Roger's hand, Tom Hudson gave a quick nod, his eyes alert and suspicious.

Roger looked at the bed. "Mr. Hudson, I am asking you purely for the record—have you administered medication in any form to Miss Powers since you've been here?"

"Me?" Hudson burst out. "Good Christ, no."

"Did you see Dr. Stone injecting or giving any pills to your fiancée any time today?"

"I went for lunch the same time as the young lady there." Hudson nodded at Margie. "When I came back, Stone had locked the door. Normally I would have kicked it in. But—" He shrugged. "There are sick people here."

Roger asked, "Mr. Hudson, can I speak to you alone?"

"You got it."

Turning to Margie, Roger ordered, "Call for an attendant to sit with Miss Powers. Tell him not to touch her if possible. Make the call while I'm talking to Mr. Hudson in the next room."

Roger closed the sitting-room door and motioned for Hudson to sit in one of the two beige plush settees.

Hudson declined with a wave of the hand. Roger, too, remained standing.

Roger began slowly. "What I have to say might be construed as unprofessional. Even slanderous. It's about your fiancée's physician."

Hudson grunted. "Slander's nothing compared to what I've got planned for that asshole."

Roger relaxed. Hudson had given him the green light to speak freely about Gene Stone.

He went on. "Dr. Stone is being very uncooperative, Mr. Hudson. He won't fill out forms. He won't supply medical facts. And now I suspect he's sedated Miss Powers to keep me from conducting tests. You can see, Mr. Hudson, I'm beginning to wonder what she's doing here."

"Coming to Tanglewood was my idea."

"Maybe so. But if we're not allowed to examine the patient, there's little point in her being here.

"That's why you heard me now giving instructions for my colleagues not to offer assistance. We cannot risk giving any aid that might later be construed as detrimental or harmful by her doctor."

Hudson's voice was a growl. "What you're saying, Cooper, is get rid of Stone."

"At least get him to cooperate. Or else I'm afraid, Mr. Hudson, we cannot accept Cat Powers as a patient. We'll have to ask her to leave. Immediately. Even if you have to hire an ambulance to remove her."

Hudson worked his jaw. "You'd do that?"

"To protect the clinic from legal action, absolutely. I've had dealings with Gene Stone in the past."

Hudson drove the fist of one hand against the palm of his other hand. "Damn it to hell. How does she get mixed up with these assholes? It's these moochers who get her on drugs. Get her back boozing. When she's not on all this junk, you couldn't ask for a nicer, better-looking, sweeter-acting lady."

"Most of our patients are good, upstanding people, Mr. Hudson. But each has his or her own reason—the wrong kind of friends, too many pressures, deeply embedded insecurities—that makes them become involved with something they should be avoiding at all costs. Jekyll-and-Hyde situations are very common around here, I'm afraid."

"But Cat can pull out of this. I know it," Hudson argued. *"I know it."*

Roger liked Hudson. Intuition told him that Hudson was the kind of guy he called a "meat-and-potato man."

He asked, "Last night at the theater, what exactly were the signs that alarmed you about Cat?"

"Before the first couple scenes she started screaming. Yelling at her dresser. Complaining one minute she couldn't breathe. Screaming the next minute her heart was racing and she was going to die. The part of that Blanche character in the play is crazy enough. I thought maybe it was getting to her. You know, making her crackers."

"Did you see Stone injecting her yesterday?"

"Yesterday. *And* the day before. *And* the day before that. Three, four times a day."

"Do you know with what?"

Hudson shook his head. "Sorry."

"Have you told Cat about your disapproval of him?"

"Cat won't hear a thing against Stone."

"Last night, did you suggest she didn't continue with the play?"

"Damn right. But she said the audience had paid to see her so she owed them a performance. Some old crap like that. But watching her getting more and more crazy between scenes, I got on the phone to you. She travels with her address book. That's where I found your number."

Roger spoke honestly. "I don't think I'm being unprofessional, Mr. Hudson, by telling you that your fiancée has a long history of alcohol and drug abuse. But under the present circumstances, she's merely taking up space here."

Looking Hudson in the eye, he added, "I squeezed the three of you into these guest rooms only because Miss Powers has been here twice before. But I must make it perfectly clear, Mr. Hudson, that we cannot place loyalty to Miss Powers above the well-being of cooperative patients."

Hudson's jaw worked as he thought. "I got a business to run. I have to get back to Chicago. But I also plan to marry Cat, and I'm not going to until I see she gets a clean bill of health."

He took a deep breath. "Tell you what. If I can't get Stone to cooperate, I'll take Cat away. Tomorrow. No fuss made."

Roger did not respond.

Hudson put his hand on Roger's shoulder. "Trust me,

Cooper. I'm not known as Tom-the-Butt-Kicker for nothing."

At that, Roger smiled. The two men shook hands.

A walk always helped solve Tom Hudson's problems. He had to walk after Roger Cooper left Cat's suite.

Apart from worrying about Cat, Hudson had to decide when he was flying back to Chicago. He had built Red Tag Food Stores from a handful of local mom-and-pop grocery shops. But every day bigger and more serious problems threatened his empire. At the moment butchers were calling a strike in New Mexico over Sunday openings. An early Florida frost had endangered the citrus crop. New Jersey Teamsters were picketing his bakery for using nonunion workers.

Hudson stopped at the end of the Orchard Pavilion, wondering what in hell he was doing there biding his time in a drug clinic in Connecticut.

The answer came quickly. He was there for Cat Powers.

Cat was going through a bad patch but, when she was in good form, there was no better woman. They made sparks fly together. Not only in bed but having breakfast, going on strolls, even letting one another in on their careers.

Hudson remembered visiting Cat on the set of a television movie. She had been making a cameo appearance in a big-budget melodrama scheduled to be aired during prime time over the Thanksgiving weekend. The male and female stars in the extravaganza were romantically involved in private life, but on set the male star was totally awed by the famous Cat Powers, while the leading lady was certain that Cat was trying to steal him away from her.

The tension had come to a head when all three personalities—Cat, the male actor, and the female lead—appeared together in one final drawing-room scene. The male lead kept forgetting his lines, intimidated by Cat sprawled across a Louis XV couch; the leading lady shot angry glances at Cat, refusing to follow the director's instructions to speak softly to her. It was getting late; the director had to call for repeated takes. Finally Cat rose from the couch and said to the director, "Love, do you mind if I take a minute to talk to a friend of mine here?"

The leading lady groaned; baffled looks were exchanged on the set; the director reluctantly consented to Cat's request.

Sauntering to the edge of the carpet, Cat called to Hudson standing in the darkness behind the cameras. "Tommy, why don't you go to Jill's party without me? I'm going to be late."

Hudson and Cat had not planned to attend any party after the day's filming; Hudson could not even think of anyone named Jill who might invite them to a party. But not wanting to argue with Cat in front of her co-stars and crew, he nodded. "Whatever you want, dear."

Cat's voice rose as she dramatically put both hands on her hips, adding "But if that bitch tries to vamp you at her shindig, Tommy, you tell her for me that I'll break every bone in her body."

Silence followed Cat's threat. Seizing the moment with perfect timing, she faced the stunned crew, saying with a playful bitchiness "A girl's got to protect her man, doesn't she?" Cat looked at the jealous leading lady. "Right, darling? Us girls all have to protect our men. They're too hard to find these days."

Laughter filled the set; even the leading lady broke into a broad grin. Seeing the mood immediately relax, Hudson understood Cat's ploy. She had recognized the other actress's jealousy and decided to show her she was not trying to steal anybody away from her. At the risk of looking like a fool, Cat had taken the situation in hand and manipulated it like a true professional.

Hudson stood in the Orchard Pavilion, smiling at the memory. He had known Cat only for a few months when he had visited her on the set that day, but already he had begun to understand that Cat—like himself—insisted on cutting through the crap to get to the important things. Cat had confidence in herself. She took chances. And she always emerged as the star.

Having found Cat, Hudson wasn't going to lose her. At least, he was going to put up a hell of a good fight to hang onto that special lady.

Hudson decided to keep looking around the clinic. If he was going to leave Cat here in its care, he wanted to make sure it was the best money could buy.

22 LILLIAN WEISS'S ANGER DID NOT ABATE BY LATE AFTERNOON. STILL FUrious at Roger Cooper for giving her an ultimatum to join the encounter group or leave Tanglewood, she knew that her final decision undoubtedly depended on money. Despite her claims to be unconcerned about money, she kept her eye on every dollar. This week's fee had already been paid, and she did not want to forfeit it. The sum equaled a month's rent for a summer house in the Hamptons. Or a winter cruise on the QE2.

Thoughts of a refund occupied Lillian's mind as she progressed slowly down the hallway of the Garden Pavilion. She moved a few yards, then stopped to rest her enormous bulk and pop a baby Snickers into her mouth. When she finished the candy bar, she moved another short distance down the hallway.

A cheery voice called behind her, "A penny for your thoughts."

Lillian looked over her shoulder and saw the frizzy-haired

nurse, Margie Clark, removing a clipboard and envelope from the cupboard under the archway.

"You look pensive," Margie said.

The bracelets clattered on Lillian's wrist as she waved one pudgy hand dismissively. "You don't need to hear *my* troubles."

"Clouds pass." Margie closed the cupboard door and moved away from it. She stopped and looked back at the small door, momentarily confused. Shaking her head, she said, "It's hard trying to remember what doors they want locked around here and which ones stay open."

Eager for companionship, Lillian decided to try to engage Margie in conversation. She asked, "So what are you doing now?"

"Pinch-hitting again for another nurse," Margie explained. "I'm on float duty this week."

"The patients here in the Garden Pavilion need special care, don't they?" asked Lillian, remembering facts she had gleaned by quizzing other staff members. "You really have to watch them, I understand."

Margie stopped at room G4. "It's not so bad."

Lillian pressed, "But this stuff here is pretty secret, huh?" Gossiping about other people made her forget her own problems.

Margie looked through her envelope for the correct card key to open the door. "Nothing's really secret. Everybody just wants to get better, don't they?"

"So whose room is this?" Lillian asked, deciding to be more direct in her approach.

"Ray Esposito. You probably haven't seen much of him."

"Esposito?" Lillian knew exactly who the man was. "That dark-haired guy who looks like a young version of Dean Martin? Yeah, I know who he is. I knew, too, what he was here for but I forgot."

"Heroin."

"That's right," answered Lillian, pleased that Margie was

so easy to get secrets out of. Pushing for more details, she asked, "So how's he doing?"

Margie shook her head. "Narcotic withdrawals can really be weird. It affects a person's sex drive. Especially men. They get an erection and there's only one way to get rid of that."

"No-o-o-o-o." Lillian's attention was now fully focused on what Margie was telling her.

Margie nodded. "It's really awful, too, if you're like Esposito and don't have a wife or girl friend around when you, you know, need someone to, you know, help out." Margie laughed nervously.

"Esposito's not married?" Lillian asked. "He's got nobody to . . . take care of him?"

"Not yet."

"So what does the guy do? A little of the old one, two?" Lillian cupped her small fist, moving it back and forth in the air.

The sudden coarse gesture surprised and embarrassed Margie. Remembering she was chatting idly when she should be working, she slipped the card into the lock, saying "Nice to talk to you, Lillian. We really have got to sit down and have a good visit someday."

Lillian stood alone in the hallway of the Garden Pavilion after Margie had disappeared into Esposito's room. She remembered seeing the man walking in the back garden. He was a hot-looking hunk. Just the kind of butch man she liked. And the poor guy had a voracious sex drive and no woman to take care of him. Lillian wondered if she was being hasty by leaving Tanglewood so soon. She certainly wasn't going to get laid at home. She glanced at the small cabinet at the end of the hallway. If she made some good plans, she might get the lay of a lifetime right here at Tanglewood.

23 "A WOMAN FROM THE *NEW YORK JOUR-NAL* IS ON THE LINE, MRS. LYELL," AN-nounced the evening telephone operator, Joe Pine.

Jackie looked at the desk clock. It was a few minutes past five o'clock and she was exhausted from what was quickly becoming a ten-hour Monday. She had buried herself in work this morning after hearing a woman answering Adrian's telephone at the Beverly Wilshire. Determined not to let jealousy and anger eat away at her, she kept herself busy with chores in Administration, trying not to make a mess of things. She had decided she should learn how to dictate on the portable Sony. She had taken all calls concerning Cat Powers. She had hounded the New York lawyer's office for a reply about Chatwyn and Lavender Gilbert, but the lawyer still had not returned her call. A bitchy journalist had demanded to be put through to someone who knew what they were talking about. The tape tangled on the pocket Dictaphone.

Her energy flagging at five o'clock, she said wearily into the phone, "What does the *New York Journal* want? Some kind of quote on poor Cat Powers?"

Joe replied, "The woman won't tell me."

"Who'd she ask to talk to, darling?"

"The administrator."

Jackie's first impulse was to shout down the phone that the bloody "administrator" had run off to Los Angeles and was having it off with a California tart.

Instead, she said with a note of strain in her voice, "I suppose I should take the call. Put her through, darling."

Joe hesitated. "Excuse me for saying so, Mrs. Lyell, but you've been cooped up in that office all day. Aren't you going to take a break pretty soon?"

Jackie was warmed by the friendly words. She said appreciatively, "Thank you for the concern, darling. You don't know how much I appreciate it. Truly. Now let's hear what your girl reporter has to say for herself."

Chuckling, Joe answered, "I do like you working in Administration, Mrs. Lyell. I hope it becomes a habit."

The matter-of-fact voice at the other end of the line introduced herself to Jackie as Carol Fleischman of the *New York Journal*. "I'm calling for your comment on Peabo Washington being a patient at Tanglewood." The journalist added, "Who am I speaking to, by the way? Your name and title, please."

The speed—and bluntness—of the questions snapped Jackie from the doldrums. She had expected questions about Cat Powers and was surprised to hear Peabo's name mentioned. She suddenly remembered that Karen Washington had not telephoned this afternoon for an appointment to see Roger.

Hedging, she asked, "Would you please repeat that, Ms. Fleischman?"

The journalist asked briskly, "Is it correct that Peabo Washington's wife, Karen, and two children, Tamara and Tyler, visited him earlier today at Tanglewood?"

"Where are you getting these details?" Jackie demanded angrily.

Ignoring the question, the woman bulldozed on. "Can you comment on why Karen Washington and her children were refused accommodation at—"Papers shuffled at the other end of the line. "—the Country Mouse Inn . . . Connecticut Highway 61?"

"I asked you, Ms. Fleischman, where are you getting these details?"

"Do you deny that race may have been the reason Mrs. Washington was turned away from the hotel?"

"Where are you getting this?"

"The *Journal* is running a front-page exclusive on Peabo Washington in tomorrow's morning edition. Tanglewood features largely in our story so we'd like your official comment on facts telephoned in by one of our field reporters."

Jackie's brain was churning. She knew that whatever she said could be twisted and used against Peabo, apart from stirring a hornet's nest of unwanted publicity for Tanglewood.

She tried, "I'm afraid I'm not authorized to speak to you, Ms. Fleischman."

"Then put me through to someone who is," the journalist retorted sharply.

"There's no one here who can speak to you," Jackie said, her own voice rising, tired of hearing that request on the phone all day long.

Remembering one of Adrian's most effective lines to terminate a nuisance call, she added, "Now I'm going to put down the receiver, Ms. Fleischman, and I'm going to instruct our switchboard to ignore all further calls from you. Good evening."

Hand trembling, she lowered the receiver to its cradle.

Jackie quickly flipped through the Rolodex until she found the listing for the Country Mouse.

A young woman answered the telephone, saying gaily "Thank you for calling the Country Mouse Inn and Tea Rooms."

Trying to keep her voice level, Jackie began, "This is Mrs. Lyell. I'm calling from Tanglewood. Near Stonebridge. Earlier today I reserved two rooms at your hotel for friends of mine. I'm ringing to see if they've arrived safely."

The woman replied, "Gee, ma'am, we haven't had any new arrivals at all today."

Jackie insisted, "But you *must* have had. They left here more than five hours ago and were driving directly to your hotel."

"I have an idea," chirped the woman. "Why don't you tell me their names and I'll look at our guest list."

Reluctantly Jackie answered, "The name's . . . Washington. They're from Philadelphia."

"Washington." The woman flipped through pages. "Gee, I'm sorry. Nobody's here by the name of Washington."

"There has to be," Jackie said. "I rang this morning. The lady I talked to promised to hold two rooms, a double and a single, until five o'clock."

"Gee, the only thing I can think of is for you to speak to Mrs. Gibbs herself. She's the owner and would've been the one you talked to if you called this morning. But Mrs. Gibbs is out for the evening, so I don't know—"

Jackie thought of another possibility. "Perhaps they checked in under another name. Do you have *any* new guests from Philadelphia? Under *any* name?"

"Uh-uh. Like I said, we didn't get any new arrivals today. Not from anyplace."

As a last resort, Jackie tried, "You don't know if anybody was turned away, do you? For any reason whatsoever?"

"Turned away? Gee, I wouldn't think so. But I just came on duty so I don't know."

Feeling deflated, Jackie murmured, "Thank you."

Line two buzzed as she lowered the receiver. In a daze, she raised the other phone. "Yes?"

Joe Pine announced, "Milly Wheeler and her mother have just arrived, Mrs. Lyell."

"Thank you, Joe," Jackie answered, numbed. "I'll come at once."

She set down the receiver, a chilling thought penetrating her daze.

Might she be responsible for all this trouble? There was only one person besides herself who knew where Karen Washington had been going this afternoon. A man had telephoned earlier—from Peabo's manager's office. Jackie had mentioned the inn to him. If the caller had really been a journalist, he could easily have gone to the inn, hoping to interview Karen Washington—and stumbled instead onto a racial incident. Jackie felt her stomach knot.

24 AS NIGHT FELL ON MONDAY, TANGLE-WOOD'S PATIENTS APPRAISED THEIR day.

Lavender Gilbert sat alone in her room. The New York–bound train had left Stonebridge an hour ago. There was one more train that night, but Lavender didn't know if she would make it. At the moment, her mind was not on trains but on the faces Dr. Cooper had shown her that afternoon in his office.

One face in particular haunted Lavender—that of the model, Candee Allen.

There had been many similarities between Lavender and Candee. Both were blonde and beautiful. Both twenty-one years old. Both from the Midwest. Candee had thought, too, that she could control drugs. It would be impossible for her to become addicted to cocaine, she had insisted. But two weeks after she had signed a contract to star in a Disney film, she had been found dead from a cocaine overdose.

Lavender told herself she should shake off these morbid thoughts and concentrate on getting back to work. She would have to get packed so she could go to New York for the Star Lady gala. But Lavender did not move from the bed. She sat still, staring at the floor, as though there were a dead body on the carpet.

At 7 P.M., around the corner from Lavender Gilbert's third-floor room in the main house, forty-three-year-old novelist Crandall Benedict entered his nightly passages into the "kook's journal" he kept to chart his progress at Tanglewood.

Tanglewood was the fourth clinic into which the bestselling novelist had committed himself in the past seven years. The first had been White Mountain in upstate New York, a privately run institution that had reminded Benedict of a Dickensian nightmare—narrow metal beds, bossy matrons, lights-on at 6 A.M. The second clinic had been Culpepper, a posh southern "rest home" where Benedict had felt like the visiting freak show, the odd man out; the other patients had recognized him from television talk shows, and they followed him around the magnolia-scented grounds, asking him for autographs, telling him their ideas for books. But the third clinic had been the worst: Industry House, located in desolate Arizona, a clinic run like a boot camp for guerrilla fighters. Benedict had been assigned to a dormitory with six other male patients, forced to do manual labor from dawn to dusk and to spend his free time reading propaganda about the dangers of drink and drugs. The regimen depressed him more than his alcohol recovery.

Tanglewood, he had learned subsequently, was for people like himself. The rich. The recognizable. The exotic.

More important to Benedict than its physical comforts, though, Tanglewood catered to the *individual* like no other clinic—at least none that he had found. It coddled you, reminding you you were human.

On Monday night in room 34 of the main house, Crandall Benedict sat in his Turnbull and Asser striped silk dressing gown, writing in his journal: "Zelda Fitzgerald could be recovering in the room next door and nobody here would give one big healthy shit . . ."

His pen paused.

Why is it that I can write in this journal without taking a single drink when I have to get sloshed to work on a manuscript?

In the Garden Pavilion, the young woman curled in the double bed looked like a little girl, red hair spread around her thin shoulders, snug in a lovely white nightie.

Little Milly Wheeler felt like a little girl again, too. Being checked into Tanglewood and given this pretty blue room made her think of the old days when she was living at home. Early to bed. Mama sitting nearby in a chair, humming a hymn as she knitted. Daddy away working someplace. Those peaceful years before Milly had had her own singing career.

The only thing Little Milly knew about Tanglewood was that Mama had said she was bringing her someplace where she could rest and get better. Where lots of nice people would help her put all her troubles behind her.

Working late, Roger Cooper stepped into his office with a handful of notes from Dispatch. One was to call Jackie Lyell "immediately re Karen Washington." It was marked 5:15 P.M.—four hours ago. Wondering if Karen had finally telephoned, Roger raised his eyes from the memo and saw Caroline hunched over the typewriter.

"What are you still doing here?" he asked.

Pushing a shank of chestnut hair away from her glasses, she replied, "Finishing correspondence addressed to you and Mr. Lyell. As Mr. Lyell's not here, Communications automatically passes them on to us."

Adrian. Roger frowned.

"No call from him yet, I suppose," he said.

Caroline dropped her eyes back to the keyboard. "No, Doctor."

Irritably, Roger turned to his office door. "Knock off for the night, Caroline. Enough's enough."

Moving toward his desk, suspecting he would have to call Jackie upstairs in her apartment to catch her at this hour, Roger thought again about Adrian.

What had got into him?

There had been no friction between them that Roger could see. No rivalry. No reason for Adrian to leave so abruptly. Their only disagreement had been over Tanglewood's future, whether it should remain a small clinic or become more of a health spa. But certainly that would be a long-term discussion. There would be time for them both to give their pros and cons. And certainly Adrian would not disappear without a word in order to transform Tanglewood into a fountain of youth with an eighteen-hole golf course.

To remind himself how long Adrian had been away from Tanglewood, Roger looked at his desk calendar. Adrian had left last Thursday.

He counted off the days.

"Friday.

"Saturday.

"Sunday.

"Today is Monday.

"Tomorrow is already . . ."

PART THREE

TUESDAY

25 AT 4:05 ON TUESDAY MORNING, JACKIE LYELL PUNCHED THREE ILLUMINATED numbers on her bedside telephone and listened to the buzz at the other end of the line.

Rita Zambetti answered the ninth buzz breathlessly, as if she had been running. "Tanglewood. Good morning."

"Catch your breath, darling," Jackie murmured softly into the phone. "It's only me. Jackie Lyell."

"Mrs. Lyell?" Rita said, surprised. "What are you doing calling at this hour?"

"Do you have the *New York Journal?*"

"None of the New York papers have come in yet this morning, Mrs. Lyell."

"Damn."

There was silence at the other end of the line.

Jackie explained, "The *Journal*'s running a front-page story today on Peabo Washington being at Tanglewood."

Rita gasped. "My God!"

"It gets worse. A local hotel refused a room to Mr. Washington's wife."

"Why?"

Jackie answered, "From what I gather, Karen Washington was refused a room because of her color."

"How awful. Which hotel was it?"

"The Country Mouse."

"Oh dear. Mrs. Gibbs was probably drinking again."

"You know the people who own the Country Mouse, Rita?"

"Yes. Emma and Len Gibbs. When Emma Gibbs drinks she's not a very nice woman."

Jackie decided not to pursue the subject of the Country Mouse or its owners at the moment. She said, "Be prepared for a flood of calls this morning, darling. They started last night and I'm sure they'll get worse today."

"What do I say, Mrs. Lyell?"

Aware of her own telephone blunder yesterday regarding Karen Washington and the inn, Jackie did not know how qualified she was to give advice to Rita. She could only venture some common sense. "Be as polite as you can and tell the truth: that you have no information on the story at the moment. I'll give you the facts when I get them from Roger. We're meeting later this morning."

"Why don't I call the train station and make sure they hold the *Journal* when it comes in?"

"Good idea, darling. Now make yourself some coffee and dig in your heels."

"Thanks for the warning, Mrs. Lyell."

"One more thing, pet. Can you check the Ansaphone while I hold? See if there are any messages on it from Karen Washington."

"Hold on just a jiff."

Rita's voice returned. "Nothing."

Jackie wasn't surprised. Roger had left the line open to his apartment last night and promised to call the moment he heard from Karen Washington. She obviously hadn't been in touch.

Setting down the telephone, Jackie saw that it was not yet five o'clock. Although it was still dark outside, she wondered if she should get up and prepare for what was probably going to be a very hectic day in Administration.

She lay in bed, her guilt returning. It was her fault that Karen Washington might be in trouble at this very moment. Then, unexpectedly, the sleep that had eluded her all night washed over her, and the next thing she knew, the alarm clock was ringing at six thirty as daylight filtered through the bedroom's Roman blinds.

Jackie jumped out of bed, grabbed her robe, and moved toward the kitchen. After filling the kettle for tea, she flipped on the TV as she drowsily scuffed past the counter to the bathroom.

She held her face toward the shower's fine pinpoints of spray as voices drifted down the hall from the breakfast television show, "Morning People."

Wrapped in a white-and-green Tanglewood robe with a towel twisted in a turban around her head, she returned to the kitchen. Now she felt ready to face Tanglewood's problems, as well as a few of her own.

As she spooned Jackson's English Breakfast Tea into her favorite Brown Betty, she realized how she had taken for granted the mornings in this small, cozy flat—when was she going to learn to say "apartment"?—built under the mansion's sloping roof. How many mornings had she spent up here not knowing that, a few floors below her in Administration, there were readmission forms to fill out? That journalists kept the phones tied up with impossible questions and tried devious ways to extract privileged information? That you needed an engineering degree to operate a pocket microrecorder?

Carrying a Victorian papier-mâché tea tray to a window seat high above the back gardens, she nestled down into the bank of chintz, brocade, and velvet cushions and began sipping her tea as she looked out over the frosty autumn trees.

Her concern about the day's work was replaced by more personal worries. Where would she go if Adrian dumped her for another woman? she wondered. Adrian would never leave Tanglewood, not after all the work he had put into it. She would be the one who would have to build a new life.

Last night, Jackie had admitted to herself that she must start being realistic about Adrian. Their love life was hopeless. She couldn't go along with his slave-master games. But

could she complain about him looking for a compatible partner? Could a wife rightfully deny her husband his sexual
needs? If not, did sadistic sex qualify as a "need"?

What troubled her more than sexual problems, however,
was the fact that she and Adrian squabbled so much these
days. He had become so critical of her, so intent on deflating
her ego; continually making snide remarks about what she
did, how she looked, who she talked to.

Their life used to be fun. They had traveled. They had
collected trinkets, searched out new restaurants, had their
private jokes. But all that had stopped some time ago. The
zing had gone out of their marriage.

Lately, too, Jackie had begun noticing unattractive quali-
ties in Adrian. He was unkind to people. Bitchy. Adrian had
always been aggressive about what he wanted in life, but
lately his aggression had turned into unmitigated selfishness.
He was becoming mean.

Adrian also was becoming increasingly critical of Roger
behind his back, calling him "self-centered," "pompous,"
saying he longed for the day to come when he could prove
to Roger that "doctors were not the center of the universe
and God's answer to mankind."

Adrian had new, restrictive ideas on how a wife should be
treated, too; he had begun ranting recently that wives should
keep their submissive places, that more men should take a
firm hand with their women. His revised philosophy of
marriage seemed to be that wives, like children, should be
seen and not heard.

Jackie told herself she had no reason to be frightened of
Adrian, that much of his gruffness was a pose. But, nevertheless, she had definitely noticed that the fun-loving bloke she
had married long ago in London was quickly becoming a
middle-aged bully.

As she was turning this thought over in her mind, Jackie
heard a familiar voice on the television set.

Glancing across the room to the small screen flickering on
the kitchen counter, she saw a squirrel-cheeked man, wear-

ing a dark business suit, announcing "Hello, I'm Sackville West. Why don't we put our heads together and give you autumn-gold hair?"

Jackie laughed at the television screen. "You old twit, you."

Years ago her first job in London had been as a receptionist for Sackville West. She had come up to London from Tunbridge Wells, wanting to go to drama school and become the new Julie Christie. But Jackie's father had advised her she'd be wiser studying shorthand and typing. Being a good girl, Jackie had obeyed. Brook Street Bureau took her on their books, sending her out on an interview to a trendy new hair salon in Conduit Street that had been opened by a young hairdresser from Camden Town who had recently won a court case allowing him to assume the old English name "Sackville West."

Memories flooded back to Jackie as she listened to the man's television commercial.

That first job in London had been during the swinging sixties, the exciting years of Jean Shrimpton, David Bailey, Vidal Sassoon, Terry Stamp, Marianne Faithful. Jackie remembered splurging on miniskirts at Biba's first shop in Kensington Church Street. And she remembered the rainy Saturday afternoon in the King's Road when she had met Adrian in designer Ossie Clarke's new shop, Quorum. Adrian had looked so "with-it" in his Mr. Fish suit, Liberty Print kipper tie, Chelsea Cobbler snakeskin boots.

A couple of weeks later Jackie had taken Adrian to lunch with Sackville West at Arethusa. The two young men immediately hit it off. In a few months Adrian quit his PR job in Soho to do for Sackville West what Brian Epstein had done for the Beatles and what Justin de Villeneuve was then doing for Twiggy. Adrian's first success was to get six pages in *Life* magazine featuring Sackville West as the latest hairdresser to Swinging London.

Sackville, thrilled with the American coverage, drew up

a partnership contract with Adrian for Sackville West International.

Easily slipping into the role of international wheeler-dealer, Adrian flew to New York and found backers for a slick salon on 57th Street. Back across the Atlantic, he signed a small Irish chemical company to produce Sackville West's first hair care line. Adrian himself designed the burnt-orange packaging and created the now-famous television slogan, *"Hello, I'm Sackville West. Why don't we put our heads together and . . ."*

Adrian's and Sackville's partnership lasted for eleven prosperous years. The company made millions. Both men, however, were prima donnas, and eventually they quarreled. Adrian sued for breach of contract, knowing that he had the trendy hairdresser by the balls. Sackville settled out of court, bitterly agreeing to pay Adrian four and a half million dollars over ten years. The money had financed Adrian's share in Tanglewood.

On the television set, anchorwoman Stephanie James said, "Welcome back to 'Morning People'. Let's go now to Los Angeles where Carole Drake is speaking to the owner of Tanglewood, the New England clinic where the world Heavyweight champion, Peabo Washington, is currently a patient."

Jackie jumped to her feet, gaping at the television screen. Grabbing the phone, she punched Roger's number.

"Quick!" She gasped. "Adrian's on TV."

Carole Drake faced the camera. "Englishman Adrian Lyell is the owner of Tanglewood, one of the most prestigious drug clinics in the world. Its list of patients reads like an international *Who's Who* of politics, finance, sports, and show business."

She turned to Adrian. "In the past twenty-four hours, reports have broken across the country about Peabo Washington being admitted to Tanglewood. What are your comments on athletes and drugs?"

Adrian was relaxed but not casual. "First of all, Carole,"

he said, "let me say that I agreed to appear on this program because I believe people benefit from hearing that celebrities have their own weaknesses. I hasten to add that drug addiction is not a new phenomenon."

Jackie clutched her robe, staring at the television screen as Adrian recited trivia she had heard him say a thousand times at dinner parties—anecdotes about Defoe's opium dreams; Pope Leo's cocaine wine, how George Washington ate marijuana.

Smoothly, Adrian continued, "Recent years, of course, have seen drug abuse soar across America's top level of society. Let me explain my philosophy for the top people who check into Tanglewood—"

"*Your* philosophy?" Jackie said aloud.

The interviewer interrupted. "What about drug abuse among athletes? How does it begin?"

Adrian ignored the camera like a professional, looking earnestly at Carole Drake. "The human body is not able to cope with modern training schedules and long periods of jet lag. Think back and you'll remember how our attention was drawn to amphetamines and steroids during the Olympics."

"Peabo Washington was an Olympic Gold medalist," Carole Drake said. "Was that the start of his drug problem?"

Adrian laughed. "Come, come, my dear. You don't expect me to discuss a patient's drug problems on coast-to-coast television."

Jackie snapped, "Then what are you doing on this show, you big phony?"

Adrian went on. "I'm in Los Angeles meeting with backers to discuss the next stage of a thirty-four-million-dollar expansion program for Tanglewood. I call my new step 'Crossover Therapy.' I believe a detoxification clinic can also be a leisure center."

"You believe—shit!" Jackie cried. "*Merde!*"

The telephone buzzed.

She knew it was Roger.

26 IN LOS ANGELES, ADRIAN SAT NAKED AGAINST THE TUFTED APRICOT MOIRE headboard, remote-control box in one hand, grinning at the blank screen of the television built into the far wall. "I looked pretty damned good, didn't I?"

"You looked fabulous," said Evelyn Palmer, the petite blonde snuggled against his bare shoulder.

When Evelyn and Adrian had returned to her home on Rexford Drive in Beverly Hills from taping "Morning People," they had gone straight back to bed, setting the timer switch so the television would turn on a few minutes before her maid brought in orange juice and coffee.

Wrapping a strong arm around Evelyn, Adrian pulled her toward him. "I like seeing myself on telly like that," he said. His other hand drew her hand toward his penis under the sheet. "I like being a media event."

"Maybe we should make videos of you," Evelyn suggested.

"For TV?" Adrian had not thought of the idea of promoting himself by videotapes.

"That, too," Evelyn said, never surprised by Adrian Lyell's enormous ego. "But I was talking about videos for home. For us here in the bedroom. To play with." She stroked him beneath the sheet.

Grabbing her by the hair, Adrian pulled back her head and stared down into her blue eyes. "Kinky bitch."

Evelyn stared up at him, promising "All for you."

"And I plan to collect." Baring his teeth, Adrian lowered his mouth and bit her lips, releasing them only seconds before he drew blood.

Pulling her back alongside him, Adrian's tone became more thoughtful. "The next time I do a TV show I'll wear a lighter shirt. Something closer to a flesh tone. I'm good in salmon pink."

"You're good in anything," Evelyn said, wrapping herself around his warm nakedness, still toying with his penis.

"And *out* of anything," he reminded her.

"Of course," Evelyn said and broke out of his grasp. "But listen. I'm serious. Considering how we only found out at the spur of the moment that there was an angle to get you on "Morning People," I just can't get over how terrific you looked . . . how professional."

"Well, you're going to be seeing a lot more of my professionalism soon."

Adrian was fully aware that Evelyn Palmer would do whatever he told her. The sex-hungry divorcée was completely under his domination. Up to now, though, she had only had a chance to express this in their lovemaking, in their games of bondage and discipline. But from now on, Adrian expected to use Evelyn by having her introduce him to her contacts in the entertainment world. Her television friends had gotten him onto the morning talk show as soon as the Peabo Washington story had broken last night.

"What time does the show come on in the East?" Evelyn asked. "Do you think anybody at Tanglewood saw?"

"If so, my only regret is that I couldn't see Roger Cooper's face while he watched."

Adrian glanced at the bedside clock. Seeing that it was almost nine o'clock, he threw back the top sheet. "Time to get going, my little slut. We're seeing your friend Warner."

Adrian had moved out of the Beverly Wilshire Hotel yesterday after meeting his backers at Doheny Insurance. Between now and a Thursday meeting with Paul Huttner, he had nothing to do except to concentrate on himself—

which included a meeting with Willy Warner, a personal publicity agent. Adrian's lawyer would be dealing with Roger and Tanglewood from New York at the appropriate time this week.

Grabbing a silk robe from the foot of the bed, Adrian said, "Are you going to get ready? Or do I have to spank you first?"

Willy Warner's home in Benedict Canyon was built around a split-level pool, all the rooms facing it and decorated in pastel-covered Donghia furniture coordinated with the outside chairs, lounges, and umbrellas.

"I called Sol Dresden when I got Evelyn's message you were doing "Morning People," said the thirty-three-year-old Willy Warner, looking, in his gray track suit, more like an aerobics instructor than a top Hollywood publicist. "Sol had another client on the show so he was watching it anyway. He made some notes and is excited to meet you. How does this afternoon sound?" Warner looked expectantly from Evelyn to Adrian.

"Excuse me," Adrian said, "but who's Sol Dresden?"

"The voice coach," Warner answered matter-of-factly, turning to Evelyn. "Sol's moved into Roland's old office on Sunset."

Evelyn seemed surprised. "Roland moved?"

"Roland's now a VP at Lorimar."

Evelyn Palmer and Willy Warner had many friends in common, people in the entertainment business whom Evelyn had met through her previous husbands and had worked hard to keep in touch with, introducing them to one another, getting mutually useful people together to keep herself part of the film-television world.

The phone rang on a low table alongside Warner's chaise longue.

Picking up the receiver, he slouched down into the pastel cushions, crossing one leg over the other as he began to speak on the phone.

Adrian turned to Evelyn. "A voice coach?"

Warner put a hand over the receiver. "The accent is great, but for serious TV exposure, you need a little fine-tuning. You do something with your vowels. Swallow them or something. Sol will explain." He went back to the phone conversation.

A few minutes later Warner bounced off the chaise longue. "I made a few notes on your clothes, Adrian. Basically I like your look. It's classic. Lots of class without being too collegiate or preppy. But before I commit myself, I want to check with Marnie and see what she thinks. Girls' opinions is what this business is all about, isn't it?"

Adrian looked quizzically at Evelyn.

Evelyn explained, "Marnie's his assistant. You'll love her."

Gulping down coffee, Warner continued. "Now, what thoughts have you had about agents?"

Adrian raised an eyebrow.

"Somebody to coordinate your career," Warner said, grabbing a handful of diet cookies from a tray.

Adrian's laugh was half impatient, half bemused. "I *am* a businessman, you know, Mr. Warner. In fact, years ago in London I did publicity work."

"Your business background is the reason I'm not suggesting a manager," Warner responded. "Lots of people have both, you know. Agent *and* manager. One to protect you from the other. But with your background, I thought you'd want to work out your own contracts for speaking tours, television appearances, video cassettes—"

The telephone rang again.

Flopping back into the chaise longue, Warner beckoned Evelyn and Adrian to step closer as he listened to the receiver; he pushed a button on the phone and a female voice said over a loudspeaker, "How's the weather out in California this morning, Willy?"

"Fabulous, Jeannie. In fact, I'm sitting outside by my pool, meeting with a British client who's talking about doing a big book. How's the health book market in New York?"

The amplified voice answered, "Keeping in shape." A feeble laugh.

"Great," Warner continued. "My client's got a very original idea for a big personality book. I want him to talk to a creative editor when he goes through New York and, of course, I immediately thought of you. . . . I'll keep you *au courant.* . . . Talk to you later. . . . And don't think I've forgotten about Liza. . . ."

Putting down the receiver, he said, "Evelyn told me you had a book idea. Something about a Tanglewood diet book."

Adrian was pleased to explain. Sitting forward on his chair, he said, "Actually, I do have an idea. I thought there might be a drink-and-diet angle—"

"Do a proposal," Warner interrupted. "No more than a couple pages. Publishers don't like to read." He motioned at the phone. "If Jeannie doesn't like it—or you don't like Jeannie after you lunch—I'll fix up a meeting with S and S."

The telephone rang.

Warner snatched up the receiver, then laughed and curled sideways on the chaise longue, lowering his voice for this conversation.

Adrian rose and moved toward a round table covered with the publicity samples that Warner had shown him on arrival. Leafing through the proposed personality sheets, sendouts, and trade ads, Adrian's excitement mounted. This was the old Hollywood treatment, true, and there was going to be a lot of empty hype. But, strangely enough, somehow he enjoyed this tinsel-town world. He understood brash, Hollywood hard-sell game tactics better than he understood what Roger Cooper was trying to do at Tanglewood. And if hype was what it would take to make Tanglewood his, Adrian was ready for it.

Evelyn moved alongside him. "What do you think?"

"About him?"

"About everything."

"As I said. I did some PR work myself years ago in London. So I know a little about it." He studied the mockups appreciatively. "The man's flash but, yes, I think we can work together."

"Willy's hot now. One of the hottest press agents in town. He coordinates an entire image."

Adrian was thinking not so much about Willy Warner as about himself. He continued. "You know what else this does?"

He took Evelyn's hand as she looked up at him.

"It makes my cock rock hard. Just looking through these promos on me is like having you worshipping my prick." He tightened his grip on her hand and his fingernails dug into her skin. "Like hearing you plead and whine and beg—"

"Shhh," she blurted. "Save it for later."

Behind them Willy Warner called, "Okay, where were we?"

27 WHEN ROGER AND JACKIE MET IN AD-MINISTRATION AT 8 A.M., A COPY OF Tuesday's *New York Journal* lay on the coffee table between them. The headline blared PEABO HOOKED above a photograph of Karen Washington and her two children gaping at the camera.

So far, Karen Washington had not been in touch with the clinic, nor could Roger or Jackie recognize where the picture had been taken.

Sitting on the leather chesterfield, Roger rested a moccasin on one knee, his manner calm. He had cancelled an eight-o'clock meeting with his juniors and told the switchboard and Dispatch to hold all calls, bleeps, and SOSs for him, that he was in an important meeting with Jackie Lyell and must not be disturbed under any circumstances.

Jackie had confessed that yesterday she had given the name of the inn to a man calling for Peabo Washington; Roger had told her not to worry herself, saying that a determined journalist would have ferreted out the facts he wanted one way or another.

He looked at the *Journal*'s headline. "At least the press is playing down the race issue and running with the drug story."

Jackie said, "What I want to know, Roger, is how Adrian learned about the story so bloody quickly out in L.A. and got on that talk show."

"The news probably broke last night on a wire service. The networks picked it up. 'Morning People' rushed Adrian's interview onto tape for this morning's show."

Roger reconsidered his theory. "The only thing I can't figure out is how the show's producers got to Adrian. Or did he go after them?"

"Adrian probably got to them," said Jackie, refilling Roger's coffee cup from a Georgian silver pot. "He's got a good nose for news and was never one to keep in the background. Don't forget, he's trained as a PR man."

Setting down the pot on the table, she looked warily over her shoulder at the large mahogany desk in front of the tall windows, studying it as if it were a symbolic reminder of Adrian's authority at Tanglewood.

"What does he hope to achieve by all this?" she puzzled. "What's the purpose of the exercise? Unless he's decided the time's come to be ruthlessly ambitious."

"What's Adrian got to be ambitious about?" His partner's television appearance had left him shocked and more than a little confused, but he kept his voice calm.

"Adrian's got everything going for him," he continued.

Jackie turned her large brown eyes back to him. "Darling, I don't mean to sound bitchy, but Adrian's a bundle of resentment. He thinks the parade's passed him by for too long."

"Are you serious?"

"Absolutely. Adrian is forty-eight years old. In less than two years he'll be fifty. He's well off, as you know, darling, but he's not rich. Not rich rich. Not as he thinks he should be. He's no Getty or Saudi prince or Texas billionaire. Nor is he famous or powerful enough. None of the things he admires most in life. Adrian feels he's spent too much time being a cog in someone else's machine."

"That's nonsense." Roger took a long gulp of coffee.

"Of course it's nonsense. You know it and I know it. But that happens to be what my husband believes about himself."

She expanded, "For eleven years Adrian was the power behind Sackville West. He pushed and promoted and polished him. But Adrian was always *behind* Sackville. Never out in front. Now the front man is you. Roger Cooper. Wonderboy of Tanglewood. And where is Adrian Lyell? In the background again."

"He tells you these things?"

"Egos like Adrian's do not allow for heartfelt confessions, my dear. Especially not to mere wives. You have to look for it in the eyes. Listen for it in their reluctant praise for other people. You've been too busy, Roger, to notice the signs."

"But Adrian and I are a team," insisted Roger. "We're partners."

"*You* think you're a team," Jackie corrected. "Adrian does not. He sees himself as a money raiser. The deal maker. But not the star."

"Is that reason to stab me between the shoulder blades? Announce on a coast-to-coast talk show a load of crap about . . . 'crossover therapy'? Jesus!"

"Get ready for more crap. If I'm right, this morning's show was only the beginning."

"Are you serious?" The gravity of the situation was beginning to hit Roger. Jackie heard it in his voice, and saw anxiety creep into his face.

"I'm very serious, Roger. I've been married to Adrian Lyell for nearly sixteen years. I know better than anyone how devious he can be."

Roger thought about what lay immediately ahead.

"Tonight's the board of management meeting," he told Jackie. "By then all the board members will have heard about Adrian being on TV. How's that bunch of upright citizens going to receive the news that Adrian's taken it upon himself to embark on expansions around here?"

"Might anybody on the board already know about it?" Jackie asked.

"Only if Adrian shared news he's been keeping from the rest of us." Roger gave a wry laugh. "It's going to be interesting to see how they react."

Looking at Jackie, his voice touched with disbelief, he asked, "Do you really think Adrian's off on some power jag?"

Jackie herself was trying to make sense out of the jumbled thoughts racing through her head, from her suspicions about Adrian becoming bored with her, to her fear that he might be hatching a takeover plot for Tanglewood. She believed the likelihood of a coup had to be seriously considered.

Settling into her chair, she said, "Adrian is off on more than a power jag, I believe, Roger. He's out to make war."

"War over what?"

"Tanglewood's future."

"Does he talk much to you about that?"

"Sometimes *ad nauseum*. I don't think I'm telling any stories out of school by saying that Adrian wants Tanglewood to be like Palm-Aire in Florida. Westicana in California. Big. High profile. A health spa with condominiums and golf courses. You, on the other hand, prefer things to stay as they are. Small. Quiet. The emphasis on detoxification and rehabilitation. *Not* rejuvenation."

Roger nodded. That was indeed his and Adrian's bone of contention. Small versus big; quiet versus high profile.

Jackie held her eyes on him. "Listening to Adrian on television this morning made me realize how much I care about Tanglewood.

"I thought about the time I put into this place myself. Maybe not as much as you and Adrian. Maybe not professionally. But, damn it, I worry about Tanglewood, too. Whether you chaps realize it or not. I've struggled right beside Adrian from the early days, hoping and planning, keeping my fingers crossed for permissions and rights and bank loans to come through.

"Tanglewood has become home to me. I made a cock-up yesterday in the office but, believe it or not, this place is my life. So this morning I decided, 'By God, Jackie, you're a fool to let Adrian ignore that you're part of Tanglewood.' How dare he pull a stunt like this behind my back? I know you're his partner, Roger, but I'm his wife. I feel just as betrayed as you do by his television announcement. Perhaps even a little more so." She lowered her eyes. "But I won't open *that* kettle of fish now."

"I'm sure Adrian intends nothing bad for you." Roger did not know if there was any problem in Jackie and Adrian's marriage. From the implications of Jackie's little speech, though, she might be angry at him for more than what he wanted to do with Tanglewood.

Jackie continued. "The important thing, Roger, is that if sides are going to be taken about which way Tanglewood goes—big and popular, or small and dignified—I'm in your camp. I want you to know that." She added modestly, "For what it's worth."

Roger tried to review the situation. "First of all, do you think that's really what's happening, Jackie? Adrian seized the Peabo Washington scandal to make points for himself? To force my hand into turning Tanglewood into a big mainstream health spa and real estate development?"

"Adrian works like that, darling. He sees a chance and he springs for it. In the dog world, he'd be a terrier." She paused. "Like a fool, I didn't tape the show this morning.

But I remember him saying something about being in California to meet backers."

Roger remembered exactly what Adrian had said in the interview. "He claimed he was meeting backers for a thirty-four-million-dollar expansion program."

"Do you know anything about such a program, Roger?"

"Nope."

He held Jackie's stare. "Now let me ask you a question. Do you truly think that's the reason for this sudden trip to L.A.? To raise money? Without discussing it with me?"

"Want my honest opinion?"

"Dead honest."

"Yes, I do think that Adrian went to L.A. to meet backers." She decided not to mention the woman who had answered the phone in the hotel room.

"What about the television show?" Roger asked.

"The Peabo story fell into his lap. That's what I think. He saw a chance to get on TV with his side of the story and he went for it."

She smiled. "But don't waste your time ringing the Beverly Wilshire to find out if I'm right. I tried before I came downstairs."

"He checked out?"

"Last night. And left no forwarding address."

Roger brightened. "Maybe he's on the way back home."

Jackie frowned. "Somehow I doubt that. Unless he's already got enough ammunition."

"Ammunition?" Roger leaned forward on the chesterfield. "Jackie, you keep talking about this being a big war."

"Hang around, soldier," she said, only half jokingly.

Reaching for the leather pad on the drum table alongside her chair, she said more seriously, "I made a few notes about things I think we should discuss. First—"

She raised her eyes, asking with mock formality, "Dr. Cooper, do you want me to continue helping here in Administration in Adrian's absence?"

"Of course I do. Why even ask? Do you think I consider you to be his spy?"

"No. But yesterday I did make quite a few mistakes in here. Apart from the Country Mouse fiasco." She glanced at the *Journal*'s headline.

"Enough about that," Roger said firmly. "There's no use flogging yourself over that now. It's not the first time the press has dogged us. Let's move on."

Jackie nodded. "Let me put my question this way, Roger. Are you willing to risk me working in Administration until we know exactly what Adrian's up to?"

"Yes." He sank back into the chesterfield and nodded at her pad. "What's your next question?"

Roger studied Jackie as she ran through the points she had compiled, straightforward questions about clinic forms, interpreting suppliers' statements, dealing with staff members. He was beginning to wonder whether this attractive but self-deprecating lady was stronger than she pretended to be. Perhaps even stronger than she herself knew. Up to now he had seen her as a rather frivolous, lighthearted Englishwoman who arranged lavish bowls of garden flowers and had a knack for finding amusing old postcards in secondhand shops. But maybe there was more to her than that. Did Jackie Lyell love Tanglewood as much as she claimed? Was she willing to fight tooth-and-nail on his side if Adrian was indeed about to wage a takeover war? Or was Jackie Lyell merely angry at her husband for some personal reason? Was she a wronged woman being vindictive?

Jackie knew Roger was questioning her in his mind. Good, she thought. She had a few doubts about him, too.

Could Roger Cooper cope with Adrian playing dirty? Or would he collapse when it came to a night of the long knives? Was the handsome, cuddly medical director a survivor? Or did he, as Adrian claimed, have a marshmallow filling?

28 BY 8:30 A.M. RITA ZAMBETTI'S SWITCH-
BOARD WAS FLOODED WITH INQUIRIES
about Peabo Washington. *Newsweek. Time. Sports Illustrated.* All the major television networks. Cable stations.
Local newspapers and radio.

Rita and her assistant, Sylvia Lundquist, busily answered
calls, terminated calls, transferred calls to Administration, to
Dispatch, to departments. Some callers were polite; some
frantic; some downright rude, Rita thought, and everybody
wanted their call put through immediately.

Inside the clinic, too, telephones were busy, calling the
outside world.

Head Nurse Shirley Higgins redialed the outside line to
Delia Pomeroy's home. After letting the phone ring ten
times, she hung up, wondering if Delia was on her way to
work. Was she sick? Or was the mousy little nurse still upset
that Dunstan Bell had called her a liar for not entering on
her job application that she had been confined to a hospital
for drugs?

The head nurse rechecked her watch. Three and a half
hours until the showdown with Dr. Bell at the meeting of
department heads. ·

Tom Hudson spoke long distance to Red Tag Stores'
national manager, Gordon Chumley, in Chicago. He did not
want to discuss business from Cat Powers's suite while Gene

Stone was hanging around there, so he used a phone in the Arboretum.

"I'm staying at Tanglewood one more day," Hudson told his subordinate. "While I stick around for the results of Cat's tests, I want you to do a little checking for me on this place, Gordon. Find out its history. Financing. Batting average. I saw one of the owners on a TV talk show this morning. I wasn't too impressed. I might want to move Cat someplace else."

Lillian Weiss sat squeezed into the armchair at the desk in her third-floor bedroom in the main house. Holding a telephone receiver to one ear, she said briskly to the operator, "Connect me with Mr. Esposito's room."

Ever since Margie Clark had told her about the hunky Italian construction worker's ferocious sex drive, Lillian had been unable to think of anything else. Her plan was to make a date with Esposito and take things from there.

"Who's calling, please?" asked the operator.

Lillian lied, "A friend of Mr. Esposito's." She added for authenticity, "He's in suite 4G. The Garden Pavilion."

"I'm sorry, ma'am, but there's a hold on all calls to 4G."

"This is an emergency," Lillian said impatiently, thinking that this time she wasn't lying. It was an emergency. For her. Oh, God, how she needed to get laid.

"I'm sorry, ma'am, but you must receive a doctor's clearance before I can connect you with 4G. Do you want me to put you through to Dr. Cooper's office?"

"No!" Lillian slammed down the phone.

Damn! There had to be some way to establish contact with Esposito. Drumming her red-lacquered fingernails against the desktop, she tried to think of how she could let him know that she was available to help him through his rehabilitation period. If deception wouldn't work, she'd just have to get pushy.

* * *

Nigel Burden took his long-distance telephone call in the pool house, a Tanglewood robe draped over his shoulders following his morning swim.

"Hello, Trisha," he said into the mouthpiece, surprised to hear his daughter-in-law telephoning him from Kennedy Airport. He had expected his son, Cyril, to report that the flight had arrived safely from London.

Forcing himself to be amicable to his son's wife, Burden asked, "Did you have a pleasant flight, Trisha? Fine. Is Cyril there? . . . No matter. . . . See you both in a couple hours. . . . Hiring a car? Good. . . . Just follow the motorway north. . . . The Americans call it the interstate."

Burden put down the phone, still puzzled that his obnoxious daughter-in-law, instead of his son, had made the call. Burden disliked Trisha immensely. He knew, too, that she considered him to be a boring old fuddy-duddy. They seldom spoke if they could help it.

What was Cyril doing at the airport that he hadn't been able to place the call? Hiring the car?

No matter, Burden told himself. They'll be here in a few hours. He must try not to fight with Trisha during the short time they would be together. The important thing was his imminent return to London. He missed his wife, Diana. He didn't know where he would be today if it had not been for her. In jail, perhaps. Or dead.

Jackie Lyell held the telephone to her ear, thankful for the shorthand course her father had insisted she should take years ago in London. Apart from calls about Peabo Washington, she was receiving increasingly more inquiries about Cat Powers. She surprised herself how calmly she was dealing with the questions.

Then came the shock call of the morning, from a social worker in Brooklyn.

"Bellevue Hospital tells me that Tanglewood's recently admitted Ray Esposito for heroin rehabilitation. I thought you should be made aware of a few facts about this patient," the woman said.

"Esposito's a Vietnam vet. You probably know that," the social worker said, "but what you probably don't know is that Esposito's a wife-beater."

Jackie began scribbling. Something told her that this news was extremely important; she ignored the other three telephones buzzing and flashing around her on Adrian's big desk.

Roger put down the phone, frustrated to hear that Tanglewood's New York lawyer, Bill Ruben, had not yet come into his office. He had hoped to get some advice on how to deal with Adrian's unexpected activities.

Ignoring the other lines blinking, he looked at the receiver in its cradle, thinking about Tanglewood's chairman of the board, Carlton Frazer.

Picking up the phone, he punched Frazer's business number at Stonebridge Savings and Loan.

"Roger, I was just going to call you," said the banker. "I saw a morning talk show and wanted you to tell me I wasn't still in bed dreaming."

Rita Zambetti cut into the conversation. "Dr. Cooper, excuse me. You said to tell you immediately when Karen Washington called the clinic. She's on line three."

"Carlton, I've got an urgent call here. Can I get back to you later this morning?"

"It'll have to wait until tonight's board meeting," said Frazer. "I'm up to Boston for the day."

His other lines continued blinking as Roger punched line three, saying "Mrs. Washington, where are you?"

Olga Turner answered the phone in the physical therapy center, where she was preparing a patient for an ice immersion.

"Morning there," greeted a friendly Nashville drawl on the other end of the line. "This is Gladys Wheeler out here in the Garden Pavilion. I'm calling to say that my daughter, Little Milly, won't be at that vapor-bath appointment you got her down for this morning. It's all been agreed she should stay right here tucked into bed for the time being. Thank you, now, and you all have a nice day." *Click.*

29 IT WAS 12 NOON. ROGER THREW UP A BARRICADE AROUND HIS OFFICE. HE INformed the switchboard, Dispatch, and his secretary to hold all calls and keep any visitors out of his office—except psychiatrist Philip Pringle, who would be arriving at 1 P.M. Karen Washington's phone call had overshadowed the shock of Adrian's appearance on the nationwide talk show. Telling himself he had no time to worry about Adrian's machinations, Roger ordered two lunch trays to be sent to his office so he could give Karen his undivided attention. She and Roger ate chicken salad as Karen recounted what had happened the day before.

Looking smart in a charcoal wool two-piece suit, Karen insisted she had fully recovered from the ugly ordeal.

Roger said, "Jackie Lyell in Administration is feeling rather guilty about letting the cat out of the bag that you'd be at the Country Mouse."

"Tell her not to be. Better the journalist was annoying me than pestering Peabo here at Tanglewood. Now let's forget about newspapers and television and concentrate on why I'm here."

Roger reflected that Karen Washington reacted as he

often did: forget land mines and barrel ahead. "Good idea," he said.

Her first question was "Does Peabo know about the stories breaking in the past twelve hours?"

"Not that I'm aware of," answered Roger. "The television set in his room plays only videos. He doesn't see papers and never comes in contact with other patients."

"How does he spend his time when he's not watching videos?"

"Therapy. Light workouts in the gym. I also asked him to write down any thoughts running through his head. Why he's here. What he thinks about the place. What he thinks about his past. But so far he's written nothing."

"But he comes into no contact with the outside world? Radio or TV or newspapers?"

"None."

"I think we should keep it that way," Karen advised.

"Only for a while."

Psychiatrist Philip Pringle arrived promptly at one o'clock. Handing out mugs of coffee, Roger filled Pringle in on what he and Karen had discussed. "It would be wrong, Mrs. Washington, to tell Peabo immediately about you and the children having this unfortunate trouble. But we mustn't keep facts from him too long. Especially if it's in the press."

"That's what Roger thinks."

Karen added, "Dr. Pringle, Roger also says that Peabo blames me for his drug problem. Why?"

Pringle was a slim man with horn-rimmed glasses. He had a relaxed, academic manner that Roger found helped put people at ease. He replied softly, "Often in drug—or alcohol—recoveries, Mrs. Washington, the patient feels his or her partner let them down someplace along the line."

"Is there any truth in that, Doctor?"

"I'd be wrong to give an opinion about your case at this point, Mrs. Washington. But I can say this. It'll be easier for Peabo to join a psychotherapy group if you're on the firing line right along with him."

"Tell me a little about psychotherapy, Dr. Pringle."

"At Tanglewood we find that therapy groups help patients come in contact with problems not unlike their own. We have three encounter groups here.

"Peabo's too assertive for the elementary group, and I feel that patients in the advanced group—what we call the Sweat Room—might eat him alive. Perhaps we should start him in the intermediate group. They'd challenge him without steam-rolling him."

Roger interjected, "Or making a pancake out of you."

"All this consideration." Karen clasped both men's hands and laughed. "Thank you. It's such a nice change."

Then she looked at Roger more seriously. "I decided to send the kids back home with my sister-in-law. I want to concentrate totally on Peabo."

Roger approved of the idea. "Are you still opposed to staying at the clinic? My offer stands to find you a room here." He noticed that Karen Washington had not once mentioned divorce, as she had done Sunday night on the phone.

"I accept." She smiled. "I think I've had enough of quaint little New England inns."

Roger turned to Pringle. "Back to the patient, Philip. I do think that Peabo should be told about the press before he joins his encounter group. Somebody's going to recognize him—a patient who's heard or read or seen something about him on TV or in a paper."

Philip Pringle proposed, "When you see your husband, Mrs. Washington, you can slowly fill him in on what's happening at home, gradually telling him that you and the children had a little problem at a local hotel, that word's out on his drug history."

Pringle's blue eyes twinkled. "Do you think you can handle that?"

"I can try."

It was agreed. Karen Washington would send her children back to Philadelphia with her sister-in-law, Desiree, and begin short, informal meetings with her husband. She would see him for the first time that afternoon. A brief session was set for three-thirty.

Philip Pringle went straight to the conference room for the afternoon staff meeting, the Huddle. Roger stopped at Administration to collect Jackie's occupancy report. Also, Jackie had told Caroline that she needed to talk to Roger urgently.

Roger stood inside Administration's door, frowning as Jackie explained what she had just learned about Ray Esposito.

Roger repeated the phrase that the social worker had applied to Esposito. "Wife-beater. . . . Jackie, do you have any idea why our preliminary screening didn't catch this?"

"No one except Esposito's wife knew about it at the time we admitted him, and she was too frightened to speak while he was at home. Finally she told her priest, who told her to contact Esposito's social worker."

"Well, we'd better keep him on a short leash."

Using Jackie's telephone, Roger called Dispatch. "Punch in a warning on Garden Pavilion Four. Nobody's to enter Esposito's room without a companion. Double his chaperones around the premises," he ordered.

30 ROGER HAD NICKNAMED THE DAILY MEETING OF DEPARTMENT HEADS THE Huddle in memory of his football days. But as he entered the conference room at 1:35 P.M. Tuesday, he surveyed the five faces around the teakwood table and thought that, instead of burly athletes, they looked more like a nestful of baby birds waiting to be fed.

At the opposite end of the table, Dr. Dunstan Bell removed his wire eyeglasses and rubbed the bridge of his thin nose. "I must admit, Roger, that Adrian Lyell looks considerably better on television than he does in person."

Laughter relaxed the group's tension; Roger was grateful for the dour man's rare display of humor.

Psychotherapist Betty Lassiter folded both arms across the chest of her plaid lumberjack shirt. "Roger, maybe you can tell us a little about—"

She looked around the table for help. "What did Adrian call it on TV this morning? 'Crossover therapy'?"

More laughter.

Roger took his place at the head of the table and answered amicably, "Sorry, guys. You've got to wait till Adrian gets back for an explanation of that one."

"When *is* our noble administrator due back from sunny California?" Bell asked.

Roger began sorting through the Xeroxed pages he had brought with him. "I expect him toward the end of the week."

Betty asked, "Are we to brush up our archery and canoeing for this leisure center he's raising money for?"

Roger made two piles in front of him, yellow pages for Administration's report, white pages for medical director's.

All eyes were on him as he replied, "That was the first time I ever heard about getting any leisure around here."

The joke was feeble, but it was the best he could muster. The alternative would be to divulge that he and Adrian held opposing points of view about Tanglewood's future. He didn't want to admit that. Not yet, anyway. Although he tried to run the clinic as a democracy, there were times when he had to play the benevolent dictator, deciding what was and was not best for his staff to know about their domain.

He said, "More seriously, guys, Philip and I have just come from a meeting with Peabo Washington's wife. You might have seen her picture in the *Journal* this morning. She's a rare lady. I was very impressed."

He looked at Pringle seated to his left. "What about you, Philip?"

"I was also." The psychiatrist nodded. "Mrs. Washington has an extremely healthy attitude about joining her husband's rehabilitation program."

Roger said, "Mrs. Washington is ready to forget about the racial trouble that sparked off this whole nasty little episode. She wants to settle down and solve her husband's drug problem."

With a glance around the table, he added, "I hope we can follow her sense of priorities."

Having chosen the words deliberately, he paused for them to sink in. Everybody had to know how far he or she could go with Dr. Nice Guy.

Head nurse Shirley Higgins raised her silver Parker pen. "I have some nurse reports on Peabo Washington."

"Mrs. Higgins," Bell said in his most officious tone, "Are we going to throw open this meeting, or follow our standard form?"

Shirley stiffened at Bell's remark. She replied icily, "I was under the impression, Dr. Bell, that the meeting had not yet commenced."

Roger cut in swiftly to forestall an argument. "Thanks, Shirley, we'll go over Peabo's reports later on. Now let's start with routine business." He began passing around the yellow sheets.

"Admissions and departures. Yesterday we accepted Milly Wheeler from Nashville. Dunstan, your sheets should show the young lady's labs."

Roger glanced around the table to see that the five chiefs had brought—and circulated—copies of their own reports.

Dr. Lonny Lamb raised his black Mont Blanc pen. "What about Cat Powers? Didn't she also arrive yesterday?"

"Actually, it was Sunday night, Lonny. Or the early hours of Monday morning. But Miss Powers won't officially be accepted until today. She's traveling with her doctor and, I'm sorry to say, he's holding things up a bit."

Bell said, "I suggest we start thinking very seriously about eliminating this practice of patients bringing private physicians to Tanglewood. It creates nothing but confusion for everybody's schedules."

Shirley interrupted triumphantly, "If I am correct, Dr. Bell, suggestions come at the end of the meeting, *not* the beginning. But if you have decided to throw open the meeting, I would very much like to raise the matter of you attacking one of my nurses."

Silence surrounded the oval table.

"What do you mean?" demanded Bell. " 'Attack' one of your nurses?"

"Delia Pomeroy," the head nurse stated. "I had to send her home, she was so distressed by your comments."

Turning to her colleagues, Shirley explained, "Yesterday Dr. Bell accused Delia of . . . lying."

Bell sputtered "The person in question kept information from her application form!"

Shirley replied that she had taken time in the past twenty-four hours to check Delia Pomeroy's record at Bellevue Hospital. The nurse had spent eighteen hours there under surveillance when she was seventeen years old.

Roger broke in. "Please! Whatever this is about, let's clear it up later. There's more pressing business at hand." Brusquely, he thrust another sheaf of papers at Betty Lassiter, sitting on his left.

Roger's display of temper—a rare occurrence in the Huddle—brought the squabble to a halt. Dunstan Bell and Shirley Higgins sat fuming but silently deferred to their leader.

After the seventy-five-minute Huddle, Roger walked Dunstan Bell down the corridor from the conference room.

"Can we stop in your office for a minute?" Roger asked as they approached Bell's door.

Bell replied, "Isn't it more in keeping for the medical director to summon insubordinate staff to his own office?"

"Dunstan, God damn it. Stop challenging me," Roger snapped with sudden irritation. "If you've got a gripe, then get it off your chest. But don't waste your time and mine being snide."

Bell removed his silver glasses. He unfolded a neatly pressed handkerchief from his pocket and wiped the lenses as he admitted, "You're right, Roger. I'm sorry. Forgive me. I'm turning myself inside out with all this damned, dithering inefficiency surrounding me."

"I'm afraid you have to be more specific."

"That Higgins woman." Bell shook his head. "Always squawking like a hen."

"Shirley Higgins happens to have twenty very productive, very impressive years at Massachusetts General behind her, Dunstan. I feel lucky to have her on our staff."

Roger looked Bell straight in the eye and added, "I also feel lucky having *you* on the staff, Dunstan. But if you're unhappy here, if you have some contention you want to air, please do it now. It's time for this back-biting between you and Shirley Higgins to stop. I plan to say the same thing to her."

Before Bell had time to reply, Roger asked, "Now what's this story about you and Delia Pomeroy?"

Bell frowned. "A storm in a teacup. The truth is that I have been troubled by more than a few items in the past days. I've been thinking of preparing a grievance list to submit to your office."

"Lists are efficient and impressive, Dunstan. But also time-consuming. If you want time to think about your complaints, though, and not discuss them at the moment, fine. Why not plan for us to have a feet-up, say, tomorrow. Have lunch together and talk things out."

"Tomorrow's my day off," said Bell.

"On Thursday I'll be seeing you again in the Huddle," said Roger. "So plan to talk to me on Friday."

It was two fifty-five when Roger continued down the corridor to his own office, opening the door to walk in on a chorus of ringing telephones.

31 AT 3 P.M. IN THE GARDEN PAVILION, NIGEL BURDEN WAS LINGERING BY the French windows in the sitting room of his suite. He kept checking his pocket watch as he waited for his son and daughter-in-law to arrive from Kennedy Airport.

Trisha and Cyril Burden would spend the night at Tanglewood. Tomorrow morning the young couple would drive him to Boston to catch a flight home to London. They themselves had come from England to enjoy a car trip across the United States.

Thinking about returning home tomorrow, Burden wondered if he would have recovered from alcoholism had he sought treatment in London. He could have gone to Charter Clinic off the King's Road or in Hampstead. Or checked into somewhere like Broadway Lodge in the country.

English clinics were reputedly good. Charter was owned by Americans. But Burden had chosen Tanglewood to protect his identity. A blast of bad publicity at home would not help him regain his seat in Parliament. But, worse, any scandal would exacerbate the blackmail demand hanging over him, the threatened exposure of a family secret. It had been the blackmail that had tipped his drinking into alcoholism.

The telephone buzzed on the table.

Certain it was Cyril at the gatehouse, Burden grabbed the receiver.

"Front gate here, Mr. Burden," the voice at the other end announced. "Two ladies have arrived who say they know you."

"Two ladies?" Burden did not understand.

"They say you're expecting them," reported the security guard.

Burden demanded, "What are their names?"

"Trisha and Joan Burden, sir."

Burden felt anger surge through his body.

"Hello?" said the guard. "Are you still there, Mr. Burden?"

"Yes. . . ." Burden's hand shook holding the phone. ". . . I'm . . . here."

"Do you give your permission, sir, for the ladies to drive down to the main house?"

"I don't see I have much choice, young man."

Burden slammed down the receiver, feeling a familiar rush sweep through him and not liking it: He needed a gin.

Nigel Burden waited on the front steps of the main house, struggling to control his desire for a drink as he watched the tan Ford stop in the driveway. Beckoning to the driver and passenger, he shouted, "Leave everything in the car and follow me."

Burden did not look over his shoulder as he led the way down the hall. Sliding back a double door, he stood aside for his son and daughter-in-law to pass in front of him into the drawing room. Both of them were wearing lipstick, skirts, and high heels.

Closing the door, Burden turned to his son and demanded, "For God's sake, Cyril, how can you do this to me?"

Cyril Burden was as tall as his father. His dark wig feathered softly over his beardless complexion. His feminine makeup was thorough but not dramatic; he wore a blue wool skirt that matched his chunky cardigan sweater and silk blouse.

"Father, we all have our lives to live," Cyril Burden answered in a voice that was neither masculine nor feminine.

"At least spare me the cliches," Burden Senior barked.

Trisha Burden, a pretty woman in her late twenties, was shorter than her husband and showed a fuller bust under her royal blue Jaeger twin-set.

"My companion's name is Joan," she said firmly. "We left Cyril at Kennedy Airport."

Burden turned to her. "Is that why *you* telephoned me this morning? Because *he* was changing into these clothes?"

"Since you ask—yes." She sniffed.

Trisha Burden exasperated Nigel Burden. She chained herself to fences at Greenham Common to protest against American cruise missiles. She broke into laboratories to free caged monkeys. She poisoned confectionery made by companies that supported vivisection. But her biggest cause was insisting that Cyril Burden—her husband, the father of her two children, and a successful solicitor in the St. James's firm of Fox, Harding and Chiswick—had the right to cross-dress as a woman.

Turning to her husband, she said, "Joan, don't let Nigel upset you. He's obviously feeling very sensitive after his recovery from alcoholism."

"Blast it," shouted Burden, "stop patronizing me, woman!"

Trisha snapped back, "And you stop being such a boring old Tory prig!"

Burden closed his eyes, trying to control his temper. "Let's be practical," he pleaded.

He looked from his daughter-in-law to his son. "Where do you two plan to spend the night?"

"Here." Cyril glanced around the large formal room dotted with palm trees and Corinthian columns. "I must say, we expected Tanglewood to be comfortable. But nothing so grand."

"You did say, Nigel, you had room for us in your suite," Trisha put in.

Burden kept his eyes on Cyril. "Do you plan on remaining dressed like that, young man?"

Trisha answered for him. "Joan's brought some lovely things for our trip across the States. She's been looking forward to wearing them. So don't ruin things. Please, Nigel."

"Well, the two of you are going to have to stop being so bloody selfish and not 'ruin' a few things yourself," Burden retorted. "More people are involved in this little masquerade than you two."

Trisha sighed. "Oh, Nigel, you're still not going on about those stupid photographs somebody sent you, are you?"

"Stupid or not, young lady, the blackmailer is threatening to send those photographs to the *News of the World*. Pictures of 'Joan' here trying on ladies' hats at Harvey Nichols. 'Joan' grocery-shopping in Harrod's Food Hall. 'Joan' and you having a night out like two bloody sisters at the National Theatre. The blackmailer's asking twenty thousand pounds to keep 'Joan' from being smeared across the front page of all the gutter press in England dressed as a typical English lady." Burden's voice had steadily risen and he was now shouting.

Trisha said, "Let the blackmailer publish and be damned. We told you we're not intimidated by blackmail."

Burden bellowed, "What about the children? What about Diana and me?"

"Mummy doesn't get as upset as you, Pa," argued Cyril. "And Trisha and I are prepared to talk to the children when the time comes."

Trisha looked at Burden. "As for you, Nigel, if Tanglewood's done the job, you shouldn't be hitting the bottle every time somebody threatens to say something about . . . Joan."

More matter-of-factly, she asked, "Now, are you going to invite us to stay here or not?"

Nigel Burden turned toward the double doors, muttering "Come along."

Lillian Weiss had been sitting behind a palm tree in the drawing room when the three Burdens had barged in through the double doors. She had stationed herself earlier in an armchair that had a clear view of the spot where Ray Esposito usually took his afternoon walk in the back garden. She had planned to exit through the French window when she saw the construction worker and approach him to suggest that it might be to both their advantage if they got to know one another better.

But the Burdens had interrupted Lillian's plan. Unable to raise her enormous weight quickly, she had remained seated in the far corner, silently eavesdropping on the heated conversation.

After the Burdens had left the room, Lillian forgot about trapping Ray Esposito in the back garden. All she could think about was telephoning her friend Myra B, the gossip columnist, and telling her the English politician's son's a drag queen! *Hot damn! What a story!*

32 BY THREE-THIRTY KAREN WASHING-TON HAD HUGGED AND KISSED HER children good-bye, packed them onto the train with Desiree at Stonebridge Station, and driven back to Tanglewood. Dr.

Pringle greeted her at the front door and accompanied her down to the Garden Pavilion for a reunion with Peabo.

Pringle told Karen, "I'll be there when you meet your husband but I think you should go alone with him into the suite. I'll return and observe you through the See-Wall in case he becomes violent." He added, "Although I seriously doubt if we have to worry about that."

Karen disapproved of the "peeping Tom" arrangement, but she accepted the necessity of being cautious. She had no idea how jealous or paranoid Peabo had become from his amphetamine withdrawal.

Peabo answered the outer door at the second buzz, wearing a brown velour track suit and holding a spiral notebook in one hand.

"Peabo, there's someone here to see you," said Pringle.

Peabo stared at Karen. "What are you doing here?"

Karen tried not to show shock over his sunken cheeks and the dark rings under his eyes.

"Excuse me," said Pringle. Karen said good-bye to Pringle, then followed Peabo into the suite's sitting room, looking nervously around her at the cheery furnishings.

Peabo pointed at the pair of settees and two armchairs. "Take your pick."

The knowledge that Pringle was watching them increased Karen's anxiety. Trying to sound normal, she asked, "Have you been writing something?"

Peabo tossed the notebook onto the round table. "I can't watch the box all day."

Karen remembered Roger saying that so far Peabo hadn't written anything in his journal. Was he starting to make a few entries?

Standing at the window, Peabo stuffed both hands into the pockets of the track jacket. "Where's the kids?" he asked.

"Desiree's baby-sitting them."

"Do they talk about me?"

"Morning, noon, and night." She opened her handbag

and unfolded a thick sheaf of paper. "Here. They sent you these."

Peabo took the pages and leafed through what he saw was Tamara's and Tyler's latest artwork. A smile cracked his face at the drawing of a stick man with oversized boxing gloves at the end of brown stick arms, and a stick lady wearing a red polka-dot apron and orange high-heel shoes. At the bottom of the tablet sheet was printed in big multicolor lettering, "I Love Daddy. I Love Mama."

Holding up a page covered with pink, yellow, and blue crayon circles, he asked, "What's this one meant to be?"

"Me."

"*You?*"

"Me taking a bubble bath."

Peabo slipped the picture back into the sheaf. "You look a lot better than that."

Was he on the verge of making a joke? Karen waited anxiously for a sign of the old Peabo.

Continuing through the drawings, he added casually, "Guess I'm looking pretty scary, though."

"Why do you say that?" Karen asked.

"You haven't kissed me yet."

The statement took Karen by surprise. She had been waiting for humor—or abuse—and instead she got a wistful plea for love. Hesitantly she stepped forward, raising her lips toward Peabo's.

Karen and Peabo's love affair had begun innocently.

Peabo Washington was eight years old when he turned to the delicately featured girl sitting next to him at the children's birthday party and asked, "Why does an alligator have more teeth than a bumble bee?"

But the girl in the ruffled yellow dress and matching hair ribbons seemed to be more interested in the party's silver balloons and gold paper horns than in the chubby-faced boy in the bow tie trying to get her attention with jokes.

Peabo was fourteen years old, no longer chubby-faced, when he approached the same girl at a Friday mixer in the school gym. "I just want you to see what I'm ready to do for you"—and he performed a perfect back flip in front of her.

The girl wore designer jeans and a red angora sweater. She smiled sweetly at the widely grinning boy, but her girl friends were tugging at her and giggling. She turned away.

In the senior year of high school, Peabo told the girl more seriously, "Maybe you'll pay more attention to me now that I'm the first black student body president this school's ever had."

The girl leaned toward Peabo. Her sweet breath tickled his ear as she whispered, "I've always paid attention to you, Peabo Washington. You've just been too busy performing to notice."

Peabo married the girl, Karen Cartwright, in June, two weeks after they both graduated from Cardinal Cameron High School. Peabo made the honor roll and was voted Best All Around Athlete and Best Sense of Humor. Karen Cartwright's yearbook entry listed: Prettiest Girl in Class, Miss Congeniality, and Best Dressed.

That fall Peabo entered Penn State on a Fulham Foundation Scholarship for academic excellence. But Karen resisted her parents' pleas to enroll in classes there. She preferred to work in the bookstore and keep house for Peabo. He seemed pleased with the arrangement.

In his freshman year, Peabo carried a full load of liberal art courses for prelaw and began to box after classes to channel his abundant physical energy. By midyear, he began fighting in intercollegiate bouts. He was spending so much time training that his grades began to suffer and the Fulham Foundation put him on academic probation.

At home, Karen said, "You better get serious, mister, or you're going to lose that scholarship."

As usual, Peabo's first reaction was to clown. First, he struck a professional pose, asking "Mr. Washington, what's two plus two?" Then, affecting a dum-dum voice, he answered himself, "Gee, teach, I don't know. I'm just a jock."

Karen remained serious. "Maybe you are a jock, and maybe

jocks don't need to pull good grades. But don't forget, Peabo, you're on an academic scholarship here. Not a sports one."

"You saying I'm not a sport?" He burlesqued disappointment.

"Peabo! Be serious! You're going to lose your scholarship."

He shrugged, answering with his first hint of earnestness "It's their loss. Not mine."

Karen stared at him. He couldn't take criticism. That was it. He couldn't admit he might be wrong. Of course. Why hadn't she realized that fact before?

Wrapping an arm around her shoulders, he said, "Don't worry, baby. I won't let you starve."

"It's not just me I'm worried about." She was pregnant with their first child.

Scooping her up from the floor, he carried her around the room, moving in waltz time, singing "Rock-a-bye baby . . . Rock-a-bye mom . . . Rock-a-bye baby . . . Rock-a-bye mom . . ." Still singing, he carried her into the bedroom.

After classes, Peabo trained with the boxing coach, Ty Johnson, working harder than he ever had in his life. Boxing became the focus of all his drives: a way to use mental as well as physical strength to do the one thing that mattered to him—win.

Coach Johnson became increasingly impressed with the big, joky kid from Philadelphia. He could see that Peabo belonged to the new breed of fighters—kids who used psychology as well as brute strength in the ring.

Peabo had the makings of a champion, Johnson recognized early on. A seventy-nine-inch reach. A knockout punch like Archie Moore. The natural hide-and-seek style of Mohammed Ali. By the end of Peabo's sophomore year, he had a 17–0 record on the intercollegiate circuit.

Peabo's first big disappointment came when the Fulham Foundation withdrew its scholarship at the beginning of his junior year for low grades. His parents stepped in to pay his tuition and cover the household expenses, but money was tight. Peabo found a job cleaning the chemistry lab. Still he refused to let Karen go back to work. She had just given birth to their second child and he wanted her home with the children.

Karen and Peabo's lovemaking was tender, occasionally ferocious, always fulfilling. But out of bed, Peabo was becoming increasingly jealous of the attention other men paid Karen.

"What do you do all day by yourself?" he asked as he sat at the drop-leaf table in the small kitchen.

Trying for one of her own jokes, Karen answered flippantly, "Oh, fly to Paris for lunch. Have tea with Bianca Jagger. Pop down to Rome and see if Valentino's got my spring wardrobe ready."

Peabo was drinking milk out of the half-gallon carton. "Any guys try to get fresh with you at the supermarket?" He wasn't joking.

Karen placed a glass on the table in front of him and filled it for him as she said earnestly, "I keep telling you, Peabo Washington—you and I are together forever. There's no reason to be jealous."

Karen truly loved Peabo. She didn't know where his boxing would lead them, but she trusted him. Though she had learned that he couldn't take criticism, she tried not to dwell on that fact. She had two beautiful children. Tons of hope for the future. So what if women's libbers called her "housebound" or "unemancipated"? She loved her man. She loved taking care of him and their children. Was that such a sin?

Peabo also took his turn caring for the children. He changed diapers. He fed them. But his favorite pastime was playing with them, making funny faces, tickling toes, getting down on the floor and pushing around rubber toys.

But not even his family interfered with Peabo's obsession to fight professionally. By the time the babies were awake in the morning, crying for breakfast, Peabo was dressed for his early-morning jog.

Coach Johnson understood Peabo's burning desire to become professional but urged, "Be patient, kid. Don't rush it."

"I'm ready for a professional card," Peabo insisted. His intercollegiate record was now an impressive 40–0. Peabo was too proud to admit that he needed the money. He hated taking *handouts from his family. Professional fights would not only bolster his self-esteem but also line his pocketbook.*

Johnson argued, "Stay in school, kid. Hang onto your amateur standing. The Olympics are just a year away. Use them for your springboard. It's the chance of a lifetime."

The advice was sound, Peabo knew. He continued to attend classes, training with Johnson at every free moment.

The next spring, as Johnson had predicted, Peabo qualified for a place on the United States Olympic team. He drew to fight contenders from Brazil, Norway, and Italy at the games scheduled to be held that summer in San Francisco.

Karen dreaded going to the summer Olympics. She hated seeing boxers pounding and battering each other in the ring, blood flying everywhere, the crowd screaming for a slaughter. But she didn't want her husband to think she wasn't behind him 100 percent.

"Be honest," she insisted two weeks before Peabo was due to fly to the coast. "Do you want me in San Francisco or not? I can easily leave the kids with Mom and Dad and be right there by your side."

Peabo joked, "Aren't you scared some fancy ringside lady's going to latch onto me when they drape that gold medal around my neck?"

"Loverboy, if you want to step out with some floozie, you go for it. Just don't bother coming home to me when the party's over."

"You're pretty sure of yourself, girl," he teased.

"No. I'm pretty sure about you."

Nuzzling her, he murmured his oldest-standing joke. "Hey, why does an alligator have more teeth than a bumblebee?"

She touched the tip of his nose. "Everybody needs their secrets, and you've got yours."

In San Francisco, Peabo won the fights with the Brazilian and the Norwegian by decision. In his final bout, with Luigi Luchese from Milan, he landed a strong right in round 1, but Luchese survived a standing count. In the third round, Peabo floored the Italian, scoring a knockout victory and earning a gold medal.

Soon Peabo had managers clamoring to handle him on the professional circuit.

Karen did not go to Miami when Peabo challenged world Heavyweight champ Sonny Moss. Apart from not liking to see the blood and the poundings, she felt that Peabo dealt better with the press by himself; he drove a hearse around Miami with Sonny Moss's name painted on the coffin; he poked pins into joke voodoo dolls; he dominated the stage better as a solo performer. Karen was content to stay at home and watch the fight, and the buffoonery, on TV.

With his stunning victory over Sonny Moss, Peabo became boxing's Heavyweight champion of the world at the age of twenty-two. He moved Karen and the children to a brownstone in Philadelphia's Germantown section. He bought a Ferrari for himself, a Seville for Karen, and hired a business manager to handle his growing fortune.

By the time Peabo was twenty-four, he had a 7–0 professional record. He owned a shopping mall in Palm Springs, a seventy-two-unit condominium development in Hawaii, a chain of taco restaurants in Colorado, and six high-rise apartment buildings in Philadelphia, as well as an impressive stock portfolio. His business manager, Harmon Gilbert, was negotiating for Peabo to represent the national airline, Air Fair, in a full-scale advertising campaign.

At home he was as happy as ever. One of his biggest joys at home was boxing with his son, Tyler. Kneeling on the floor, he let Tyler swing his tiny brown fists at him, then suddenly fell to the carpet with a thud as if the boy had knocked him out, playing unconscious as Tyler squealed with delight. Against Karen's better wishes, he also let Tamara climb into the "ring."

Peabo's next championship match was with San Salvador's Juan Elvirdor.

Scheduled to fight Elvirdor in Las Vegas, Peabo trained in Los Angeles to minimize travel time and conserve physical energy. It was during this training schedule that he first began to feel tired. He guessed that his personal appearances, business obligations, and increasing endorsement commitments were taking a *toll on him. He even didn't have much energy for clowning with the press.*

His L.A. trainer, Clem Meyers, noticed Peabo's lethargy early in the training camp in the San Fernando Valley. One day Meyers said, "Why don't I give you a little of my rattlesnake juice to get you through Vegas?"

Peabo agreed to Meyers's offer of injections. The so-called rattlesnake juice was methamphetamine.

In Las Vegas, as Peabo weighed in, he joked to the reporters " 'Juan Elvirdor' means 'Stop! I can't take no more!'." He posed for pictures with a photograph of his daughter in one hand, and one of his son in the other. It was becoming known around the world that Heavyweight champion Peabo Washington was not only a very funny man but a family person who kept his wife and children well away from the bloody world of prizefighting.

After knocking out Elvirdor in the fifth round, Peabo won a purse of four-and-a-half million dollars, plus a percentage of the fight's cable television rights.

"Great news," Harmon Gilbert announced the next morning when he telephoned Peabo in the hotel's presidential suite. "Air Fair wants to cinch the endorsement deal immediately. This is going to make you the biggest money-spinner in the history of the sport."

Peabo grunted. He wanted nothing but sleep.

Without the rattlesnake injections, Peabo felt lifeless. Deep down inside, he knew he had developed a need for them. But he could not admit to himself that he shared a problem with thousands of other people—students who had to find instant energy to study all night for exams, truckers who had to stay awake to drive from Alaska to Florida in one uninterrupted stretch, and executives who had to be alert for meetings all day and company dinners all night.

Before flying home, Peabo cornered Clem Meyers for names of contacts back east where he could score shots of rattlesnake juice.

As soon as the needle bit Peabo's skin, he felt a surge, as if he had been plugged into a high-voltage socket. He relied increasingly on the injections, using the chemical boost not only for training sessions and business meetings but for the filming of the television commercials in which he now was appearing.

On the Air Fair set, Peabo shared bursts of comical energy with the crew. Mugging for the makeup girls and set dressers, he shouted, "You all expected Peabo Washington to be some ugly, beat-up old boxer, didn't you? Admit it! But lookee here. See how pretty I am!" He ducked his head behind a chair and came up holding a cauliflower along each side of his head.

As weeks of dependency on the injections passed, Peabo made the dosages stronger, but their effects lasted for shorter periods of time. Peabo found less and less time to play jokes and clown for the crew.

Also, Peabo began to suffer physical reactions: loss of appetite, weight loss, no sexual drive, his sense of humor replaced by edgy behavior, obsessions over details. He spent hours on end pursuing meaningless pastimes, taking apart his alarm clock, rearranging his compact discs by artist name, then pulling them all from the shelves and rearranging them by category . . . .

Karen noticed the changes in Peabo on his rare visits home. She saw that his sense of humor was gone, that he had less time for the kids. She wondered if he might be having a drug problem—cocaine or pills—but she was too frightened to broach the subject to him and risk the vile temper tantrums he also was having.

Then came the worms.

One night at home, Peabo's scratching awoke Karen from sleep.

"What's the matter, honey?" she whispered in the darkness of their bedroom.

"Worms are crawling under my skin. Thousands of little worms."

Worms? Was it a joke? Karen turned on the bedside light and saw that Peabo was serious. Collecting the minuscule "worms" from the sheet, she carried them to the kitchen.

Under a bright fluorescent light, she saw that the "worms" were bits of dried skin that Peabo had dug from his arm in his obsessive scratching. He was fast asleep when she returned to the bedroom.

Should she insist they have a serious talk? Should she beg him to see a doctor? Remembering how Peabo was always unwilling to admit he had a fault, she kept her mouth shut, praying for a solution.

The problem surfaced when Peabo flew back home from Japan and accused Karen, "Who've you been sleeping with, bitch, while I've been away?"

Karen stared at him, waiting for a joke. Certainly he couldn't be talking to her in such a way. The outburst had to be some kind of setup for a joke.

He repeated, "You been sleeping with anyone while I was away?"

Realizing he was serious, she snapped, "How dare you talk to me like that!"

"Why in fuck don't you make love to me any more?"

Peabo's crude words and brutal tone devastated Karen. What had happened to the old tenderness they used to share? The loving way he had always talked to her? She could put up with Peabo's craziness. But she wouldn't stand for him calling her unfaithful.

She retorted, "I've been here waiting for you to come home to your bed, mister."

"Are you saying I'm not a good lover?"

"I'm saying you have no reason to accuse me of stepping out on you, that's what I'm saying."

The next day Peabo ordered a Rolls-Royce to be sent around as a gift for Karen when he was in Florida opening an adventure amusement park.

The night after the Rolls arrived, Karen put the kids to bed and sat alone in her bedroom, wondering if she should keep the expensive car or send it back. It was beautiful. She loved the plum-red color. But it represented a part of their life she was beginning to hate. She and Peabo had been so much happier living in two rooms, shopping for bargains at K-Mart, wondering how they were going to make ends meet. She longingly remembered the days when he had held both hands behind his back, giving her a choice between a used paper towel and an old sweat sock.

Karen's attention turned to the television set beyond the foot of the bed. One of Peabo's latest commercials for *Air Fair* was on.

On the television screen, Peabo and two children ran along an airport runway, hands joined together. They took off, becoming airborne, soaring over Manhattan, D.C., New Orleans, the Rocky Mountains, the Grand Canyon, San Francisco. Descending across Disneyland, they circled to land at Los Angeles as a voice-over said, "This used to be the cheapest way to fly to California . . ."

Karen flipped off the TV by her remote-control unit. Burying her head in the pillows, she wondered who she could talk to about Peabo. His parents would never in a million years accept the fact that their champion son was dependent on drugs. Her own parents would be frightened for her and the children's safety and insist they immediately move out of the house.

Karen did not want to divorce Peabo. But was that the only solution? She had wanted nothing except to be a loving wife and mother, but had she carried her role too far? In her devotion to Peabo had she lost track of herself? Had she played the retiring wife too well? Was it too late now to stand up to him and demand some changes?

Karen decided to call Peabo's manager, Harmon Gilbert, while Peabo was still in Florida. She asked him if he had noticed a change in Peabo's behavior.

"Karen, Peabo's a busy man. He has a lot of important commitments, and he has a full training schedule as well. I agree he looks a little fatigued, but it's nothing a little R and R won't cure."

"Herman, I'm not talking about 'fatigue.' And what about his commitment to his family? We hardly ever see him any more."

"Just try to be patient. Peabo is crazy about you and the kids, it's just that. . . ." Gilbert stopped, as if searching for the right phrase.

"It's drugs, isn't it?" The words popped out of Karen's mouth.

There was a pause at the other end of the phone. "Well, you know, Karen, that does happen in the sports world."

Karen let loose. "You bastard. You got him into this mess. You and all your big deals. Your slick promotions. Your brainwave syndication schemes. You're ruining his life. But I'm not going to let you ruin mine and my kids'."

"Hold it, Karen. Hold it right there. What exactly are you saying?"

"I'm saying it's impossible to live with Peabo Washington anymore. I never thought I'd hear myself say this, Harmon, but Peabo's not a fit husband or a fit father. I've decided to file for a divorce."

"Now, hold your horses. Calm down. You can't walk out on Peabo. Not at a time like this."

" 'Walk out'? He's never home to 'walk out' on! And when he does come home, he makes life hell for all of us by his craziness. How am I supposed to raise two kids in this kind of environment?"

"Karen, it'll ruin Peabo's life if you leave him now."

"What about my life? My children's life? Don't we count anymore?"

"Karen. Hold on. Listen to me."

Harmon Gilbert hurriedly said, "There's a drug clinic in Connecticut I've heard about. It's called Tanglewood. Lots of high-profile people go there. It's very discreet. Peabo will be protected from the press at Tanglewood. Nobody will ever know he's there."

Karen calmed her temper long enough to admit, "In theory, Harmon, that's a good idea. But in practice it stinks."

"What's wrong with it?"

She explained, "Peabo will never go to a drug clinic for the simple reason he'll never admit anything's wrong with him."

Gilbert argued, "I'll tell him it's a health farm. That he's going there for a rest. Do some light training."

Karen was shocked by the man's ignorance. "Peabo's not stupid, Harmon. It'll take him exactly two seconds flat to figure out what the place is."

She added, "What's more, to get somebody off drugs, they have to admit they've got a problem in order to deal with it. I tell you,

Peabo Washington will never admit he does one . . . thing . . . wrong."

"Leave it to me."

Karen put down the phone, more convinced than ever that the sooner she went ahead with a divorce, the better it would be for her and the kids.

Dr. Pringle walked Karen down the corridor of the Garden Pavilion. "How'd it go?"

Karen and Peabo's introductory reunion had lasted forty-five minutes, and Karen felt drained.

"Let's just say it broke the ice," she answered, not disillusioned but not encouraged.

They continued along the carpeted hallway. Pringle nodded hello to the frizzy-haired nurse, Margie Clark, who was letting herself into the foyer of Little Milly Wheeler's suite with a medication tray. As he continued walking Karen down the corridor, he asked, "How do *you* feel?"

"Dr. Pringle, I read once that drugs are a family disease. I'm beginning to understand why they say that. Not only is the whole family affected, the whole family might be a little bit to blame."

For the moment that was all Karen would say.

33 IT WAS NEARLY 5 P.M. WHEN GLADYS WHEELER MET MARGIE CLARK HALF-way across the sitting room of Little Milly's suite.

Glancing down at the tray Margie carried, the Nashville

matron smiled. "I guess your hands were too full, dear, to press that little buzzer outside the front door."

Margie ignored the honey-coated barb. She was tired and it was time to go home. Moving past Mrs. Wheeler into the bedroom, she saw Little Milly propped up in bed on pillows, wearing a pink knit bed jacket. Her long red hair fell in loose ringlets around her shoulders in the old-fashioned style of other country and western singers.

"Evening, Milly," said Margie, setting down the tray.

Little Milly smiled thinly and kept her eyes shut, hands tucked under the top bedsheet.

Margie leaned forward to fluff the pillows.

"Stop!" Gladys Wheeler grabbed Margie's hand. "Don't touch her."

The nurse froze in surprise.

Stepping between Margie and the bed, Gladys's face softened and, as she picked long threads of hair from Milly's damp forehead, she added more sweetly, "I've been taking good care of my little gal, haven't I, sugar plum?"

Milly's eyes remained tightly shut.

In addition to the detailed information available on patients at checkpoint, every room had a coded sheet showing what treatment, medical or psychotherapeutic, had been completed or prescribed.

Margie reached for Milly Wheeler's progress chart. She had undergone urinalysis and blood tests. The coded record showed a high count of alcohol and amphetamines. Poor girl, Margie thought. No wonder she looks like a corpse. First, she has to be weaned off the speed, then the booze. Thorazine would replace the uppers before phenobarbital could be used for the alcohol. Or perhaps her doctor, Lonny Lamb, would prescribe Nembutal for alcohol withdrawal. Whatever, it would be no bed of roses.

Margie also noted that Dr. Piciska had visited that afternoon and had listed her in the red stratum, a danger zone. She's really in bad shape, Margie realized. Surprisingly, Margie saw no checks for physical therapy. Did that mean she was too delicate to move about?

She asked, "Milly, have you been downstairs today for treatment? Your massage and vapor bath?"

Gladys Wheeler answered for her daughter. "Little Milly's been right here with me all day, ain't you, honey? I've been busy with my knitting and talking to Milly about old times."

"Didn't any attendants come to take her to physical therapy?"

Gladys laughed. "Is that what you call them boys, honey? 'Attendants'? The last thing Little Milly needs is more boys helping her. She's got one too many of them back home."

Margie, bemused, replied as kindly as she could, "If you object to male attendants, Mrs. Wheeler, you could have called for a female. Or me. I would have taken her."

"Now I know, don't I, dear?"

Gladys glanced at the tray Margie had set alongside the Boston fern on the bedside table. "What you bring there, honey?"

"Milly's medication," Margie answered, at a loss to understand what was going on.

Peering from the glass of orange juice to a small white paper cup, Gladys asked, "Drugs, honey?"

"It's best to ask Dr. Lamb what he's prescribing for your daughter, Mrs. Wheeler."

A buzzer sounded in the sitting room.

"That must be my supper." Gladys looked at Margie. "Get the door for me, will you, dear? Have them leave my supper on that little table out there in front of the TV. I'm going to watch some news and then get a very early night. I'm plumb tuckered."

Margie moved from the bedroom, feeling that something was definitely wrong here; somebody was hiding something from her. But she couldn't guess what.

Following Gladys Wheeler's instructions, Margie told the room waiter to set a place on the coffee table. She returned to the bedroom, deciding to give Milly her medication and get home. Her own fatigue was making her jittery. Maybe she was merely imagining trouble where none existed.

Seeing the juice glass and paper cup both empty on the tray, she turned to Gladys. "Did you give that medication to your daughter?"

Gladys blinked. "That's what you wanted me to do, wasn't it?"

"No. That is *not* what I wanted you to do, Mrs. Wheeler. That's why I'm here."

Gladys corrected her with a smile. "No, dear. You're here to help me. But as I've done all your work for you, you can go."

"Mrs. Wheeler, I understand your concern for Millie, but please leave the medication to me next time." Exasperated, Margie turned to leave. Gladys continued to nod and smile.

"You will close the door behind you, won't you, dear?" she asked.

Gladys heard Margie shut the outer door but waited a few seconds before checking the foyer. Satisfied that the nurse had gone, she returned to the bedroom, fluffing the Boston fern into whose pot she had emptied Milly's orange juice in case it was medicated, too. Removing the pills from her pocket, she stepped into the adjoining bathroom and flushed them down the toilet.

As she returned to Milly's bedside, Gladys said, "If your mama had known they were going to give you all this dope, I would never have brought you here. We want to get you *off* this junk. Not replace one crutch with another."

Throwing back the sheet, Gladys Wheeler checked the wide leather belt buckled around Milly's waist, restraining both arms tightly to her abdomen.

"Mama, *please,*" Milly begged, trying to move her hands from under the belt. "This belt's hurting me, Mama."

"Shhh, baby. If them nurses hear you, they'll bring you more drugs and you'll never get better."

"Take off the belt, Mama," Milly pleaded. "I'll be good."

"We'll just keep it on till your danger period passes." Gladys reminded her, "The doctor says the next couple days are not going to be easy for you. You're not going to be yourself. But it'll pass and then Mama will take off the belt."

"The belt hurts, Mama. It hurts!"

"Course it hurts, Little Milly. But it's better to control you with this belt than with all them drugs they give you here."

Gladys Wheeler pulled the sheet back over the makeshift straitjacket, assuring her daughter, "This ain't much to pay for all them years you've been poisoning your system with pills and liquor, now is it, Little Milly?"

Milly knew it was useless to argue with her mother. How stupid she had been to think that Mama was going to let other people help her. It was the same old story: If Mama doesn't approve of how other people do things, she changes the rules to fit herself.

At the moment, though, Mama and her belt was only one threat. What Milly feared more were the brightly colored streaks that came flashing across the room without warning and the shrill voices that taunted her about what a mess her life was in. No belt would control those lights and sounds that haunted her like demons.

34 AS DAYLIGHT BEGAN TO FADE ON THE CHILLY OCTOBER TUESDAY, LIGHTS blinked on inside the windows of Tanglewood.

Inside a second-floor window of the main house, Charles

"Chips" Ashford, senior vice president of Amenco Electronics, wrote in his therapy journal of how he had begun drinking in college to feel like "one of the boys."

Across the hallway, Patricia Cacoyannis composed a letter to her married daughter in Cleveland, thanking her for insisting she seek help with her "secret drinking" and suggesting the family all get together in Shaker Heights for a celebratory Christmas dinner—with cranberry juice for cocktails.

In the gymnasium on the lower level of the Orchard Pavilion, Ray Esposito worked his way around the Nautilus equipment. The physical exertion helped him fight the sluggish effect that Methadone had on his system—as well as distracting him from his obsessive sexual drive.

On the ground floor of the Orchard Pavilion, Dr. Evan Isaacs III, acting junior to Philip Pringle, listened to cabaret artist Marilyn Joel confess, "I'm scared to go out on the road without Quaaludes. I get so lonely at night. I get so insecure on my own. When I was touring, Quaaludes were the only constant in my life. They went everywhere with me."

Outside the main building, Roger Cooper cut across the staff parking lot, hurrying to the old coach house to change clothes for tonight's board of management meeting in town. He checked the time on his wristwatch in the fading daylight. Tanglewood's New York lawyer had not returned his call. He would telephone the office again tomorrow morning. Or would Adrian be back by then?

In the parking lot, the day staff was leaving Tanglewood, the night workers arriving, the clinic moving smoothly into the next shift.

As Tuesday darkened into night, Jackie Lyell's bravado began to wane.

Sitting behind Adrian's oversize desk in Administration, she remembered how she had spoken so bravely to Roger that morning about defending Tanglewood against Adrian's changes. Now, ten hours later, her mind was a jumble of uncertainties.

Where would she live if she had to fight Adrian to remain at Tanglewood? Could they occupy their flat—apartment—as rivals? Or would they move into separate accommodations? What would she use for money? Everything was in Adrian's name. She had no stocks. No bonds. No savings. Nothing to pawn or sell except for the string of pearls around her neck and a few kitschy nineteenth-century paintings.

The idea of being nearly destitute increased Jackie's anger at Adrian. She told herself: That's even more reason to get your independence from the swine.

But how could she support herself on her own? Certainly not as a typist! This afternoon she had not wanted to overload Adrian's secretary, Joanie Hemphill, so she had decided to do some of her own typing. It had taken forty-five minutes to prepare an eight-line letter. Also Accounts had sent back a long list of queries on yesterday's checkouts. Two newspapers telephoned for updates on Cat Powers and asked for Roger, refusing to talk to "that Englishwoman in Administration."

As she wondered what she should do to avoid sitting upstairs alone tonight and brooding about tomorrow's work and Adrian and the future, she thought about Roger. Maybe she could buzz him to see if he was free to join her for dinner in the dining room.

Then she remembered. Roger had that board meeting in town tonight.

Poor guy, she thought. I think *I* have problems. He's the one who has to face that bunch of fogeys and explain Adrian's shocking behavior.

Looking at her watch, Jackie had a sudden inspiration. There was just enough time to change clothes and catch Howard Jefferson's seven-o'clock exercise class. A good workout would relax her nerves and help her have a sound night's sleep.

* * *

Pull your left knee across your right thigh . . . pulllll . . .
*Reach for those ankles . . . you can do it . . . sure you can do
it. . . .*

Seven people—three men, four women, all patients except
Jackie—stood facing the sinewy black gymnast as he
stretched upward, reaching for the sky, urging them to follow him.

Feeling her body tingle from the exercise, Jackie recalled
how Adrian teased her for coming to the exercise class,
saying she was mutton trying to be lamb. But the physical
effort made Jackie feel good, kept her figure in shape, and,
most important, helped her fill uneventful days—and nights.

Forty-five minutes sped by. Jackie was sorry the class
seemed to end almost as soon as it had started; she beat the
bottom of her T-shirt back and forth, fanning herself as she
lingered behind three women dragging toward the shower
room. One was Marianne Turnbull, the Westchester housewife who was in the final stages of a Valium withdrawal,
complaining bitterly, as usual, about the rude way people
acted in her advanced encounter group. Jackie tried to avoid
the woman whenever she could.

She decided to shower upstairs instead of using the aero-
bic room's showers. Tossing a Tanglewood robe over her
shoulders, she moved down the hallway to her office. She
had left a stack of work to take upstairs and finish over
supper.

"Jackie?" a man's voice called.

She turned in front of Administration and saw Roger
coming out of his office.

"How's everything going?" he asked.

"Surviving." She smiled, one hand on the door handle, the
other pushing hair from her perspiration-soaked forehead.

Seeing his eyes lower, she realized that the robe was open,
showing her tattered old T-shirt, leotards, and droopy leg
warmers from the exercise class—and, with a shock, she
realized that Roger was studying her figure.

Pulling the robe tightly across her, she quickly said, "I thought you had the board meeting tonight."

"I do." He raised his eyes back to her face, a smile on his lips, as he said, "But I'm glad I ran into you like this. Now I know what to give you for Christmas."

"What's that?" She felt herself blush.

He lowered his eyes again, nodding at the exercise clothes under her robe. "A new T-shirt."

The smile played on his lips as he added, "Got to go now. Bye."

As the front door closed, Jackie's ears burned red hot. She felt as if he had been looking at her totally naked.

Outside the front door, Roger bounded down the steps, still grinning. Who would have thought that Jackie Lyell looked so dishy under all those ladylike clothes she wears every day? In fact, the lady is downright sexy.

35 AMONG THE GUESTS IN THE DINING ROOM WERE TWO DINERS SEATED AT table 7, both wearing evening gowns.

Trisha Burden was dressed in black jersey. Her husband, Cyril, wore a long flowered skirt with matching top. The young Burdens enjoyed the slivers of chicken breast in walnut oil. They finished the bottle of Montrachet. They agreed that the *crème brûlée*'s crust was perfect—not too burnt. The evening's only discordant note was that Cyril's father, Nigel Burden, had not joined them for supper.

Despite the excellent food and gracious atmosphere, Trisha and Cyril remembered they must make an early start tomorrow morning on their car trip and decided to forgo coffee in the drawing room. They strolled arm in arm back to the Garden Pavilion, hoping to find Nigel Burden in his suite.

He was not there.

Cyril Burden, naked in front of the bathroom sink, rubbed cold cream on his face to remove his makeup as he called, "Trish, do you think we should worry about Pa?"

"Not at all." She was repacking their evening dresses into the suitcases. On the bureau in front of her stood a wigstand holding Cyril's wig for tomorrow morning. Their freshly pressed skirts and blouses hung in the closet.

After removing his makeup, Cyril reached into the shower. "Are you going to shower after me, dear?"

"I showered before supper," answered Trisha. "I want to finish packing so that we can leave straightaway after breakfast."

"Where do you think Pa's gone?" Cyril called, his lean body half in, half out of the tiled stall.

"Don't worry," Trisha urged. "He's a big boy now. Let him walk off his sulk."

"Have you noticed how glad he is to be going home?"

"Hmmm. To your mother," Trisha answered. "He's obviously beginning to realize how important she is to him."

"It's Mother who saved him."

Trisha was in bed reading when Cyril's weight disturbed her.

Smiling, she put aside the road map she had been studying and looked up at her husband. Brushing the damp hair from his forehead, she said, "Ummm, you feel warm and lovely, darling."

"You *look* lovely." He kissed the tip of her nose.

Wrapping both arms around him, Trisha groaned. "Oh, thank you for the super evening."

"Thank *you*." He lowered his mouth to hers.

Their kiss became prolonged, and Cyril pulled back the sheet, his penis bobbing hard in its erection.

As Trisha welcomed her husband's nakedness, she thought what a lucky woman she was. She had two bright, wonderful children. A husband who loved her and gave her a perfectly healthy sex life. A career and opportunities to travel. The only blight on their marriage was that Cyril's father could not accept the fact that Cyril enjoyed dressing as a woman. Trisha had long ago stopped trying to find a psychological reason for this need. Cyril was not a homosexual; they enjoyed an active love life together. The simple fact was that he enjoyed wearing women's clothes in public places, and Trisha lived with this situation by telling herself that Cyril had a multifaceted personality to express. Their relationship had become even stronger, after she had helped him choose his clothes and makeup.

Trisha and Cyril's problem was to help Nigel accept Cyril's multipersonalities. But that could be done, Trisha felt, only when Nigel Burden threw away his gin bottle and got on with his own life. Nigel had to learn how to tell the world to be damned.

Tom Hudson also ate in the dining room that Tuesday night.

After a whiskey on the rocks, he ordered onion soup, followed by a steak filet and salad. As he ate he reread the sales report on Sunbakers, the Florida fast-food chain he was trying to buy. Hudson gulped down a cup of coffee and hurried from the dining room to make one last telephone call before returning to Cat's suite.

Pleased to find the Arboretum empty, he went to his usual phone in the corner and placed a long-distance, credit card call to Red Tag's Honolulu office. It was still a working day in Hawaii and Hudson could check on the Japanese bid for canned tuna.

As he finished the Hawaii call, Hudson decided it was too chilly to take his evening stroll without an overcoat. Rather than go back to the suite for one, he decided to explore inside the clinic.

At 10 P.M., the corridors were nearly deserted except for an occasional white-jacketed waiter pushing a trolley of dirty dishes back to the kitchen, a junior doctor making nightly rounds. The loudest sound was the tick-tock of a grandfather clock. There were no clanging bells. No intercoms blaring from wall speakers. No obtrusive alarms. Who would ever guess this was a medical facility?

Hudson approved of the way in which Tanglewood kept its workings behind closed doors. He had seen the Hub, studied its impressive dispatch console and high-tech computer station, seen how it functioned as the nerve center for doctors, nurses, therapists, orderlies. He had visited Security's basement headquarters, too, impressed by their scanners, videotapes, surveillance systems connected to all the buildings and around the twenty-eight-acre grounds.

Tanglewood was a clinic of the future, Hudson realized, as he moved along the hushed corridor. But it wasn't like a corny space-age movie. Tanglewood boasted the latest equipment blended with luxurious appointments, rich woods, lush carpets, antique furniture, fine oil paintings.

He paused in front of a birch fire crackling beneath a shoulder-high carved marble mantelpiece in the entrance hall. Facing the dancing flames, he realized that, yes, he felt safe leaving Cat there. Then he could get back to his own work. His only stipulation would be that Roger Cooper should supervise Cat's recovery. Hudson could see Cooper was the driving force behind Tanglewood. The head honcho.

As he stared into the fire, an idea teased Hudson's brain. He did not know whether he should pursue it, or whether he already had too much on his plate. It was at that moment that he remembered asking Chumley in Chicago to get him some details on Tanglewood. Chumley had not yet produced them.

* * *

While Tom Hudson had been eating in the dining room, Cat Powers lay in darkness in her bedroom, feeling the warmth of Gene Stone's hand fondling her breast. She giggled. "I'm engaged to be married."

Stone goaded, "Once a slut, always a slut, right . . . bitch?"

Cat enjoyed verbal abuse. She had developed an appetite for dirty talk during the years she had been becoming dependent on pills and liquor. Stone had discovered that. He also knew how to deliver the raunchy talk she had learned to enjoy. Apart from being Cat's traveling physician, he was also, on occasion, her lover.

Today was Cat's first full day off his hypodermic cocktails. Stone was nevertheless certain that she had enough junk in her system to prevent her from becoming hysterical or from experiencing acute withdrawal symptoms. She was able to enjoy sex as usual—in fact, she seemed to be as horny as a bitch in heat.

Tom Hudson had little enthusiasm for making love to Cat while she was racing on drugs or drink, and he had certainly not thought to come to bed with her at Tanglewood.

Gene Stone had no such reservations.

Cat was a vital part of his practice. She gave him great cachet, making him a celebrity himself, certainly a millionaire. The Rodeo Drive doctor did not want to lose Cat Powers when she married Tom Hudson.

Hudson was the root of all Stone's problems. Today Hudson had given him an ultimatum: either to cooperate with Tanglewood and let Cat have her tests or go straight back to Los Angeles.

Stone had capitulated. But he was tired of giving in to people who were stronger, more powerful, richer than he was.

Someday he would be top dog. Then he wouldn't need the Cat Powerses and Tom Hudsons and Roger Coopers of this world. Meanwhile, he thought with a grin, he didn't mind screwing them on the sly.

* * *

Snoring rose from the sitting room of Little Milly Wheeler's suite in the Garden Pavilion. Gladys Wheeler was fast asleep on the sofa bed there, while in the bedroom, Little Milly lay wide awake, wondering if she should call out for her mother. The demons, as Milly called them, had come again.

Bright colors had started flashing around the room, tormenting Milly. The voices laughed at her for being so weak all her life. They scorned her for having let her mother run her life for so long. They hooted at her for letting her husband try to replace Mama's domination in both her career and private life. Even Little Milly's daddy had taken a toll on her—perhaps the most destructive one—and the demon voices would not let her forget it. The worst part was that there was no whiskey, no beer, no pills to quiet them. Not even a sleeping pill. Mama had banned everything.

Lying in bed with both hands stuffed into the leather belt buckled and tied around her, Little Milly looked to the bedside table and saw that Mama had removed the emergency call button. It was useless. Mama had also pulled out the telephone's jack from the wall.

The only way to get attention was to scream. But Milly knew that Mama would just make up excuses if anybody outside the room did hear Milly's cries. Mama had also put a wadded handkerchief into her mouth earlier today, to demonstrate the discomfort she would have to endure if she decided to start hollering and shouting and screaming.

Milly's anguish increased in the darkened room as the red and yellow and green flashes became brighter around her bed, and the nagging voices taunted her for being so weak, so dependent, always tied to Mama's apron strings, always listening to her daddy, always trusting her husband.

36 "SO WHAT'S THIS ABOUT ADRIAN LYELL ANNOUNCING THIS MORNING on television there's plans to expand Tanglewood?"

The question came from Carlton Frazer. The silver-haired man was president of Stonebridge Savings and Loan and chairman of Tanglewood's board of management. The board was meeting in a private dining room at the Cherry Hills Inn, located on the outskirts of Stonebridge. Supper had been served and the meeting commenced after the waitresses had served coffee and brandy.

Roger sat at the far end of the table from Carlton Frazer, replying to the chairman's question with one of his own.

"Has Adrian said anything to you, Carlton, about plans for expansion?"

"Not a word," answered Frazer. He looked the length of the table and said, "That's why I'm concerned. Because of Adrian's silence on the matter."

Roger surveyed the other members: Senator William Baird. Sharon Gizer from the County Clerk's Office. Clive Gower, administrator of Stonebridge General Hospital. Warren Tolan, publisher of the *Stonebridge Herald*. Dorothy McCall, owner of McCall and McCall Realty.

"Did Adrian say anything to any of you about expansions?" Roger asked them.

He singled out the members one by one. "Bill, you saw Adrian last Tuesday. Sharon and Clive, I was with Adrian on Wednesday when he ran into you at the Road Safety

Show. The three of you went off and had coffee. Warren, Adrian was at your office last Monday. Dorothy, Adrian talks to you about real estate and investments. Has he said anything to you about expanding Tanglewood into a health spa?"

One by one, the members denied that Adrian Lyell had spoken to them about changes at the clinic—or about flying out to California to meet potential backers for an expansion program.

Roger proceeded. "For the record, I want to say that I was as surprised as anyone when I saw that TV show this morning. Unlike you, I knew that Adrian wanted to expand Tanglewood. He even went as far as showing me plans. But I certainly didn't know he had approached investors."

Frazer broke the hush. "What does Adrian's wife have to say about all this, Roger?" he asked. "Have you spoken to her?"

"Indeed I have. Jackie Lyell was the first—and only—person I've discussed this matter with. I would prefer this not to go any farther than this room, but Jackie is as surprised as any of us. I think I can even say 'distressed'."

He went on. "Adrian left Jackie working for him in Administration, and she's been holding up extremely well under pressure."

Frazer asked, "Mrs. Lyell's acting as Administrator?" The banker kept any surprise from his voice.

Roger's nod was confident. "Yes. And I have no complaints on the arrangement. Naturally, I'm as anxious to talk to Adrian as anyone, but the clinic is functioning quite smoothly at the moment."

Frazer addressed the other board members. "I would like to put it to a vote that we grant Adrian, say, seven days to return to Tanglewood before calling an emergency meeting to discuss this matter with the seriousness it deserves."

With a vote of hands, the members agreed to accept the chairman's proposal.

Before the meeting broke up, Roger cautioned the group,

"I might suggest that none of you leave town in the next few days without telling Carlton. If Adrian comes back, he might have to call that emergency meeting before the week's out."

37 IN MANHATTAN, FASHION DESIGNER CHATWYN DID NOT KNOW WHAT TIME it was—late Tuesday night or early Wednesday morning—when he drowsily reached for the ringing telephone in the bedroom of his Trump Tower triplex on Fifth Avenue. Hearing the name "Lavender Gilbert," he jumped out of bed, gripping the cordless phone to one ear.

Monica Silvers, head of San Trop Agency, said at the other end, "Fabulous news. We tracked down your Star Lady."

"This better be good," said Chatwyn.

"You've heard of Tanglewood?" Monica asked. "And I don't mean the music festival in Lenox, Massachusetts."

"Keep going."

"Let me backtrack. You know that Lavender flew back from the Antigua shoot on Sunday. She was traveling with Bev Jordan."

Monica laughed. "After a little arm-twisting, Bev told me where she was."

"Spare me the detective story, Monica. Just tell me where the girl is."

Monica sighed. "Lavender's checked into Tanglewood for a coke cure."

"*Now?*" Chatwyn snarled. "At the eleventh hour of my Star Lady campaign?"

"She has a problem."

"So do I have a problem!" Chatwyn screamed into the phone. "I've got an opening on Friday at the Waldorf and no Star Lady."

"Calm down, dear. Calm down," urged Monica. "We can drive up and get her for you. Tanglewood's no more than a couple hours away."

"No, leave her to me." Chatwyn's voice had leveled; his brain was whirring with plans. "You just keep your mouth shut about all this, Monica, and wait for my next instructions. Understand, Monica? Leave Lavender Gilbert to me."

Chatwyn clicked off the phone.

So Lavender Gilbert was having problems with drugs, thought Chatwyn. The athletically built thirty-four-year-old designer stood naked in front of a floor-to-ceiling plate-glass window fifty-six floors above Fifth Avenue.

Staring blankly down at the twinkling lights, he wondered: Why is Lavender Gilbert so misguided? Everything's going her way. The Star Lady contract runs twenty-six months. Then she can renegotiate or walk or have her drug rehabilitation or whatever she needs. Why does she have to run off to a hospital now? When I need her?

The answer was simple.

Cocaine. It fucked up so many people. So many careers. It was true that Chatwyn's personnel chiefs often paid photographers and stylists with coke, and they in turn gave it to models. But so what? Every fashion house did. He didn't make the rules.

To Chatwyn, doing drugs was a personal choice. Nobody forced you. Nobody held your nose down to the table.

For the zillionth time, Chatwyn was thankful he had the strength to succeed in his career without depending on coke or uppers or any of that shit.

Looking down at Manhattan stretching north, south, east,

and west, he wondered how many people out there in apartments and hotels and clubs were ruining their careers at that very moment with drugs. How many bright, talented, pushy people who had come to New York to make it big were throwing away everything on cocaine or crack?

Poor, dumb, misguided assholes. They didn't have the drive it took to make it big in New York so they had to rely on drugs. And, then, when a few did make it big at the top, they depended on drugs to stay there.

A half smile flickered on Chatwyn's face as he gazed out at the diamond-twinkling city and remembered Robin Williams's line: Cocaine is God's way of telling you that you're making too much money.

38 IN SOUTHERN CALIFORNIA, TUESDAY NIGHT'S WARM BREEZE WAFTED through an open bedroom window in Evelyn Palmer's Tudor-style house on Rexford Drive. Inside the bedroom, Adrian Lyell stood naked, except for a pair of black leather boots, in front of a mirrored wall.

Evelyn Palmer knelt on the floor in front of Adrian; she wore black satin pumps, a lace G-string, and a leather bra with cups pierced to show her nipples.

"Look at me, slut," Adrian ordered.

Evelyn raised her eyes toward the mirrored wall.

"Not the mirror, bitch. Look at *me*." He grabbed her short blond hair and held back her head so she would have to stare at him.

Working his penis with one cupped fist, Adrian glowered down at her, cautioning "You've got to start listening to me better, cunt face."

"Yes," she answered with fear flickering in her sea-green eyes; she added devotedly, "You look so beautiful."

In their ten-month relationship, Adrian and Evelyn had dispensed with the mock sadomasochistic ritual of sex partners addressing one another as "master" . . . "sir" . . . "madam." During their sessions, Adrian called Evelyn any derogatory term he chose.

Planting one foot in front of her on the champagne-color carpet, he pushed down her head, ordering "Go to work on them, bitch."

Evelyn eyed the pair of California Highway Patrolman's boots she had bought for Adrian as a welcome-to-Los Angeles gift. The tops of the black leather boots reached his midcalf. He was wearing nothing but the boots and a thick silver cock ring around the base of his penis and scrotum.

"Kiss them," he ordered.

Obediently Evelyn moved her mouth toward the boots.

Adrian toyed with his penis as he watched approvingly as Evelyn kissed, licked, and ran her cheek against the front of the round-toed boots.

Leather sex was not new for Adrian. He had participated in games of domination and submission since his bachelor days in London. In the seedy Soho district near Piccadilly Circus, Adrian had visited the prostitutes who posted small white cards in newspaper shops, using coy double entendres to advertise their specialized services: "Schoolgirl needs strong discipline" . . . "Stern teacher requires willing students" . . . "Naughty Nanette won't say no-no to a firm voice of authority" . . .

Adrian continued paying visits to the Soho "models" even after he married Jackie; he was certain she had no suspicion of his sexual forays. Their own lovemaking was lively enough at home but, inevitably, they reached a point in their passion that Jackie refused to pass: She did not enjoy suffering pain, nor did she want to see others suffer, and she refused to allow Adrian to introduce domination and submission into their relationship. His recent insistence on trying to dominate Jackie had been the beginning of the end of their sex life.

Adrian realized that, as he grew older, the cruel streak in him was getting stronger. The more frustrated he became in work, the more sadistic he became with his lovers. He was learning, too, that many American women longed for strong-handed men.

Evelyn Palmer was one of the most ardent lovers Adrian had ever met. She was also one of the most unique, insisting on equal time playing master and slave. The demand to alternate roles often frustrated Adrian, but he allowed Evelyn her way because the rewards were always so fulfilling when she was passive to him.

The touch of Evelyn's hand on Adrian's thigh brought him back to the present. Seeing her reaching longingly up to his crotch, he grabbed her by the upper arm. "Who said you could touch me?" he hissed.

He yanked her across the carpet, then sank down on the edge of the bed and shoved her across his knees. Bringing the flat of his hand down across her buttocks, he began spanking her, thinking how he would like to be using a leather paddle. Or better, a whip.

Holding her down by the neck with one hand, he increased the force of his blows as another image flashed through his brain. He saw himself wrapping a long steel chain around Roger Cooper's neck. Slowly, with relish, he pulled the chain tighter and tighter.

PART FOUR

WEDNESDAY

39 WEDNESDAY MORNING WAS GRAY, RAINY, AND MISERABLE. A STORM HAD moved in from Cape Cod shortly after midnight, bringing lightning and thunder, followed by a heavy downpour of rain. The rain had slackened in the early hours of the morning, but a slight drizzle kept the fallen leaves a soggy, slippery blanket covering the chilled ground.

Roger Cooper hesitated under the pillared stoop fronting Tanglewood's main house. He wore his old canvas fishing hat and wondered if he should go back inside to grab an umbrella. The walk to the gatehouse wasn't long, but the rain might start falling more heavily.

Wryly, Roger told himself that rain was the least of his worries. He pulled up his jacket collar and set off.

A few minutes earlier Roger had been working in his office—his mind drifting to Adrian—when front gate Security telephoned, saying that a Space Challenger courier had arrived with a letter for him and needed his signature to release it. Should the car be allowed to drive down to the main house?

Roger seized the call as an excuse to get out of the clinic. He had been working through progress and lab reports since six-thirty, and he wanted a break. The time was eight forty-five.

Hands stuffed into his jacket pockets, he walked slowly up the drive between the oaks. Their leaves had been stripped by last night's storm. Many branches were bare and twisting in dark shapes against the morning's gray sky.

Roger's thoughts returned to Adrian, how he had to have a confrontation with him, and soon, if he was to salvage any future for Tanglewood.

"Roger?"

Looking over his shoulder, he saw a flapping apparition hurrying toward him, someone in a long coat and scarf holding an open umbrella to one side like a tightrope walker.

Running toward him, Jackie called, "Wait for me. There's a letter for me, too."

She hurried to catch up with him, explaining between gulps for air, "Security told me you were walking . . . up to the gatehouse to collect a letter, too . . . so I decided to try . . . to try to catch up with you."

Roger saw that Jackie wore Adrian's old Burberry raincoat and a pair of tennis sneakers.

Reaching for her umbrella's wooden handle, he offered his arm. "Be my guest."

"How did last night's meeting go?"

"The board agreed to wait a week for Adrian to come back and answer questions himself."

"That should be interesting," she said, sliding her hand around his crooked elbow.

Arm in arm, they continued up the avenue of oaks, Roger holding the umbrella over their heads, neither of them speaking about who might have sent each a courier letter. They both had the same suspicion.

Attempting to be cheerful, Roger asked, "How you feeling after another long day at the grindstone?"

"Stiff, thank you very much."

Roger remembered his glimpse of Jackie in her exercise outfit the night before. "How did you feel after your workout?"

Pulling down her scarf, she pushed up wayward shanks of hair into an improvised topknot as she replied, "I haven't gone to Howard's class for over a month and it almost killed me."

Roger smiled. "You sound chirpy enough."

Jackie laughed. "I don't know why I should. I took a pile of work upstairs to finish over supper. I fell asleep on the couch in the middle of Renee's financial forms."

Jackie looked as attractive this morning to Roger as she had last night. Despite her sloppy raincoat and tennis sneakers, she seemed to be more feminine, less brittle than usual.

She added, "I've got a list of questions for you today."

"I hope I can answer them." Roger's thoughts shifted to the list of things he himself had to do that day. He must meet with his juniors. Report to Accounts about Management's approval of their unit cost sheets. He must not forget, either, to make an appointment with Tom Hudson to break the bad news about Cat Powers's blood tests. The surprise results added to Roger's glumness. He had discovered the shocker this morning.

Jackie interrupted his thoughts. "I'm trying not to be a nuisance by asking too many questions."

"Ask all you want. That's how you learn." He added, "I must tell you, Jackie, I'm very impressed by the way you're tackling that job. You're hanging in there."

She frowned. "I'm also making more than a few mistakes, darling."

"I have one-hundred-percent faith in you," he assured her.

"You mean that?"

"Absolutely."

"Why, thank you for the confidence, Roger. That makes my day."

Keith Wendell, the front gate security guard, stood talking with the Space Challenger courier under the shingled overhang of the gatehouse. After Roger and Jackie signed for their separate letters, Roger stuffed a ten-dollar bill into the courier's hand and followed Jackie into the small building to open his blue, silver, and gold envelope.

Roger flipped through a sheaf of Xeroxed pages. "Adrian," he murmured.

Jackie studied a near-blank sheet of paper. "Mine, too."

Neither sounded surprised. It was the threat they had both secretly expected.

Rereading the letter accompanying the stapled pages, Roger asked, "Want to hear mine?"

"If it's not too personal."

"It's very personal. But as it involves you—directly or indirectly—I think you should know."

First, he held out the stapled pages. "A copy of our partnership contract. Along with a letter reminding me please to note—"

He read, " '. . . according to paragraph seven, you must submit a counteroffer within two months to buy my half of Tanglewood or accept my offer to buy yours . . .' "

"Adrian wants to buy your half of Tanglewood?"

Roger's face was pale, his jaw working. "Yep."

"Is he offering you a fortune?"

"I'm sure it's the market value."

Jackie looked back at her own letter, reading " 'Never ending, still beginning, fighting still. Love, Adrian.' "

Puzzled, Roger waited for more.

"Dryden," she explained. "A poem I learned years ago at school and always remembered whenever the struggle got me down. But Adrian leaves out the best part."

She recited, " *'Never ending, still beginning/ Fighting still, and still destroying/ If the world be worth thy winning/ think, oh, think, it worth enjoying.'* "

Folding the letter, she muttered, "How dare that bastard misuse my poem."

"Dr. Cooper."

Roger and Jackie turned. The guard stood in the doorway.

"Sorry to bother you, but there's a policeman asking to see you, sir."

Roger and Jackie had been too involved in their letters to notice a police car stop in front of the iron gates.

A uniformed officer stepped alongside the guard. "Roger, sorry to bother you this morning."

"Kyle. Good to see you." Roger held out his hand, greeting the local policeman. "What brings you to our neck of the woods?"

Officer Kyle Sells said, "I've got somebody in the car who says you know him."

Roger looked from the ruddy-faced officer to the black-and-white police car beyond the window.

Sells explained, "We booked a guy for drunk and disorderly conduct last night at The Sandpiper and threw him into the tank to cool down. This morning, when he was sober enough to talk, he told us he's a patient here at the clinic. I wonder if you could identify him."

Roger and Jackie exchanged glances; Roger stepped to the door.

Handcuffed in the backseat of the police car sat the British politician Nigel Burden.

40 BURDEN FOLLOWED ROGER AND JACKIE DOWN THE DRIVEWAY TO THE main house, necktie unknotted around the open collar of his shirt, unshaven face turned toward the misty rain, seemingly having not a care in the world.

The threesome reached the house. Roger opened the front

door, saying to Jackie "You and I will talk later this morning."

"I'll be in the office." She passed in front of him, taking the umbrella from his hand to replace in the umbrella stand. "Was my report okay yesterday for the Huddle?"

"You're on the right track. But I need photocopies of all admission forms. I made a note of that fact. You should find it in your memo tray." He added, "Also, today's Huddle meets earlier so I'll pick up your report around twelve."

"See you then," she answered. But she did not walk away. Jackie still had a glow of confidence from the faith Roger had expressed in her. She wanted him, too, to have a word of encouragement from someone. She stepped closer to him and murmured, "You'll work out something about Adrian." Then, with a brief smile at Burden, she turned toward her office.

Roger beckoned Nigel Burden toward the door marked MEDICAL DIRECTOR. "Wait here with my secretary, please, Nigel. I'll be right with you."

After closing the door inside his inner office, he lifted the receiver to his private line and called Carlton Frazer at Stonebridge Savings and Loan.

"Sorry to bother you first thing in the morning, Carlton, but I thought you should know about the latest development out here."

Roger explained the gist of Adrian's letter offering to buy Tanglewood. He concluded, "I'll have a copy made and sent around to you right away."

"Have you spoken to Bill Ruben in New York?" Frazer asked.

"No," replied Roger. "I tried all day yesterday but he didn't return any of my calls. Now I think I understand why. The letter came from his office."

"You're going to need a lawyer to act independently for you," Frazer advised.

"I was thinking of Avery Brennan. He's retired but still has a few clients."

"Excellent choice, Roger. Brennan represented Stowe Williams in the Standard Land trouble. He's brilliant."

Roger added, "I also had the idea of flying out to L.A. to confront Adrian personally. I can find out from Ruben where he's staying."

Frazer's voice became grave. "I would suggest holding off on that, Roger. You'll have time for a confrontation. It might well be at the emergency board meeting I see I'll have to call. Adrian will be informed of it, of course. Through Ruben."

"What day will you try for, Carlton?"

"As soon as possible," the banker answered. "What's your schedule like?"

Roger laughed. "This obviously takes precedence over everything."

"I'll try to make it as soon as possible. Friday. No later than Saturday."

"All right. I'll let you know if anything else develops."

Determined to put Adrian and his purchase bid out of his mind, Roger opened his office door. "Nigel, excuse me. Come in now please." His adrenaline was pumping but he told himself that he had a clinic to run and patients to care for.

When the British politician was seated, Roger said, "Your son and daughter-in-law arrived here yesterday, right?"

"I have two guests, yes," Burden confirmed.

"Your son and daughter-in-law?"

"Whatever," Burden said dismissively.

Roger pressed the intercom button. "Caroline, buzz Mr. Burden's suite. Tell his family that he's with me in my office. Ask them please to join us."

To Burden, Roger said casually, "Want some coffee? Tea?" He pulled off his jacket.

"No, thank you," Burden said, then added, "I like your

style, Cooper. You don't make me feel like a schoolboy who's sneaked into town to get drunk."

Roger leaned back in his chair. "Because you're not a schoolboy. You're a sick man. With a serious drinking problem."

Burden nodded. "I appreciate your honesty."

"Cures depend on honesty, Nigel. A man's honesty with himself. *If* he wants to stop drinking."

"Oh, I have the desire. But I'm not alone in my decision."

"Explain that."

"That's the rub, Cooper. I can't explain. I can't talk about my problem. You see, it involves more than myself."

Roger could buzz Betty Lassiter's office for Burden's encounter group file, to see what he had said over the past week in the Sweat Room about not being able to discuss his drinking. But something told Roger that now would be the wrong time to disturb this interview.

Burden looked at his hands. "You see, it involves my son . . ." He paused.

"Go on," said Roger.

The intercom buzzed.

Damn it. Roger pressed the button.

Caroline announced, "The Burdens are here, Doctor."

Roger looked at Burden. "Shall I ask them to wait?"

Burden sighed. "No. It will be simpler than my explaining."

"Send them in," Roger said into the intercom. He rose as the door opened and two women entered the office.

Burden sprang to his feet. He stabbed one finger toward the taller woman. "*This*, Dr. Cooper, is my son."

Cyril Burden, dressed in a paisley skirt and matching shawl, ignored the introduction and faced his father. Irritably he demanded, "What happened to you last night? We were worried sick."

Trisha Burden said, "The important thing is that you're safe."

"One can rely on you, Trisha, to be so understanding," Burden snapped sarcastically.

Roger stood back from the confrontation, shocked by the fast exchange of hostilities, the inexplicable fact that Burden's son was wearing women's clothing.

Trisha Burden asked her father-in-law, "Where did you go last night, Nigel? Out somewhere to look for courage in a bottle?"

"It was better than looking at fruit in my sitting room!"

She said cattily, "One can rely on you, Nigel, to be so predictable."

Nigel Burden turned to Roger. "Here before you is part of the reason why I can't stop drinking. These two. My shining heir and his charming wife."

Roger made the most of the rancorous introduction. He shook hands with the couple, deciding he would wait for an explanation for the younger Burden's costume.

He addressed Burden Senior. "You say 'part' of the reason, Nigel. What's the other part?"

"Blackmail." Burden glowered at his son. "*He* swans around stores, the opera, the theater, God-knows-what places, dressed like this. Finally some chap followed him and took a few pictures. He sent them to me, demanding twenty thousand quid."

Trisha interrupted. "Have you ever considered, Nigel, that your problem might not be the blackmail but your coming to terms with Joan?"

"Sod Joan!"

Trisha explained to Roger. "Dr. Cooper, my husband feels there's a personality inside him trying to emerge. Her name's Joan. Nigel can't accept this fact."

Burden bellowed, "I'm being blackmailed for twenty thousand quid because of bloody 'Joan.' *Blackmailed!*"

"Dr. Cooper, may I speak?" asked Cyril, hands folded across the knotted paisley shawl. "Trisha and I begged my father to go to the police with the blackmail demand. We have nothing to hide. We believe our careers can withstand any adverse publicity."

"What about *my* career?" snapped Burden.

Trisha sneered. "You know you don't have a constituency at the moment, Nigel. What kind of seat can you hope to win in Parliament if you continue this drinking of yours?"

Roger saw the time had come to pull them apart.

"You three have obviously had this argument before," he said.

"Too many times." Burden sighed. "I'm sick and tired of these two."

"Then perhaps we should speak separately." Roger gestured to the chair. "Nigel, why don't you sit quietly here while I go down the hall with your family?"

"Splendid idea!" Burden sank back down on the chair. "I'll tell you right now, I'm not going anywhere with those two. Not even to the airport."

He looked at Roger. "I confess. It was my idea that they come here. I thought we should spend at least a short time together as they were going to be in the States. But I had no idea he would be arriving in . . . *costume!*"

Trisha sniped, "Nor did we suspect you'd still be so badly off."

Burden ignored her. "I'll stay right here at Tanglewood. Let them go merrily on their way as they should've done in the first place. I'll get on with my own life."

"Bravo for you," Trisha complimented. "Smashing idea. The wisest thing you could do is stay in treatment, Nigel, and get to the real root of your problem."

Burden closed his eyes. "Oh, piss off, you wretched do-gooder."

Roger eased the young Burdens from the room, calling to his secretary "Caroline, can you get some coffee for Mr. Burden?"

Continuing across the outer office, he caught sight of the clock on the wall. It was nearly ten-thirty. One hour had already elapsed of the time in which he had either to raise nine million dollars to buy Adrian's share of Tanglewood or sell his own half of the clinic.

Nigel Burden sat alone in Roger Cooper's office and reflected how a combination of problems had contributed to his drinking.

The first person to recognize his drinking as a grave illness had been his wife, Diana.

Stumbling as he walked. Never home in time for meals. The constant need to decline social invitations for fear of how he would act. Time with family and friends ruined by insulting behavior.

A tall woman with silver hair and a patrician manner, Diana Burden had told her husband, "Nigel, I think the sooner you admit you're an alcoholic, the sooner you'll lance the boil and be on the way to healing it."

Burden had admitted to his wife that, yes, he might possibly have an alcohol problem, but he continued to drink. However, drinking was no longer so enjoyable after Diana had spoken to him. Every time he lifted a glass, he asked himself, "Am I really a sick man? Does each swallow make it worse?"

Alcoholism and being a member of Parliament went hand in hand for Nigel Burden. On his arrival at the House, Burden collected his mail at the Members' Post Office and went immediately to the Smoking Room to look for the day's drinking companion. If nobody agreeable was lounging there in one of the brown leather chairs, he ambled down the hall to the Members' Dining Room and took a place at the center table, a sure spot to find a companionable drinking crony amid the Tory backbenchers.

Diana Burden hovered close by her husband during his campaign for reelection in Sussex, making certain he accepted no alcoholic drinks, attentively listening to his conversation if she knew he had been drinking before they had left home.

But Labour's sweeping victory over the Tories in the spring election also cost Nigel his seat. More important, gone were all his chances to be selected for a Conservative Prime Minister's cabinet.

Determined to accept disappointment without drowning himself in Bombay gin, Burden threw himself into work at North Sea Investment, the City merchant bank where he held a partnership. But then arrived the photographs of Cyril.

Burden did not inform Diana about the initial blackmail demands. He also tried to keep from her the fact that he was drinking heavily. Through alcohol, he was trying to find courage to face his fears of being made a laughingstock by the gutter press, having scandal hurled at the family.

Full of guilt, Burden followed an established pattern of many alcoholics. He sneaked drinks. He hid bottles. He surreptitiously added alcohol to his glass. He always ordered doubles in a bar.

Nigel entered Harley Street Clinic when he began vomiting blood. Fearing an ulcer, he was astounded when the surgeon told him his acute gastritis was as severe as that of a Soho derelict dependent on rot-gut wine.

A fire crackled in the Adam-style hearth of Burden's London home on the night that Diana Burden spelled out Nigel's choices.

"You can go to Alcoholics Anonymous. You can seek private help. You can try—as people say—to go 'cold turkey.' You can kill somebody in a car accident and be sent to prison. Or you can continue drinking and kill yourself in the process. Now which is it going to be, Nigel?"

Alone in Roger Cooper's office, Burden wondered if he had the strength to spend more time at Tanglewood. Considering the question, Burden asked himself if his priorities had been wrong all along for coming here. Shouldn't he be breaking his habit not because of Cyril and Trisha but for himself and Diana? It was for *their* future he wanted to live.

In any case, he would rather face another month at Tanglewood than three hours cooped up in a car with Trisha and "Joan."

41 SEATED BEHIND THE BULKY DESK IN ADMINISTRATION, JACKIE LYELL sorted through the photocopies she had made for Roger for today's Huddle. It was impossible not to think about the courier letters Adrian had sent them. The more she thought about Adrian's offer to buy Roger's half of Tanglewood, the more inevitable, in retrospect, the move seemed.

Adrian was gifted at managing money. Roger was the medical talent. Adrian intended that this, the strength of their partnership, should become the tool for its dissolution.

But would it?

Roger had appeared surprised, but not crestfallen, at the letter. Adrian's gibe that Roger had a marshmallow center might be wrong. Maybe Roger would surprise Adrian as a businessman.

Jackie remembered how stoically Roger had received the news of the purchase offer. She could understand why women were so attracted to him. He displayed a very real confidence—low-key, but no less potent for all that.

Next, Jackie considered Adrian's letter to her. What about that presumptuous little note?

If Adrian had had any feelings for her at all, he would not have sent her a letter by courier. He would have telephoned her. Explained why he had gone to California, what he planned to do about Tanglewood, asking for her trust and understanding. But he hadn't. The most contemptible thing about this morning's letter, though, was that Adrian had totally ignored her place at Tanglewood, merely patting her on the head like a pet dog, saying "There, there, old girl," and tossing her a bone of poetry.

Perhaps he didn't love her any more—or she him. She must learn to accept that time marches on, people change, et cetera.

But when Adrian turned a blind eye to the years she had spent encouraging him, worrying for him, nursing him through Tanglewood's conception and budding—when he decided to deny her an even teensy-weensy little voice in its future, that meant war.

The telephone rang.

Jackie snatched for the receiver, the British Army on the march.

Rita Zambetti said from the switchboard, "Mrs. Lyell, Chatwyn's on the line from New York. He wants to speak to the patient Lavender Gilbert."

"The designer Chatwyn?"

"He just said 'Chatwyn,' Mrs. Lyell."

Jackie remembered that Lavender was due to be Chatwyn's Star Lady at the Waldorf on Friday—the day after tomorrow. She recalled, too, that Tanglewood's lawyer still had not returned her call about the clinic's legal position should there be a dispute about Lavender not honoring her contract with the New York designer.

She said, "Put him through."

Chatwyn's voice sounded warm, touched with a masculine note of concern. He began, "Mrs. Lyell, I've heard that one of my girls is at Tanglewood. I'm very worried about her and want to know if there's anything I can do to make her stay with you easier."

The offer took Jackie by surprise. Chatwyn did not sound like the awful ogre that Bev Jordan had painted him to be.

"How nice of you to show your interest," she replied guardedly, still ashamed of the dreadful blunder she had made the day before yesterday by saying too much on the telephone to the journalist who had called about Peabo and Karen Washington.

Chatwyn continued. "I know these cures can really screw up a person's head. I just want Lavender to rest assured that her place with me will be waiting when she gets out."

Jackie breathed more easily. She knew that Chatwyn's support might swing Lavender's decision to stay at Tangle-wood for treatment.

"It's very considerate of you to let her know," she said. "People do get paranoiac."

Chatwyn added, "Perhaps it would help if I told Lavender myself that she has nothing to worry about."

"A word from you might be just the boost she needs." Jackie looked at the extension numbers listed alongside her telephone. "If you will hang on, I'll see if she's in her room."

Jackie was impressed that a busy man like Chatwyn should spare time from his day to encourage a young model. It made her feel a little more kindly toward the business world.

She dialed Lavender's suite.

CHATWYN: We've been so worried about you.

LAVENDER: Chatwyn?

CHATWYN: Who else? I heard last night you're at Tan-glewood and I want to know if there's anything you need.

LAVENDER: You aren't . . . mad at me?

CHATWYN: Why should I be mad? But you should have told us where you were going. We've been running around looking for you. So what if we now have to terminate your Star Lady contract? That doesn't affect our feeling of friendship for you. Our con-cern for your health.

LAVENDER: You're going to . . . terminate my con-tract?

CHATWYN: Friday's show still's got to go on.

LAVENDER: What about when I come out?

CHATWYN: I can't cancel the opening or hold back the campaign, waiting for whenever that might be, Lavender.

LAVENDER: No. But . . .

CHATWYN: In fact, I've got to get off the phone now because Monica's sending a new girl around from the agency to replace you on Friday. She's fabulous. Chiseled features. A neck like a swan. Hair to die for. I just wanted to call you and say "hi" and wish you good luck in whatever you decide to do next.

LAVENDER: But I want to be Star Lady.

CHATWYN: And I want you. But it's a little late for that now.

LAVENDER: No, it's not.

CHATWYN: Well, for starters, you're there and we're here.

LAVENDER: But I can be there.

CHATWYN: Aren't there a few complications, Lavender?

LAVENDER: Like what?

CHATWYN: Like you're checked into Tanglewood.

LAVENDER: No, I'm not. Not officially. And even if I was I can check myself out.

CHATWYN: No. I don't think that's a very good idea, Lavender.

LAVENDER: I can leave whenever I want. And I'm going to do it. Right now.

CHATWYN: I guess I *could* send a car for you. But you'd have to check out of that place right away, this morning. The car would be there by one, two o'clock.

LAVENDER: I'll be ready.

CHATWYN: You're sure, Lavender? This new girl can
           step into your shoes. Literally. Everything
           fits her like a dream. She's a younger ver-
           sion of you.
LAVENDER: I'll be ready when the car gets here.

42 LAVENDER STOOD IN HER ROOM, MIND
RACING, HEART BEATING, THE INSIDE
of her head feeling as if it were made out of tin and somebody was hammering it with a spoon.

She had to get back to New York.

Relieved that she had put off formally admitting herself
for treatment, she wondered if she would have a hard time
getting out of the clinic. Would Roger Cooper and the
nurses argue for her to stay?

She remembered the faces of the cocaine victims Roger
had shown her on the monitor. Thinking about Chatwyn
cancelling her Star Lady contract, she next imagined that
she might have to return home to Iowa, a failure, somebody
who hadn't been able to make it in New York. She flashed
on herself twenty years from now, living exactly like her
parents, complaining that life had passed her by.

She had to get to New York, she decided. The important
thing at the moment was to salvage her career. There would
be plenty of time later to worry about drugs.

As she looked around the room for belongings she could
pack, Lavender reconsidered her conversation with Chatwyn.

What if he turns out really to like that new girl the agency's sending around to replace me? What if he decides he doesn't need me and changes his mind about sending the car to Tanglewood? I'm stuck here.

She couldn't depend on Chatwyn to send a car for her, she decided. She had to find her own way back to New York, and quick. Only she and she alone could truly watch out for her future.

She moved to the closet and reached for the luggage on the high shelf.

Thinking of the confrontation she might have with Roger Cooper and the nurses if they were to see her leaving Tanglewood with a suitcase, she looked down at the clothes she was wearing—pink track suit, a pair of silver Nike running shoes.

She glanced at the dressing table, knowing there was money inside her purse. A few dollars. Enough for a train ticket back to New York.

She didn't need a suitcase. Her career was more important than these few clothes. She would leave them.

Outside Lavender's room, the coast was clear.

Raising three magazines above one shoulder, she called to checkpoint at the end of the hall, "Going downstairs to get something new to read."

A voice answered, "Don't forget, honey, Dr. Cooper wants to see you at twelve."

"I know," she said. Dr. Cooper was expecting her decision about whether she'd be staying at Tanglewood.

But Lavender was convinced she was doing the right thing by going back to New York. She bounded down the stairs, reminding herself that she had done pretty well in the last couple of days without cocaine. She had been nervous and high-strung, yes, but she hadn't gone screaming mad without drugs. She told herself she could cope with her drug habit when she got back to New York. After the Star Lady launch.

At the bottom of the stairs she passed a white-jacketed

attendant escorting a woman wearing a Tanglewood robe. "Morning," she said politely and continued toward the foyer.

As she dropped the magazines onto the tapestry chair by the front door, she glanced at the brass umbrella stand and remembered the morning's showers. She wondered if she should take an umbrella.

Opening the door, she saw the rain wasn't too heavy. She forgot about umbrellas and quickly stepped outside.

She pulled the door shut behind her and told herself to act natural, to amble across the driveway as if she were out for a harmless stroll.

Out of sight of the main house, she scrambled over a fieldstone wall, hopping and lurching through wet grass in an apple orchard as she headed in the direction of the highway.

When she reached the paved road, she saw a car speed past her and had another idea. Instead of waiting for a train to leave for New York, why not hitchhike? Another car came into view. Lavender stuck out her thumb and flashed her best girl-next-door smile.

43 ADRIAN LYELL CHECKED HIS TIE IN THE MIRROR FACING THE SIDE TABLE where he sat in the fashionable West Hollywood restaurant, L.A. Mood. He was waiting for Pegasus Chemical chairman, Paul Huttner, to arrive for their one o'clock lunch.

Ordering a second gin and tonic, Adrian looked back to his watch: 1:45. He presumed that in southern California business executives, as well as film stars, liked making late entrances.

Adrian's mind returned to his plan.

Everything was falling into place. Roger should have received the purchase offer by now. He would scream and moan at first about selling his share of the clinic, but when the complaining died down, they could proceed with the negotiations.

Adrian rechecked his watch.

Two o'clock.

He began to be impatient for Huttner's arrival. As he sat twisting the signet ring on his small finger, he caught the eye of an attractive blonde at a nearby table. *Does that woman think she knows me, or did she see me on TV yesterday?*

He might not be a Hollywood superstar, but the ladies of Tinsel Town fancied him rotten. The elegant features. The Huntsman suit. The St. James's tie. Hair combed back from his forehead with a little ruff at the nape of his neck à la Trumpers, the London gentlemen's barber in Curzon Street. And, quite simply, an aura of money and success. In L.A., there was no bigger turn-on.

He took another sip of the gin and tonic and mused about Jackie. He was glad he had taken time to send her the snippet of poetry. He had to coddle her for the moment. He knew he was making the right decision by keeping her a permanent fixture in his life. She had good breeding without being stuffy; the right accent; smart clothes sense; a ready line of chit-chat for parties while still being a long-suffering listener. She was quality set dressing.

It was good having a wife you could confide in, Adrian knew. But it was better having one like Jackie to whom you didn't have to explain a damn thing. Adrian told himself he must stop being so critical of Jackie, not let her know he was finding her old hat, in fact, damned tedious—especially in the sack. But he couldn't afford to let her revolt. Not at the moment. Bad image.

The thought of lovemaking reminded him of Evelyn. She

really knew how to give him what he wanted. Evelyn, too, kept his dick as hard as a seventeen-year-old farm boy's. No worry about going soft in middle age with Evelyn nearby. The perfect playmate.

He rechecked the time: 2:25.

He decided to give Huttner's office a call to find out what had happened to him.

Adrian pushed back his chair.

As he turned, he faced the last person in the world he wanted to see.

Adrian looked from Sackville West to the high-cheeked young woman on the hairdresser's arm. He recognized her immediately from magazine photographs as Sackville's new Tahitian wife.

Affecting a big smile, he held out his hand. "Good to see you, old man."

Sackville ignored Adrian's proffered handshake and said dryly, "I thought it was you sitting all by yourself over here in Siberia."

Adrian glared at Sackville, but before he had a chance to reply, the hairdresser took his wife's arm and walked away. Sackville called over his shoulder, "If the person you're waiting for ever shows up, Adrian, try the salmon. You'll like it. It's fishy."

Adrian, still standing by his table, did not see Paul Huttner entering the restaurant.

"Sorry I'm late," said Huttner.

Adrian was twisting the signet ring, his lips pressed into a thin line. He forced himself to turn politely to Huttner. "No problem. I just ran into an old friend."

Huttner took a long gulp of his vodka and apologized again for being late. "I was on a conference call with Nolan and Demetrious."

The mention of his other two partners brought Adrian's attention back to Tanglewood and the purpose of the day's lunch. Reaching for a plump green olive in a small dish, he asked, "How's everything with them?"

"They agree with me on one point."

Adrian chewed the green olive slowly, surprised to find a big pit at its center.

"Roger Cooper's got to go," Huttner said.

Adrian spit the pit into the palm of his hand and dumped it into the ashtray. He did not understand. "Go?"

"I know it's in your contract that Cooper can stay at Tanglewood in a minor capacity if he accepts your offer. But we decided it'd be better with him out of the picture completely."

Adrian studied the square-featured executive in the Ivy League suit. "I shouldn't worry about that. Roger won't want to stay."

"You never know. That *Time* article changes everything, doesn't it? The piece focuses on Cooper. Throws attention on Tanglewood as a medical clinic. With him gone, it'll be a hell of a lot easier for us to change the image." Huttner took a deep drink. "That's our stipulation, Adrian. We don't step in till your situation with Cooper is resolved. Completely."

"There's nothing to resolve."

"To our way of thinking there is." Huttner insisted, "Either you make sure Roger Cooper takes the money and runs or—" He pointed a thick finger at Adrian. "—*you* get paid off by him and *you* leave . . . and we all call it a day."

Adrian's voice was low, his eyes on the table. "Even if he wanted to stay, Roger would never be able to raise the money."

"Then you've got nothing to worry about. Except to get him out of there as soon as possible. Have you talked to him recently?"

"Not since he received my offer," answered Adrian, considering the complications this sudden demand could make. Damn it.

"Talk to him," Huttner insisted. "Hear his reaction to it. You might have to add a little sweetener now to get him out of there. Bonus cash or removal benefits. But do it. Then we can sit down and finalize our own agreement."

"Very well. I'll take care of Cooper." Adrian twisted his gold signet ring. Once more he saw the image of Roger with a chain around his neck. It was time to pull the chain tighter.

In Beverly Hills, Evelyn Palmer lounged alongside her swimming pool, surrounded by small iron tables holding sun lotions, magazines, a cordless telephone, and bottles of Evian water. When Adrian Lyell was in town, Evelyn cancelled all lunches with her girl friends to keep herself at his beck and call. Today she was waiting for him to come home from his lunch with Paul Huttner and discuss how he wanted to progress with his press image.

Hearing the French door open across the white-bricked patio, Evelyn looked up from the trade paper of the entertainment industry she had been leafing through.

Seeing it was him returning from lunch, she waved the glossy tabloid at him, calling "Look! You're in the gossip columns again today!"

Adrian's dark mood had not lifted.

After leaving the West Hollywood restaurant, he had ordered the driver of his hired limousine to drive slowly through Beverly Hills as he collected his thoughts.

He knew it might not be easy to get rid of Roger, as his new partners were now insisting. What if one of Roger's stipulations was that he'd sell his half of Tanglewood only on the condition that he remained as a consultant?

Originally Adrian had not been troubled by the idea of Roger staying on at Tanglewood. In fact, such an arrangement would have perversely pleased him. He would have a chance to beat Roger into the ground, to pay him back for all the years he had played the bright, young, high-and-mighty medical director. Who would have predicted that Huttner, Demetrious, and Nolan would want Roger out of Tanglewood more than he himself did?

There had to be a way to insure that the bastard sold his partnership and cleared out of Connecticut. But Adrian would have to find it quickly.

Adrian was unable to show much enthusiasm to Evelyn's mention of the gossip column item.

Crossing the bricked area to her chaise longue, he asked without interest, "What is it?"

Evelyn handed *The Hollywood Score* to Adrian. "There's a bit in Taxis Mariachi's column about Cat Powers checking into Tanglewood for a cure," she said "It says she's taken Gene Stone with her."

"Gene Stone?" Adrian considered the name, trying to recall how he knew that name.

"You know," Evelyn said. "Hollywood's chicest Dr. Feelgood."

"That's right." Adrian recalled something Roger Cooper had said about Gene Stone and how they had been young doctors together out here somewhere in California.

His interest increasing, Adrian asked, "What does it say? Stone is staying at Tanglewood?"

Evelyn waved toward the daily. "According to the Bible."

Adrian's first thought was that maybe his good luck had not deserted him after all. The details of Roger and Stone's unpleasant history were coming back to him.

"Tell me about Stone," he said, pulling up a chair to Evelyn's chaise longue.

She scooted up higher on the pink canvas cushions. "I've seen him around. I always thought he was kind of a flake. But who knows? If he's with Cat Powers, he must be hung like a—" She touched her lower thigh.

Adrian's idea became more of a temptation and he reached for the telephone.

"Who're you calling?" Evelyn asked.

Adrian shook his head, punching a New York number into the phone. He waited for an answer, finally saying into the receiver, "Adrian Lyell calling from Los Angeles for Mr. Ruben please."

When Tanglewood's New York lawyer, William Ruben, came onto the line, Adrian sat to the edge of his chair. With renewed enthusiasm in his voice, he asked, "Bill, did you get that purchase offer sent off to Roger? . . . Good. . . . Now, there's another thing I need you to do for me, Bill. In Roger's and my contract, there's a morals clause. . . . We had to put it in to satisfy federal guidelines on drug supplies. It's also a safeguard against disreputable conduct. . . . Bill, I want you to go over that clause very, very carefully. . . . We'll discuss it in detail tomorrow. . . . I've decided to fly back to New York tonight."

He lowered the phone, smiling.

Evelyn asked, surprised, "New York? Tonight?"

"Something's come up."

She eyed him suspiciously. "Why am I thinking you're up to no good, you naughty boy?"

A half smile on his lips, Adrian said, "You just lie there and look sexy while you tell me everything you know about Dr. Gene Stone."

44 AT TANGLEWOOD, THE FOUL WEATHER KEPT SOME PATIENTS IN-doors. Others, ignoring the rain, took their daily outings in the fresh air.

Male attendants Reg Walker and Art Bailey stood out of the rain under the gazebo's overhanging eaves, watching Ray Esposito following the flagstone path that edged the rose garden, skirt the jardinières flanking the lily pond, pace the length of the pool house. Since yesterday's cautionary warning had been posted on Esposito, attendants accompanied him in pairs; nurses visited him in tandem.

Esposito, head bent forward, walked with both hands stuffed into the pockets of his raincoat, one cupped fist working through the torn lining, masturbating himself as he kept his back to the attendants.

Inside Esposito's head, he was picturing a wide-hipped wife as he masturbated, remembering how he had beaten her for always looking at him, always waiting for him to make a pass at her, always wanting him to make love to her.

Across the garden from Esposito, Lillian Weiss held an umbrella over her head and pretended to be taking deep breaths of fresh air. In a few minutes she had to attend her first group therapy session. But she lingered on the walkway, watching her new dream man.

Was it her imagination, or was Esposito moving his hand back and forth under his raincoat?

The idea that the sexy construction worker might be masturbating as he walked in the garden thrilled Lillian. She cursed the two attendants for loitering nearby. Why were they hovering around Esposito so closely? Drat! When could she catch him alone to make a date?

Tom Hudson forgot about the gloomy weather when he got the phone call with good news from Florida. The fast food chain, Sunbakers, had agreed to sell to Red Tag Stores.

Eager to fly down to Miami the next day to close the deal personally with Sunbakers' president, Hudson put down the phone in Communications and asked to be connected to Roger Cooper's office. He wanted to tell Cooper he'd be leaving Cat here alone for a few days.

Roger's secretary answered the first buzz.

"Tom Hudson here. Doc Cooper in?"

"Sorry, Mr. Hudson. Dr. Cooper's in a meeting. But he's been trying to contact you. He wants to know if you can join him for dinner tonight. The dining room. Eight o'clock. Just the two of you."

"Tell him I'll be there."

Hudson put down the receiver, wondering: Now why in hell does Cooper want to have dinner alone with me? What's up?

Thinking of Roger, he remembered the tempting business idea he had entertained last night about investing in Tanglewood or a place like it. But now, with Red Tag buying Sunbakers, the idea was out of the question. Too bad. A clinic like Tanglewood would have certainly been a sound venture. Especially with Roger Cooper as the brains behind it.

In the basement of the main house, Chief of Security Leo Kemp studied the camera image of Ray Esposito walking alone in the garden as two attendants lingered nearby.

Kemp turned rows of knobs and flipped switches but the alert remained silent. He wasn't picking up any reading from Esposito's body heat. The system had not even registered movement in the garden when Lillian Weiss had been standing on the walkway with her umbrella. Weiss's body heat generally set off all the sensors. But now, today, nothing. Damn this temperamental equipment, Kemp grumbled. Had the rain short-circuited the infrared system?

45 ON THAT GRAY, RAINY WEDNES-
DAY AFTERNOON, PSYCHOTHERAPIST
Betty Lassiter convened Tanglewood's advanced encounter
group at one end of the arboretum. The lush ferns hanging
from its glass ceiling and gracious palm trees placed around
the red brick floor helped cheer the bleak day.

Presiding at a round table, Betty listened with five patients
as the sixth member of the group, nineteen-year-old Skip
Ryan, spoke about angel dust.

"The real name for angel dust is PCP. Phencyclidine. I
read up on it when I first began smoking and learned that
Parke-Davis began making PCP back in the fifties as an
anesthetic."

"It must be nice being a rich kid," David Terranova wise-
cracked. "Lying around your Newport estate. Doing research on what drugs to drop."

Terranova was a New York playwright, thirty-seven
years old, alcoholic, burnt-out, currently the most cynical,
sharp-tongued member of the group. Like most of Betty's
other patients, Terranova was also at the final stage in treatment.

Over the past week, Betty had noted a curious relationship
developing between David Terranova and Skip Ryan. Re-
clusive, nineteen-year-old Skip seemed almost to hero-wor-
ship the abrasive New York playwright. He never took
offense at Terranova's sharp remarks about the Ryan family,
their reputed millions, even gibes at Skip's controversial

father, Jimmy Ryan, the former President of the United States. What was the attraction? Was young Skip in awe of the playwright because of his secret ambition to be a writer himself?

Betty was proud of Skip's progress; there had been no need for more "handholding" since last Sunday. But he still refused to let her read his journal. How could she break through that wall?

Skip continued, "As I was saying, Parke-Davis first made PCP back in the fifties. They tested it on humans but quickly decided it was safer on animals. Now, legal PCP is used on horses and elephants and grizzly bears out west in Yellowstone Park. The stuff you buy on the street is stirred up in somebody's bathtub. You take it in tablets, or inject it. Me, I spread it on joints."

"What's the effect?" asked Dieter Biddlehof, the towheaded art dealer from Amsterdam whose wife had committed him to Tanglewood for a heroin cure.

Skip shrugged. "Angel dust acts a lot like grass. You feel weightless. You become disoriented. Your eyes do funny things. You think you can *hear* colors. *See* sounds."

"You make it sound enjoyable," said Biddlehof. "Why did you stop?"

"For one reason—" Skip hesitated, searching for the right words. "Dust took me places grass doesn't go. Panic places. Through little trapdoors into dark attic rooms. Down into spooky deep cellars. Sometimes you think you're never going to escape. Lots of people don't. You know, more people flip out on angel dust than acid. It's classed as a hallucinogen. Like LSD and MDA. But it's way-y-y more unpredictable."

Skip was speaking fluently now, caught up in his explanation. He continued. "When you come down from a high, you really crash. Sometimes it takes more than a day to land. Dust also repeats on you. Crystals linger in your system. You often get, you know, a druggy *déjà vu*. You might think you're straight but you're not. You can be walking down the street, looking into store windows, feeling really normal, and then wham, the dust hits you and you suddenly start tripping. It's scary, man."

Terranova said, "You're almost intelligent when you talk about dust, Skip. Not the preppy airhead you usually are. Or maybe you're not just a snotty airhead after all. Maybe you put on the act for us *common* Americans. Do you look down on us, Skip? Be honest."

Skip picked at a cuticle on one finger, agreeing "Okay, maybe I do have attitude. But maybe a lot of my attitude stems from dust."

To the rest of the group, he continued. "Dust puts you in a world all your own. You *do* look down on things. On everything. You're never part of the world around you. You're always above it. Literally."

Betty Lassiter thought: *Good for you, Skip. Good answer to such a bitchy question.*

Biddlehof asked, "Why did you give up? Why come to Tanglewood?"

"Dust was beginning to control me. Not the other way around like it should be. I was cutting classes. I didn't date. I had no ambitions. I just thought about dust, dust, dust. I lived for it.

"I was rolling my joints thicker and thicker. Making them stronger. When a gram used to make a hundred joints or so, it began making ninety. Then eighty. Then seventy-five. I was smoking, six, eight times a day.

"But what really freaked me out was when I lost four days out of one week. Four whole *days*. Wow! They just disappeared, and that's scary, man. I floated through four days with no memory at all of what happened. Like I could have been killed or dropped dead."

Terranova reminded him sarcastically, "Just like your cousin, Tommy Ryan, did down in St. Bart's last year, right?"

"Yeah. Tommy did dust, too."

" 'Yes, Tommy did dust, too'," Terranova mimicked in a

New England lock-jaw drawl. "How do you feel when the *National Enquirer* ran pictures on Tommy's funeral? And about you getting busted in Chinatown last year?"

Skip tried to be lighthearted. "Yeah, okay. So I'd rather read about myself in *The New Yorker.*"

"Oh, *The New Yorker.* We read *The New Yorker,* do we?" Terranova sneered. "Do you just read the cartoons or what?"

"Actually, I read some of the profiles. In fact, I've even once sent in one of my own. On my English Lit professor."

"A writer? Little Skippie's a writer! Ho-ho-ho-ho!" teased Terranova.

Skip's ears burned red.

Lillian Weiss snapped at Terranova from across the table, "Do you always act like everybody's critic and conscience, mister?"

Terranova glared at the group's newest member. "And don't you ever wash your cunt, lady?"

A hush fell over the round table.

Lillian pulled herself high on her chair. "I beg your pardon!"

"You stink." Terranova curled his upper lip with disgust. "Go away and don't come back till you take a good bath."

Lillian retorted, "You are a very rude man."

Terranova welcomed the challenge. "Why are you here, lady? You've been quiet all morning. So what's your problem. Booze? Pills? Smack? No. It's none of those things, is it? It's food. You can't say no to Sara Lee cheese cake. Famous Amos chocolate chip cookies. Häagen-Dazs ice cream . . ."

Betty interrupted. "David, if you're going to ask our newcomer a question, at least let her answer."

Terranova turned to the psychotherapist, who was wearing her usual jeans and sloppy lumberjack shirt. "What is this? Time for the Fatties of the World to unite?"

Marianne Turnbull, the Westchester housewife, asked,

"David, what do you have against women? You always go for such negative things."

Betty looked at her watch. At last, momentum seemed to be picking up. Betty had blamed everybody's sluggishness on the wet, dreary weather. Better progress was always made when people argued. Hostility broke down defenses. People got to the truth about each other when they felt aggressive and mean.

Across the bricked floor of the arboretum, Roger Cooper approached the group. "Sorry to disturb your good time, guys," he called.

"You're always welcome," Betty replied jovially. "Pull up a chair."

Roger said, "I'm bringing back somebody who decided to spend a few more days with us."

Behind him, Nigel Burden sheepishly entered the room.

46 IT WAS 3:20 P.M. IN SECURITY'S BASEMENT OFFICE, LEO KEMP WAS STILL watching replays from outdoor scanner cameras 7, 8, and 9.

The wiry ex-police detective from Boston had learned two hours ago that Lavender Gilbert was missing from the clinic. Kemp had been interviewing third-floor checkpoint about the model when he received word from Communications that Stonebridge police had driven another patient—Nigel Burden—back to Tanglewood after he had spent a night drinking in town.

Two disappearances in twenty-four hours. And Security

hadn't heard about the first until four hours after the local police had brought back the guy. Leo wondered if his worst fears had come true. It was hard to believe a few drops of rain had knocked out the entire heat alarm system. But there was no doubt that two patients had waltzed through their expensive surveillance.

So far, the brass upstairs had not started complaining. But Kemp was worried and more than a little embarrassed.

Kemp heard the office door open behind him. Turning from the video screen, he saw his twenty-two-year-old assistant, Calvin Curtis, soaked from the rain.

Curtis shed his canvas parka and cap and moved across the office to the coffeemaker, reporting "Keith and I searched the garages, the pool house, and all the outbuildings. No sign of her."

"Did you search the back woods?" asked Kemp, his eyes back on the screen playing the tapes of the front property.

"With a fine-tooth comb. That's how I got so wet. All that underbrush."

Curtis held out a mug that said *Make My Day*. "Coffee?"

Kemp declined with a grunt. "You didn't tell anybody? No patients? No unauthorized staff?"

"Not a soul."

"Good. Apart from making us look like a horse's ass, if word gets around that somebody's disappeared, patients start to worry. They whisper. They spread stories. Rumors get started. They're paranoid enough in their cures without us adding to their problems."

Curtis nodded at the monitor. "You spot anything?"

Kemp froze the video. He removed his aviator glasses and rubbed his tired eyes as he muttered, "Three squirrels. Old Luther Brown gathering leaves. The young gardener, Colman, taking a leak against a maple tree."

He shook his head. "I doubt if the broad's around here. I think she's taken a hike."

"Drugs do screwy things to your head." Curtis sipped at

his coffee. "I guess there's nothing to do but call the State Patrol."

"Mrs. Lyell took care of that in Administration."

"*Mrs.* Lyell?" The boy smiled. Like all clinic staff, Calvin Curtis was fond of the gregarious Englishwoman. "I hope her old man never comes back."

Kemp frowned. "Maybe we better invite her to come down here and straighten us out."

Looking around him at video screens, rows of red, yellow, and white lights, computer hookups, room-to-room surveillance links, he said dejectedly, "More than a cool million in equipment and two people slip through our hands." He held up his fore and middle fingers. "Two people!"

"Don't take it so personally," urged Curtis. "The sensors just went on the fritz. It's not your fault."

"What about Burden?" Kemp demanded. "He strolled calmly up the driveway!"

The phone alongside him rang.

He answered, "Security. Kemp here."

His face brightened.

To Curtis, he repeated the news. "It's front gate. . . . A limo's just pulled up. . . . The driver claims he's been sent to drive Lavender Gilbert back to New York."

Swinging around in his chair, Kemp raised his eyes to screen 10. Outside the locked gates, a black limousine was waiting, and a uniformed chauffeur was pacing alongside the gatehouse.

47 AT THE SAME HOUR, MARGIE CLARK WAS WALKING THE TEXAS DEPART-ment store heiress, Bunny Duncan, to the ice immersion unit in physical therapy where she would be injected her with phenobarbital. The drug stabilized alcohol withdrawal, but, as it also irritated sensitive skin, a medicated ice bath was used to control blemishes and eruptions.

Margie, on float duty all week, left Bunny with the physical therapist and decided to grab a sandwich in the Hub, where she could check for her next assignment.

As she climbed the stairs, she glanced at the call screen over the staircase and noticed a flashing green "3G."

3G was Little Milly Wheeler's suite in the Garden Pavilion. Flashing green meant emergency.

Margie remembered yesterday's trouble with the country-and-western singer's mother.

Margie pulled the Weatherhead call-pack from her pocket and punched in her code to accept duty.

Lunch would have to wait.

Gladys Wheeler stood in the suite's doorway, delivering a sharp diatribe to attendant Glen Schaeffer.

Margie hurried forward. "Trouble, Glen?"

"I have instructions to take Miss Wheeler to her counselor," he said, waving a clipboard in one hand. "But this lady won't let me into the room."

Margie turned to Gladys. "Ma'am, maybe you'd be more comfortable if I walked Milly to her appointment."

"When I need your assistance, miss, I'll ask for it," Gladys retorted.

Margie tried to maintain her calm. "Your daughter's on a strict program, Mrs. Wheeler. You must help keep her to it."

"You're all a little too drug-happy around this place for my liking, young lady."

"I don't think I understand," Margie said.

Gladys stepped farther in the hallway. "The drugs you push here. It's shocking. A snip of a nurse brought more drugs a little while ago and tried to insist Milly take them."

"Did you keep a nurse from administering medication?" Margie asked.

"I brought Little Milly here to get her *off* drugs. Not to stuff more down her gullet."

"Mrs. Wheeler, the dosages ease off gently. They should stop altogether next week. Total withdrawal could cause Milly serious mental as well as physical damage. Whether you realize it or not, your daughter has a very serious condition of alcohol and amphetamine—"

"Shush! How dare you discuss Little Milly's private life in front of"—Gladys glared at the attendant—"in front of outsiders."

"Outsiders?" Margie pointed at Glen. "This man is a qualified paramedic. He's been at Tanglewood longer than I have."

"I don't care who he is or where he's been," Gladys insisted. "He has nothing to do with my daughter—and he won't while I'm around."

Margie could no longer hold her tongue. "Mrs. Wheeler, if you don't approve of Tanglewood's treatment, why did you bring your daughter here in the first place?"

"I'm beginning to wonder the same thing myself."

A shattering noise came from within the suite.

Margie and Glen exchanged glances.

Gladys Wheeler reached for the door handle, ordering "You can go now. Both of you."

Beyond the foyer came another crash, followed by cries.

Margie Clark, twenty pounds heavier than Gladys Wheeler, easily shouldered her to one side. Gladys thumped against the door as Margie rushed into the room.

Little Milly knelt on the bedroom floor, hands to her abdomen, blood streaming onto the carpet.

"Call the ambulance," Margie shouted to Glen.

"My baby!" screamed Gladys. "Leave my little girl alone!"

Glen pulled Gladys from the bedroom as Margie tried to loosen Little Milly's grip on—*What's in her hands? Why is that leather belt strapped around her arms?* Then she saw.

"Oh, my God," she said.

The young woman was gripping two pairs of steel knitting needles under the belt, stabbing herself with the needles and crying "Let me die . . . let me die . . ."

Little Milly had depended on too many things, too long, and the demons would not let her forget it.

Little Milly Wheeler was ten years old when she first got drunk.

Carrot-topped, with rusty freckles smeared across her pug nose, Milly lay in her pink canopy bed, waiting to hear the last car crunch down the gravel driveway.

Throwing back the violet-sprigged bedsheet, she slid her bare feet into a pair of Minnie Mouse slippers and crept from the bedroom.

The house was in a shambles. Yesterday Milly's father had returned to Nashville from the state penitentiary. To celebrate his parole, Donny Wheeler had invited all his old friends to the Wheelers' home in southwest Nashville. From the house, the party would drive in a cavalcade to Old Hickory Boulevard where Donny Wheeler was making his first welcome-home appearance at Walt's Armory. The singer insisted that his wife, Gladys, be on stage with him. But because Walt's Armory served beer and liquor, Gladys Wheeler refused to let Little Milly appear as part of the reunion show.

Tiptoeing down the carpeted hall, Milly peered into the living room. Her baby-sitter, Colleen McCruder, was necking on the couch with Joe Bob Harper. Milly had caught Colleen and Joe Bob kissing and hugging before, but never quite like this. One of Joe Bob's hands was hidden under Colleen's tartan skirt, and Colleen was rubbing the crotch of Joe Bob's Levi's. They did not notice Milly as she passed.

Looking for potato chips and clam dip for a late-night snack, Milly continued down the hall, finally reaching the pine-paneled room called the den. Glass-fronted cases of rifles and shotguns lined the walls; the pegged floor was layered with Indian carpets; antique wagon wheels hung from the ceiling, wired to make chandeliers.

The den also held Donny Wheeler's collection of gold records, show business awards and trophies and photographs of him with other Nashville singers—Roy Acuff, Minnie Pearl, Hank Williams.

The den was Milly's favorite room in the house. But tonight she turned up her nose at the mess. Paper plates, empty beer bottles, and half-filled highball glasses were strewn everywhere. Cigar butts were stabbed into plates of potato salad. Half-eaten barbecue ribs and chicken drumsticks were thrown on the floor. The potato-chip bowl was soggy with tomato juice.

Disgusted by the mess, Milly decided to forget about a snack and have something to drink.

Donny Wheeler had allowed his daughter to sip from his beer bottle ever since she'd been a little girl, laughing at how much she liked Coors, beer brewed from Rocky Mountain water and shipped especially to him from Denver, Colorado.

Little Milly flip-flopped around the den in her Minnie Mouse slippers, finishing the remains of one, two, three Coors bottles. The buzz made her feel less lonely. Pleased that Daddy was back home, she began to hum softly, making up one of her little nonsense songs.

Next she tried a highball glass. Ick! The bourbon burned her throat. But Milly knew her daddy liked Jim Beam as well as Coors, so she forced herself to drink an entire glass. She wanted to be just like her daddy in every way—drinking and singing and having everybody love her.

The next morning Milly's head throbbed and she couldn't keep down her breakfast.

Donny Wheeler laughed at the idea of his ten-year-old daughter having a hangover. But Gladys Wheeler didn't think it was quite so cute.

She swore, "Over my dead body is that McCruder hussy going to baby-sit in this house again. I can tell you right now her career as a baby-sitter is over."

"Calm down, old girl," said Donny, looking bleary-eyed himself that morning. "It's not the end of the world."

"This is not how we lived when you were away, Donny Wheeler," Gladys said sharply. "We may be common people but our house is no beer hall."

"Well, I'm home now, and I want to hear less of your yapping."

Listening to her parents arguing, Milly knew things were back to normal, like they had been before her daddy had been sent to prison.

In the three years that Donny Wheeler had been in the penitentiary, Gladys Wheeler had kept his singing career afloat. Rather than hide the fact that Donny Wheeler had killed a man in a drunk-driving accident, Gladys had invited reporters to interview him in prison, getting his side of the story printed in magazines and newspapers across the country—receiving valuable publicity at the same time for the old records she pushed Four Bell Records to re-release.

Gladys Wheeler's determination paid off. Donny was paroled and emerged from prison a folk hero. His single, "God Didn't Build the Jailhouse," went to number one on the country-and-western charts.

As Milly grew older, Gladys also made career plans for her. Being an obedient girl, Little Milly followed her mother's dic-

tates. Using the family nickname of "Little Milly," Gladys found a place for her on Donny's Welcome-Home Tour and persuaded Four Bell Records to include three duets by Donny and Little Milly on Donny's new album, Home Cookin'.

When Little Milly was thirteen, Gladys commissioned a novelty song for her to record and release in time for Christmas. "Santa Cat" had a modest success, which Gladys pushed Milly to follow with a ballad aimed at high-school students for a springtime release. To promote "Patchwork Prom Queen," Gladys booked a limited concert tour for Milly at the larger high schools in Tennessee, Alabama, and Georgia.

Donny protested. "Little Milly's too young to get caught up in all this tour crap."

"What about Marie Osmond?" asked Gladys. "Or those Wright Sisters? They're hardly more than girls themselves and they've got their own TV shows. All I want is for Little Milly to sing pretty at a few high-school dances."

"Gladys, why you driving Little Milly like this? What's your reasoning?"

"Money and independence, that's why. My daddy played fiddle all his life. Billy Boy Beard played the best fiddle in all Tennessee. But we never had a penny. Sometimes not even enough money to buy a loaf of bread.

"Donny, things haven't always been rosy for you, either. When you got in trouble with the law, I had to dust off the cobwebs from your old records to pay the rent. I don't want my baby dependent on nobody."

Donny's and Little Milly's careers flourished under Gladys's shrewd guidance. She supervised their contracts; moved them from one record company to another; advised them to branch out into other media. CBA signed Donny for a holiday television special, but he was reluctant to play the part of a boozer in one skit, frightened that people might say he was typecast as a drunk. It was no secret that Donny Wheeler had been in and out of clinics for his drinking problem. But Gladys pushed him to play the television role, insisting that the public loves to forgive a man his weaknesses, that Donny must show the world he was just a common, ordinary, hard-working man.

Gladys also had definite opinions about Little Milly's future. When Milly graduated from high school, Gladys advised her against going to college, saying she'd make a fortune in a musical career, and insisting she'd get no better preparation for one than by touring in a road show. Milly was young and had no other ideas of what to do with her life; she reluctantly accepted her mother's advice. For apprenticeship, Milly signed on with Round-up of Stars, a road show of established country singers and musicians. On stage, her red hair, her small eager-to-please face, her plaintive voice appealed to audiences, and they immediately took Little Milly to their hearts.

Gladys traveled with Milly from town to town on the bus, making certain she got the right billing, had her own dressing room, wasn't molested. But even when Milly traveled unchaperoned, nobody bothered her. Everyone knew Gladys Wheeler would blackball them from every music circuit in the country if anything happened to her freckle-faced daughter.

On tour, Milly's taste for liquor graduated to Jim Beam. The Kentucky bourbon gave her confidence, making her feel she was singing almost as well as the artist everyone compared her to— Brenda Lee.

Drinking also gave Milly confidence off stage, helping her relax with strangers and make new friends. But most nights Milly sat alone in her room after the show, drinking by herself, making up nonsense songs as she had done as a little girl, giggling when she sang them off-key. The solitary motel parties were her only escape from being sad and lonely.

When Little Milly was twenty-three, Gladys commissioned a Motown artist to write a disco song. Kissy Missy became an immediate cross-over hit for Little Milly, moving her from country-and-western charts to the wider market of pop music. The album went platinum.

Little Milly, suddenly a mega-star, followed her mother's advice and bought two buses for her own traveling show and three semitrucks to carry sound equipment. Gladys hired Holly-

wood designers to create costumes, as they had done for Cher and Marie Osmond. Little Milly appeared on Merv Griffin. Her photograph was on the front cover of People *magazine.* Variety *categorized her with Olivia Newton-John. Success on the pop charts also meant that northern cities booked her show. Despite her new glitter and fame, Little Milly did not lose the waiflike presence she had always exuded on stage, and the audiences cheered for her more wildly.*

Soon, though, the extensive traveling began to exhaust Little Milly. By the time she reached the end of the northern concert tour, she was relieved to be going home to Nashville.

But Gladys Wheeler had added a surprise.

Detroit represented a stronghold of country music fans in the north, and the management of Detroit's Seymour Hall planned a jamboree for country-western entertainers who had relatives in the entertainment industry. They invited Johnny Cash. June Carter. Loretta Lynn. Crystal Gayle. The Oak Ridge Boys. Grandpa Jones.

For Detroit's Country Family Show, Gladys Wheeler booked Donny and Little Milly to appear with the cream of Nashville, as well as agreeing to walk onstage herself and say a few words about her own father, Billy Boy Beard.

On the night of the performance, Gladys commandeered Little Milly's dressing room, more nervous than any performer about her makeup and hair and the blue lace gown she had had flown in from Neiman-Marcus in Dallas.

Little Milly gladly abandoned her dressing room to her mother, pleased to be with her daddy in his. She'd spent too little time with him in the past three years.

Donny complimented Milly on her red beaded jumpsuit, adding in his gravel-throated voice "But I got to say, honey, you look dog-tired tonight. Your tour take it out of you?"

"I'm beat, Daddy." Milly laid her head against her daddy's broad shoulder, long red hair combed to one side of her freckled face. "Do you ever get so tired your bones feel like one more step's going to break them? Your mind becomes nothing but fuzz? All you want to do is . . . throw up?"

"Lots of times I feel like that," Donny admitted, patting Milly's hand. "Mostly on the road, too."

"Don't be surprised, Daddy, if you got to carry our numbers tonight. I don't have it in me."

"You that bad off, girl?"

"Worse." She confided, "If it weren't for Mama, I'd have flown home."

She lowered her head to the dressing table, moaning "Oh, I just want to curl up and die."

Donny Wheeler took a brown plastic tube from the pocket of his shirt. Handing Milly two small pills, he said, "Take these. But don't tell your old lady. She'd kill me."

That night Little Milly and Donny Wheeler sang three duets and received uproarious applause from the Detroit audience. After four encores, they still had enough energy to go on to The Cattle Yard and jam until six o'clock in the morning.

Ever since that night, Dexedrine was part of Little Milly's life. She had energy for concert tours, for practicing, for recording late with the session players. Calming herself down with Jim Beam, she partied with friends, caught a few hours' sleep, and the next morning her drug-and-liquor cycle began all over again when she popped her first pill.

Milly had been mixing Dexedrine and Jim Beam for two years when she met Stu Travis at Pegler Brothers' Studios in Nashville.

Twenty-six-year-old Travis managed the hit gospel group, Fly Eagle Fly. After finishing the master tape for their new album, Stu hung around in the control room to listen to Little Milly record "Freight Train." Impressed by her finger-popping rendition of the classic oldie, he invited her across the street afterward for supper at Biddy Hen's Chicken Farm.

Over predinner cocktails, he asked, "How long you been on speed, boss?"

The blunt question caught Milly unawares. She had noticed the mustachioed young man around the studio for the past few weeks, hearing him call everybody "boss" and watching secretar-

ies swoon in his wake. Milly had heard the girl talk, too, about Stu Travis's masculine endowments.

"Speed?" she asked. "What you talking about?"

"Cut the down-home crap, boss. I know the signs. Dilated eyes. Twitchy fingers. Nervous talk."

He reached across the red-checkered tablecloth and, patting Milly's slim hand, said, "Hoss, I ain't out to arrest you. I'm just saying that if you want to do drugs, you shouldn't monkey around with uppers. Your pretty little face will last longer on downers and grass. So'll your voice."

Milly tried to sound sophisticated and worldly. "Is this some kind of invitation to . . . fly?"

"Could be." The ends of his thick black moustache rose as he smiled. "What do you say to buzzing around my lake cabin this weekend?"

Stu Travis's mountain retreat at Bear Lake was a log A-frame equipped with Jacuzzi, a mirrored headboard over a king-size waterbed, and a deep freeze full of T-bone steaks and frozen French fries. Smoking marijuana and sipping margaritas, Stu and Milly spent the weekend moving from the waterbed to the bear rug in front of the fireplace.

Milly was not disappointed in Stu's body, nor in his performance as a lover. The bonus, though, was the keen interest he showed in her career.

"Stop being Donny Wheeler's good little girl," he urged. "'Kissy Missy' changed your life. But if you go back to shit-kicking, you're going to be a freak show. People's going to come see you because you're Donny Wheeler's kid. Not for who you really are. You've got your own magic with your own audience, Milly. Don't throw it away."

Milly became besotted with Stu Travis, physically, emotionally, professionally. Apart from weekends at the lake, she was soon spending weekdays at his house in town, going back to her own apartment only to get clothes. From Stu she was receiving encouragement that someday she would have a home and a family, be a happy, normal person.

One Saturday afternoon Milly popped into Safeway to buy

lobster tails and salad fixings for Stu's supper. He had gone to Macon, Georgia, for three days and she wanted to have an extra-special meal for him when he came home.

As she carried the bulging grocery bag across the parking lot, she was surprised to see her mother sitting in the front seat of her gold Eldorado.

Stuffing the groceries in the backseat, she asked, "Mama, what're you doing here?"

Gladys held her handbag primly on her lap. "You never come see me any more, honey," she said, "and I don't know where to find you these days."

"Mama, come off it. A smart lady like you knows exactly where I've been hanging my hat."

"Milly, why're you doing this to yourself?" Gladys asked seriously. "You're a star. Granted, you've got a long way to go till you get to be Dolly Parton. But do you really think you should be lugging home groceries for the likes of Stu Travis?"

Milly slid behind the steering wheel. "Mama, who says I want to be Dolly Parton? For that matter, who ever said I wanted to be Brenda Lee? Don't you think I might have fun just being myself? With a home and a husband and babies?"

"Stu Travis putting these ideas into your head?" Gladys smirked. "While he has you bringing home the bacon?"

"What have you got against Stu, Mama? You don't even know him."

"No. But I hear enough about him. And what I hear ain't good. Stu Travis sounds like he's the kind of young man who forgets he's common people like the rest of us."

"Common people." Milly laughed, shaking her head. "Mama, you're always talking about common people. Well, tell me the name of one common person who'd give up his home to follow this life. Sleep in dirty motel rooms. Eat supper night after night in greasy spoons. Travel all cramped up in a tour bus. No, Mama. I'm not common. But I want to be. I want to be plain and ordinary so bad that it hurts."

Outside the car window, a voice interrupted. "Excuse me, Little Milly."

Milly turned. A stranger stood next to the Cadillac.

A young, short-haired woman in a cotton housedress, with two freckle-faced children behind her, said, "I saw you in Safeway shopping, Little Milly, and I wondered if you'd please autograph this for me." She held out a folded brown-paper grocery bag.

"I'd be honored to," Milly said with sudden professionalism. Such approaches were usual. Milly's fans sought her out everywhere, and she was always kind and friendly to everyone. As she scribbled her name and a brief message across the grocery bag, she asked the two children questions about where they lived and urged them to study hard at school.

After the fan and two children walked happily away from the car, the woman clutching the prized autograph, Milly turned to her mother. "Well, Mama, do common folk get asked for their autographs in a Safeway parking lot?"

"Milly, the truth of the matter is that your fans love you. They live for your tours. They flock to see you in the flesh. Now you sit there and tell me you want to stop touring and stay home and nest build."

"Stu's offering me a nest, Mama. He asked me to marry him."

Gladys studied her daughter, hair tied back by a shoestring into a pony tail, man's cowboy shirt knotted over her jeans.

Milly turned away her head, unable to face her mother as she told her the most difficult part. Oh, why was it so hard to stand up to Mama?

"Mama, Stu also wants to . . . manage me."

"Manage your career?"

"He knows the business, Mama. He manages Fly Eagle Fly." *She added more eagerly, "He'll manage me like you manage Daddy. Stu loves me, Mama. And, oh, I love him. I love him so much."*

Gladys frowned. "I won't waste my breath commenting on gospel singers. You know what a racket I think they have. And as far as love goes, what do you know about love, Little Milly? You haven't even had a steady beau. Love? You don't have a clue what it means."

Milly turned on her mother. "When was the last time Daddy made love to you, Mama?"

Gladys slapped her face.

Holding one hand to her stinging cheek, Milly let it all pour out. "Mama, I hear what people say about you and Daddy. That Donny Wheeler only goes home long enough for his wife to balance his checkbook. That he keeps his boots under other women's beds."

Gladys's face turned ashen. "Little Milly, you listen to me and you listen good. Because I'm only going to say this once.

"Your daddy and me don't have a normal life together. That's true. But I've stayed with him all these years because he's my husband. We've been joined in the eyes of the Lord. For better or worse. For richer or poorer. You were born into this world because of that marriage. You're part of my God-given vow. So I'm not going to abandon you, either. Understand? To nobody."

After stepping out of Milly's Eldorado, Gladys Wheeler hurried across Safeway's parking lot, not looking back as she moved toward the chauffeur holding open a rear door of her white limousine.

The next day, Little Milly and Stu Travis flew to Las Vegas and were married in a civil ceremony. In the flourish of publicity following the wedding, Milly topped the bill at the Golden Horseshoe on the Strip, playing to packed houses, introducing Stu at every performance.

From Las Vegas they chartered a plane to Los Angeles. Renting a house in West Hollywood, Milly interviewed songwriters, auditioned Broadway choreographers, pursued Flashdance designer Michael Kaplan to create her a whole new wardrobe, with Emmy-award winner Jeremy Railton to do sets. As Milly developed a Hollywood look, Stu met regularly with the William Morris Agency, discussing a package by which they would represent Little Milly as an artist and him as a producer.

The result was the television special, "Hot to Trot." The album and video would be released the week the show aired coast to coast. But the ratings were so poor, the reviews for the costumes and sets so much better than Little Milly's performance as a

dancer and comedienne, that Columbia pulled the record and
ABC dropped their two-show option. The final consensus was
that Little Milly's devoted fans were not television viewers.

Following this disappointment, Milly and Stu agreed that
Hollywood was not what they had expected it to be. They were
disillusioned, too, that country stars were not the one big happy
family they pretended to be, hurt that not one of them had
invited Little Milly to their homes, let alone asked her to appear
on their shows. Disenchanted, they moved back to Nashville.

Milly and Stu chose a sprawling white colonial house in
northeast Nashville for their new home. Stu renegotiated Milly's
contract with RCA Records in Nashville but, still keeping open
his connection with the William Morris Agency, flew out regularly to Los Angeles to discuss film and television packages. He
signed Milly to record a soundtrack but the studio balked at her
appearing in the film. To prove she could act, Stu flew to New
York to discuss her making a cameo appearance in a soap opera.

In Nashville, Milly was becoming less interested in movies,
television, and concert tours. She wanted to settle down and raise
a family. But when Stu reminded her how high their monthly
expenses were, she temporarily agreed to do the next soundtrack
or to embark on a new concert tour. She was as powerless in
standing up to Stu's dictates for her career as she had been against
her mother's professional plans; it was as if her mother had
seasoned her for a life with a willful husband.

Preparing for her annual Florida appearance, Milly returned
to Dexedrine and Jim Beam. But old dosages were no longer
strong enough; her drinks had less ice and more bourbon.

It was at this time that she also began to suffer delirium
tremens. Apart from shaking, she imagined she was seeing streaks
of bright colors flash across the room, like a racing neon animal.
Inevitably, when she saw the imaginary streak across the floor,
she also heard a shrill voice taunting "Milly's weak . . . Milly's
weak . . . Milly needs another drink, another pill . . . Milly's
weak."

Frightened that the voices meant she was going insane, she did
not report them to Stu. She did not want to increase the risk of

losing him. Already she was beginning to fear that he was becoming emotionally involved with other women.

Stu did not hide his promiscuity from Milly. Cradling her in his arms, he explained, "I eat meals when I'm away from you, boss, don't I? Sex is the same to me as food. I need my nourishment. But that don't mean I wouldn't prefer stuffing myself—and you—right here at home."

"When I'm away on the road," Milly whimpered, "do you take women up to the lake cabin?"

"Those women don't mean more to me, boss, than something warm and plump to cover in Wesson Oil."

Donny Wheeler settled into success easier than his daughter. In growing demand since his song, "Big Daddy USA," topped the mainstream pop charts, he flew around the country in his new Learjet, opening supermarkets, making speeches at youth centers, appearing in concert.

Gladys was left at home alone. Having little work to do, she used her time to renew old ties with her daughter.

Knowing Stu was away in New York, she visited Little Milly at Talk of the Town Costumes, saying she had come to give advice on Milly's Florida wardrobe.

Alone with Milly in the dressing room, she attacked Stu Travis once again, telling Milly what a bad choice she had made for a husband and manager, that she had chosen to spend her life—and career—with a loser.

"Stu's one of those swingers you read about. He chases anything in skirts."

"Mama, Stu's a red-blooded man." Milly had taken three Dexedrines and still felt exhausted. But pills were the only way she knew how to find strength to go on with Stu's plans; whiskey quieted the demons that were running more frequently—streaking in brighter flashes of yellow and red and green—across the floor, shrieking at her she was a fool to be listening to her husband; "Silly Milly . . . Silly Milly . . ."

Gladys persisted. "How can you work when you know Stu's doing these things? How can you be happy?"

"Mama, are you happy with Daddy?"

Gladys repositioned her rhinestone eyeglasses. "At least my husband has the decency not to tell me about his floozies."

The Florida tour was both a critical and financial success. In Tampa, fans broke through the police barrier during Little Milly's lilting version of "God Bless America" and hoisted her to their shoulders. A physician had to give her a sedative that night to calm her hysteria.

Stu telephoned Milly the night she returned home from Florida. "I'm in Atlantic City, boss, and just about to cinch the deal for you to open with Joan Rivers at Caesar's Palace. Ain't that great?"

"Sounds exciting," Milly said unenthusiastically.

"In the meantime, I got you top billing at Prairie Dog Town in Vegas."

"Prairie Dog Town?" Milly had never heard of it.

"It's not on the Strip, boss. But the money's great, and you got free time to do it, so I signed you for two weeks."

She protested. "Stu, I'm tired. I just finished twenty-seven days on the road. . . ." She wondered if she should tell him about the streaking visions she was seeing, how they were getting worse, more frequent, their voices becoming louder as they goaded her.

"Baby," he argued, "you know our money situation."

As before, Milly honored the contract Stu had made for her, and again the demons chided her: "Milly's weak . . . Milly's foolish . . . Milly's nothing but a skinny minnie . . ."

Milly's Las Vegas dresser was a kindly Hispanic woman named Rosa who noticed her weak, nervous condition on opening night.

"You have a nap this afternoon, Miss Milly?" she asked, brushing Milly's hair in front of the dressing-room mirror.

"Ummm," answered Milly, draining a Dixie cup of Jim Beam.

"You maybe want coffee?" asked Rosa. "Something to eat? You eat nothing all day, Miss Milly."

"Stop nagging me." Milly pulled away from Rosa's brush and sprang from the chair. "You're just like my mama. Always nagging me."

"Oh, Miss Milly, I mean nothing bad."

Milly paced the dressing room, shouting to quiet the voices chattering inside her head, holding both hands to the side of her eyes so she wouldn't see the flashes of color darting past her like Technicolor cats.

"Sometimes I just want to curl up and die," she screamed. "Sometimes I think: Is all this work worth it? Everybody nags me. Everybody tells me what to do. Tells me to sing this. To do that. To work there. To tour here. Sometimes I just want to scream enough, enough, enough."

"Oh, Miss Milly," Rosa soothed, watching Milly holding her hands to her temples. "You're tired. Maybe you lie down before your show, yes?"

That night, the audience cheered Milly's entrance, applauding and stamping their feet when she began her opening number. Halfway through "Freight Train," though, Milly stopped and peered out over their heads.

Holding one hand above her eyes to block the blinding spotlights, she surveyed the tables, calling "Stu, honey? You out there to surprise me?"

A silence fell over the audience.

A few people laughed nervously, unsure whether Milly's behavior was part of the show.

"She looks sick," said one voice.

"Hey, Milly, you all right?" called out another.

Ignoring her fans, Milly continued to speak. "Stu, I've got a little surprise for you tonight, too, honey."

Like a child, like a young girl all alone in a motel room left to entertain herself, Little Milly began to sing, making up words to a nonsense song that she sang off-key: "This old boss is yellow and wants a bowl of Jell-O if you say see-saw-swing in the apple tree—"

Rosa the dresser led Little Milly offstage as the audience sat silently. After a few minutes, they became restless. They rose to their feet, clapping loudly in unison, chanting "Bring back Milly! Bring back Milly!"

But Milly did not come back.

* * *

Gladys Wheeler arrived the next day and found Milly hospi-
talized for amphetamines, alcohol, and exhaustion. Gladys im-
mediately realized what she must do. First, get legal custody of
Little Milly. Second, obtain a divorce for her from Stu Travis.
Third, move her to a clinic where her mother could take care of
her just like in the old days. And she would find Milly the best
clinic in the United States.

48 FROM A DISTANT VANTAGE POINT IN
THE MAIN HOUSE, LILLIAN WEISS
watched the white-jacketed paramedics lifting the stretcher
into the back of the ambulance. She had not learned any
details about the accident except that the victim was the
country-western singer, Little Milly Wheeler. Lillian would
snoop later and unearth the facts. Right now she was obsessed with Ray Esposito.

Lillian loitered a few more minutes in front of the window, waiting for the ambulance's siren to disappear into the
distance, before deciding it was safe to make her move.

Slowly, waddling from the main house, she progressed
toward the Garden Pavilion and reviewed, for what seemed
like the hundredth time, what she would say to the horny
construction worker.

Lillian had decided to put all her cards on the table. Esposito needed sex. She was on fire, too. Esposito could only
masturbate himself. But she—expert lover that she was—

could suck him, let him fuck her in the cunt, up the ass, could fondle and massage and tease him . . .

Lillian stopped under the archway. The Garden Pavilion was deserted. Not a soul was in sight.

Glancing to her left, she saw the wall cabinet from which she had seen Margie Clark take the card keys a few days ago and not lock it behind her.

Lillian looked around her one more time before stepping toward the cabinet. The small door was exactly as she had expected—unlocked.

Inside the cabinet, she spotted a buff envelope. Digging through it, she found plastic card keys marked "G1," "G2," "G3" . . .

Card key in hand, Lillian moved across the hallway, extremely pleased with herself.

After listening one more time for approaching footsteps and hearing nothing, she inserted the card key into the lock.

It wasn't until Lillian heard the *click* of the lock that she remembered she hadn't freshened her makeup.

Oh, well, she decided, passing into the suite's foyer, the Italian Stallion's going to have to take me as I am.

Ray Esposito raised his eyes at the sound of the opening bedroom door. He made no move to cover his nakedness as he sat on the end of the bed, his fist gripping his penis.

"Who are you?" he demanded. "What are you doing in here?"

Lillian flashed her most winning smile. "Hi, there!"

Esposito did not move. "You want something, lady?"

Lillian did not reply, her eyes glued to his crotch.

"Who are you?" he repeated. The conversation had not softened his erection.

Lillian tore her eyes from it with difficulty. She stepped forward, beginning her rehearsed lines. "I've seen you around and I was wondering if—"

"How did you get in here?" he asked sharply.

Lillian told herself to be confident, to remember her story

exactly as she had rehearsed it. But her throat had gone dry. She had lost her *chutzpah*. She was unable to do anything but stare at his—What a beautiful pecker!

"What's your name?" Esposito folded both arms across his hair-matted chest, organ wagging from his crotch.

"Lillian . . ." She took a deep breath. Esposito would be the crowning glory of her sexual career.

"You've been staring at me for the past couple days, haven't you?"

"You're a nice-looking man." She flirted, regaining some of her old boldness. "I bet a lot of girls stare at a nice-looking man like you."

"I seen you. I wondered why you were gawking at me."

She repeated, "You're a good-looking guy."

"I know what you're after, lady."

She leapt at the opening. "You maybe want the same thing yourself?" She flashed her million-dollar smile, rolling her irresistible eyes.

He replied sourly, "You're just like my wife. You know that? Always looking at me. Always waiting."

"You're married?"

"Sure I'm married. My wife. She's just like you. Gawking at me. Following me around. Waiting."

Lillian didn't like the surly tone in Esposito's voice. She wondered for the first time if she had made a mistake. But, then, if he didn't want her in here, why didn't he cover his big dick?

Esposito said, "I get tired of being bothered. Especially by a tub of lard like you."

The crack about her size irritated Lillian; she snapped back, "Don't knock it till you've tried it, bub."

Esposito laughed but suddenly his swarthy face sobered and he sprang at Lillian, knocking her off her feet and shoving her to the floor.

Lillian Weiss was a big woman, and strong. But Esposito was stronger, and when Lillian tried to pull away from his clench, he began to beat her, hitting her on the shoulders and head and back and repeatedly in her baby-doll face. The last thing she knew she was having trouble gasping for breath. Pain shot through her chest as she lost consciousness.

49

Dear Peabo,
I've been a fan of yours since I first discovered guys could do more with their fists than stuff food in their face. I'm writing to say me and my buddies are all behind you, champ. Beat that junk like you beat that Swede over in Stockholm last year and you'll be proving to everybody you're the latest and greatest.

Phil Hinds
Carbonville, North Carolina

Dear Peabo Washington,
I have never written a fan letter before. I have never taken the time to express my admiration to an actor or musician or sports figure when they have given me great pleasure. That's a fault on my part, I feel, because the artist or athlete lets me in on their own experience of greatness. Therefore I am taking this moment to tell you how much I admire the form, grace, and intelligence you have brought to the ring. You are more than a champion boxer. Your are an admirable athlete. I am only sorry that I have waited so long to write you this letter. But then

maybe it will help you get back on your feet before the
last count. I am certain I am not the only person out
there cheering for you to overcome your drug
dependency. Sincere good wishes for your recovery.

James T. Gillete
Long Beach, California

Hey, Peabo Washington! What's happening, man? Why
you doing that dope shit? Everybody down here in
Austin, Texas, looks up to you, man, and wants our kids
to grow up to be just like you. So don't let us down.
Drugs are real bad news. Keep smiling.

Charley Joe Langdon
Austin, Texas

Dear Mrs. Washington,
Due to the sad state of affairs in this wicked world I must
begin this letter by telling you what color my skin is. It
is necessary to say I am white so I can also say I am so
very much ashamed of some other white people, that you
and your dear little ones were not allowed a room at that
snooty hotel up there in New England. Hats off to you,
Mrs. Washington, for sticking by your husband in his
time of need. The papers love making a fuss about
famous people having hard times. But knowing human
nature like I do (I turned ninety-two last September
30th) I bet that next week the same papers and TV
shows will be calling him a saint. But you're the saint in
my book. Congratulations on being such a lady.

Miss Jocasta Phlug
Montgomery, Alabama

Dear Peabo,
I am writing you this letter to tell you you've got one
hell of a good woman. Most men would give their eye
teeth to have a woman stand by them like you have. Plus
she's a fine-looking girl. So take this as a warning, champ.

Treat her good because the line is already forming
around the block with men ready to step into your shoes.
No offense meant neither to her because she's a real
classy lady.

> Bubba Rodriquez
> Dayton, Ohio

Dear Tamara and Tyler,
I am seven years old and live in a big house with my
Mama and Daddy in Seattle. They told me that if you
have no place to go when your Daddy's in the hospital
sick, you and your Mommy can come stay with us here
in Seattle. The only house rule is that you have to make
your own beds and not talk while Grandpa says Grace
before supper.

> Tiffany Sandell
> Seattle, Washington

Letters of praise. Letters of hope. Letters of advice and
encouragement and love. The few crank letters were vastly
outnumbered by the avalanche of support from people
around the country. There also came packages of toys, clothing, homemade cookies and candy and sweet potato pies
carefully wrapped in aluminum foil.

"I'm overwhelmed." Karen Washington sat in Philip
Pringle's office, the letters heaped in front of her on a folding
card table. "What do I do?"

Pringle and his junior, Dr. Isaacs, stood side by side in
front of Pringle's desk; the psychiatrist said, "Enjoy the fact
you have lots of friends out there."

"Do I dare tell Peabo?" She looked from Pringle to his
junior.

Pringle answered, "It's a good way to break the news to
him that the public's behind him. That there's no shame in
his dependency."

Isaacs reminded her, "The post office called to say there's

four more bags of letters and packages waiting in town. But it was too late to deliver them today."

Karen could only shake her head. "All this mail . . . all these people. All this . . . *love!*"

50 IT WAS 6:15 P.M. WHEN ROGER RE-TURNED TO TANGLEWOOD FROM Stonebridge General Hospital. His secretary had gone home for the night. Roger was relieved. Tonight was the first time Caroline had got away before 7:30 all month. She worked far beyond the call of duty.

As Roger stepped through his office door, a telephone was ringing on his desk. He was relieved to hear Jackie Lyell's voice in the receiver, not another distress flash from Dispatch or the switchboard.

"How is Lillian Weiss?" she asked.

Collapsing into the chair behind his desk, he answered, "Two cracked ribs and a broken jaw. God knows why she ever went into Esposito's room. But she'll live. That's the important thing. I'm sorry I can't be so optimistic about the Wheeler girl."

"What's the verdict on her after surgery?"

"Not good. She punctured the upper lobe of the left lung, jabbed the bronchus, and tore muscle fibers in her diaphragm. She's in intensive care with acute internal bleeding."

"The mother?"

"Under sedation."

Jackie reported, "I located Donny Wheeler in Lake

Tahoe. He's on the way here now. A gospel group in Nashville gave me a lead on the husband. I'm staying in the office trying to track him down."

"Good girl."

"Roger, how do we stand legally in these cases? Can Lillian Weiss seek damages against us? Can the Wheelers sue, too?"

Roger admitted, "I don't know. They might try. My only advice for the moment is to watch what we say, and to whom. I admit, I'm concerned about that, too."

Jackie continued, "In all this commotion, Roger—were you told that Lavender Gilbert is missing?"

"Missing?"

"Her clothes and suitcase are still in her room," Jackie reported, "but nobody can find her anywhere."

"Security on it?"

"Everybody but the Canadian Mounted Police."

"Did anything unusual happen earlier?"

"Chatwyn called this morning from New York, wanting to assure her she still had a job with him."

"That was thoughtful."

Jackie let out a sigh of relief. "I'm so glad to hear you say that, Roger. I was beginning to wonder if I had made another major telephone gaffe. I put through Chatwyn's call to Lavender and that's the last anybody heard of her."

"Have you called Chatwyn back to see if he might have any explanation for the disappearance?"

"I tried. He was out and didn't return any of my calls. Next I got a call from Leo Kemp in Security saying a limousine had arrived at the front gate asking for Lavender."

"But she had gone."

"Vanished."

"And Chatwyn's still not answering or returning your calls?"

"Not one. So I've been onto the Highway Patrol. FBI. Local police. Leo's scoured the place top to bottom but isn't having much luck."

"Maybe she just decided to go." Roger paused before asking "Any other bombshells? Problems or questions needing answers?"

"I've got a few questions about book work. But they can wait."

"Questions on what?" he asked.

"Unit costs and drug supply companies. I hate to bother Renee in Accounts about everything but—"

"Let me stop around and see if I can answer some of your questions," Roger offered.

"Thank you, Roger, but you must be exhausted."

"A little rushed but not too busy to give you a couple minutes." He thought about his evening plans. "I'm going to grab a quick shower right now. Then have a bite with Tom Hudson in the dining room to discuss Cat Powers. How long are you going to hang around in the office tonight?"

"About tenish."

"Why don't I stop around and have coffee with you there. I can look at the supply sheets and see what the stickler is."

"It'd be terrific if you could."

"I'll be there."

"Smashing."

Roger put down the receiver. Lavender Gilbert's disappearance troubled him. But there was nothing he could do about it at the moment. Weary from his evening at Stonebridge General, he wanted to lock the door and go home to bed. There was still Hudson to see, though. He also had to start sometime, somewhere putting feelers out for investors. Where was he going to find nine million dollars to meet Adrian's purchase offer?

Sorting through the messages that Caroline had left on his desk, he found a note that the old gardener, Luther Brown, had telephoned him.

What did Brown want?

Roger glanced at the desk clock: 6:37. Luther Brown had gone home long ago.

As he looked at the clock, Roger's thoughts returned to the need to start approaching potential investors. He remembered that the time was two hours earlier in the Midwest, and thought of two people—one in Illinois, one in Minnesota—whom he could put the pitch to for money. They were both long shots but he had to start somewhere.

Flipping open his private address book, he found the office number of his old college buddy, Reg Clore, in Chicago. Clore headed a safe deposit company and was personally listed in the Forbes 400. He might be a possibility to help save Tanglewood.

"This is Roger Cooper calling for Mr. Clore," he explained into the receiver. When the secretary said that Reginald Clore was out of town for the rest of the week, Roger was not too displeased. He had never enjoyed fundraising.

Next he tried his cousin, Chuck Trunkey, in Minneapolis, to discuss a loan from the family trust. He got no reply from the home phone number he had written in his address book. Realizing he should be asking his new lawyer about the possibility of offering stock options to potential investors, he put down the receiver and decided to check before making further calls.

Roger turned off the desk lamp and moved toward the door, thinking about the inevitable changes soon to be happening at Tanglewood. Both administrative and medical.

His hand froze on the light switch as a question struck him.

Even if he sold to Adrian, the partnership contract allowed him to continue working at Tanglewood. But Adrian would certainly not want him there under a new regime. So who would Adrian put into his shoes? Somebody new, or somebody already on the staff who would be familiar with the clinic?

Was there a shadow medical director among the doctors at Tanglewood?

51 JACKIE LYELL WAS ALSO THINKING ABOUT LAWYERS.

Jackie stayed in her office, making calls to track down Milly Wheeler's husband, confirming the lunch she was having tomorrow with actress Carol Ann Rice. Then she again tried the telephone number at the top of her list—for a lawyer, Tom Schweider, in Hartford, Connecticut.

To her relief, someone finally answered the Hartford number.

"Mr. Schweider?" Jackie asked.

"Who's calling, please?"

"My name's Mrs. Lyell—Jackie Lyell. I got Mr. Schweider's name from the American Bar Association. When I called his office earlier, I got this number from an answering machine. But the line has been either busy or no one picks up."

"This is Tom Schweider speaking."

Jackie asked, "Am I disturbing you at home?"

"I'm working at home while my offices are being refurbished. Now what can I do for you?"

"I'm married, Mr. Schweider, but . . . I want a divorce."

"Where do you live, Mrs. Lyell?"

"Near Stonebridge. My husband's a partner at the clinic, Tanglewood."

"Ah, Tanglewood. Of course."

Schweider paused, then said, "Mrs. Lyell, do you mind if

I turn on my tape recorder? It will save me repeating a lot of questions later."

"Does that mean you agree to represent me, Mr. Schweider?"

"Let's presume for the moment that it does. Now give me some background, Mrs. Lyell."

Jackie proceeded.

52 IN FIFTY MINUTES FLAT, ROGER HAD SHOWERED, SHAVED AND CHANGED into a fresh shirt, yellow tie, gray flannels and blue blazer. By eight o'clock he was sitting in the candlelit dining room, enjoying the burn of a whiskey inside his chest.

Tom Hudson had not yet appeared. Roger was grateful. He enjoyed the time by himself, mellowed by the whiskey, relaxed by the evening's string quartet playing Scarlatti on the corner dais.

Sipping his drink, he realized that if he did decide to sell to Adrian, and chose to leave Tanglewood, he would be free to go wherever he wanted in the world. He would be a very rich man.

But he was not sure he wanted such freedom. More than he wanted a fat bank account, Roger wanted to work at something he believed in.

Money would not be new to Roger. He had resisted its temptations before. He had learned the hard way about its many dangers.

* * *

Money had been the cause of all Roger's troubles.

*Roger's mother had been a Trunkey, a member of the Trunkey
family headed by Coleman Trunkey, the Minnesota farmer who
had invented the Trunkey harvest rake in the 1930s. As the
United States was emerging from the Great Depression, the
revolutionary way of raking hay with a bounce spring became
a popular fixture on farms across the country; its sales formed
the basis of a considerable fortune. Elizabeth Trunkey was one
of six children; she married Walter Cooper, a young Air Force
wing commander; they had one son, Roger. Elizabeth and Walter Cooper moved with their child from air base to air base, living
comfortably, showing no ostentatious signs of wealth. But the
fact that his wife was a millionaire ate away at Walter Cooper's
masculine pride, leading him into a severe alcohol problem.*

*Roger Cooper went through childhood and school years un-
spoiled by the advantages rich parents usually showered on their
children. He attended public schools; his first car was a jalopy;
his clothes came from Sears, Penney's, the store on the corner that
sold Levi's and Wranglers. He had money for college and med
school but his allowance was not lavish. He planned to continue
living in the same unpretentious life-style when he finished medical school and married Deborah Hurley.*

*With money from his mother's share of the Trunkey family
trust, he bought a medical practice in Santa Barbara from Dr.
Hewittson, a doctor who owned two practices and was becoming
too old to manage either one.*

*Roger was attracted to the practice not for its patient list, but
for the corner lot on Anapamli Street on which the white stucco
building stood. The space promised great potential for expansion.
Roger was fresh from residency at California Health but already
had vague dreams of opening a multipurpose clinic. Expansion
was a long way off, however.*

*A few months after Roger hung out his shingle, a new patient
telephoned for a late-morning appointment. She gave her name
as Mrs. Bentley.*

Patricia Bentley was an attractive woman in her early thir-

ties, dark-haired with blue eyes, a woman who wore expensive clothes well, not allowing them to "wear her." Roger noticed, too, that she had more than a fair share of arrogance.

Sitting in Roger's office, she lit a king-size cigarette, announcing as she slipped her gold lighter back into a lizard handbag, "Dr. Cooper, you don't look like a rich man."

Roger thought the statement was odd for a patient who had come to discuss having an IUD put in. He had been prepared to warn about a possible psychological effect on her, how some doctors prescribed painkillers for the initial discomfort. His bank account was the last thing he had expected to be discussing.

After emptying paper clips from the one ashtray in his office, he pushed it toward her, deciding to try for an old joke. "There's a rumor going round that doctors make a lot of money. Don't believe it, Mrs. Bentley."

Her eyes were ice-blue. "There's a rumor, too, Dr. Cooper, that your father's recently set you up with a very nice trust fund."

A few people in Santa Barbara knew that Walter Cooper had signed over his inheritance from his wife to Roger. The money, coupled with Roger's own inheritance, made him comfortable but certainly no multimillionare. Elizabeth Trunkey Cooper had seen how her money distressed her husband and had allowed the bulk to remain in the family trust. Roger was growing to share his mother's point of view about money. He had seen how her wealth had dogged his father's life. He had watched rich classmates rebel, ruin their lives, destroy others; he had long ago decided to make his goals mundane, hoping to experiment with a clinic, working with a variety of doctors, perhaps even somehow involving his new love for pediatrics.

To counter the woman's remark about his private finances, he half joked, "Mrs. Bentley, are you from the IRS?"

She took a long drag on the Benson and Hedges. "No, Doctor. I'm just interested in rich men. Big, blond, broad-shouldered rich men. I make it my business to meet them when they move in under my nose."

She added, "Santa Barbara has more than its fair share of

millionaires. But, believe it or not, you're one of the few attractive ones around. I noticed you immediately."

Roger did not ask Patricia Bentley where she got her information. Nor did he inquire where she had seen him. He wanted to
return the conversation to a professional footing.

Patricia Bentley was a very desirable woman, and she knew
it, which only made her allure more powerful. Roger had immediately recognized that. But blinding himself to her physical
attractions, he said solemnly, "Mrs. Bentley, are you here to
discuss my finances or your problem?"

"My problem is you, Dr. Cooper. I think you're an extremely
attractive man and I want to know how I can get to know you
a lot better."

Roger folded his arms on the desk. Taking a deep breath, he
began, "Mrs. Bentley—"

"Call me Patty," she interrupted.

"Mrs. Bentley," he insisted, "let me be equally honest with
you.

"As you know, I'm new in the community. I'm starting out
in a new practice. I'm soon to be married to a very fine woman.
And, well—"

He shrugged, struggling to be as honest as he could. "I don't
know how to deal with the embarrassing situation you're putting me in."

"There's no need for embarrassment," she assured him, rising
from her chair, allowing her skirt to ride up her thigh.

As she moved toward the desk, Roger caught the scent of her
perfume. He could literally feel the animal warmth from her
body.

He pushed back his chair, rounding the opposite side of the
desk, moving to the door.

She warned, "Open that door, Doctor, and you'll regret it."

He did not look back as he answered, "I've turned down good
chances before, Mrs. Bentley."

Her voice sharpened. "But I don't like being turned down, Dr.
Cooper. You leave me standing here—feeling like a fool—and
you'll regret it till the day you die."

Roger was angry. "Mrs. Bentley, some regrets are easier to live with than others."

"Open that door and I scream rape."

He opened the door; the scream that followed shattered the next four years of his life.

Roger's painful memories were distracted by a hand on his shoulder.

"Sorry I'm late," said Tom Hudson.

Tom Hudson ordered a Jack Daniel's on the rocks. After the waiter left, he said, "This is one of the things I like best about this place, Doc. A guy can drink here. A drying-out clinic with an open bar."

"Patients have to learn to live with alcohol after they leave Tanglewood," Roger explained. "Why not face reality while they're here?"

"I approve, I approve." Hudson looked around the dining room. "When's Adrian Lyell coming back?"

"You know Adrian?" Roger asked, surprised.

Hudson's eyes lingered on the surrounding tables, assessing the dancing candles, the sparkling crystal, the antique silver. "Before we talk about Tanglewood," he said, "let's settle my problem."

He looked back to Roger. "All this special treatment, Doc. You obviously have some bad news to tell me. So let's get it over with."

Roger was grateful for the man's directness.

"Something showed up in Cat's blood," he began.

Hudson folded his arms across his chest, waiting for details.

"When was the last time you had a blood check?" Roger asked.

"April. I send all my executives for a complete physical once a fiscal year. I make a point of following my own rules."

Hudson held his piercing brown eyes on Roger. "What's wrong with Cat, Doc?"

"Syphilis."

Hudson's eyes instantly glazed.

"I'm sorry, Tom," Roger said, watching Hudson's face turn a spectrum of colors, his fist tightening on the table.

When Hudson did speak, his voice was cold. "You think I gave it to her?"

"I'm just reporting the labs."

Hudson appeared to be collecting himself, fighting down his anger. Finally, he growled, "I had clap twice in my life. But that's it. No herpes. No scabies. No syphilis."

"Will you let me test you?"

"Of course. But it's got to be fast," he said, his face returning to its normal color. "I fly to Miami tomorrow night. I should've gone today."

"You know where the lab is?"

"Hell, I know where everything is in this joint. I've had nothing to do but wander around finding out where you guys bury your skeletons."

"Be in the lab at eight-thirty sharp tomorrow morning."

The waiter brought the whiskey; Hudson took a long drink as if to fortify himself for his next words. Finally, he said, "Why not test Gene Stone while you're at it?"

The suggestion stunned Roger. Was that why Hudson had looked so angry? Did he suspect Stone and Cat might also be lovers?

In a noncommittal tone, Roger answered, "I don't think Dr. Stone would agree to that."

"I'll give him one of my ultimatums." Hudson crunched down hard on an ice cube.

It had not occured to Roger that Cat and Stone might be sleeping together, but he put nothing past Gene Stone.

He agreed, "Why not?"

Another wave of fury crossed Hudson's face, then he continued more conversationally, "Okay. Let's put that little matter aside for the moment."

"No," Roger insisted. "We can talk about it. I'm only sorry I had to tell you at this moment."

Hudson shook his head. "You're a busy guy. I see you running around the place. You do what you have to do, when you have to do it. I just don't want to pursue it at the moment because I tend to let my temper run away with itself. And that's not good. Not good at all when important matters are at stake."

He looked directly at Roger. "Now what's this I hear about Adrian Lyell being out in California trying to raise money to expand this place into some kind of play farm?"

"You saw yesterday's TV show."

"That shit." Hudson took a longer drink.

Roger saw that Hudson was controlling his anger, at least temporarily. Not only did Roger, too, think it was a good thing to change the subject for the moment but he was pleased to be able to discuss his own dilemma with someone not personally involved with the clinic. He began, "Adrian wants to buy me out. I received his formal offer this morning."

"By the sound of your voice, Doc, you're not exactly over the moon about selling."

"Our contract doesn't leave me much of a choice."

"You've got a topping clause." Hudson's words were not a question.

Briefly, Roger explained the terms of his partnership contract. He concluded, "Do you want to invest in a clinic?"

Hudson crunched his ice. "You're about twenty-four hours too late."

Roger stared at him. "You don't seemed surprised by the questions. You sound as if you've been thinking about it. How? Why?"

Hudson gave his answer slowly. "When I saw your partner on that TV talk show . . . he was a little too slick for my liking, if you want to know the truth about it, and I began wondering if I was leaving Cat in the right kind of place. So I started snooping around here. I looked in your Hub. I saw your nerve center. Your checkpoints. Your dispatchers. The more I saw around the place, the more interested I became. I began thinking maybe I should talk to you. Discuss investing. If not in Tanglewood then maybe in another place. A sister clinic out on the coast. I saw how you fill a need and fill it very professionally."

Roger listened, encouraged by Hudson's enthusiasm. He was also impressed that Hudson could put his own problems momentarily aside to discuss another man's business.

Hudson continued. "Then something came up. I've been wanting to buy the Florida food chain, Sunbakers, for a couple months. It just came through. Fact is, that's why I'm flying down to Miami tomorrow. To cinch the agreement. Buying Sunbakers changed my mind about pursuing Tanglewood. I'm a man who doesn't like heaping too much on his plate.

"But the idea of going to Florida started me thinking of another angle—of approaching drug companies I've been doing business with down there. I play poker with a couple of their officers, and I thought of letting them in on the word that there's a sound future for pharmaceutical companies in places like Tanglewood."

Hudson smiled wryly. "Which only goes to show—great minds think alike."

Roger shook his head. "You lost me."

Hudson asked, "Remember? I told you that seeing your partner on TV made me suspicious?"

Roger nodded.

"The day I saw him I asked my Chicago office to run a check on Tanglewood. I just got the report from them today."

Roger waited.

"Among the information my source gave is that your partner, Adrian Lyell, is out in L.A. meeting with three companies about investing in Tanglewood. One is Pegasus. My ears really perked up at the mention of their name as I also was thinking about pharmacy companies getting involved with drug clinics."

"Adrian is seeing Pegasus?" Roger asked, astounded. "The chemical company? For financing?"

"None other. Your partner's been meeting with their chairman, Paul Huttner. His office is in Century City. The other two parties are Doheny Insurance and some outfit called Omega Catering."

Hudson's jowls lifted into a grin. "I see this is all news to you."

"Yes," Roger said grimly.

"What you probably *do* know is that Pegasus is blue chip. Conservative. They've got inroads to Mitsubishi. Japanese as well as German giants. Anything Paul Huttner at Pegasus is interested in must be good. Which only reinforces my hunch about Tanglewood."

"You've learned all this since you've been here?" asked Roger. He felt remarkably inadequate.

"I have to do something. I don't play tennis."

Hudson turned his empty glass between his thumb and middle finger, then continued. "Now for my angle.

"A lot of my stores have pharmacy counters. Among my suppliers are a couple drug companies that have made windfall profits this past year off the changes in the generic prescription laws. Companies that need to invest before the end of the year or take a hell of a beating in taxes."

Roger felt his excitement growing.

"It would mean you'd have to give them a few pertinent details about Tanglewood as a hook. Profits. Loan history. That sort of thing."

"Sounds fair enough," Roger said.

"Can you have a few figures together by tomorrow?"

"Absolutely. You've never seen me crack the whip," Roger said enthusiastically, breaking into a broad grin.

53 ROGER LEFT THE DINING ROOM IN JU-
BILANT SPIRITS. TOM HUDSON MIGHT
not be able to help him find potential backers for Tanglewood, but at least now he had some investor alternatives
rather than going directly to schoolfriends or to his cousin.
After Santa Barbara, he had sworn never to approach the
family trust unless it was absolutely necessary. He was a man
who liked to keep relatives at a distance.

He rapped on Administration's door jauntily, adjusting
his tie as he waited for a reply.

Jackie opened the door; smiling, she said, "I was beginning to give up hope."

"What time is it?" Roger asked.

"Almost ten."

"Hey, I'm sorry. Why don't we put it off till tomorrow
so you can get some sleep?"

"It's you I'm worried about." Jackie stood back from the
door. "You're the busy one."

Roger glanced past her into the office. Papers were strewn
across the chesterfield and the coffee table, and piled on the
desk. "Looks as if you started without me."

"Actually, I think I solved my biggest problem. If you've
got a minute, perhaps you can just check my calculations."

Closing the door, Jackie offered, "Coffee?"

"Please. Black."

"Brandy?"

"No thanks. Coffee's fine."

Jackie pouring two cups from the silver pot, then moved to the desk and handed Roger one. He had begun studying the lists of supply costs she had compiled, lifting the long white streamers of adding tape on which she had tallied the clinic's receipts.

"You did all this tonight?" he asked.

She sipped her coffee. "It's one way to find out where money goes."

"Good for you." He smiled. "You're doing Renee's work, as well."

"Renee's been doing a lot of my work," Jackie said in fairness.

Setting her cup and saucer down on the desk, she showed Roger tabulations she had made on money owing from patients who had accrued extra-service fees.

Roger laughed. "I can fire half the bookkeeping staff with you around, Mrs. Lyell."

Jackie blushed. "Wait till you start stumbling across my mistakes!"

"Hey, come on. Everybody's allowed a few human errors." He tapped her paperwork. "With dedication like this, I'm beginning to see we were silly not to have put you to work in here long ago."

"Tell that to Adrian."

"I will. If I get the chance."

Jackie eyed him. "You sound as if you might never see Adrian again."

"I wonder."

"I know the feeling. I wonder, too."

"It's a little different for you, Jackie. You're married to Adrian. He and I are"—Roger laughed—"mere partners."

"In the loose sense of the word, yes, we're married. But in the very loose sense of the word."

Roger did not know whether to press Jackie for an elaboration on that remark or to change the subject.

"As you know," she went on, "Adrian's trip to Los Angeles was as big a surprise to me as it was you."

Roger watched her turn toward the window and suspected there might be something she wanted to get off her chest.

"But there's one thing I didn't tell you, Roger."

He listened.

"I telephoned Adrian," she said. "When he was still at the Beverly Wilshire. . . . A woman answered the phone in his room."

Roger kept his silence.

"I'm not one to wash dirty linen in public, Roger, so I won't go into details about Adrian's and my marital history. I'll only say that things haven't been rosy. For some time now I feared there might be another woman. Or two. Or three. The voice on the phone only strengthened my suspicions."

Roger felt an urge to comfort Jackie, to offer her some kind of consolation. Instead, he forced himself to stand quietly and listen to what she obviously needed to tell him.

She continued, "I guess that's one of the reasons I've been throwing myself into work in here. To keep myself from exploding with frustration. And anger. Everything I did here in the office seemed to go wrong but I kept on slogging away—for better or worse. It was either that or disintegrating into one big disgusting heap of jelly."

Roger said softly, "You must remember, Jackie, it could have been an innocent accident. There could be a number of reasons why a woman might be answering the phone in his hotel room."

"Of course. And it's extremely generous of you to defend him like that. But the woman in the room—the voice on the phone—is really unimportant when all is said and done. It's the trip to Los Angeles. All his trips. All his secrecy lately. All the—"

She closed her eyes, gulping back a rush of tears.

Roger took a step forward and gave her his handkerchief, saying "Jackie, you should have said something to me sooner. I'm just at the other end of the phone, you know."

She was regaining her composure. "Thank you, darling. I appreciate that. I really do."

Taking the handkerchief, she dabbed her eyes. "But you are terribly busy."

"Maybe so. But I'm always here when you need me. I mean that, too."

"Thank you, Roger. Thank you very much indeed. It's reassuring to hear those words. Especially in the present circumstances. But the truth is, I think I'm better at lending a shoulder to cry on than asking for one for myself. I suppose it comes from having a military man for a father—stiff upper lip and all that."

Looking at the handkerchief in her cupped hands, she smiled at the contradiction and added slowly, "Besides, Roger, I've already talked to somebody. I've talked to a . . . divorce lawyer."

This was obviously the news she needed to share with somebody. Roger understood Jackie's decision, but he still felt a sense of shock.

He asked, "Are you being hasty?"

"Hasty? More like slow. More like—why has it taken me so bloody long to do it?"

Breaking into tears again, Jackie shook her head. "You don't know what it's been like. Adrian's become such a bully. Such an awful, mean-spirited bastard . . ." Sobbing overtook her.

Jackie looked lost and miserable and vulnerable. Impulsively, Roger wrapped his arms around her, saying, "Shh, don't take it too hard. Everything will work out. You'll see."

Jackie was trying to stop her tears, shaking her head. "I'm so embarrassed. I don't usually do things like this. I'm so ashamed of myself."

"Shhh." Roger put his hand under her chin and, raising her face to his, kissed her gently on the lips.

He felt her respond to his kiss. He kept kissing her, holding her more tightly in his arms, until she moved to pull away. He quickly let her go and took a step backward.

It had seemed so natural to Roger to be kissing Jackie. But now, after she had withdrawn from the embrace, he wondered if his impulse had been bold and exploitative of her vulnerable situation.

Taking a deep breath, he avoided her eyes. "I guess I better say good night on that one."

Jackie stood in front of the desk, staring at Roger as he closed the office door behind him.

Her mind was a jumble. Roger had stopped by the office to look over her work, but she had swamped him with all her personal problems.

A few moments ago I was crying, she thought, but now my stomach is full of butterflies. What's happening to me?

54 IT WAS PAST MIDNIGHT WHEN THE TELEPHONE RANG IN GENE STONE'S Orchard Pavilion room and a voice announced at the other end of the line, "Dr. Stone? This is Adrian Lyell. I know we've never met but I feel I can speak to you in strictest confidence."

Gene Stone sat up in the darkness. The telephone had awakened him from a deep sleep, but he immediately recognized the name of Roger Cooper's partner.

Adrian continued. "I'm calling from Los Angeles, but I'll be arriving back in New York tomorrow. I won't be returning immediately to Tanglewood. I'll be staying on for a few days in New York and wondered if you could meet me there to discuss a matter of mutual interest."

"Can you tell me what you have on your mind?" Stone asked, his voice hoarse from sleep.

"I'm aware you're at Tanglewood as a private consultant to Catharine Powers, Dr. Stone. Also, I want to say that I'm a great admirer of your work with figures from the entertainment industry. In fact, that's the reason I want to talk to you. I'd like you to consider working at Tanglewood on a permanent basis."

Stone laughed, reaching for a cigarette. "Roger Cooper and me work together here? Forget it."

"No, no, no." Adrian quickly protested. "I would never propose such a thing. Not to a man of your singular reputation. Not with Roger Cooper's history in Santa Barbara. In fact, I understand you are more familiar than most people with Roger's, shall we say, weaknesses on the job."

Stone swung his bare feet out of bed and switched on the bedside lamp. "Yeah. I know about Roger Cooper's wild oats."

"That's another reason I'm calling you, Doctor," Adrian continued more cautiously. "I'm worried Roger might be placing a Tanglewood employee in an extremely precarious situation. I'm particularly concerned about Delia Pomeroy because I hired her myself. I know she has weaknesses, too."

"Delia Pomeroy." Intuition told Gene Stone to forget about lighting his cigarette and to grab for a pencil; he spelled aloud as he wrote "D-e-l-i-a."

" 'Pomeroy,' " Adrian supplied. "Naturally I'm talking to you strictly off the record, Dr. Stone. You'll appreciate this is an extremely delicate situation. But knowing Cooper's history as you do, I thought you might be able to speak to Miss Pomeroy while you're up in Connecticut. Away from the clinic, of course. I thought you might be able to go to her home and see if she's willing to give an affidavit on Roger approaching her."

This is some cookie I've got on the line, Gene Stone told himself. Into the phone, he asked, "Do you know for certain if this nurse has something to talk about? In terms of Cooper?"

"Delia Pomeroy has certain needs. Physical as well as financial. That's all I can say at this moment. On the telephone."

"I think I'm getting your drift," Stone said, thinking: This Adrian Lyell character is a real son of a bitch. He's asking me to help frame his partner in some trumped-up charge and he doesn't even know me. What's he heard? Who's he been talking to in Los Angeles to take this chance with me?

Adrian pressed on, leaving Stone no time to raise questions.

"You'll find Miss Pomeroy's number in the local telephone directory. Tell her you're a friend of mine who wants to discuss something that might be to her advantage."

This unexpected conversation appealed increasingly to Gene Stone's sense of mischief. He also saw a way of showing Roger Cooper that he, Cooper, was not such a hot shit after all.

Stone decided to be as blunt as Adrian Lyell. "What if I have to, say, refresh the young lady's memory about Cooper putting the make on her?"

The question did not give Adrian pause. "I suspect that Delia's wants are not too exorbitant. A small apartment . . . someplace out here in California for a fresh start . . . an introduction to a new job . . . maybe a little sports convertible . . ."

You bastard, Stone thought. You really want to nail Roger Cooper, don't you? What's he done to you? Why are you taking such a desperate chance like this with me? And what are you willing to pay me for doing your dirty work, you old scumbag?

Keeping those questions to himself, Stone instead asked, "So what's the other subject we'll be discussing, Mr. Lyell, if I come down to see you in New York after talking to Miss Pomeroy?"

"Dr. Stone. I would first like to explain to you my vision of Tanglewood's future. Then I would like you to consider replacing Roger Cooper as our medical director."

PART FIVE

THURSDAY

55 IN NEW YORK CITY, ADRIAN HAD A MORNING MEETING WITH HIS LAW-yer. "Bill, I want you to study the morals clause carefully in view of Roger's recent involvement in immoral activities similar to those he was accused of in Santa Barbara."

Adrian had arrived in New York three hours earlier on the night flight from Los Angeles, feeling surprisingly fresh and rested. Evelyn had traveled cross-country with him. After they had checked into the luxurious Park Regent Hotel on Park Avenue, Adrian had walked the six blocks to William Ruben's Madison Avenue offices.

"I remember you telling me about Roger's malpractice suit," said Ruben, resting both hands on the blue waistcoat of his dark-blue suit. A thick-chested man in his midfifties, Ruben had small, twinkling dark eyes. "But didn't you also tell me the case was thrown out of court?"

"True. Roger was never charged. But rumors still circulate." Adrian twisted his gold signet ring. "Perhaps that's why my new backers have now added this surprise stipulation."

"Stipulation?" Ruben was instantly curious. "What's come up?"

"The backers want a clean slate on Roger or they won't come in on the deal. It's that simple." Adrian had decided not to explain to anybody—including his lawyer—that the three L.A. businessmen wanted Roger completely out of

Tanglewood before they signed the investment contract.

"You've got worries about Roger's private life?" Ruben's shoe-button eyes narrowed.

"Unfortunately, yes," answered Adrian, affecting grave concern. "I've heard rumors about Roger and a certain young lady at Tanglewood. So I've got no choice now but to investigate."

"How?"

Adrian replied, "I've got somebody on the scene asking questions for me. That's all I can say at the moment, Bill. I'm sure you appreciate that. It's a sensitive matter and I've got to look into it carefully."

"Absolutely."

Ruben was no fool. Adrian knew that fact well. If the lawyer had guessed that Adrian was resorting to muck-throwing, he wasn't saying so. The two men had made a private deal: Adrian promised Ruben shares in the new Tanglewood real estate development in return for Ruben's acting for him against Roger in the purchase bid. The deal was irresistible to Ruben, but he hoped to avoid getting too involved with Adrian's manipulations. He knew when the smart move was not to ask questions.

A telephone rang on the glass-topped desk.

Ignoring it, Ruben said cautiously, "But you're acting with great care."

"Of course." Adrian enjoyed having the lawyer in his control.

The phone rang again.

"Answer your phone," Adrian ordered.

Ruben picked up the ivory receiver and announced himself. Listening, he motioned for Adrian to remain seated.

Bending over the desk, Ruben jotted notes, nodding his head, finally saying "Thank you, Mr. Schweider, for this prompt communication. Please put all your points in a letter to me. In the meantime, I'll contact Mr. Lyell and see if I'll be representing him in this personal matter." Ruben lowered the phone.

"Personal matter?" Adrian sat forward on the chair. "What's that all about?"

Ruben looked down at his notepad, reluctant to deliver the news. "Jackie. She's suing for divorce."

Adrian's face showed a flash of surprise, then darkened in anger.

Ruben nodded at the phone. "That was her lawyer. Calling from Hartford."

"On what grounds?"

"Irreconcilable differences." Ruben added, "There's more."

Adrian's jaw worked.

"Her lawyer's trying to get a restraining order to keep you out of Tanglewood. On the grounds that Jackie's domiciled there."

"The bitch." Adrian's voice was a snarl. "The low, sneaking . . . *bitch.*"

56 AT TANGLEWOOD, AS JACKIE LYELL HURRIED TO LEAVE ADMINISTRATION to meet Carol Ann Rice for lunch, she was trying not to think about last night's kiss with Roger.

Digging through the desk drawer for her car keys, she jumped as the telephone rang. Every time the telephone had rung this morning, she had had the same thoughts: Was it Roger? What would he say about last night—or would he pretend it hadn't happened?

At the switchboard, Rita Zambetti said, "Little Milly

Wheeler's husband, Stuart Travis, is on the line, Mrs. Lyell. He wants to speak to the person in charge."

"I'll take the call," Jackie said confidently. She had spoken briefly to Travis earlier that morning after he had arrived in Stonebridge—a few hours after his father-in-law, Donny Wheeler—and checked into a nearby hotel.

Stuart Travis was angry. "Nobody's telling me how Milly ended up in intensive care, and I'm not going to stop asking questions till I find out."

"We'll give you the information when we receive it, Mr. Travis," Jackie assured him, mindful that the singer's mother was suspected of having interfered with treatment.

Travis said, "Old lady Wheeler railroaded Milly into a divorce. I know that for a fact. But she's still my wife and I demand to know what's happening."

Jackie repeated her promise that Tanglewood would contact him at the hospital. After urging him to rest, she put down the receiver.

The telephone buzzed again.

Annoyed with herself for acting like such a giddy schoolgirl every time the telephone rang, she snatched for it and scolded the operator, "Darling, I'm running very late. I can't take any more calls."

As she hurried across the room, she caught her reflection in the mirror by the door. Pausing, she eyed her electric-blue suit. The chunky orange and yellow Ken Lane jewelry. Were the colors too vibrant for a woman of her age? Was she going out as Adrian accused her—mutton dressed as lamb?

Oh, well, she decided. In for a penny, in for a pound. Grabbing the fox tails she had brought downstairs to wear with the outfit, she hurried out of the door and decided not to dwell on the most important age question in her mind: How much older than Roger was she?

Jackie had never heard of Carol Ann Rice until she had moved to the United States and saw a television situation comedy called "Jim and Jenny." It was about an unmarried couple sharing an apartment in Manhattan. Carol Ann played their bubbly next-door neighbor who wrote soap operas. Because of the brunette comedienne's enormous popularity on the show, the producer spun off a second series, "The Carol Ann Rice Show," about the madcap adventures of the soap-opera writer.

During Thursday's lunch at the Pepper Pot, Carol Ann looked as exuberant as the day she had left Tanglewood eighteen months ago, following her recovery from alcoholism. Since then, Jackie had met her twice for lunch in New York, enjoying her company. They usually ended up talking about Carol Ann's old flame, Roger Cooper.

At today's lunch, Jackie tried to keep the subject away from Roger and strictly on Carol Ann. The last thing she wanted was for the actress to suspect that she had the slightest interest in Roger. She didn't even know herself if she did. Last night's kiss had happened so quickly . . . but the kiss and its after-effect had been electrifying.

Glass of Perrier in hand, Carol Ann talked about her new project. "*Heart Strings* is my first feature film and I'm scared stiff. It's all drama. No pratfalls. No funny faces. No kooky Carol Ann."

"Can you tell me about it?" Jackie asked, struggling not to visualize Roger kissing Carol Ann, holding her exactly as he had held Jackie.

"Cora Granville's a Texas widow," said Carol Ann. "She's left alone on her farm to raise her blind son. Her family and all her friends say she's crazy not to move into town. But Cora's got a steel backbone. Like me, she's stubborn as a mule. She stays alone on the farm with the child, doing the chores, raising her son, teaching him Braille, putting her own life on the line in a terrific scene in a snowstorm. When I read the script, I bawled and bawled. I knew I had to do it."

"It sounds challenging. How old is the child?"

"He was a baby in the first draft. We've made him eleven

and signed Berry Dwight from *Grim Secret* for the part."

Jackie scoured her brain for more questions about Carol Ann's work. "So now you're in New York casting the rest of the parts?"

"Actors. Designer. The works."

She leaned closer to Jackie, confiding, "My television contract promised me a production company if my series went into reruns. It has. So . . ."

She raised both hands. "Madam producer."

The bowls of vichyssoise arrived. Carol Ann asked for freshly ground pepper and said to Jackie, "You told me you've been working in Administration. How do you like it?"

Jackie explained casually that Adrian had gone to Los Angeles, and how she was becoming more involved in the day-to-day running of Tanglewood than she had been in her five years at the clinic.

Carol Ann broke off a piece of black Russian bread. "Adrian and Roger have been fools not to put you to work long before this."

"I've arranged a flower or two around the place but never anything like this. I love it. I make more than my share of mistakes but"—she laughed—"I'm learning."

"What are you going to do when Adrian comes back?" Carol Ann broke off another nibble of bread.

"I don't know," Jackie answered honestly.

When the luncheon plates were removed, Jackie and Carol Ann resisted the cream pies and layer cakes on the dessert trolley and ordered coffee, laughing when the waitress brought a footed dish of *petit fours* with the pewter pot.

The mood turned serious. Carol Ann ventured, "Jackie, you mentioned that Adrian's in L.A."

"Since last week." Jackie was relieved that Carol Ann had not yet asked about Roger.

"Where does Adrian stay when he's there?" Carol Ann asked nonchalantly.

"This time he's at the Beverly Wilshire." Jackie thought: That's an odd question.

"Does he ever mention the name 'Evelyn Palmer' to you?"

"Evelyn Palmer?"

"Mmm." Carol Ann toyed with the Apostle coffee spoon. "Should he?"

"No . . ." She set down the spoon. "Not unless he wants you to know he has a mistress."

Jackie froze.

Carol Ann raised her brown eyes. "Jackie, I hate busybodies. But you're very dear to me and I have to interfere."

"What do you mean?"

"Jackie, a woman named Evelyn Palmer is going around Los Angeles saying she's going to marry Adrian and help him run Tanglewood when he takes it over."

Jackie tried not to sound bitchy. "Darling, how do you know what's being said in Hollywood if you've been in New York for the past month?"

"Because Evelyn Palmer's been bragging about it for almost a year."

Jackie remembered the mysterious voice answering Adrian's phone at the hotel on Monday, the weekend trips he had taken over the past year.

She asked, "Is she a friend of yours, this woman? Do you see her in Hollywood?"

"Evelyn Palmer?" Carol Ann laughed. "Not if I can help it. But Hollywood's a very small town."

Confused, Jackie shook her head. "I don't know what to say."

"I'm sorry if I shocked you."

Jackie opened her mouth to speak but stopped.

Carol Ann leaned forward. "Jackie, we haven't known each other very long. But in the short time we've been friends, I've learned you're a very generous, very special person. I've also seen how innocent you are. Surprisingly naive sometimes for such a worldly woman. . . . Darling, I'm telling you about Adrian playing around because I don't want him catching you unprepared."

"How can he do that?"

"By leaving you in the lurch. You must admit, a year with another woman is getting pretty serious.

"It's hell being dumped for someone else," Carol Ann went on. "I know. I've been that route myself. But I fought. Oh, God, did I fight. Like an alley cat. It helps, too. It eases the pain. That's why I want to plant a seed in your head. I want you to think about talking to a lawyer. You don't have to take any drastic steps. Just let Adrian know you've seen a lawyer. That you're serious about protecting your rights if he insists on playing hanky-panky away from home. Women don't have to stand for that kind of thing any more. Like the cigarette ad says, 'We've come a long way, baby.'"

Jackie admitted, "I've already talked to a lawyer, Carol Ann."

It was Carol Ann's turn to be surprised.

"Yesterday."

"So you *knew* Adrian was seeing somebody."

"I suspected. But I never knew her name."

"Are you suing for divorce?"

"Yes."

"On what grounds? Mental cruelty usually does the trick. Or you can go for the big one: adultery."

"But I have no real proof that Adrian was unfaithful, have I?"

"Get a detective. They're not as expensive as you think. If you prove adultery, your lawyer can get you a fabulous settlement."

Jackie wondered whether she should confide that she had already decided on "irreconcilable differences."

Carol Ann lifted her handbag from the floor, saying, "In fact, I think I still have the card for the agency I used for Stan. They're nationwide."

Jackie held up both hands. "No, no, no, no. I don't even

know if I can go through with a lawyer, let alone hire a . . . detective."

Carol Ann removed a small white business card from her wallet and pushed it across the table. "Think about it. If you can prove adultery, you've got an automatic divorce."

Suddenly Jackie was confused. Not only about changing her plea to adultery but also about the direction in which the conversation was now going. She had come to lunch, expecting Carol Ann to want to talk about Roger, and now they were discussing herself and Adrian, another woman in Adrian's life.

Her eyes lingering on the white card, she said, "Tell me more about Evelyn Palmer."

Carol Ann took a sip of coffee. "She divorced the film director Drake Palmer a few years back. Before him she was married to Jolly Montgomery. You know, the shoe store chain, Jumping Jolly's. Evelyn's thirtyish. Pretty in a bobbed-nose sort of way. The kind of woman Hollywood's crawling with. No apparent ambition except to keep trim and suntanned and be taken to all the right parties. Preferably by somebody rich and famous."

"Adrian's neither of those, compared to a lot of people in Hollywood."

Carol Ann smiled. "If Adrian gains control of Tanglewood as she says, he could be both."

Then she asked, "What *is* this about Tanglewood, anyway? Has there been a rift between Adrian and Roger? Is that why these stories are going around about a takeover?"

"There've been a few disagreements between Adrian and Roger, but nothing major."

"Lovely Roger." Carol Ann savored the name. "Without Roger there could be no Tanglewood."

She held her eyes on Jackie. "You *do* realize that, don't you?"

"Roger's importance at Tanglewood? Of course I do."

Carol Ann admitted, "In fact, that's Roger's one and only flaw. He has a single-track mind. Tanglewood."

"Hmmm." Jackie could still feel the pressure of his lips, the warmth of his arms holding her.

A nostalgic smile came over Carol Ann's face. With a little sigh, she said, "Roger and I had our little fling after my recovery. It was short and sweet and totally enjoyable. We both knew there was no future for us. So we just enjoyed ourselves. He's a divine companion. A perfect escort. And an *unbelievable* lover."

Jackie could feel her smile—crooked and nervous.

Carol Ann asked, "Haven't you noticed Roger's magnetism?"

"Magnetism?"

"Come on," the other woman coaxed. "Roger Cooper's a very sexy man."

"Roger's attractive, yes, but . . ."

"Jackie Lyell, you're blushing!"

Jackie's ears burned red. "I've known Roger Cooper for over five years and—"

"So?"

"Roger's like the man next door. A good neighbor."

"So?" repeated Carol Ann. "Lots of ladies have flings with the man next door. Even run off with him."

As Jackie struggled for composure, she wondered if she was trying to prepare herself for a rude shock from Roger, as well as trying to convince Carol Ann—and herself—she had absolutely no interest in him. She had reminded herself all last night that Roger had a reputation for being a lady's man. That tens—possibly hundreds—of females had flipped over him. Long ago she had decided that the suit against him for sexual misconduct in his office had been fraudulent. But it still lingered at the back of her mind—along with the realization that Roger Cooper was indeed a very sexy man.

"Roger's a professional," she tried. "Tanglewood comes first and foremost to him. The last thing he wants is to get involved. With anybody."

For good measure, she added, "You know about Crista? The girl who broke off their engagement?"

"Yeah, what about her?" asked Carol Ann, curious.

"It's simple. Crista left Roger because she said he was married to Tanglewood. Roger is so professional, so involved with his work that there's no time left for wives or girl friends in his life."

Carol Ann said, "It's because of Roger's professionalism that I'm here today. He waited until I was back on my feet before he let it be known he was interested in me."

"Do you mind talking about your stay at Tanglewood?" asked Jackie, trying to change the subject.

"No. Do you know why I'm a Tanglewood fan?"

"Why?"

"Jackie, I've been in three clinics in the past four years. The first time when Stan dumped me. Then when my daughter was killed. And I became a basket case when my series folded. That's when I came to Tanglewood. It cured me. For good. The reason is very simple."

Jackie nodded, feeling her face return to a more normal temperature.

Carol Ann continued. "There're no straitjackets at Tanglewood. No cold-shower treatments. No taking out of garbage or washing dishes or making your beds. It's the trust that Tanglewood puts into patients that's important. Not the shock treatment. Not cold-shower tactics. You don't feel like you're suddenly in Hitler's Youth Movement."

Gripping Jackie's hands across the table, she insisted, "I meant it when I said I'm glad you're taking a more active part in the clinic. I hate to say it, dear heart, but Tanglewood's only flaw is Adrian.

"Adrian's grasping and avaricious. He reeks of being a money man. On the other hand, Jackie, you're a very warm, concerned person. You belong in Administration. Greeting new patients. Meeting the public. You and Roger would make a great team."

Jackie smiled nervously as she fingered the private detective's business card.

* * *

Carol Ann Rice wheeled out of the parking lot in her new red Mercedes 500SL, honking, waving, blowing good-bye kisses to Jackie.

Sitting behind the wheel of her four-year-old silver BMW 320I, Jackie did not turn on the ignition.

Instead, she stared at the detective agency's card, wondering how her life could suddenly be in such a muddle. Only a week ago she had been a quiet housewife whose husband worked with a doctor named Roger Cooper. Although she had not been a particularly happy housewife, she still had had order in her life, and she had clung to that orderliness like a life raft. Now she felt as though she were spinning dizzily on the edge of a whirlpool.

57 AT 2:45 P.M. IN STONEBRIDGE GENERAL HOSPITAL, CRITICAL CARE NURSE Sharon O'Neil emerged from Little Milly Wheeler's room and hurried down the hallway to a yellow metal door marked PRIVATE.

The pudgy nurse studied the patient's family gathered in the private waiting room—mother, father, husband.

She announced, "Milly's been given her anticonvulsant and I'm pleased to report the monitor is constant again. But until further notice nobody will be allowed in to see her."

Her voice softened. "Why don't you folks go back to your motel rooms and get some rest?"

Gladys Wheeler moved to the edge of the blue plastic couch. "I'm not leaving my baby."

Donny Wheeler jabbed a finger at the floor. "We wait here until we talk to some guy who knows what the hell he's doing."

Stuart Travis moved from the window. "Has Dr. Nathan talked to the specialist I told him to call in Houston?"

Nurse O'Neil remained calm. "Dr. Nathan's spoken to each and every doctor you've instructed him to call."

She added, with some satisfaction, "Your doctors all concur with Dr. Nathan's diagnosis."

Donny Wheeler demanded, "How the fuck can somebody 'concur' when they haven't even examined her?"

Nurse O'Neil backed away from the singer's foul breath. "If you thought enough of your doctors to give their names to Dr. Nathan, I assume you have faith in their intelligence, Mr. Wheeler."

"Listen, smarty pants—"

Tired of listening to their insults and rude language, Nurse O'Neil moved toward the door. "It's my break," she said. "I only stopped by to give you folks an update. So if you'll excuse me now—"

Donny Wheeler grabbed for her. "Hold it, lady."

The nurse looked from the singer's grasp on her forearm to his bloodshot eyes. "I have nothing further to say, Mr. Wheeler."

Wheeler held his grip. "When do we see Nathan?"

The nurse answered frostily, "When *Dr.* Nathan arrives back at the hospital."

She held his stare, letting him know she was not intimidated by his size or his fame.

Donny Wheeler released the hold, waving her toward the door. "Go on. Get out of here."

Sharon O'Neil disappeared into the hallway, the swinging door slapping behind her.

Gladys Wheeler resumed rocking on the plastic couch after the nurse left the room. "Why, Lord?" she asked. "Why did You let this happen to my little girl? Why?"

Donny Wheeler was pacing back and forth across the linoleum floor. He frowned at his wife. "Go fix your face. You look like hell."

"I *feel* like hell."

"Then take a walk. You're getting on my nerves."

"How do you think *I* feel?" she cried. "Our baby's going to die."

Across the room, Stuart Travis leaned against the window frame and pulled one end of his bushy black moustache. He looked from Gladys to Donny. "Nobody's told me yet what happened to Milly," he said angrily.

Gladys ignored her son-in-law, rocking back and forth on the couch, tears rolling down her cheeks.

Travis stepped from the window. "Why'd Milly try to kill herself, Gladys?"

Gladys closed her eyes.

Travis leaned toward her. "What happened, Gladys?"

Covering her face with both hands, she began crying in gulps.

Donny Wheeler stopped pacing. "Now see what you've done, jerk-off. Leave her alone."

"Leave her alone?" Travis pointed a thumb at the door. "My wife's down the hall dying and you tell me to leave *her* alone?"

"Your wife? Shit, boy, I don't know if you've noticed but divorce papers have been served on you."

"I don't give a damn. Milly's still my wife."

"Then why haven't you been treating her like one?"

"I suppose you've been a model husband all your life?"

"Yeah." Wheeler nodded. "Leastwise better than you, jerk-off. You treat your wife like other men treat their whores. Fact is, if you weren't making a fat living off Little Milly's singing, I'd say you'd probably have her out on the street hooking for you."

Travis sprang at his father-in-law. His fist cracked Wheeler's jaw.

Wheeler saved himself from a fall and swung his right arm.

Travis ducked the punch and swung his right fist, striking Wheeler's face as he hit him in the stomach with his left.

The two men fell in a clinch, hands choking one another's throats, fingers gouging eyes, rolling across the floor as they fought.

Gladys sprang from the couch. She grabbed a yellow fiberglass desk chair by the hind legs and swung it at the men, screaming "Stop your fighting. Stop it right now."

Her cries and the sound of crashing furniture brought two orderlies into the room.

As the white-jacketed men pulled apart Wheeler and Travis, Gladys stood alongside her son-in-law. "You did it!" she screamed. "You put Little Milly on pills! You gave her whiskey! You did it!"

Catching his breath, Stuart Travis nodded at Wheeler. "Ask him what happened in Detroit. The night him and Milly topped the bill at the Country Family Show."

"Shut up, boy," growled Wheeler.

Travis continued goadingly. "Ask him, Gladys. Go on. Ask how he helped Little Milly go on stage that night in Detroit. Milly told me all about how her dear, loving daddy helped her through that Country Family Show."

Donny Wheeler threatened, "Shut up, boy, before you go too far and I have to kill you."

"See, Gladys," Travis cried. "He don't deny it."

Donny Wheeler broke from the orderlies and pushed through the swinging door, the two white-jacketed men chasing after him.

Gladys stared angrily up at Travis's bloodied face. "Can't you see how destroyed that poor man is by what's happening?" she demanded.

" 'Destroyed,' my ass." Travis said accusingly, "Donny's as guilty as you are, old lady. The two of you put Milly in this place. But neither of you can face facts."

"What do you know about facts? You . . . degenerate."

"I know you and Donny have a piss-poor marriage. I know you've been so lonely, so sexually frustrated all your life that you're about ready to scream."

She slapped his face.

"You've wanted to do that for a long time, haven't you? You knew from the start you couldn't control me like you control everybody else. You saw I was a threat to you running things. You knew I was giving Milly good loving, too. Damn good loving. Something you never got from Donny. And that drove you crazy."

"Shut your mouth," Gladys hissed. "Shut your no-good white-trash mouth, Stu Travis."

"Not until you know the truth."

Stu Travis grabbed her by both shoulders. "*Donny's* the one who started Milly on pills, old lady. In Detroit. She was tired. Her tour was over. She wanted to go home. But, no, you pushed her to do that Country Family Show. You wanted her to represent the third generation of country music in your family. You told her a Wheeler and a Beard can do anything they set their minds to."

Gladys's upper lip curled. "What do you know about Wheelers and Beards, scum?"

"I know they're nothing but boozers. That's what I know. Hell almighty, Gladys. Donny can't go on stage unless he takes a handful of pills and tanks up on Jim Beam. It was Donny who gave Milly her first Dexedrine. That night in Detroit. Milly told me so."

"You liar!"

Travis laughed. "I know stories, too, about your own daddy, Gladys. How the great Billy Boy Beard used to stop by Ruthie Sidcup's every night to buy a jug of corn liquor— and whatever else Ruthie might be selling if her old man wasn't at home."

"Is nothing sacred to you?" Gladys's voice shook with rage.

"Why should it be? You wrecked my marriage. Why should I respect anything about your life?"

Travis sneered. "Gladys, what about *your* dear momma and poppa? You go around Nashville sobbing how poor Billy Boy Beard had to work his butt off to support eight kids. But that's a lie, ain't it, Gladys? Billy Boy Beard needed money to pay hospital bills for your ma. Your ma was a boozer, too, wasn't she, Gladys? Her mind had rotted away from too many years of bad moonshine. So your daddy had to work his butt off to keep her in that private rest home up at Iron Springs."

Gladys broke away from Travis's grip.

He followed her across the room. "You can't go around ruining other people's lives, old lady, and expect them to leave you lily white and untouched."

Gladys stopped in front of the window. Looking beyond the hospital's parking lot at the narrow river, she admitted in a low voice, "Work . . . that's all us Beards ever knew."

"And booze," Travis added.

Gladys ignored him, continuing softly "My daddy used to tell us kids that work was the only thing you can be sure of in life. Work and dying."

"You tried to raise Milly with the same old break-ass philosophy, didn't you, Gladys?"

Gladys still ignored him. "Daddy had a little saying: 'If you want something done well, you got to do it yourself.' " She wiped the tip of one forefinger across the window ledge and looked at the dust she had collected.

The unexpected action puzzled Travis. He fell silent, watching her.

She rubbed the tips of her thumb and forefinger together, feeling the grime. "So much work to do around a place," she said.

"Hey," Travis muttered. "What the hell you talking about, old lady?"

She wiped her finger tip across a windowpane and looked at the smudge on her finger. "Filth."

Travis shook his head.

Gladys Wheeler faced the window, folding both arms across her chest, reminiscing. "I used to sew Donny's fancy shirts. Book his appearances. Do his contracts and agreements. When Little Milly came along, I bundled her up all warm in a blanket and took her over to Four Bell Records where Donny was recording in those days. Despite all my work, I kept a clean house. Nobody could say Gladys Wheeler didn't keep her place spic 'n span."

Travis backed away, leaving her standing by the window.

Alone in the room, Gladys continued talking to no one. "People used to say, 'Donny Wheeler, he might be a drinker. But Gladys Wheeler, she's a *work*aholic. That's what Gladys Wheeler is. A *work*aholic. . . .' "

She angled her head to one side. "I was just a little tyke myself when my daddy taught me Life's Golden Rule. Daddy used to preach, 'Gladys, honey. Never say, *What* can I do now? Always say, *Now* what can I do?' "

Gladys nodded at her reflection in the window. "That's the secret of success in this life: Never say, *What* can I do now? Always say, *Now* what can I do?"

58 THE CLIMATE IN THE POOL HOUSE WAS TROPICAL, LIKE A GREENHOUSE. CRANdall Benedict uncinched his Tanglewood robe, wondering if the man sitting in the chair at the end of the pool was who he thought it was: playwright David Terranova.

"Don't let the splash frighten you," he called jokingly.

The man turned in the chair and, sure enough, it was Terranova, a younger man than Benedict, much slimmer, almost gaunt.

"I just want to warn you," called Benedict. "I get into water like a polar bear."

Terranova waved and moved to return to reading his paperback.

"Now that I've disturbed you, Mr. Terranova, let me say one thing," the novelist continued affably. "I'm a great admirer of your work. I've always been. I enjoy reading *Nantucket Light* as much as seeing it."

Terranova moved to the edge of the chair. "Why, thank you, Mr. Benedict. That's a great compliment coming from a man of your talent."

"Talent?" Benedict waved his small hand. "What's talent? The ability to sit down and get the job done. That's the trick. It takes me a half bottle of Chivas Regal even to turn on the typewriter. That's what I'm doing here. Trying to learn how to work without first falling over in a dead drunk."

Moving to the edge of the pool, he continued. "I didn't mean to disturb you. I just wanted to say how much I enjoy your work. Not enough writers are willing to admit that these days, don't you feel? This new wave of bitch-criticism has become epidemic. And as far as encouraging young writers—forget it. Established writers don't have the time of day for young talent. That's a shame. A great shame."

Holding his nose, the chubby novelist jumped into the pool with a loud splash.

David Terranova sat watching the lapping waves, thinking: That was pretty thoughtful of the fat little fag. He's respected. Rich. Famous. Won the Pulitzer prize. Yet he took time out to give me a professional compliment. Would I ever do such a thing?

59 FOR LUNCH THURSDAY, KAREN WASH-
INGTON ATE WITH PEABO IN HIS
suite. They talked comfortably about Tamara and Tyler, the
work Peabo's mother was doing with Philadelphia's Martin
Luther King Trust, how Karen's parents were planning to
visit China next year for their summer holiday. The conversation was easy and relaxed, almost like old times.

Karen waited until the waiter removed the lunch dishes
from the suite before she produced a large manila envelope
of letters from her handbag. Roger had convinced her that
they had to tell Peabo soon about the news stories breaking
on him; he believed that the best way to do this was by
reading Peabo a few of the letters. Roger had promised to
be nearby when that moment came. They had decided that
Karen would begin after today's lunch.

Hoping Roger was in the suite's foyer as planned, Karen
removed a sheaf of letters from the envelope. "Peabo, it's
been on the news that you're here at Tanglewood."

"Where?" Peabo was standing in front of the round
wicker coffee table.

"In the newspapers and on television and radio," Karen
explained softly. "The press knows all about you and amphetamines, Peabo."

"How'd they find out?"

Karen had rehearsed her speech with Roger and now
forced herself to say, "It started with the same old problem—"

"What old problem?" His anger was mounting.

"Oh, some white woman thinking I wasn't good enough to stay in her hotel. The kids and Desiree were with me. One thing led to another. A newspaper man overheard us and—"

"Where'd this happen?" he demanded. "When?"

Karen did not answer the questions; instead, she proceeded with the explanation she had carefully prepared with Roger.

"Peabo, before I continue with the negative side of what happened, I want to tell you about the positive side. I want to read you some of the lovely, supportive letters you—we— got from people who've heard about you being here in the clinic."

"*Letters?*" He spun around on the carpet.

"Peabo, calm yourself."

Pacing the carpet, he hit his fist into the palm of his other hand, stopping in front of a wall, driving his fist against it. "Letters to me here? In this . . . *drug* clinic?"

He turned and kicked his foot into the television screen.

Karen sat rigidly on the couch. But, strangely, she did not feel threatened. Although Roger was presumably waiting in the foyer, she still did not feel she needed his help.

Seeing Peabo grab for a picture on the wall, she said more forcefully, "That's enough temper tantrums now. Cool it."

He glared over his shoulder at her.

Karen knew it was now or never. She must criticize him at this moment or forever hold her peace.

Sitting on the sofa, she crossed one leg over the other, calmly observing "If you weren't so pig-headed, you could talk about all this."

"What do you want me to do? Go on TV? Talk about how I'm a junkie?"

Karen took the remark seriously. "That's one idea. But I doubt if you would do it. If you *could* do it. You can't even talk to *me* about your dependency."

"Since when do you know so much?"

"Peabo, I've known since the first year we were married

that you can't take criticism. That you can't stand looking
bad. Oh, sure you can tie big leather pillows around your
fists and hit away at some other guy inside a boxing ring.
You can make jokes about it to reporters. You can charm
them on the talk shows. But you can't face people across a
table. You can't calmly and sensibly discuss any of your
problems one to one."

A vein stood out on his forehead in anger. "That's what
you think?"

Karen nodded. "That's what I think."

He pointed a finger at her. "You think I'm a coward?"

"Yes, I do. The same way I think I'm a coward for not
standing up to you before now and telling you what I think.
I loved you so much, Peabo Washington, I wouldn't dare
criticize you. I wouldn't dare disagree with you. I didn't
want to upset you. Even after you started living on speed,
I kept my mouth shut. I made excuses to myself why you
were doing it. I told myself you were under a lot of pressure.
Traveling too much. Tired. But do you know how far that
got me? Straight to the divorce lawyers!"

"What you talking about? Divorce lawyer?"

"I'm saying that if we—notice I say *we*, not you, not me,
but *we*—if we don't make some changes, Peabo Washington, there's no future for us together. Two cowards can't go
on living under one roof."

"You can't divorce me."

"I most certainly can."

Karen told him of the decision she had made privately
since coming to Tanglewood. "I don't want to divorce you,
but if we can't sit down and talk husband to wife, I'm going
through with it."

"There's another guy," he said accusingly.

She frowned. "There's your old male ego. Thinking I
wouldn't leave you for myself. Thinking there has to be
another man. Well, there's not, Peabo. I'd be leaving you for
me. For the kids."

"What about *me?*" he wailed with sudden panic. "Don't I get any consideration?"

"Yes. What about you?" Karen asked, holding her large brown eyes on him. "You're supposed to go into group therapy and you're dragging your feet about that."

"Who says?"

She answered by holding up a handful of letters. "You can't even listen to compliments from strangers. How can you hear criticism in a therapy group?"

He pointed at the letters. "Those strangers put bread on our table. They're fans, girl. Fans! People who do not expect me to be strung out."

"But you *are* strung out, and you have to admit it before you can get better."

He glared at her, fury in his eyes.

The suite's doorbell buzzed.

Peabo turned to the window. "Tell whoever it is to go away."

"Why? Ready to hide again?" asked Karen, standing up.

He shouted over his shoulder, "Woman, I want you to stop challenging me."

"And I want you to come out of your shell," Karen called as she moved with determination to the door.

"Roger!" she said cheerfully, better at play-acting today than she had been yesterday. "Come in. Peabo and I were just getting ready to read a few fan letters."

"Mind if I listen?" Roger looked at Peabo, trying to gauge if the boxer suspected this meeting was a set-up.

Peabo stood at the window, his back to the room.

Roger called louder, "Mind if I come in, Peabo?"

"Suit yourself," Peabo grumbled.

Roger still did not know how good his idea was but he felt that if Peabo acknowledged a few faults in front of him— along with Karen—he might have less difficulty facing a larger group.

Karen sank back down to the couch, sorting through the selection of letters. "Here's one: 'Dear Peabo Washington,

I'm writing to tell you it's time for you to get on with the show. The money I won from your Harrow fight bought my baby girl her first cot. Now Tina's almost four and needs a bigger bed very bad. Please let me know when your next match is so I can start placing my bets.' It's signed, 'Smoky Gable, Denver, Colorado.' "

Roger tried to sound lighthearted. "Peabo, I guess you didn't know you furnished more than your own house!"

Peabo grunted, unamused.

Karen continued. "Here's another one. 'Dear Peabo, Please settle an argument for us. My better half tells me you're a clown because you're covering up your nerves before a fight. I say that's not so.' "

Karen picked another letter from the collection she had carefully selected for this meeting. "Ah, yes. Here's one of my favorites. 'Dear Karen, It must be difficult for you living with Peabo during his present troubles. Do you think the problem is because you're a younger woman married to an older man?' "

" 'Older man?' " Peabo roared, turning around.

Karen held up her hand for him to hush. Smiling, she continued. " 'On the brighter side, Peabo will have you to nurse and care for him when he gets old and gray—like I do my old man.' "

"Who wrote that?" Peabo demanded. But Roger thought he saw a trace of a smile on Peabo's lips.

"Lorna Jane Wilkes. Miami, Florida." Raising her eyes from the letter, she handed a sheaf to Roger. "Your turn."

Roger took the thick pile of letters and began with the top one. "Dear Peabo Washington, I am eight years old and think you will always be the champ. But my older brother says you can't even lick a stamp. I'm sending you a stamp and a blank postcard. If you would please put the stamp on it—along with your autograph—you would settle a big fight here in our house. Signed, Junior Smith . . . Washington, D.C."

Peabo pointed his finger at the letter in Roger's hand. "Now that's a smart kid. I need somebody like that for my manager."

Looking from Roger to Karen, he joined them in a laugh.

"That wasn't so hard now, was it?"

"What?"

"Laughing." Roger looked at Peabo. "Do you think you can do it in a therapy group?"

"You two in this together?" Peabo's smile had disappeared.

Karen answered, "You better believe it. We want you better."

"What about those letters?" Peabo asked suspiciously.

Roger said, "The people who wrote you these letters are fans of yours, Peabo. They want you better, too. Everybody's on your side. Except you."

"What you saying, man?"

"I'm saying give yourself a chance, Peabo. Why don't you sit down and listen to me for a minute, okay?"

Seating Peabo and Karen side by side on the couch, Roger paced the room. "This is how it is," Roger explained. "Your body's kicking the chemicals. Your labs are looking good. The only thing that's off course is your mind. You're fighting your own recovery, Peabo." He stood in front of him. "So why don't you want to get better?"

"Don't talk shit." Peabo worked his hands nervously.

"Then why are you resisting a therapy group?" Roger asked. "You think those other patients are all that concerned about you? Do you think they've all come to Tanglewood to find out what they can about Peabo Washington? Or do you think they might have their own problems? Might be more concerned about their own recovery?"

Peabo dropped his head. "I hear you, man."

"So you're willing to give it a chance?" Roger asked.

"I'm ready?" Peabo asked.

Karen put her arm through his. "I don't know about you.

But I am. Ready for you to get out of here and come home where you belong."

Peabo nodded. "Okay. You guys win. I go to that group therapy."

"No," Roger said firmly. "We don't win, Peabo. *You* win. This is *your* battle. Nobody can fight it except you. You have to understand that now or you might as well throw in the towel."

Peabo repeated, "Okay, okay. I'll go to your circle jerk."

Roger closed the door on Peabo's suite. His gut reaction told him that the time spent with Peabo was going to pay off; not only was he going to a group therapy session but also he might start admitting some important facts about himself.

Roger moved on to other items on today's list.

The Huddle. He had five minutes to get there.

Also, he had to remind Accounts again to prepare the fact sheet for Tom Hudson to take to potential investors in Miami. He had a meeting with Hudson at four o'clock this afternoon.

The biggest question was Jackie.

Hurrying to the Huddle, Roger remembered the way they had kissed last night. He didn't regret it. Not at all. But why was he suddenly finding her so attractive?

Also, why was he having so much difficulty in approaching her today?

How do you follow a kiss like that?

60 DR. DUNSTAN BELL ADDRESSED THURSDAY AFTERNOON'S HUDDLE IN his usual acerbic tone. "As two patients have walked out of here in the past thirty-six hours, I think we should face the fact that we have a very serious security problem."

"Forced restraint creates prisons," argued Philip Pringle.

"True." Bell removed his wire eyeglasses and squeezed the bridge of his nose. "But once treatment begins, a patient changes, often experiencing paranoia. Disorientation. Therefore I suggest we reevaluate our entire surveillance system. Consider posting guards at outside doors. Patrol the grounds day and night. Install more scan cameras in trees."

Seated at the head of the table, Roger listened to the give-and-take, trying to keep from thinking about Jackie. Recalling he had a meeting tomorrow with Dunstan Bell to discuss his complaints, he added it to the list of tomorrow's important things to remember.

Then he raised his yellow pencil and interrupted. "Dunstan, let me clarify a few facts."

The group gave Roger its attention.

"First, Lavender Gilbert was not officially a patient here. Not yet. Nor did disorientation or shock seem to have been a motivating force for her disappearance. I believe everybody in this room is aware of how her employer telephoned from New York, and sent a limousine to collect her a few hours later."

Heads nodded; theories about the designer's ulterior mo-

tive in getting his star model back to New York had circulated throughout the clinic.

Roger continued. "The same holds true for Nigel Burden.
I do not believe he left here in a state of disorientation."

Betty Lassiter hoisted her Zippo lighter. "Can we save
Burden till later? He's back in my therapy group and I'd like
to make a few observations about him when it's time."

The table agreed.

Roger said, "Dunstan, I've discussed these problems with
Security, but I'm waiting for a full report from Leo Kemp.
But I agree with you that a review of our system is in order."
To the table in general, he said "Over the next week, I'd like
each of you to submit your ideas on Security to my office.
No tapes, please. Caroline has enough transcribing to do."

He looked around at the five faces. "What's next on the
menu?"

"Milly Wheeler," Bell said.

Roger looked at his notebook. "The news about Milly
Wheeler isn't good. Nick Nathan telephoned this morning
from the hospital. The right lobe's filled with blood. The left
lung's in rapid process of collapse."

His remarks were greeted with silence.

Bell glanced at the head nurse. "Has any of your staff
verified the rumor that Mrs. Wheeler interfered with treatment?"

Shirley Higgins flipped through her spiral pad, murmur-
ing to herself.

Bell interrupted irritably. "In brief, Mrs. Higgins. In brief.
Did any of your nurses find anything unusual or alarming
about Mrs. Wheeler's conduct?"

The head nurse glared at her rival. "They did after comparing notes about Mrs. Wheeler."

Bell spoke harshly. "I find that very unprofessional, Mrs.
Higgins. Waiting for staff to compare notes on a patient.
Was there no suspicion, no report whatsoever about the
mother on arrival?"

Roger was fed up with Bell's baiting of Shirley Higgins.

He rapped his pencil once on the table. "Dunstan! Drop the cat-and-dog fight, okay?"

To Shirley Higgins, he said, "Let's talk about that leather belt around the patient's waist. Did anyone see it there beside Glen Schaeffer?"

"Margie Clark also saw it," replied the head nurse. "It's in her report. You'll have it tomorrow."

The subject moved to Lillian Weiss and Ray Esposito.

Again Bell spoke up. "What happened? A very explicit order had been posted on Esposito's room when we heard that he was a wife-beater. If she hadn't fallen against the emergency button, we could have had a homicide here."

"Lillian Weiss hasn't spoken about it yet," Shirley Higgins reported. "She's still in the hospital, with her jaws wired."

Pringle raised his Tiffany pen. "This morning I interviewed Esposito. He was inarticulate on the subject of Lillian Weiss."

"Does he say anything at all about yesterday?" Roger asked. "About the attendants pulling him off Mrs. Weiss?"

"Whenever I try to discuss the incident with Esposito, he changes the subject. Looks blankly into space."

"What's your opinion?"

Pringle clasped his hands on the table. "I believe the attack on Mrs. Weiss had nothing whatsoever to do with drug withdrawal. I'm willing to stake my professional reputation on the fact it was totally psychotic."

Betty Lassiter said, "The interesting story will be hearing what Lillian Weiss has to say." Her eyes twinkled.

"I'll talk to Esposito this afternoon," Roger said.

Pulling Esposito's file from the stack in front of him, he added, "I'll also transfer him to Security in the main house. Keep him there till the final stages of treatment."

At the far end of the table, Dunstan Bell coughed, twice. Faces turned.

Bell said, "There's something I want to mention that involves—at least indirectly—everything we've been discussing this afternoon."

All eyes studied the dour physician.

"Jackie Lyell." Dunstan Bell shook his head disapprovingly. "Should a . . . housewife really be running Administration?"

Roger jumped from his chair. "Mrs. Lyell's working in Administration with my full agreement. If you have any complaints about Jackie Lyell, make them directly to me. We have a meeting scheduled for tomorrow, if you remember."

Looking around the table, Roger saw everyone staring at him in stunned silence. Without even realizing it, he had been shouting.

61 RAY ESPOSITO WAVED ROGER CASUALLY INTO THE SITTING ROOM OF HIS suite, as if Roger had come to read the gas meter, fix the telephone, or repossess the furniture.

Still a little bit embarrassed about defending Jackie Lyell so emotionally in the Huddle a few minutes earlier, Roger moved slowly into the sitting room, remembering exactly why he had come there: Esposito had to be transferred to strict security accommodations. Roger also had to try to get him to talk about how and why he had attacked Lillian Weiss.

Esposito's dark eyes shone with hatred, his lantern jaw

was set with rigid defiance. As Roger took note of this, he recalled Philip Pringle's diagnosis of psychotic behavior.

Roger gestured at two chairs. "Do you want to sit down and have a talk, Ray?"

Esposito shook his head, running one hand through his curly black hair.

"It might do you some good," Roger persisted. "I understand you had some trouble you might want to talk about."

"Naw. It's too late for me to talk now. When I needed to talk to somebody in New York, there was nobody around to talk to. Just that pig of a woman I was married to."

"Don't you like women, Ray?"

The question neither surprised nor offended Esposito. He shrugged his broad shoulders. "I don't like women staring at me."

"Is that what happened yesterday?"

Esposito's voice was soft, touched with a slight Brooklyn accent. As if he were bashful, he did not look at Roger as he spoke. "You've been decent to me, Dr. Cooper. Real decent. More open than anybody in a long time. But let me tell you something. I learned a long time ago to live inside my head. It's better living inside there because I'm the only person asking questions."

He smiled, showing a broken tooth. "I also know all the answers so I don't have to talk back to myself, right?"

He turned to the window, saying more innocently "So when are you kicking me out? Is that what you come to do now?"

"I've come to move you to another accommodation, Ray. You're not ready to leave us yet."

"Where you moving me?" Esposito asked. "Someplace where you keep the wild animals?"

"Someplace where you might feel safer from prying eyes."

"What then? What if I have no place to go when it comes time for me to leave?"

Roger knew from the social worker's report that Esposito's wife was filing for divorce on the grounds of assault and battery. He answered, "We'll work out that problem if and when we come to it, won't we, Ray?"

Of all the patients at Tanglewood, Roger was most confused by this New York City construction worker whom his juniors dubbed the "hardhat junkie."

Ray Esposito's drug habit began in Vietnam.

Boredom, rather than a fear of being killed in action, was what started his experiments with heroin. Bangkok brown was readily available and cheap to American GIs. It looked similar to unrefined sugar, and Esposito sprinkled it on cigarettes or inhaled its fumes from a piece of tinfoil, whiling away hours in what he and his buddies in Charlie Company called "chasing the dragon."

Heroin made Esposito feel as if he were living in his own little world. America might be fighting a war in Vietnam, but it was the first time Esposito had ever felt at peace with himself.

By the 1970s, Vietnam had become a drug supermarket. Heroin. Cocaine. LSD. When U.S. bombers destroyed supply lines across Cambodia during Esposito's first winter in Saigon, Bangkok brown became scarce and Esposito was forced to try China white. Compared to brown heroin, the white variety was disappointing when smoked or sniffed. The alternative was to inject it into a vein.

Afraid of poking hypodermic needles into his body, Esposito asked bunkmate Tommy Taylor to give him the first injection.

Taylor, a rancher's son from Helena, Montana, eagerly pulled off his webbed belt. "First we got to pop out a vein, old buddy."

Esposito cringed, turning away his head as he extended his muscled arm.

"Next we got to make sure the needle's nice and clean and—"

Taylor studied the syringe against the light. "I don't want to pump no air bubbles into your vein and kill you on your first fix."

The prick was surprisingly painless; the high, immediate and far stronger than any of Esposito's previous experiments with narcotics. He injected himself later that night to reexperience the euphoric rush, and by the time he returned to the United States fourteen months later for military discharge, Ray Esposito was addicted to mainlining heroin.

Esposito had married his high-school sweetheart before going to Vietnam. When he arrived at their one-bedroom apartment in the Fort Greene section of Brooklyn, he expected to find the same curvaceous Latin beauty, but instead he saw a chubby woman waiting to cook his meals, wash his laundry, bear his children. How could anybody have changed so quickly?

Laura Esposito was surprised, too, by the drastic changes in the person to whom she can had been writing faithfully in Vietnam. Once a handsome, happy-go-lucky boy, her Prince Charming had come home a gaunt, hollow-eyed man. He didn't talk to her. He didn't eat her cooking. He told lies. Worst of all, though, he never made love to her. By the end of their first six months of being reunited, they were quarreling regularly. Laura complained that he never asked about her day, never took her anywhere, never gave her any compliments.

Their lack of money was also the subject of arguments.

"What do you do with your paychecks?" Laura demanded as she dug through their secondhand refrigerator to find something for supper.

"Buy things." The languor that followed a three-minute heroin rush could last up to twelve hours, making Esposito lethargic, his voice slurred, his head nod.

"Buy what things? We've got the same old clothes. Same old clunky car. Same tacky old junk"—she kicked at the fridge—"that Mama threw out years ago."

Esposito's job was with Janni Brothers Construction, working on a building site on Madison Avenue in Manhattan. There he met other Vietnam veterans who had been hired not for heroic war records but for their willingness to ride open elevators far above street level to work in all kinds of weather, risking their lives to score the next fix.

Esposito learned that many skyscraper sites hired junkies. Job accidents were frequent, maiming or killing the workers, sometimes involving innocent passersby—a steel girder falling to the sidewalk, lift cranes tumbling down into Manhattan's congested traffic. Despite the safety hazard of junkies nodding off at work, construction companies continued to employ them.

Esposito also discovered that heroin was easy to buy in New York. Dealers sold smack from parked cars in Harlem. Newspaper boys peddled it with the New York Times on fashionable midtown streets. Mafia pushers set up shop in derelict buildings in the ramshackle section of the Lower East Side known as "Alphabet Town," because of the street names of Avenues A, B, C . . .

After a day's work, Esposito caught the F train downtown, taking his place at the end of a line that formed along Avenue A. As if waiting in line to buy a ticket to a movie, he stood with other hardhats as well as with denim-clad college students, Brooks Brothers–suited executives, commuters to Connecticut, the homeless who roamed the streets of New York City—all there to score drugs.

Police cars cruised Alphabet Town, but they only troubled the drug lines when a dealer had not paid protection money or if City Hall ordered a cleanup before an election. Most times, NYPD ignored the addicts waiting to buy a fix.

The transaction itself was quick and anonymous.

After reaching the head of the line, Esposito shoved his money through a crack in a door, or sometimes a hole in a wall where a few bricks had been removed to make a small, low window. A hand passed back a white paper packet. The customer and pusher never saw one another, never exchanged words except for the customer saying what he wanted and how much.

From Alphabet Town, Esposito went to Johnny Ferraro's place in Little Italy. After injecting himself there, he lounged around his army friend's railroad apartment, chain-smoking cigarettes, reminiscing with Ferraro and other buddies about good times in Nam, sometimes going around the corner to Mulberry Street for a plate of spaghetti. Unlike Esposito, Ferraro had no regular job; often he was not in the apartment but out on the street, hustling money for his next fix: stealing, or pawning radios, cameras, gold chains he had stolen to buy drugs. It was money from Ferraro's life of crime that kept him one step away from joining New York's homeless—the city's transient "bag people" who slept on the streets, all their possessions in shopping bags.

In Brooklyn, Laura Esposito waited impatiently every night for her husband to come home. On evenings when he did appear early, he sat like a zombie in front of the television, nodding in a stupor.

"You never talk to me," Laura complained from her own chair. "You never ask if I'm happy, if I feel good, if I want to go dancing. Ray, what's the matter with you? Vietnam make you nuts?"

He ignored the questions. He sat, hands clasped in the lap of his ragged trousers, fingers swollen like sausages from his heroin addiction.

"Look at you. You look like a bum. Why don't you buy yourself some new clothes? Get a haircut? Or shave, at least?"

Esposito had been back in the States almost three years. In that time his appearance had grown steadily worse. His skin was blotched under the stubble of his beard. His clothes were torn. His hands swollen and encrusted with dirt. His only concern was for heroin.

He felt worse, too. His limbs ached. He was constipated. His muscles were sore. As an excuse for his ailments, he told Laura he had contracted a tropical disease in Vietnam, showing her the needle marks on his skin and claiming they were gnat bites that wouldn't go away.

Esposito was now injecting himself not to get high but merely to feel normal. The condition would continue that way, too, he knew, as long as he had money to support his ever-increasing habit, or until he accidentally killed himself.

From the Madison Avenue building site, he moved with Janni Brothers to a new site off Columbus Circle. He was earning more money than many advertising executives, but the street price for

heroin—coupled with his growing habit—left him with less
money to take home.

Laura was becoming concerned that she was getting too old
to have a baby. At night she stared at Esposito sleeping next to
her in bed, as she fingered herself to satisfy her physical needs,
ashamed that she had to do such a disgusting thing, hating him
for not satisfying her as a husband should, not giving her a
family.

One evening she finally challenged him.

"You know what I think, don't you?" she said when Esposito
came home late. "I think you're a fairy. I think you and your
friend, Johnny Ferraro, are fruits. The only thing I can't figure
out is who screws who. Who is it, Ray? Do you wear your
underwear backward for Johnny?"

Esposito struck her. He hit her again, harder, stopping only
when she ran from the apartment, screaming to the neighbors for
help.

After catching the subway to Manhattan, Esposito scored a fix
in Sheridan Square and injected himself in a dark doorway. But
instead of feeling the usual hit, he blacked out, awakening the
next morning in a crowded ward in Bellevue Hospital.

Esposito's first reaction on awakening was anger. He was
outraged that he had passed out and missed his high.

His next shock was the hostile way in which the hospital staff
treated him. Doctors, nurses, and orderlies frequently considered
drug accidents to be self-inflicted, seeing drug users as nuisances
who took away valuable time and space from more worthwhile
casualties.

Bellevue kept Esposito for the first phase of his withdrawal—
the cold sweats, initial nausea, and retching—then sent him
home to recover. They told him he would feel as if he was having
a bad case of flu. But at the beginning of the new week, Esposito
was back standing in a drug line.

At home in Brooklyn, he apologized to Laura for hitting her.
He burst into tears, explaining that he had been delirious from
his tropical fever, that he had gone to Bellevue Hospital for

treatment because his pain had become so unbearable. As always, Esposito's lies contained a shred of truth.

Laura was touched by his tears, but nevertheless she remained secretly leery. When he did not return home the next night, she decided to check the story.

Bellevue Hospital verified that Ray Esposito had been a patient there. But not for a tropical disease. For a heroin overdose.

After talking to her mother, Laura consulted the parish priest and family doctor. Both men advised her to wait for the right moment to confront her husband with the truth.

Laura prepared Esposito's favorite supper, lasagna and endive salad. She didn't complain when he came home three hours late and gave no excuse for where he had been. Such conduct was normal by now.

Toying nervously with the layered pasta, she began, "I bought a copy of Newsweek today, Ray. Have you noticed how many articles about drugs there are lately?"

Esposito was not listening. That afternoon he had been fired from his job. As he stared at his untouched supper, he wondered how he was going to support his habit.

Laura tried a more direct tack. "Ray, you know those gnat bites you got overseas. Well, I went to Bellevue Hospital and they told me they're not gnat bites."

Esposito did not respond. He was wondering if he was going to be like Johnny Ferraro, forced to steal and mug people for money. And what came after crime? Would he end up as an itinerant, moving from flophouse to flophouse, all his possessions in a couple of paper bags? That was his worst fear—becoming a "bag man."

"Ray, I talked to somebody at Bellevue Hospital," Laura said again, louder.

The name penetrated his haze.

He looked at her, scowling.

Laura elaborated. "I went to Bellevue Hospital, Ray. They told me your gnat bites are track marks from a needle. You've been lying to me, Ray, haven't you?"

" 'Track marks'? What the hell are you talking about, Laura?"

"Ray, don't play games with me no more. I know you're a drug addict. The hospital told me so. I feel so stupid for not guessing it sooner. But I know now for certain. Because I'm your wife, they showed me your records."

"What hospital?" he asked, still playing innocent. "What record? What are you talking about?"

"Bellevue Hospital. They told me you spent three days there. For a heroin overdose. You're a drug addict, Ray. A junkie."

Reaching across the table, she patted his hand consolingly. "But don't worry. I talked to Father Genovese about your problem. I talked to Dr. Morgan, too. They told me they'll help you turn yourself in for—"

Esposito sprang from his chair, dishes and glasses crashing to the floor. Before Laura had time to flee, he began hitting her, striking her face, knocking her to the floor, kicking her chest, buttocks, legs.

Rolling under the kitchen table, Laura grabbed a chair for protection, screaming "Help me! Help me! He's gone crazy again! Help me!"

Esposito fled the apartment, his one thought to get a fix. But as he ran down Atlantic Avenue, he realized he had to be clever if he was to survive and not end up living on the streets. Laura would divorce him this time for beating her. Maybe even have him arrested. He would have no place to go. He would be thrown into the gutter with the garbage.

He decided to go back to Bellevue Hospital. Showing his needle marks to the nurse in Emergency, he said he desperately needed to talk to somebody about his habit. He cried as he spoke, sobbing that he was the scum of the earth, just another guy turned into a piece of shit by the senseless war in Vietnam.

This time his reception greatly differed. Everybody loves helping a repentant junkie, he told himself, and he was more certain than ever that Laura would not throw him out on the street when she learned he was trying to kick his habit.

Beginning a new stay in Bellevue, Esposito reexperienced the *withdrawal symptoms, aches, pains, vomiting, diarrhea. Two days passed and he didn't hear from Laura. This troubled him. But not as much as the nagging thought of being out of work. He could always sweet-talk Laura. But what could he use to buy smack when the hospital released him tomorrow or the next day? Despite his fears of becoming a bag man, he had no intention of giving up heroin.*

On Esposito's third day at Bellevue two doctors visited him in the ward. He thought they had come to discharge him, but the younger doctor asked Esposito if he would consider transferring from Bellevue to a private detoxification clinic in Connecticut.

Esposito became interested when he heard that the private clinic gave methadone as a replacement in a heroin withdrawal. New York City gave methadone, too. But as an outpatient service. The patient needed somewhere to live before he could register for it. Esposito still hadn't heard from Laura and didn't know if she was going to let him go back home.

Thinking of how he had no money to buy smack and remembering that some junkies swore methadone was better than the real stuff, Esposito decided to accept the invitation and go to the private clinic.

Tanglewood was a total surprise. Esposito had expected to see a sterile sanitorium in a New England factory town, drab and depressing. Instead, he found a stately mansion sitting at the end of a long wooded driveway. He had never before seen such luxury. There were thick carpets on the floor. Gold-framed pictures on the walls. Quiet music tinkling in the background. And peaceful scenery outside every window.

There was methadone as Dr. Roger Cooper had promised, too. It was administered daily in Esposito's orange juice. Methadone did not give him a rush like heroin, no instant euphoria or languorous nods. But it did control his aches and pains, minimizing the withdrawal discomfort.

Depression became the worst part of withdrawal. He was certain he was going to end up on the streets of New York City when he was released from Tanglewood. Counselors assured Esposito, however, that his low spirits would not continue, that there was light for him at the end of the tunnel. His attention was diverted with massages, whirlpool baths, physical exercises on Nautilus equipment in a gymnasium.

Toward the end of Esposito's first week at Tanglewood, he began experiencing a sexual drive. He had not felt horny since Vietnam, but now he began masturbating morning, noon, and night.

He began to have sexual fantasies; he thought about Asian prostitutes' small brown bodies, their total willingness to please him. He thought farther back, to high-school years, remembering Laura's high-standing breasts, the way heavy petting had always made her panties dampen. He then thought of how Laura looked today, how she was always whining for him to make love to her, how she had finally hounded him too much and he had had to beat her.

Late one afternoon that week, Esposito had been masturbating—thinking about punishing Laura for staring at him— when he looked up and saw another woman watching him. It had been Lillian Weiss.

Roger Cooper sat in the Garden Pavilion suite after the attendants had escorted Ray Esposito to high-security isolation adjoining Leo Kemp's basement office.

Roger remained alone in the sitting room, appraising its spaciousness, its comfortable furnishings, the gleaming rows of buttons on the teakwood paneling for a ready supply of video movies and a wide choice of music channels.

Studying the luxurious accommodation, Roger saw the rooms through Esposito's eyes and realized the ironies in Tanglewood's charity patient scheme.

Hospitals that knew about Roger's limited charity program frequently provided him with names of potential candidates. Bellevue had drawn his attention to the Vietnam veteran, Ray Esposito.

Maybe bringing patients like Esposito into the refined atmosphere of Tanglewood only confused them, giving them the message: You can stay here in the lap of luxury with the fat cats as long as it takes you to recover—but then you get your ass back out into your own struggling little world.

Gene Stone's words echoed in Roger's ears, that Tanglewood was nothing but a "doll hospital," a haven for the elite, for movie-star dolls . . . rich-and-famous dolls . . . celebrity dolls . . .

Should that be changed? Should Tanglewood be less of a . . . doll hospital? But if so, how?

Lower the level of medical attention? Lower therapy standards? Reduce comforts? Think less about providing first-class service?

But those were the ideals on which Tanglewood had been built. To fill a gap in treatment and rehabilitation centers. Too many clinics were gray and bleak and slipshod or run like boot camps.

Roger stood alone in the empty sitting room, his thoughts again on the gratis patient program. It was the fees of the so-called fat cats that paid for patients like Ray Esposito and the parish priest, Father Hawkes. In a way, the gratis program was a Robin Hood enterprise, taking from the rich to help the poor.

One choice would be to abandon it. But Roger thought of an alternative. Why not consider *increasing* the number of gratis patients at Tanglewood? The list of potential charity patients referred to him by hospitals was endless; at present, he could accept only a small fraction of 1 percent of referred names. He would never be able to convince his partner to increase their number. But if he was able to raise money to buy Adrian's half of the clinic, perhaps he could increase his charity admissions, and at the same time, perhaps improve the program to prepare those less fortunate patients for their return to the outside world.

It was definitely a thought to consider.

62 IN HER DARKENED SUITE, CAT POWERS FLUTTERED HER EYELIDS.

Drifting into consciousness, she did not know what time it was, but she remembered that she was at Tanglewood and that her sleep had been troubled by bad dreams, nightmares about falling out of airplanes, about opening her clothes closet and finding nothing but tiny red dresses.

Seeing a shaft of daylight slanting through the bedroom door, she knew it was day. But what day?

As she lay in bed, covered by a white cotton sheet, she felt a weightlessness to her body, as if she were as light as a feather, as delicate as the creamy lace of her nightie.

Cat had made enough visits to Tanglewood to recognize the airy sensation in her arms and legs as the effect of phenobarbital. Her troubled dreams, too, were because of the barbiturate drug. Soon her brain would turn into an egg beater.

Cures were hell. Twice as bad when you had to kick more than one habit.

Despite the feathery feeling of her body, Cat knew she was overweight. She inched one hand from under the sheet and felt her neck, touching the folds of flesh lining her throat.

Moving her fingers higher, she gripped a handful of tangled hair. Had the roots gone white in the short time she had been there? Were gray hairs threaded through the black dye job?

Thankful that there was no mirror in the room, she wondered what the people who saw her thought about the way she looked.

What did Tom think? Would he think she was too fat? Too ugly? Too old? Would he change his mind about marrying her?

All of Cat's insecurities tumbled forth.

She fretted until voices in the next room attracted her attention.

Listening, she recognized the voices—Hudson and Stone.

Her heart sank. They were arguing again. Was it futile to hope they would ever become friends?

Their voices rose.

Cat wanted to call to them, please, to bury the hatchet. But she knew that phenobarbital slurred her words, that it would be difficult to call out to them.

One word in their argument caught her attention.

Hudson and Stone were arguing about *syphilis*.

"I don't have syphilis," Gene Stone insisted.

"Somebody gave it to her," Hudson argued.

Stone bluffed for confidence. "What I'm interested in knowing is how you think I've been able to give syphilis to Cat. That's what I'm interested in."

"You don't want to hear what I think, creep," Hudson warned.

"No. This interests me. This interests me very much. How long do you think I've been knocking off a piece . . . man, she's my patient!"

"Don't push me, Stone. Don't push me."

Stone called behind him. "What about other guys?"

Hudson didn't hear. He stared at the bedroom doorway; Cat was collapsed on the carpet, hands clinging to the door. Her mouth was open, her eyes rolling in their sockets.

Hudson rushed for her. "What are you doing out of bed?"

"Syphilis . . ." she slurred.

Hudson and Stone exchanged glances.

"Who gave me . . . syphilis?" she asked.

Hudson shoved one arm behind Cat's knees, the other across her back, and hoisted her.

Carrying her into the bedroom, he called to Stone, "Get a nurse in here. Quick."

"That's okay." Stone moved toward the door. "I'll get my bag."

"Fuck you," bellowed Hudson. "Get a nurse."

Cat struggled against Hudson as he lowered her to the bed. "Who gave me . . . syphilis?"

Hudson eased her onto the pillows. "That's what we're going to find out, puss. That's why Stone's having a blood test this afternoon. Just like I did this morning."

"Did Gene give me syphilis?"

She called to Stone, "Gene, did you give me syphilis?"

Hudson froze.

Cat's question answered something for him: Stone *had* been fucking his fiancée.

63 TOM HUDSON'S FROWN WAS DEEPER THAN USUAL AS HE SAT IN ROGER'S OFfice after coming directly from Cat's suite. His voice was uncharacteristically sullen as he complained, "The only thing she cared about was—who gave her syphilis. *Who gave her syphilis!* Not one worry about me finding out Stone's been knocking her off. Not one consideration of our engagement. Not one damn question about me."

"Cat's beginning her treatment," Roger reminded Hudson. "Her mind's jumbled."

"I told myself that."

Hudson grunted. "One thing, Stone's going to have that blood test. Mark my words on that. I want to hear the results."

Roger looked at his watch. "He'd better hurry if he's going to make it today. The lab closes at six." The time was 5:10 P.M.

"He'll be there. She's got him on the run. The old meal ticket's at stake."

"What about you?"

"What about me?"

"How's this affecting you?" Roger remembered Hudson's furious reaction last night in the dining room.

"What do you mean?"

"Do you have your temper in control?" Roger suspected that Hudson needed to talk about the relationship between Cat and Stone before it got blown out of proportion. He couldn't believe Cat could be seriously interested in Stone.

Hudson began opening and closing one hand, palm upward. "I knew what kind of woman I was getting mixed up with. I knew she wasn't some fading wallflower. It's crazy to think she's going to change for me." He paused. "I'm no angel myself. I've taken my own walks on the wild side."

"Do you love her?" Roger rose from his chair and moved around to the front of his desk.

"Love her? Or love the idea of loving her? Maybe I love a picture I got inside my head."

Hudson added, "One thing I know for certain. I make a hell of a husband. I tried once and fell flat on my face. No matter what's happening at home, I've always got a phone in one hand, shouting orders around the company about canned peaches or late openings on weekends."

He looked at Roger sitting on the edge of the desk. "But, Doc, you've got to give it all you got to put Cat back on her feet—regardless of what happens to her and me."

"I'm going over her records now. Trying to find some clue why she might keep having these relapses."

"Got those figures on the clinic I asked for?" Hudson asked unexpectedly.

"Right here," Roger answered, but he didn't reach for the buff envelope behind him on the desk. He felt that the conversation about Hudson and Cat was far from complete.

Hudson said more brightly, "Oh, yeah. I didn't tell you. I talked to my friend, Joe Marino, at Triathlon Chemicals in Miami this morning. I fed him a little hook about maybe there might be a slight chance for him to get involved with Tanglewood. He got excited as hell and wants to hear some figures when we get together tonight at The Reef for our poker game."

Roger held up both hands. He was eager to hear about Joe Marino and Triathlon Chemicals—whoever they might be—but he first wanted to finish discussing the professional matter at hand.

"Whoa, Tom," he said. "Hold it. One thing at a time. We're discussing you and Cat."

"There's nothing to discuss."

"I think there is." Roger added, "And don't tell me it's none of my business."

Hudson shrugged. "If something's going to happen between Cat and me, it's going to happen."

The telephone buzzed.

Roger ignored it, saying "Tom, I don't like you leaving like this. Twenty-four hours ago you were head over heels in love with Cat Powers. I refuse to believe it's cooled down. You're upset. You've got reason to be. But don't you also have reason to weigh Cat's side of the matter, very seriously?"

The telephone buzzed again.

"You're right. I love her," Hudson admitted. "And, okay, I'll tell you. I'm a little hurt by what happened. Hell, I'm more than a little hurt. I'm mad. Damned mad. You saw that last night. I feel she cheated on me. She *did* cheat on me."

"Tom, I'm going to have to come on strong as the medical director and say that maybe there's a reason for her actions.

Maybe she needs your understanding about now. People don't change overnight, you know. She was lost and alone before she met you. She was searching. Stone obviously took advantage of her situation. Give her a chance."

The telephone had buzzed three more times.

Roger said, "Excuse me," and lifted the receiver. Listening, he glanced at Hudson, nodding. "Good. Come on down to the office, Gene. I'll wait for you here."

He lowered the phone.

"Stone?" Hudson's face flushed.

"He wants to talk to me," Roger said.

Hudson checked his watch. "Damn it. I wish I could hang around for the score. But my car's been waiting out front for an hour. I've got to get to that airport."

Roger stood up from the desk. "Are you coming back here after Florida?"

"I'll call you from Miami tomorrow morning."

He held out his hand to Roger. "Let's have those papers."

64 ROGER WAITED THIRTY MINUTES FOR GENE STONE TO COME TO THE OFFICE before trying to reach him by telephone. After getting a busy signal on the line, he decided to go to the Orchard Pavilion and try Stone's rooms.

"You're leaving." Roger stood inside the doorway of Stone's bedroom, seeing a raincoat and a suitcase on the bed.

"Why spend all my time around here?" Stone was packing. "I've got other fish to fry."

"You wanted to talk to me."

"I was coming to say *ciao*—" Stone stood in his stocking feet, looking around the room for the mate to a crocodile loafer he was holding. "But I decided I'd heard enough about that fucking blood test shit. Who needs the hassle?"

"Gene, you just told me on the phone that you were coming to my office. I waited there for thirty minutes."

"I had some of my own phone calls to make."

Stone's eyes were glassy, his hands shaking. As Roger watched him searching for the other shoe, he wondered if he had injected himself with one of his cocktails.

"Gene, don't put off having a blood check," Roger said.

Holding the crocodile loafer in one hand, Stone slid back the closet's louvered door. "You think this is playing right into your hands, don't you?"

"What is?"

"This VD business." Stone looked from the closet floor to its overhead shelf. "You and Hudson think it's a good way to get me out of here."

Still carrying the loafer, he moved back across the room and, dropping to the carpet, looked under the bed. "But let me tell you this. Don't you and Hudson get too puffed up with victory. This isn't the last act."

"You seem to enjoy causing trouble, Gene," Roger said, his temper rising. "Don't you see how this could seriously harm Cat and Hudson's future?"

Stone got to his feet. "They're rich. They can handle it."

"Rich?" Roger asked. "Are you really that naive? To think money makes a difference?"

Stone laughed. "A rich boy from Santa Barbara like you can talk about money."

"I'm not rich."

"Bullshit. You started at the top with that practice up at Santa Barbara."

Roger stared at Stone, understanding something for the first time.

He said, "That's why you gave that deposition against me

in Santa Barbara, wasn't it? You were jealous. Because you thought I was rich."

"Forget it." Stone dropped the crocodile loafer into the wastebasket with a thud. "The case was dismissed. You survived."

"Yeah. But a lot of mud was flung and some of it stuck. I lost my practice. My dad died. Deborah left me. All because of that suit. Your deposition didn't help things."

"Don't overplay the scene, old man." Stone moved to the bed and pulled a pair of brown Top-siders from his bag.

"Fine. Forget about me. But what about Cat?" Roger asked as he watched Stone slip into the shoes.

"What about her?" Stone turned to the bedside table, lifting a half-smoked joint from the ashtray and pulled a gold Cartier lighter from his jeans pocket.

"Have you told her you're leaving?" Roger asked.

Stone sucked on the joint, holding the smoke in his lungs, shaking his head.

He released the smoke, saying "I never leave anyplace for long."

Roger frowned, impatient with Stone's self-satisfied remarks.

"Anyway," Stone said, "why should I have any loyalty to that fat, washed-up old cow?"

After taking another toke, he exhaled and continued. "The only reason people pay to see Cat Powers any more is to have a look at a freak show. Elephant Woman in sequins." He took a third drag.

"You sound like you're trying to convince yourself about something, Gene. What is it? Do you think Cat's going to drop you? So you're pulling out first?"

"Keep thinking that, Rog," Stone said, smirking. "You just keep thinking that."

The cryptic remark further enraged Roger; he turned to leave when the telephone rang on the bedside table.

"That's probably my cab." Looking suddenly disoriented,

Stone asked, "What do I do? Tell them to drive down here from the gate to pick me up?"

"Let me do it." Roger reached for the phone. "Nothing will give me greater pleasure."

Gene Stone slumped in the backseat of the taxicab, grinning to himself about the recent turn of events as the cab drove up the driveway to the gatehouse.

The nasty little scene with Cat and Hudson—as well as the latest with Roger Cooper—had convinced Stone that he should definitely pursue Adrian Lyell's offer to consider becoming the new medical director of Tanglewood.

The only difficulty he had encountered so far with Delia Pomeroy was finding her telephone number. The number listed in the local directory was out of service. After making a few fruitless calls around the clinic, he had decided to try for the obvious—call information. The decision had been the right one: Delia Pomeroy had merely changed apartments.

The cab stopped at the gatehouse; the driver handed his metal pass-chip to the security guard.

The guard looked into the backseat, asking Stone "Name, please, sir?"

"Stone. Dr. Gene Stone."

The guard checked his list, ticking off "Stone" and asking "Are you returning, Dr. Stone?"

"You better believe it," said Stone, chuckling to himself.

The guard touched his cap's visor. "Have a nice evening, Dr. Stone."

The taxi driver passed through the opened iron gates. As he pulled out onto the highway, he called over his shoulder, "So you're a doctor, then?"

Stone didn't answer; he was lighting a joint.

As the pungent odor filled the cab, the driver said, "Hey, what's that you smoking back there?"

"Himalayan moss. I use it for my bronchial condition." Stone pounded his chest, coughing. "This cold weather does me in."

"Oh. I thought for a minute it might be some of that pot. But you being a doctor, I guess you wouldn't touch that junk."

Stone took a third, deeper puff, frowning. Nosy jerk.

Exhaling, he called, "You know how to get to that address in Stonebridge I gave you?"

"You take care of the sick people, Doc," answered the driver. "Leave the driving to me. Okay? You've got nothing to worry about."

As the driver prattled on about his career behind the wheel, Stone took another drag on the joint. He was feeling gradually lighter, dreaming about his future at Tanglewood.

When Gene Stone was a boy, medical school—and drugs—had not been part of his plans, at first.

Gene's first dream was to be Elvis Presley. He saw himself arriving at Hollywood premieres, emerging from the backseat of a limousine, dressed in a gold lamé jumpsuit, greeted by cheers and screams from adoring fans and the pop of flashbulbs.

"Gene's going to make it big in this world," bragged his mother, Yvonne Stone. "Gene's a real charmer. I call him 'Mr. Charm.' "

Gene didn't know his father; he only knew that his mother had worked as head bookkeeper and office manager in Schultz's Lumberyard in Tobago, Oregon, for as long as he could remember.

Yvonne Stone managed to provide young Gene with whatever he needed—clothes, a bicycle, pocket money. She sent him to the movies twice a week, on Tuesday nights and Saturday afternoons. Gene didn't learn until later that those were the times Yvonne entertained her boss, pot-bellied Bert Schultz, in the bedroom of their small house.

Gene's first drunk was on gin; he awoke on a Sunday morning in his bedroom, a pool of vomit spread across the floor, his head aching.

Yvonne stood in the bedroom doorway in her bathrobe, a pink net nightcap on her head. Holding a mug of coffee in one hand, she joked, "Guess you're not going to church this morning, Mr. Charm."

"Mom, don't be angry," fourteen-year-old Gene pleaded from his bed.

"Angry? Why'd I be angry? You're the one who's got to clean up all that puke."

Scuffing in her slippers back to the kitchen, she called, "You're not the first kid to go out on Saturday night and tie one on, and you won't be the last."

When Gene was a year older, Yvonne told her son her version of the facts of life.

"The last thing you want is to knock up one of the high-school girls around here. They might look pretty tempting in the back-seat of a car. But in a few years' time, they'll be as flabby and ornery as their old ladies. Save yourself for something better than these local skirts."

She made one stipulation. "If you do knock up some gal, just tell me. We'll work something out so you don't have to marry her. You won't be the first kid caught with his pants down. And you won't be the last."

Yvonne got tuition money for Gene to go to Oregon State. She also had ready advice about career choices.

"You're no dummy. School comes natural to you. Especially the sciences. So there's two things I think you should consider going into: dentistry or being a chiropractor. They both rake in the green stuff."

"Doctors make more," Gene reminded her.

"If you think you can hack med school, I'll get you through it hook or by crook. If you flunk out—well, you won't be the first one."

Yvonne Stone was bursting with pride when Gene was ac-cepted by UCLA med school. But to him she talked common sense. "Don't get any ideas of trying to become one of them movie stars when you're down there in Hollywood. Those stars are on top one day, out on their butts the next. But doctors . . . Honey, doctors always stay on top. You're good-looking enough to be a movie star. I'm not denying that. But, honey, oh, just think of

*the bankroll a good-looking sawbones can make. Especially a guy
with a lot of charm like you."*

Gene shared his mother's respect for money and concentrated
on social contacts more than romance. From his mother he had
also inherited an easygoing approach to all his relationships. He
never became closely involved with one person, and his suave,
blond good looks attracted many women.

In Los Angeles, Gene learned to be especially attentive to
privileged people. He met many rich kids. Sons and daughters
of powerful families. They were attracted to the streetwise manner that came naturally to him, to his ready line of praise, his
constant invitations to try new things, the latest thrills.

But certain types of privileged people niggled Gene Stone.
One was Roger Cooper, at California Health Hospital. It wasn't
that Roger Cooper was a goody-goody. He was just too much of
a straight arrow. He showed no interest in the recreational drugs
Gene was experimenting with. He had no sense of trends in
clothes, jewelry, disco. He was headed straight for what Stone
considered to be a graveyard—family life. Roger Cooper's only
diversion from being a normal straight arrow was that he wasn't
married to his old lady; he was just shacking up with her. This
struck Gene Stone as being odd at the time. He later used it when
he heard—also to his surprise—that Roger Cooper was involved
in a malpractice case up in Santa Barbara. In his deposition
Stone stated that Roger's sexual habits had surprised him during
his residency at California Health. Stone felt satisfaction in
making a body blow to the worst kind of rich kid—one who tried
to pass himself off as Joe Average.

The taxi driver stopped in front of an old red brick apartment building in the unkempt west side of Stonebridge.
Gene Stone instructed the driver to wait. "I've got to pop
in here for five, ten minutes, then you can take me on to the
train station."

Stone did not know how long this exploratory visit with
Delia Pomeroy would take. The young nurse had sounded
noncommittal but curious on the telephone when Stone had

announced that Adrian Lyell had told him they should meet to discuss something to her advantage.

A slim woman in her midtwenties answered the door; she wore an inexpensive but colorful jumpsuit and no shoes.

"Miss Pomeroy?" Stone asked, smiling.

"Dr. Stone?"

Stone could tell by the eagerness of her smile—and the generous amount of eyeliner she had applied—that she was ready to talk business.

Standing in the hallway, he feigned a shiver. "This New England cold! I don't know how you can stand it up here. Why aren't you living in southern California?"

"You tell me," she joked.

"Invite me in, Miss Pomeroy, and maybe we'll be able to find a way to improve everybody's lifestyle."

65 SIX O'CLOCK AND A RUSH AGAIN IN THE PARKING LOTS. DAY VISITORS were leaving; early supper guests arriving; night shift staff straggling to work; husbands and wives and lovers collecting mates from the day shift.

Roger dashed across the parking lot, waving to the green Chevrolet sedan leaving in the exodus of day workers.

"Luther!" he called. "Hold on a minute."

"Dr. Cooper!" Luther Brown stopped his car, surprised to see Dr. Cooper chasing him. He rolled down his window.

"Sorry I missed you on the phone," Roger said to the old gardener. "I understand you had something to tell me."

"Maybe it's nothing all that important, Dr. Cooper, but—"

Brown repositioned the wool cap on his head and said, "Remember how it was so rainy yesterday?"

Roger nodded.

The old man continued. "I was working over there"—he pointed beyond the treelined driveway—"gathering piles of wet leaves so they didn't ruin none of that new lawn we put down. I was hurrying because I was getting wet myself when, all of a sudden, I see this girl go lickety-split through the trees. She didn't see me. No, sir. She was too hell-bent on getting over that fieldstone wall up yonder."

Turning to Roger, he looked up through the car window. "I guess the most natural thing to have done was told Security. But they get mighty ticklish about who knows what around here. So I decided to hold my peace till I got a chance to talk to you, Dr. Cooper."

Roger thanked Brown, assuring him he had done exactly the right thing. Wishing him good night and sending best regards to his wife, Roger watched the green Chevrolet drive from the parking lot and thought that, yes, he might have stumbled on how to improve Tanglewood's sophisticated surveillance system.

As Roger continued to the main house for an evening meeting with all five junior doctors, his thoughts returned to Jackie.

He hadn't spoken with her all day. She had gone into Stonebridge for lunch, he knew, but she had obviously returned to the clinic long ago.

Wondering when—and how—he should approach her, he heard a car honking behind him across the parking lot. Turning, he saw the Dodge van that drove employees into Stonebridge to catch local buses to outlying districts.

He waved; among the passengers was attendant Art Bailey, who had sat with Cat Powers after she'd been sedated earlier that afternoon.

Roger glanced at his watch: 6:15. Still enough time to drop by the Orchard Pavilion before meeting the junior doctors.

Roger continued toward the main house. He thought it was important to check on Cat, but he wondered if he was creating excuses for not dropping by Administration to see Jackie Lyell. Was he frightened of something?

66 CAT POWERS WAS GROGGY FROM THE AFTERNOON'S INJECTION. SHE SEEMED

to Roger to be less troubled about having syphilis than about the whereabouts of Tom Hudson.

"Where's Tommy?" she asked Roger as he stood beside her bed.

"You remember," he reminded her. "He had to fly down to Florida on business."

Cat turned away her head on the fluffy, fresh pillows. "He won't marry me now."

"Tom Hudson's not a fickle child," said Roger, trying to sound reassuring yet, at the same time, not willing to pledge Hudson's love to Cat. Perhaps Hudson would decide to break off the engagement because of her involvement with Gene Stone.

"Look at my career," she mumbled. "I screwed that up, too."

"You needed a rest," Roger answered, too familiar with patients' low self-esteem, their pessimistic views of the future.

"I walked out on a show," Cat said miserably.

"You were a sick lady."

"But I'm also a professional," she argued. "It's not like me to walk out on a show. Even when the reviews are rotten."

Remembering a small notice he had seen in a New York tabloid, Roger said, "*The Examiner* thought you were terrific. They compared you to Vivien Leigh."

Cat considered. "Yeah . . . they did like me, didn't they?"

"Absolutely. And you haven't seen all your reviews yet." He said encouragingly, "Give yourself a break, Cat. If you aren't rooting for yourself, who will?"

A little more enthusiastically, she said, "I hope Linda's clipping all the reviews."

"Who's Linda?"

"Linda Lawrence—my new secretary," Cat explained. "She's a jewel. She's also got a great eye for new material for me. In fact, there's a miniseries she thinks I should seriously consider for television."

Roger was pleased to see Cat trying to be optimistic. It gave him an idea: He would have her secretary come to Tanglewood, bringing a few scripts and all the fairly decent reviews she could find for *Streetcar*.

Cat explained, "The part's not big but the character's good. An older American woman who becomes the head of a French perfume empire . . ."

She stopped. "But look at me. I'm so fat. So sloppy. Who would ever believe somebody like me could run a perfume empire?"

Roger said lightly, "Hey, girl. Where's your fight? You've gone on diets before, or got a new look from the hairdressers'."

"Yes, but—" She looked up at him. "Kid, that's always been when I had something to live for. To work for. To fight for. I don't know if I have that fight left in me anymore, Roger."

Her sincerity touched him. "I think you do."

"Do you think Tommy's going to come back? Be honest," she insisted.

"I'm always honest with you," Roger said. "So you be honest with me. Do you love Tom Hudson?"

"Like a crazy woman."

"Are you willing to pull yourself together for him? Go through the recovery for him?"

"I'd cut off my arm for the man."

"Answer yes or no."

She dropped her eyes. "Yes . . . but will Tommy be there at the end of it? Will he ever be able to forgive me for the syphilis? If not, it will all be in vain."

"Don't *you* count anymore?" Roger asked.

The question puzzled her. "How do you mean?"

"Can't you get better for your own sake?"

She sighed. "That's what I've got to find out, don't I?"

Roger's call-pack bleeped as he was hurrying away from Cat Powers's suite. Stopping by the house phone in the Orchard Pavilion, he punched the Hub's number; he had an urgent telephone call.

"Roger, sorry to bother you like this," apologized Carlton Frazer, chairman of Tanglewood's board. "But I'm calling to say that the emergency meeting's set for this Saturday—the day after tomorrow. Is that okay with you?"

"Fine. The sooner the better."

"Good," replied Frazer. "Adrian's also agreed to be there. The lawyer, William Ruben in New York, confirmed this only an hour ago. The meeting is set for the Burlingame Club. Eleven o'clock. See you then." *Click.*

67 IT WAS CHILLY IN NEW YORK ON THURSDAY EVENING WHEN BEV JORdan returned home, exhausted from working a ten-hour day as a temporary house model for Summer Palace Fashions on West 35th Street. Four days had passed since Bev had driven Lavender Gilbert to Tanglewood.

Bev let herself into the Columbus Avenue apartment, wanting nothing more than to kick off her shoes and have a cup of coffee. She stopped halfway across the narrow entrance. A blond woman in a pink jogging suit was stretched out on her couch.

"Lavender," she called, rushing into the living room. "Where have you been?"

The telephone had rung all day yesterday and all last night. People had said Lavender had disappeared from Tanglewood, wondered if she had turned up at home.

"What happened to you?" asked Bev, falling to the floor alongside the couch, staring at the mud and grease stains on Lavender's pink outfit.

Lavender's eyes were bleary with sleep and her hair snarled. Groggily she answered, "I've been trying to get back to town."

"Are you okay?"

Lavender forced a smile at Bev's concern. "Mmm. I just need some sleep now."

"Where have you been?"

"Hitchhiking."

"From Tanglewood?"

"Uh-huh," Lavender answered sleepily. "Through the rain and sleet and dark of night. Some people took me way out of my way. One woman's car broke down on a back road. An old man in a pickup got rammed by a milk truck. It wasn't easy."

"So how do you feel?"

"Tired." Lavender pulled a pillow over her eyes to block out the light.

"Why don't you go to bed?" Bev asked.

"Let me snooze here."

"What about food?"

"I'm famished. But let me crash for a couple hours. Okay?"

Bev tucked a knitted afghan around her roommate and promised to wake her in a couple of hours with some supper.

Halfway across the living-room floor, she stopped and called back over her shoulder, "What about Chatwyn? Do you want me to call him and tell him you're here?"

"I already did," Lavender answered from under her pillow. "He wants me at the Waldorf bright and early tomorrow morning."

The pillow over her eyes, Lavender lay on the couch as faint sounds drifted in from Bev puttering around the kitchen. As she fell back to sleep, her mind jumped from image to image. She saw the photographs of drug victims that Roger Cooper had shown her. Her whirling mind next flashed on images of her parents in Iowa, bickering in front of the TV set. She then pictured Candee Allen lying dead on the floor, a coke spoon in her fingers.

Lavender hadn't done any cocaine for the last four days. Her body was too strained from being on the road, though, for her to know if the pain she felt was caused by a drug withdrawal or mere exhaustion.

Could she give up cocaine on her own? Could she go cold

turkey? She now knew for certain that she wanted to kick her drug habit completely. But could she resist temptation? Tomorrow morning at the Waldorf would be the big test: the final countdown for the Star Lady launch.

68 IT WAS MIDNIGHT WHEN NIGEL BURDEN'S WIFE, DIANA, HEARD THE BAD news in London.

The family solicitor, Ian Stevenson, stood beside her wing chair in the lower sitting-room of the Burdens' home in the Boltons, SW10.

Ian Stevenson looked tired; midnight was late for him. But he had come to see Diana as soon as he had received the tip on a gossip column item set for Sidney Cripps's column in tomorrow's *Morning Horn*.

Fortified with a large brandy, Stevenson lifted a pair of half-moon eyeglasses to his nose and read from a piece of paper, " *'Surprise Visit—Nigel Burden, Tory old boy currently in search of a constituency, reportedly did not recognize a visitor this week at the New England health farm where he's resting . . .'* "

Diana interrupted. "That's not libelous. Nigel could be 'resting' for a good many reasons."

"Of course. Cripps is too clever to mention drink. The sting's in the tail. Listen."

Continuing, Stevenson read, *"Son Cyril, city solicitor and father of two, known for his fancy dress flair, appeared at the Yankee spa looking like an English rose at the Chelsea Flower*

Show. Who says British eccentrics are all in the closet? The question is: Does wife Trisha find hubby as much of a drag as Pa Burden?"

Diana sat back in the chair. "How did that dreadful Sidney Cripps find out that Cyril had visited Nigel at Tanglewood?"

"Not merely visited him," Stevenson reminded her, "but what he wore."

"Perfectly dreadful," Diana complained. "Doesn't anybody have any privacy any more?"

Folding his glasses, Stevenson said, "We obviously have to prepare Nigel for the shock before anyone tries to get to him for a comment."

"Poor darling."

Stevenson offered, "Do you want *me* to telephone him?"

"No," Diana sat forward. "This is a family matter. I shall do it."

She reached for her diary, looking for the telephone number of Tanglewood.

69 COULD RENEE NEWBY IN ACCOUNTS HAVE ACTUALLY MADE A MISTAKE?

Working late in Administration, Jackie rechecked her own figures for New England Power's monthly account and found that, sure enough, Renee had double-added four of the clinic's collective electricity bills and had overpaid the power company by $718!

The telephone rang as Jackie totaled the figures for the third time.

It was the salad chef, Buck O'Reilly, calling from the kitchen. "Mrs. Lyell, do you want coffee sent down to Administration again tonight?"

"No thanks, Buck. But what a wonderful supper tray you fixed me. The paté was heavenly. Did you make it yourself?"

There was a knock on the office door.

"Come in," Jackie called to the unexpected late-night visitor, saying quickly into the telephone "Darling, somebody's at my door. Thanks again for the delicious supper. I'll leave the tray in the hall. Bye—"

As Jackie put down the receiver, the knock repeated on the door.

"I'm coming," Jackie called as she moved around Adrian's big desk.

When she was halfway across the room, the door opened and a hand reached in through the partially ajar door, holding a cinnabar rose.

Recognizing the luscious rose from the floral arrangement she had made for the foyer, Jackie wondered who was playing games with her.

Roger stepped into the room, a cautious smile on his lips as he held out the dark-red rose to her.

Jackie accepted it, heart racing.

Reaching behind him, Roger closed the door and locked it.

As an afterthought he asked, "You don't mind, do you?"

"Not at all." She smiled. "In fact, I've been hoping all day that you . . ."

Her voice trailed off as he moved in front of her.

Taking the rose from her hand, he laid it on the drum table and turned back to her.

He held her. The embrace was so strong and delicious that Jackie told herself she had to be imagining it. Nothing this romantic had happened to her in a long time.

As she tasted his lips, her mind struggled with her emotions. Was she doing the right thing? Or was she being incredibly stupid? Where would all this lead?

Roger sensed Jackie's hesitation. He didn't know whether he was making a mistake by coming back to romance Jackie. After all, she was still married to Adrian. This might only complicate everything at Tanglewood still further. But somehow, at this moment, he didn't care.

When he felt Jackie's mouth slowly and gently return the pressure of his kiss, he knew he had not made a mistake.

Encouraged by her response, he caressed her breasts. Jackie's quick intake of breath told him he was exciting her. Soon they were both fondling one another as their mouths worked hungrily together.

In a fleeting moment, Jackie observed herself in the embrace with Roger. She saw herself losing all control. She had been starved for love for so long that now she was a woman gone mad.

The wild embrace, the electricity between them, unleashed all their passions. In unison, they began removing one another's clothes.

Naked, they stood embracing. Roger ran his hands through Jackie's hair; she kissed him, her hands clenched behind his bare back. She cried out when he returned his attention to her breasts.

Slowly, Roger lowered her down to the chesterfield, his desire changing to tenderness, returning to passion.

This isn't happening to me, Jackie told herself as she thrashed her head back and forth. I'm not this lucky. I'm dreaming.

As she clung to Roger, they reached a steady rhythm. When they did speak, it was only to whisper one another's name, as if to reassure themselves that this was really taking place.

From the chesterfield, they moved to the carpet. Roger grabbed cushions to place beneath Jackie. He found himself thinking: I want to take care of this woman. I want to take care of her as I never suspected I would.

Jackie did not know how long they lay intertwined on the floor until she felt Roger lift her, kissing her as he carried her across the room in his arms.

She clung to his neck, feeling his heart beat against her bare skin, not thinking about where they were going until she heard a telephone clatter to the floor. They were making love on top of Adrian's desk.

Then she lost all sense of time and place as she felt Roger's lips on hers once more.

Oh, can this man kiss, Jackie thought. He's an incredible lover. He knows what to do with his body. But why is it the kisses I love? Oh, don't stop the kisses.

PART SIX

FRIDAY

70 "WAKE UP, DOC. TIME TO GET OUT OF BED AND START MAKING SOME money."

Roger held the phone to his ear, glancing bleary-eyed at the bedside digital clock: 5:47.

"You awake, Doc?" nagged the voice in the receiver. "Or did you go back to sleep?"

Recognizing the voice of Tom Hudson, Roger croaked, "What time do people get up down there in Florida?"

"Who's been to sleep? I've been playing poker all night with Joe Marino and telling him about Tanglewood. He likes what he hears and wants his accountants to look at your books. That story about you in *Time* magazine didn't hurt—"

"Hold it." Roger groped in the darkness for the bedside lamp. He was awake enough to be disappointed that the early-morning call was not from Jackie. They had stayed in Administration talking late last night, neither of them embarrassed or self-conscious about their voracious lovemaking. But, also, neither of them had dwelt on the subject; for both of them, it was a pleasure just to have someone they could talk to freely.

"Let me turn on a light," Roger said to Hudson.

"Get a pen and paper while you're at it," Hudson said.

Roger clicked on a lamp and swung his bare feet onto the floor. "Okay. Got a pen . . . got my pad . . ."

"Sorry to come on like gangbusters so early in the morning, Doc," Hudson said. "But Joe Marino's excited as hell and wants to move fast to beat his tax fix. He looked at the fact sheet you sent with me and wants to see more. I thought you'd like the good news seeing you're on a countdown yourself. Ready to take down a few notes?"

Hudson gave Roger the specifics on Joe Marino and Triathlon Chemicals. "Tell your new lawyer to expect a call from Marino. Marino also said that he might make an exploratory call to Lyell's lawyer, Bill Ruben, in New York this morning. That okay with you?"

"Why not?"

"Let them know you're not sitting on your can."

Would Adrian be surprised by the prospect of a counteroffer? And so soon? Roger suspected so.

Hudson added, "Before I hang up and start taking care of my own business, I want to say thanks for yesterday, Doc. I needed that little pep talk you gave me about Cat. It got me thinking on the flight down here and I decided, what the hell? Cat and I enjoy each other's company. We know each other's faults as well as our good points. So why not go for it? We can't be worse off than we are now."

He paused. "What about Stone? Did he take the blood test?"

"He left yesterday."

"Left Tanglewood?"

"About an hour after you did." Roger added, "He was acting rather strange. Saying things I didn't quite understand. But he left without taking a blood test."

Hudson laughed. "Why, that yellow-bellied fuck. He pulled out when the going got rough. Good riddance."

Listening, Roger glanced at his list, making certain he could make sense out of his scribbling before Hudson hung up.

"What'd Cat say about Stone leaving?" Hudson asked.

"She took it relatively calmly. But don't forget, she's on

medication and has very abrupt swings. It could be a different tune this morning."

"You tell her you heard from me, Doc. You tell her you heard from me and that I'm going to call her later today."

"That'll make her very pleased," Roger said. "I talked to her yesterday and she worries about you walking out on her. For good."

"Hell, she's got no need to think that. I love her."

"She needs to hear that from you."

"Doc, when's the best time for me to phone her?"

"Toward evening. When she's calm. Today's an important transition day for her."

Hudson repeated his love for Cat and promised to assure her of it on the telephone. Before he hung up, Roger put in, "Tom, I also want to thank you for what you're doing for me and Tanglewood."

"Glad to do it," said Hudson. "It's a wild chance but who knows? It might pay off."

He added, "You get Cat back on her feet and that's all the thanks I'll ever need."

By 7:10 A.M., Roger, shaved, showered, dressed in corduroy jeans and a Pendleton shirt, sat in his office, second mug of coffee in hand, two important telephone calls already under his belt.

The first call had been to his new lawyer. Knowing that Avery Brennan went for an early-morning jog, Roger called him at his Bluejay Ridge home, telling him to expect a call today from Joe Marino of Triathlon Chemical. Roger also reminded Brennan about Saturday's emergency board meeting at the Burlingame Club.

Roger's second morning call had been to Cat's secretary, Linda Lawrence, at her New York hotel; he had invited Linda to Tanglewood tomorrow with a few potential scripts for Cat to consider as well as all the positive reviews she could find for *Streetcar*.

After talking to Linda, Roger had wondered if he should

make a quick call to Jackie. Ask if she felt as good as he did this morning.

No, he decided, remembering last night's promise. They were going to try to be adult and not bug each other with frivolous phone calls; no chitchat until they met for a quick lunch.

Alone in his office, a thick stack of Cat Powers's past files piled in front of him on the desk, he sipped his black coffee, thinking: *Now why does Cat have these relapses?*

Environment? Lifestyle? Was there some physical imbalance, with the clue lying hidden in her medical notes? Or should he go to the computer and pull up her psychotherapy records?

Cat Powers was a spoiled, self-indulgent egomaniac who boozed and played around with drugs for cheap thrills. That was one diagnosis. Another was that she was a sick, lost, very lonely lady crying out for love and affection.

One thing was certain: Cat Powers was a fighter. In her two previous visits to Tanglewood she had found her strength quickly and pulled herself out of her dependencies.

But what gave her the will to fight? Was it her need to work? Being a diehard professional actress? Or did she also need a man in her life?

Thinking of Cat's marriages, divorces, and love affairs, Roger pictured the two men she had been with most recently: Tom Hudson and Gene Stone.

What would Cat's opinion be this morning about Gene Stone leaving Tanglewood? Past records showed that she had a history of panic in early phases of withdrawal, and this morning Cat's phenobarbital would be reduced by 10 percent. If she began suffering anxiety attacks, would she interpret Stone's disappearance as personal rejection? Would she feel abandoned by a friend? Possibly a lover? Or would she see his departure as the loss of her drug supply? Either way, she could panic.

What about Tom Hudson? Would Cat think Hudson was dumping her because of Stone and the syphilis? No amount of loving telephone calls from Hudson in Florida would remedy that. Paranoid patients needed tangible reassurances.

Family or religion supplied strength for many recoveries. But Cat Powers had neither. Even professional coddling from her private secretary might not be enough.

This was Cat's third visit to Tanglewood. Roger had to do something positive for the woman or she might soon start seeing herself as resistant to cure.

A voice deep inside him said to concentrate on Cat's professional side. She had always been an entertainer. An old showhorse. There had to be some way to appeal to her show-business grit to make a breakthrough in treatment. Roger scrawled absently on his notepad: THE SHOW MUST GO ON.

71 IN NEW YORK, THE OCTOBER MORNING FOG WAS LIFTING FROM MIDTOWN Manhattan by 8:30 A.M. as fleets of yellow taxicabs commenced the day's race on either side of Park Avenue's central flower beds; speeding to catch a run of green traffic lights, tires hissing, screeching, thudding over the ravaged pavement.

In front of the Waldorf-Astoria's gilt doors on Park Avenue, a taxi pulled to a stop and, as the rear door swung open, Lavender Gilbert stepped out onto the sidewalk.

Behind her, Bev Jordan followed, opening her shoulder bag and shoving ten dollars at the driver.

At the same moment, a group of long, shiny black limou-

sines surrounded the taxi. Doors opened, people poured out
to encircle Bev and Lavender.

"Chatwyn!" Bev said to the tall man clad in denims. She
moved to protect Lavender from Chatwyn's milling entourage.

Bussing Bev's cheek, Chatwyn ordered, "Bev, love.
You've been a brick. Go with Freddie and choose something
from my fall fur collection."

A strong arm pulled Bev toward a limousine as Chatwyn's
followers swarmed around him and Lavender on the sidewalk.

Inside the circle of personal assistants and advisers, Chatwyn crooked a forefinger under Lavender's chin, turning
her head left to right.

He asked, "What do you think, Pierre?"

Cosmetician Pierre Gautier studied Lavender's face. "A
few blemishes. A few zits. Nothing catastrophic."

"Ira?"

Ira Cassims felt her hair. "I've seen it worse."

"Dr. Edelman?"

A bespeckled man in a Van Dyke goatee removed a penlight from his pocket and tilted back Lavender's head to
study the inside of each nostril.

He snapped off the penlight. "No sign of dripping or
damage caused by recreational inhalation."

Chatwyn turned to a tall young woman with bicycle clips
around the bottom of her blue jeans and an orange backpack
on one shoulder.

"Tracey, don't let her out of your sight all day. You even
pee with her."

"You got it, boss," said the muscular woman.

To a young man in a cardigan sweater and a red bow tie,
Chatwyn ordered, "We're ready to move out, Lee. Go clear
an elevator."

The young man hurried past the gold-braided doorman.

To a female assistant with a two-way radio, Chatwyn

instructed, "Tell the Starlight Room we're on the way up."

Orders given, the party began to move. Assistants remained grouped around Chatwyn and Lavender as they passed through the gilt doors, across the marble lobby, oblivious to staring hotel guests as they hurried toward the west elevators.

Inside the elevator, Red Bow-Tie engaged the elevator man in conversation as Bicycle Clips removed a glass vial from her backpack and held it to Lavender's nose; the female assistant with the two-way radio took a small silver box of pills from her pocket.

Lavender shook her head at Bicycle Clips. "No, thank you."

Bicycle Clips looked from Lavender to the assistant holding the open pill box.

To Chatwyn, Lavender said, "I'm going straight."

"Straight?" he asked, surprised. "Do we have a new Lavender?"

"No," Lavender said firmly. "Still the same old girl with a drug problem. The only difference is that now I'm trying to do something about it."

There was silence in the speeding elevator.

Lavender admitted, "I've gone cold turkey. Two days at Tanglewood. And two on the road. Now I'm trying for the fifth day."

"That's all fine and well, darling," Chatwyn said with a forced smile. "But what about my show? I don't want you hyperventilating in the middle of it. Collapsing with the D.T.'s or something."

"Don't worry about me," Lavender calmly assured him. "I'll make it through the day."

Chatwyn's voice became more impatient. "It's not just today I'm worried about. You've got a run-of-campaign contract, my dear."

Lavender met his eyes, her own voice becoming more assertive. "I remember exactly how long my contract runs . . . *darling*. I also remember it doesn't call for—"

She looked at Bicycle Clips and the girl with the pillbox. "—little perks like this."

"Well, that *is* impressive," Chatwyn said bitchily. "Do we have Tanglewood to thank for this breakthrough?"

Lavender remembered the faces Roger had shown her, her friend, Candee Allen, and all the other models and actors and entertainers who had ruined their careers and their lives with drugs.

"I guess we do," she said.

The elevator doors opened; photographers waited on the landing.

Chatwyn took Lavender's arm, whispering "I just hope you can handle this."

"As they say, 'One day at a time.'" With a dazzling smile, Lavender emerged from the elevator, as the cameras flashed all around her.

72 "MY BIGGEST CHALLENGE WAS GETTING DELIA POMEROY'S HOME PHONE number," Gene Stone said brightly to Adrian Lyell over a late morning Buck's fizz in the lobby of New York's art deco hotel, Mallett's, in Murray Hill. "From there on it was a breeze."

Stone recrossed one leg of his raw silk trousers over the other leg, crystal flute of orange juice and champagne in hand. "To begin with, the girl's unhappy working at Tanglewood. Hell, she doesn't even like nursing. When I said I could find her a cushy job in a Brentwood or Westwood clinic, she asked if I had any connections for something a little more glamorous like, say, in television or movies." He laughed at the idea.

Adrian was twisting his signet ring. He shared none of Stone's high spirits. He was still smoldering with anger at the discovery that Jackie was not only suing for divorce but also trying to obtain a restraining order to keep him off the grounds of Tanglewood. He would take care of Jackie. But first there was Cooper to deal with.

To Gene Stone he said, "You *did* make it clear to Delia Pomeroy what is expected from her in exchange for a few . . . favors."

Stone said, "Let me give you the whole scenario.

"She invites me into her apartment. We exchange a few pleasantries, then I move in for the kill. I say, 'You know, Delia, your boss, Roger Cooper, has a history of being a lady's man.' She doesn't miss a beat; she responds, 'I wasn't surprised when I heard those stories about Roger. He'd been making eyes at me, too.' "

"Eyes!" Adrian exclaimed. "We need more than some nurse claiming that Roger Cooper made *eyes* at her."

"Calm down, old top," Stone said soothingly, patting Adrian's knee. "Calm down. Hear me out.

"The young lady continues, 'If you want me to, I can say Roger and I got very close on a couple occasions. Closer than I wanted to be.' I asked her if this is true and she asks, 'Does it matter?' "

Adrian asked, "She's willing to give a deposition?"

"She says the only thing to keep her from making a formal statement that Roger Cooper made work uncomfortable for her at Tanglewood by his amorous advances would be if she had to continue working there. She doesn't want to continue working alongside people who might 'speak ill' of her." Stone smirked. "The girl's no dummy. She sees a break when it's offered to her. She'll say what we want as long as we pay for it."

"You mentioned a job out in California?" asked Adrian.

"A job and her own apartment. Someplace in West Holly-wood." He waved his hand dismissively. "One of those new complexes with a tacky little pool. They're a dime a dozen."

"So how did you leave it?" Adrian asked.

"I told her a lawyer would contact her in the next few days. I also said that she would be wise to remain on sick leave from Tanglewood—as she is at the moment."

"Perfect." Adrian nodded.

Stone added, "I also gave her a couple hundred bucks cash to tide her over."

"For which I'll reimburse you, of course."

Stone finished his Buck's fizz. Setting the stemmed crystal down on the Odeon table, he said, "Now what about me?"

"Since we spoke on the telephone, Dr. Stone, a board meeting's been called for tomorrow morning. In Stone-bridge."

"How does that affect me?"

"I won't go into the intricacies of the situation at the moment," Adrian said. "I will only say that, tomorrow, I will prove to the board that Roger Cooper will be best advised to accept my purchase offer immediately and resign from his position as Tanglewood's medical director."

He considered the information Stone had given him con-cerning Delia Pomeroy. "Unfortunately, tomorrow might be too soon to produce Delia Pomeroy's deposition. But leave that to me. I'll discuss what you've told me with my lawyer."

Looking at Stone, he asked, "You'll be here at Mallett's?"

"As your guest," answered Stone, eyes twinkling.

"Of course."

Stone raised one hand to the white-jacketed waiter, saying to Adrian "One personal question. Have you ever balled Pomeroy?"

Adrian remembered a SoHo party, a girl in black leather who had spoken flirtatiously to him about bondage and dom-ination, but whom Adrian suspected was one of those people who talked a lot but had had little experience with S/M sex.

The prospect of being her teacher had been tempting to Adrian, although he had not been wildly attracted to her physically. He had found her a job at Tanglewood to have someone around for a potential playmate if things ever got truly dull in Connecticut. In the following months, he had never resorted to playing around with Delia Pomeroy but she had always been there, waiting, like an emergency stash.

To Stone's question, he replied with satisfaction, "If I had ever 'balled' Miss Pomeroy, she would have been sent on her way long before now."

73 BY 11 A.M. AT TANGLEWOOD, ROGER'S OFFICE HAD BECOME FORT APACHE. HE was trying to keep everybody at bay so he could concentrate on patients.

Over the past three hours, Roger had briefed his juniors for the day. He had warned Leo Kemp in Security that he was coming downstairs to shake up the hierarchy there. He had sent a scribbled memo to Dunstan Bell reminding him that they had a private meeting immediately after the day's Huddle. And he and Jackie were keeping to their promise of not interrupting each other's morning with telephone calls.

The morning's bad news was that Dr. Nick Nathan reported from Stonebridge General that Little Milly Wheeler was convulsing in intensive care. Roger made a note to stop at the hospital after Saturday's board meeting. On the brighter side, Philip Pringle called to say that Karen Wash-

ington wondered if she and Peabo could attend Betty Lassiter's Sweat Room today. Roger readily agreed, hoping
yesterday's reading of fan letters with Peabo had truly
worked. Maybe Peabo was breaking out of his shell. Roger
decided to make time to sit in Lassiter's therapy group. He
then slammed the gates to all outsiders, giving his undivided
attention to patients.

The first name on the list was Cat Powers.

Roger began by punching up the staff list on his computer
to see which nurses and attendants were assigned to Cat that
day.

The day's nurse was Elizabeth Kravetz.

Punching up her profile, Roger read that Kravetz was
fifty-eight years old, a widow who had been in nursing for
the past thirty-two years. He kept punching the keyboard
until he came to hobbies and pastimes.

Nurse Kravetz enjoyed travel and—

Roger grinned.

She was also a film buff.

Swiveling around in his chair, he reached for the telephone.

74 UPON AWAKENING ON FRIDAY MORN-
ING, CAT POWERS FELT MORE CON-
trol over the light-and-feathery effects of the phenobarbital
than she had yesterday. Her limbs seemed less weightless,
somewhat more manageable. She could cope with the
spongy feeling in her fingers. But more important, she could

talk more easily than yesterday, forming her thoughts more clearly into words.

But for the first time all week, Tom Hudson was not sitting alongside Cat's bed when she awoke, asking how she felt, listening to her recount her vivid nightmares. Instead, she saw the gray-haired, scrub-faced nurse, Elizabeth Kravetz, seated in the armchair.

Cat remembered her fiancé had gone to Florida.

Then she remembered Gene Stone. Tommy and Gene had argued about VD. *Syphilis.* Someone had given her syphilis and—Cat remembered clearly after drinking her orange juice—Gene had left last night without even saying good-bye to her. Gene must be the guilty one. He had to be. Tommy was not promiscuous. Gene was a tramp. His sudden disappearance verified his guilt.

Nurse Kravetz sat reading *National Geographic.*

Cat said, "Nurse, I have to make a long-distance call." She was worried that Hudson might not forgive her about the syphilis. Oh, my God! Did he have it, too?

"No phone calls for the first week, Miss Powers," Nurse Kravetz reminded her, turning another page of the magazine.

"It's a very important call," Cat insisted.

"Of course it is. And you're a very important patient, Miss Powers. That's why we have to take extra-special care of you."

"What if my fiancé calls?" asked Cat, frustrated by nurses who had all the answers.

"I'm sure if Dr. Cooper thinks you're doing well when he comes to see you today, he'll let you talk to Mr. Hudson."

Cat's mind was jumping. "How do I look?"

Nurse Kravetz replied, "More important, Miss Powers—how do you feel?"

Cat sniffed. "That must mean I look like the *Titanic* going down."

"You've been a very sick girl."

"I've been a very gullible girl, that's what I've been," said

Cat, thinking of Gene Stone. She was furious that he had abandoned her in her time of need. How was Roger Cooper treating the VD? She must ask him.

To Nurse Kravetz, she said grumpily, "People take too much for granted from doctors. When a doctor prescribes something, you should demand to know what it is and what its effects will be and why he's prescribing it. Look at me. *Look at me!* How did I end up in a situation like this? And it's not the first time! What's the matter with me? Am I crazy?"

"I don't think so, Miss Powers. Anyone can get mixed up with the wrong people sometimes. But next week you'll see your psychotherapist. You can get all that off your chest then."

"What I want to know is, do I have to suffer every humiliation on the face of this earth before I die? That's what I want to know."

"You're not going to die, Miss Powers," the nurse assured her. "You've just had a very full life."

"Full life?" Cat laughed. "Tell me!"

Cat Powers lay on the heaped bed pillows, reflecting that her life had always depended on perseverence, on chutzpah—and not always her own.

Cat Powers first appeared on stage at the age of eight in the juvenile chorus line of the 1941 revue Stamp Your Foot.

Her father, Leonard Powers, waited in the wings of Broadway's Schubert Theater during rehearsals with the stage mothers keeping watchful eyes on their daughters.

Leonard Powers, a dapper man with an Errol Flynn profile, was crippled in both legs and dependent on two oak walking sticks. He was also as ambitious as any stage mother. Ten days before opening night, he pushed his way through the crowded women, clearing a path with his sticks, calling "Catharine! Catharine, dear! Show the nice man the number we saw last season at the Palladium in London."

Neither Leonard Powers nor Cat had ever traveled out of New York City. But Leonard had read in Variety that the show's director was an enthusiast of English music hall songs.

Eight-year-old Cat obediently, stepped forward from the line of eighteen curly-headed girls and, raising one finger as her father had coached her to do at home, sang without accompaniment, "He stuck his toe in my coconut, in my coconut, in my coconut . . ."

The orchestra in the pit picked up the lilting rhythm and soon Cat was prancing around stage in Marie Lloyd fashion, imitating music hall entertainers.

The mothers in the wings clucked disapprovingly at the song's sexual innuendo, glowering at Leonard Powers for being so pushy.

But in the darkened stalls, the show's producer and director broke into applause. "Get the young lady's name. Write her a vaudeville song into the show."

Opening night reviews for Stamp Your Foot were tepid. But critics hailed Cat Powers—"A small wonder" . . . "Little Miss Powers steals Footlights" . . . "A short candle shines brightly in a dull season" . . .

In the blast of Broadway acclaim, Twentieth-Century Fox invited Catharine Powers to Hollywood to discuss a featured player contract. Leonard Powers quit his desk job at American Field Insurance Company and moved his daughter to California. But before reporting to Fox, he visited Metro-Goldwyn-Mayer, intent on proposing a full star contract for Cat to Louis B. Mayer.

Mayer refused to see Powers, sending a message through his secretary that he had enough kids.

Disheartened by the rebuff, Powers reluctantly accepted Fox's contract. His spirits lifted when the studio quickly put Cat in Klaus Heinrich's new film, Little and Biggs.

Accompanying Cat to daily shooting, Leonard coached her with lines, making corrections on the script where he saw necessary, sending notes to the director on how to interpret various *scenes. After the second week, Heinrich banned Powers from the set, claiming he interfered too much with filming.*

When another young actress, Elizabeth Taylor, was out of the running for Fox's production of Bleak House *and scheduled to appear in a new MGM film called* National Velvet, *Fox hurriedly signed Cat to take over Taylor's part in the lavish production of the Charles Dickens novel—with the proviso that Leonard Powers did not participate in his daughter's professional life.*

Bleak House's *success brought a stream of new offers to Cat from Fox as well as MGM.*

As Cat's salary grew with her popularity, Leonard found a Spanish-style home for them in Hollywoodland. Studio cars collected Cat for work; top agents handled her contracts; studio designers and dressers chose what she wore; Leonard Powers became more and more of a recluse as the Hollywood star machine took over his daughter's life.

Cat's beauty grew as she matured, her hair ermine black, her eyes brilliant blue; she developed an aura of being part child, part woman, a quality that helped her make the transition from juvenile to adult parts that other young stars like Shirley Temple and Margaret O'Brien were finding it difficult to do.

During the filming of Cat's first adult role, Royal Princess, *she returned home unexpectedly one afternoon and smelled a sweet, pungent odor as soon as she entered the hillside house's vaulted foyer.*

Following the scent down the red tiled steps into the sunken living room, she passed the white baby grand piano. The odor became stronger as she climbed the half-moon stairs that led to the upper floor.

By now she could also hear the soft hum of a voice coming from her father's bedroom at the end of the hallway.

Was somebody with him? Did he have a secret lady friend?

Her heart beating, Cat crept along the hallway to the bedroom's elaborately carved door.

She listened.

Mumble, mumble.

"Daddy?" she whispered, heart beating.

Mumble.

"Daddy?" she called louder.

Silence.

Slowly turning the crystal door knob, Cat pushed open the door and stopped when she saw her father lying on his gondola-style bed, dressed in a black silk kimono, satin cushions propping a long Chinese pipe in front of him, a ribbon of sweet smoke curling from the pipe's carved ivory bowl.

Leonard stared blankly at his daughter, not seeming to see her, mumbling to himself as if he were in a wide-awake dream.

Cat kept her father's opium addiction a secret, blaming herself for pursuing a career while he was forced to stay home alone. In the following weeks, she also discovered that Leonard Powers was dependent on another opiate, morphine, to ease the pain in his withered legs.

By then in her late teens, Cat knew little—and wanted to know nothing more—about drugs. She was blossoming into womanhood, and her curiosity was targeted on the opposite sex.

Athletic young Derek Hartman was cast opposite Cat in the film of the 1950s best-selling war novel, The Long Way to Hell. Their love affair on camera continued into their private lives . . . kissing, petting, but never consummating in sex.

Leonard Powers had instilled a terror in Cat of becoming pregnant and ruining her career. But she longed to become a full-fledged woman. She dreamed of going all the way with Derek Hartman, becoming his wife, having his children. The young couple agreed to wait until the picture wrapped to elope.

A virgin on her wedding night, Cat discovered that her young husband was sexually inept. During the war, Derek had accidentally fired a pistol while removing it from his holster, shooting himself in a testicle. The misadventure had not made him impotent but it did cause him to suffer mentally. He needed to be led on in lovemaking.

"Talk to me, honey," he whispered in the darkness of their Laguna honeymoon bungalow.

"How do you mean?" Cat asked, curled around him in her satin negligée.

"Tell me what you want. Tell me how you want it. Tell me stories to . . . get me going."

Cat thought she understood the request.

Taking his forefinger in one hand, she began, "Once upon a time a very handsome young prince decided to take a trip through his kingdom, so . . .

"His wife kissed him good-bye when he left their palace . . ."

She kissed his fingertip.

"And he set out to enjoy all the delights and mysteries waiting for him. . . ."

Moving his finger to one breast, she said, "He first came to a very big, very soft, very sweet mountain . . ."

She encircled one breast.

"Then another mountain. . . ."

Tracing his finger around her second breast, Cat centered it on the nipple, rubbing herself into hardness through the satin nightie.

"He did not want to leave the mountain peak but decided he should see what other wonders lay ahead in the kingdom—"

Moving his finger across the flat of her stomach, she said, "He especially wanted to see the magic forest. . . ."

She rubbed his hand over her pubis, feeling his masculinity harden against her thigh. Increasing the pressure of his hand on her groin, she moved her lips toward him, whispering "The magic forest was warm . . . and dark . . . and all wet with heavy, heavy dew. . . ."

The public welcomed the sensational report that Cat Powers had eloped with handsome young Hartman. But the news devastated Leonard Powers, and he overdosed on morphine while Cat was still on her honeymoon.

The suicide shattered Cat; her mother had shot herself when Cat had been only a child in New York. Throwing herself into work, she told herself she must concentrate on her career and her new husband.

Cat was twenty-two years old, filming in Mexico, her marriage to Hartman going badly, when she met Jack Castle.

Castle was everything Derek Hartman was not. Confident. Mature. Potent. A building contractor, he was in Mexico discussing a tourist complex in Acapulco. It was refreshing for Cat to be involved with someone who wasn't in show business. And someone who did not need coaxing in the bedroom.

Cat obtained a quickie Mexican divorce from Hartman and married Castle in Acapulco.

Back in Los Angeles, Castle bought Cat a twenty-two bedroom house in Bel-Air and presented her with a carpenter's tool box full of signed checks "to go wild with" in decorating her new home.

Cat announced at a press conference, "I'm giving up my career until I fill every room with babies. I'm going to be 'Mrs. America.'"

Cat was six months' pregnant with her first child and decorating a nursery in pink-and-blue stripes when news came from Alaska that Jack Castle had been killed in a car accident. Rushed to the Cedars of Lebanon Hospital, Cat lost her child in a miscarriage.

For the next year, Cat remained a hermit, turning down film scripts, drinking tequila in memory of her Mexican wedding to Castle; she told friends she believed she had put a curse on his life.

The first photograph of Cat to appear in a newspaper after Castle's death was an uncomplimentary shot of her glowering at Helen Strand, the singer married to the South American orchestra leader, Chico Mocambo.

Coast-to-coast gossip columns dubbed Cat Powers a "homebreaker" for taking Chico away from his ladylike wife.

Helen Strand divorced Mocambo in Reno; a week later Cat married him at the Top of the Mark in San Francisco.

Like Jack Castle, Chico Mocambo was older than Cat. He was also a worldly man and tutored her, mostly in drugs.

Tall, with a hawk nose and a pencil-thin moustache, Mocambo lounged with Cat alongside the pool of their Palm Springs home.

"*Marijuana and hashish are from the same plant, my little gata,*" *he said, translating Cat's name into Spanish.* "*But hashish is ten times stronger than grass. See how it looks like a bit of old rubber tire.*"

Mocambo held out a small piece of black tar in the palm of his hand.

"*You sprinkle this on cigarettes or you smoke it in a little pipe. But for your birthday, my gata, I shall have cook bake it in a be-e-e-e-g cake. Then all our guests will rip off their clothes and jump into the pool. Yes?*"

Less enjoyably, Cat also learned about promiscuity from Chico Mocambo. After discovering that he was secretly dating Cuban dancer Yolana Solez, she divorced him ten months after their wedding.

By the time Cat reached her thirties, she was playing a wide range of roles, from sultry dramas to lighthearted comedies. She was a favorite at the box office. In the press, she was lauded not only as a star but also as a warm-hearted woman who cared about her fans. Cat flew stricken children to big-city hospitals for expensive operations. She sent overly generous checks to families whose homes had been devastated by fire. She set up scholarships for needy students.

Despite her philanthropy and good works, the public loved seeing Cat best on the screen as a temptress. Monogram Pictures decided to cast her in the title role of Jocasta, *a historical epic filmed in Puerto Rico.*

Cat's co-star in Jocasta *was the brooding young actor Benedict Kraft. Cat and Benedict—"Dickie"—became immediate chums on the San Juan locations. Monogram's publicity department exaggerated their platonic friendship into a torrid romance, hoping to hide Kraft's homosexuality from the world. Cat loved Dickie as a friend and went along with the story to help his career.*

Dickie kept an apartment in New York's Greenwich Village and invited Cat there with him at the end of filming. Cat wanted to work on Broadway and she accepted Dickie's offer. She enrolled in acting classes to develop her stage skills.

Cat and Dickie began a Manhattan spree, sampling new hallucinogenic drugs available in the early sixties, such as LSD, and exploring Greenwich Village nightlife. Together they laughed at the gossip columnists who wrote about their steamy love affair.

Cat's sojourn in New York was cut short by her agent securing her a plum stage role in London's West End. Cat signed the contract, remembering how her father had fabricated stories about London so many years ago to get her her first part.

In London, Cat's co-star for the two hander, Mouth to Mouth, was the respected pillar of British theater, Sir Roland Haskins. Arrogant and temperamental, Sir Roland treated Cat like a parvenu, referring to her as "that bosomy wench from the colonies."

Cat, unaccustomed to being dismissed as an underling, terminated her contract by a sickness clause. But she stayed in London to star in Ex Cathedra, an English black comedy being filmed at Pinewood.

Ex Cathedra's storyline was too intellectual for mass distribution. Cat also discovered too late that she was miscast as an Englishwoman. The British critics roasted her film performance, and the tabloid press dredged up details of her private life, details about her past marriages, her café society life, the weight she had recently added to her curvaceous figure.

The critics' personal attacks devastated Cat. She had never claimed to be a great actress. She had never set out to hurt anybody intentionally. She had been married only three times—a low figure compared to many Hollywood actresses. Cat saw herself as somebody trying to make a living like anybody else; she could not understand why the critics had picked on the negative things in her life, ignoring all the good she tried to do.

Hurt and disillisuioned, Cat abandoned England for the Continent.

Setting up home in Paris in a luxurious apartment on Avenue Foch, Cat signed to star in Fernando Devoti's new film being shot in France. She followed it with a spy thriller in the Mediterranean and, next, a caper romance set in Corfu.

In Europe, Cat's private life was filled with a string of love affairs. French matinee idols. Petty noblemen. Powerful industrialists. She listened to all the men's problems. She supported them emotionally and, sometimes, financially. But she turned down proposal after proposal of marriage, discovering that each suitor wanted something from her besides romance—either to ride to Hollywood on her coattails or to flaunt her like a trophy rather than a loving bride. Discouraged, she moved back to Los Angeles after ten years of living abroad, hoping to pick up the pieces of a long-ago life there, to find a man who loved her for herself.

Famous back in the United States as the woman who'd spurned some of the world's most eligible bachelors, Cat was showered with film offers, particularly for roles of sexy, worldly-wise females. Fan magazines and supermarket tabloids ran more and more stories about her glamorous existence, her love affairs, the charity benefits she hosted, the poor and needy she helped out of her own pocket.

In private life, however, Cat remained alone and unfulfilled.

A pattern was emerging in her life, she grimly realized. Ever since her father had groomed her for stardom, she seemed to gravitate toward older men. Also since childhood, she had struggled to balance her private and professional life. An early exposure to alcohol and drugs—even dirty talk begun with her young husband, Derek Hartman, during lovemaking—was part of the burden she now carried through life. To her Brentwood analyst, she complained, "I'm not a woman. I'm a baggage car on a runaway train."

Cat's feeling of helplessness was aggravated by her growing addiction to sleeping pills. Pep pills. Diet pills. Recreational pills popped with friends. And bourbon to calm her between dosages. Finally Cat committed herself to the new detoxification clinic that had opened in Connecticut.

After a three-week cure at Tanglewood, Cat settled in New York, staying at a friend's Central Park West co-op, trying to organize a new life for herself.

Still on the prowl for the ideal husband, she had a succession *of love affairs but became quickly frustrated that most of the men she met used amyl nitrate to excite their passions. It seemed that the total male population of New York City needed a popper to get a hard-on.*

Before the year was out, she returned to Tanglewood with an alcohol and Valium dependency, complicated by recreational drug use. After a month in residence, she flew back to California and checked into the health farm, Westicana, for a facelift and supervised diet, more determined than ever to find a husband.

After emerging from Westicana thirty-five pounds lighter, Cat began making the Los Angeles social scene, only to discover that many of her old friends had either overdosed on drugs or spent all their money on the newest drug craze, freebasing cocaine. But one thing remained the same: All the men wanted something from her.

It was later that same year in Texas that Cat met Tom Hudson at the youth charity ball. She was immediately drawn to the solid, middle-aged man, and the relationship soared. Hudson had presence without being flashy. He headed his own empire but still had time for quiet suppers, arm-in-arm strolls, a fun night out on the town. He was a robust lover but not interested in Cat solely for sex; he did not brag to his friends that he had banged the famous Cat Powers.

Hudson understood the enigmas in Cat's life. "You're a star performer. The public idolizes you. All you have to do is pull together your personal life."

"Maybe I should give up my career for a year or so and work at just being a woman." Cat had just received the offer to play Blanche Dubois in Streetcar Named Desire *on Broadway.*

Hudson disagreed. "Acting is part of your life. To abandon it, even temporarily, would be like giving up an arm or a leg."

"I don't know if I have the strength for a Broadway show," Cat confessed. "Or the courage to let a live audience and critics see me without the benefit of cameras and lighting men and editors."

"The least you can do is try it."

"I might need a few crutches."

"I'll come along and take them away from you when it's time."

Cat signed to do Streetcar. *Still unsure of her ability to cope with the demands of a live performance, she hired Gene Stone to travel with her to New York as her personal physician.*

In a candid interview about drugs and alcohol and marriage in The New York Times *a week before her Broadway opening, Cat was quoted as saying: "You might say I've been dependent, at one time or another, on everything except the one thing I want to depend on—a husband."*

75 IT WAS TWELVE THIRTY—THIRTY MIN-
UTES UNTIL ROGER WOULD JOIN
Jackie for lunch in Administration. He decided to use the
half hour to make a couple of quick visits on his Friday list.
Moving around the clinic would also help him burn up some
of the nervous energy building inside him.

In Security, Roger spoke to Leo Kemp.

"I just wanted to drop around and let you know what a
fine job you're doing down here. I also wanted to bring to
your attention something we've all overlooked. The importance of *people* in security.

"Oh, these cameras and bells and alarms are all fine, but
people are what count. Leo, I'm sure you've been thinking
about the same thing, but I didn't realize our mistake until
yesterday when I talked to Luther Brown—you know, one

of our men in the garden. He told me how he had spotted Lavender Gilbert. Now, I know it's policy to keep Security at a strict, low profile. But maybe we should think about including more opinions in our work, asking more staff members in other areas to help join in on the watchouts.

"Next week, Leo, I'll be calling a meeting of all the staff. I mean everybody. Doctors down to potato peelers. Naturally I want the authority—you—to address the meeting. So between now and next week's meeting, Leo, kick around my 'people' idea inside your head."

In Shirley Higgins's office, he told the head nurse, "I'll be seeing you later this afternoon in the Huddle. But I wanted a minute or two alone with you, Shirley, to say that the bad blood between you and Dunstan Bell has not gone unnoticed. I'm having a word with him after today's Huddle. We all have to remember that bickering is not only time-consuming but interferes with everybody's work. Worse, though, it's unbecoming to the splendid job you're doing for Tanglewood."

Shirley Higgins stood alongside her tidy desk. "Thank you, Roger, for the compliment. I also accept the rebuke. It's true. Dr. Bell and I often don't see eye to eye, but . . ."

She hesitated, checking her words. "I'll try harder, Roger. It might be difficult to bite my tongue but I'll try harder."

Smiling, she added, "Also, I always learn a great deal from you on the matter of diplomacy."

"The compliment was in earnest. You *are* doing a splendid job for Tanglewood. I'm proud to have you on the staff."

As Roger turned to leave, Shirley called, "While you're here, Roger, there's something I think I should mention to you."

"What's that?"

She explained, "Yesterday I received a call from one of our patients—actually, from one of our patient's physicians, Dr. Gene Stone."

Roger was instantly alert.

"Dr. Stone telephoned me here in the office," Shirley continued, "saying that he knew of a good job opening suitable for Delia Pomeroy and wanted her home telephone number. I explained as politely as I could that I never gave out my staff's home numbers."

"Delia Pomeroy?" Roger asked. "How does Stone know Delia Pomeroy?"

"I—I don't know," the head nurse stammered. "I assumed he'd seen her working around the clinic."

"This was yesterday?"

"Shortly before noon, I believe it was."

Gene Stone had left Tanglewood late yesterday afternoon. Why would he have wanted to talk about job opportunities to—of all people—Delia Pomeroy, a nurse whose work was satisfactory but certainly not noteworthy?

Turning to the door, he said, "Thanks for telling me this, Shirley."

"Yes. I thought it was some nerve of him," she admitted indignantly. "Visiting Tanglewood and trying to lure away one of our staff!"

Roger kept silent. He was certain that Stone's intentions were more devious than mere nurse rustling.

76 JACKIE MET ROGER AT THE DOOR OF ADMINISTRATION, EXTENDING ONE hand toward the luncheon trolley behind her. "You're right on time, Dr. Cooper."

"You're being kind," he said, checking his wristwatch. "I'm five minutes late."

"I needed those five minutes." Jackie laughed. "It's a madhouse here again today."

After closing the door behind him, Roger kissed Jackie's cheek. "I feel strange kissing the occupant of this office. Especially with what I have to say to you—"

The casual remark caught Jackie's attention. Last night's lovemaking had left her with mixed feelings, from euphoria to second thoughts about the wisdom of their utter sexual abandonment. She was glad that Roger had gone to his own apartment last night, so they both could arise fresh and early this morning and get on with the business of the day.

As Roger moved past her to the wheeled table covered with a white damask cloth, he studied the serving dishes and two place settings. "Shall we eat first and talk later? Or shall we talk and then eat?"

A tone of mild rebuke in her voice, Jackie chided, "Now, Roger Cooper! How am I going to have an appetite after hearing a question like that?"

He lifted a tureen's lid, a whiff of tempting steam rising from a golden rich vegetable soup. "Mmm. Smells delicious. But it also looks like it'll keep warm until I finish saying what I have to say."

Jackie sank to the French chair, nervous yet relieved that she wasn't pinning all her hopes on having an affair with Roger. If last night's wicked fling had done anything, it had given her faith in herself as a woman. What more could she ask for—at least, for the moment?

Roger remained standing. "Jackie, if I'm lucky enough to find financial backing to top Adrian's offer, how would you like to run this office for me?"

The question stunned her.

"That is," he said quickly, "if you see there's no future for you and Adrian . . . as you've intimated there might not be."

"You mean, work in here"—she waved around the book-lined room—"permanently?"

"Nine days a week. Fourteen months a year."

Roger had considered the proposal carefully last night after retiring to his apartment, mulling over all the changes happening in his life, for better or worse. He could not be certain of Joe Marino's continuing interest in Tanglewood. But such immediate excitement to put money into Tanglewood convinced Roger that it wasn't going to be as difficult to beat the bushes for investors as he had first suspected.

To Jackie, he explained, "You've been at the clinic as long as anyone else. This week proved you can perform the practical side of this job."

"Roger, I don't know what to say—"

"I can understand that you might be surprised," he said sympathetically. "Also, our behavior last night was a little . . . different from our usual conduct in the past."

Turning to her, he said, "What I'm proposing at the moment is a purely business arrangement, Jackie. As two adults, we must be able to discuss—and at a later date, hopefully soon—our personal future. Do you agree? That they're two separate matters?"

"Absolutely." Jackie was not ashamed of her compartmentalized mind; she was relieved to hear that Roger, too, could separate work and personal life.

"I must warn you, too, Jackie. There will probably be some opposition to you being my administrator." He quickly added, "If and when I'm lucky enough to find investors."

"Opposition from Adrian?"

"No. If I buy Adrian's shares, he's out."

"From your new backers?"

"No, again. I'll insist on having approval of who's to become administrator."

He cocked his head at the door. "I'm talking about the gang of five. The Huddle."

"Somebody's said something about me?"

"I just wanted to warn you."

Jackie's head was still spinning from Roger's offer to run

Administration. She tried to think of arguments why she should not accept but couldn't produce one.

Pacing the carpet, Roger continued. "You know me well enough, Jackie, to know that work comes first with me. Tanglewood is the center of my life. It's also been a large part of your life. You know how it runs. You've caught on extremely quickly here in Administration. The staff loves you—"

Stopping, he turned to her and blurted, "I've never said this to a woman before, and I'm surprised that—when I do say it—it's in a professional situation . . . but, Jackie Lyell, I need you!"

Jackie laughed. "And I never thought I'd hear somebody say they needed me . . . for a job! You don't know how I love hearing it!"

Becoming more serious, she said, "Obviously, though, I'll have to think it over, Roger. There are a number of issues I must take into consideration."

"Of course," he agreed. "Absolutely. Adrian, for one."

She nodded but failed to elaborate; at the moment she did not want to discuss with Roger how far she had already gone in pursuit of a divorce.

But Roger asked no more questions. Motioning toward the small table, he asked, "Now how about something to eat?"

"I'm starving!" Jackie jumped to her feet and pulled a chair up to the table.

Over lunch, Roger talked about clinic matters, noting that he hoped to visit Betty Lassiter's therapy group later to see if Peabo Washington could relate to the other patients, and that Shirley Higgins had just told him of Gene Stone's unusual request.

Folding his napkin and placing it alongside his plate at the conclusion of the brief lunch, he returned to the important subject of Jackie's position. "As for the possibility of you becoming full-time administrator, Jackie, I wanted to men-

tion it to you before tomorrow morning's board meeting.
have no idea what's going on with Adrian."

"Nor do I," she answered solemnly.

"I'm not pushing you for an answer but I want to know
if I have some options."

"Do you have to know by tomorrow morning, Roger?"

"No. Not a definite answer. But I'd like to know if the
idea appeals to you at all."

"I can answer that now," she said. "It appeals to me very
much."

"Good." He rose from his chair. "That's all I want to
know."

Thinking of his next appointment, he said, "At the moment, I'm going to make an announcement in today's Huddle. Say that Adrian and I might very possibly be dissolving
our partnership."

Jackie raised her water glass. "Good luck."

Roger reached for his glass, accepting the toast and adding
"To the future. Whatever it holds. Professional *and* private."

The telephone rang as they both sipped their ice water
eyes locked on one another.

Rising from her own chair, Jackie waved good-bye to
Roger, calling as she moved to the ringing telephone "Talk
later."

Jackie said into the receiver, "Yes. This is Mrs. Lyell . . ."

She glanced at the office door. Good. Roger had gone
This was one conversation she didn't want him to hear. She
was still uncomfortable with what she was doing.

"I see," she said into the telephone. "Yes. I authorize you
to proceed in place of your Los Angeles bureau. Contact me
here at this number with any results."

She reminded the caller, "Remember, this is extremely
urgent. I would like any proof as quickly as possible. Need-
less to say, it's also highly confidential."

She lowered the receiver.

Adrian was at the Park Regent Hotel in Manhattan. The New York bureau of the detective agency she had hired reported that Adrian's lover, Evelyn Palmer, had accompanied him to New York and was staying with him at the hotel.

Of all the information that the detective agency had reported, Jackie was most confused by the news that Adrian had met Dr. Gene Stone yesterday at a small New York hotel, Mallett's. She didn't even know Adrian knew the Beverly Hills doctor. She remembered what Roger had said about Stone asking for Delia Pomeroy's home telephone number. Jackie didn't know Delia but she did remember from the nurse's file that Adrian—who seldom became involved in the hiring of the clinic's medical staff—had recommended her for a job. . . .

Checking the desk clock, Jackie saw that Roger was probably already in the Huddle. But he definitely should know as soon as possible that Adrian had met with Stone in New York. She could smell something fishy all the way up in Connecticut.

77 ROGER RUSHED DOWN THE CORRIDOR FROM ADMINISTRATION TO THE CONFERENCE room, pleased with the way things had gone at lunch with Jackie. His brain whirred as he prepared himself to deliver one of the most important speeches he ever had made in the Huddle.

It was a speech Roger had never thought he would give.

* * *

The partnership with Adrian had been meant to provide the perfect professional solution for Roger. Adrian would run the business side of a clinic while Roger was free to concentrate on patients.

The Santa Barbara suit had left Roger exhausted; the dismissal of charges for improper conduct was no more than a hollow victory for him.

Deborah had packed her bags, and her grandmother's china, and moved back to Denver. The final straw for Roger had been when his father had died from cardiac cirrhosis, having returned to drink during the trial.

Deciding to try for a new life away from Santa Barbara, Roger applied—and was accepted—for a position at the Mandell Clinic near Arlington, Virginia.

The Mandell Clinic treated high-ranking figures from the government—senators, congressmen, military—suffering from alcohol and drug dependencies. More than a few patients there reminded Roger of his father: proud, patriotic old warhorses unwilling to admit that they had a fatal disease—the inability to drink alcohol—whatever the reasons might have been that they had taken to the bottle. Working at Mandell helped ease Roger's guilt that he—the legal action against him—had caused his father to return to drinking.

At Mandell there was a sprinkling of international personalities who had been unable to find discreet, anonymous cures for drink or drug problems in their own countries. Among them was the British hairdresser, Sackville West, who was suffering from anorexia after an amphetamine dependency.

Roger met Adrian and Jackie Lyell when they came to visit Sackville West. Adrian's charm and easygoing manner had immediately won Roger's friendship. After a week of visiting Mandell, Adrian presented Roger with an idea for opening their own clinic. Offering high-quality, extremely confidential care, their clinic would be close to New York City but set in quiet rural

*surroundings. Most of the financing would come from interna-
tional merchant banking houses.*

*It took Adrian exactly three days to find the site and the first
two million dollars. It took him considerably longer to extricate
himself from Sackville West International.*

*Throughout all of Adrian's problems with Sackville West,
Roger admired how Jackie had stood supportively by his side.
During that time, Roger was living with Crista. He had met her
after his wounds from Deborah had healed, and had asked her to
marry him. But Crista was already complaining that he spent
too much time working.*

*"I wish you were as obsessed with me as you are in getting
Tanglewood off the ground," Crista said.*

*"Just be patient till we open," Roger pleaded. "I'll make it
up to you."*

*But Crista had had every reason in the world to complain
about him, Roger later realized. He did ignore her for work. As
Tanglewood took shape, the patients' problems became the main
concern in his life. Crista finally left him.*

Opening the door to the Huddle, Roger mused that his
ideal woman would work at Tanglewood as the other half
of a team.

Roger addressed the Huddle from the head of the table.

"You all deserve to know that changes are in the air for
Tanglewood," he began. "I cannot tell you yet exactly what
those changes will be. But Adrian has offered to buy my half
of the clinic."

A stunned silence filled the room; the department heads
exchanged glances around the table.

Roger promised, "Of course, I'm not going to sit still for
that—"

The Huddle broke into applause.

Betty Lassiter raised a power fist over one shoulder.
"Right on, Rog!"

"We're all behind you," Philip Pringle called.

Lonny Lamb clapped and nodded his approval.

Roger warmed at the show of instant support. Raising both hands to silence his colleagues, he said, "Thank you, guys. Thank you. It's nice hearing that. Real nice. But let me give you a little more background."

He proceeded to explain the opposing views he and Adrian held for Tanglewood's future.

78 BETTY LASSITER LEFT THE HUDDLE AT TWO FORTY-FIVE, GRABBED A HAM-and-cheese croissant in the Hub for a late lunch, and dashed to convene her Friday afternoon psychotherapy session in the drawing room. The morning had been hectic. She had met with Karen Washington and discussed Peabo's domestic history, then interviewed Peabo himself. She'd decided to give him a chance inside her cage of lions and tigers.

Seven patients were waiting in the drawing room. Betty introduced the two new members and suggested, "Why don't we pull up those four armchairs around these two sofas."

Keeping her own chair a short distance back from the group, Betty tried to forget the bombshell that Roger had dropped in the Huddle.

Betty forced herself to concentrate on the patients, pleased to see that the group looked more spirited than usual this afternoon. She had already dubbed the day "Electric Friday."

*   *   *

David Terranova began the session by announcing, "I've got a complaint."

Groans rose from the chairs and two couches.

"No, I'm serious," insisted the bearded playwright. Looking at Skip Ryan, he continued. "Everybody pours blood, sweat, and tears into writing their journal, but young Ryan here hasn't been producing."

Betty watched Skip shift nervously in his chair, remembering how Terranova had mocked him for submitting a piece of his writing to *The New Yorker*.

Terranova said, "This week Skip gave us a brief history of his experience with angel dust. Personally, I thought it was very good. Very informative. I would like to see what it reads like."

Silence.

"Put it down on paper," Terranova urged the young student. "Maybe it won't help you in therapy. But it could be interesting for you as a writer. You have a good narrative, Skip. Maybe it's a little 'golly gee' and 'scary, man.' But that could work, too. In a Salinger sort of way. I'd be glad to read whatever you write and make any suggestions. I'm serious."

Skip nodded, lowering his eyes. "Thanks," he mumbled.

Terranova glanced back to the other patients. "That's all I have to say . . . for the moment."

Nodding at Nigel Burden, he said, "The spotlight's on you, Nigel. You were quiet yesterday and didn't tell us what you're doing back with us again."

Nigel Burden picked up the gauntlet. "I'm certain that the others, like myself, are stunned by your sudden show of good will, Mr. Terranova. But perhaps I can top you for shock value."

He looked at Betty. "I feel as if my life's been restored by God."

"God?" Dieter Biddlehof snorted from the depth of his club chair. "Were you struck from your horse on the way to Damascus, Burden?"

"No. My thunderbolt came on a transatlantic telephone call from London last night."

Burden looked at Peabo and Karen Washington seated side by side on one couch and explained, "Most of our little group here knows that, for my sins, I hold—or held—public office in England."

He said to the others, "I've always considered the press a necessary evil. Never to be trusted. Occasionally to be made use of. But last night I learned that a London newspaper is printing a scurrilous little story about me and my son which is, ironically, saving me from blackmail."

Biddlehof asked, "Is that why you drink, Nigel? Blackmail?"

"I always enjoyed a nice gin," admitted Burden. "Blackmail merely plunged me headlong into the vat."

David Terranova cut in, "You left Tanglewood earlier this week. Supposedly recovered. Then you unexpectedly returned. What happened?"

Burden eyed the swarthy New York playwright. "You're back to playing the devil's advocate, aren't you, young man?"

"Isn't the basic object of these meetings to ask questions?" Terranova reminded him.

Less amicably, Burden said, "As I stated, young man, the newspaper story does not involve only me. It also involves my . . . son."

"Stop dragging your feet," Terranova exclaimed, his old fire returning. "Why were you being blackmailed? Facts. Give us the facts."

Biddlehof came to Burden's defense. "Perhaps he can't talk about it yet. For legal reasons."

Marianne Turnbull spoke up. "If it's in the newspaper, all we have to do is get a copy and read it."

The others waited.

Terranova observed, "That moisture collecting on your brow, Mr. Burden, happens to be the reason why we call these meetings the Sweat Room. So 'fess up."

Burden reluctantly resumed his story. "It's true, I was due to leave Tanglewood this week. Tuesday, to be precise. My son and his wife were coming here to collect me. But when they arrived, my son was . . ."

The drawing room was silent.

Burden continued in a halting voice. "I don't know how the press learned that Cyril—that's my son's name, Cyril—was here . . . but they did. And you see, a year or so back, somebody sent me photographs of Cyril dressed . . . dressed as a . . ."

"Having trouble, Nigel?" Terranova taunted.

Burden glared at him.

Terranova would not let up. "Need a drink, Nigel? Need courage to talk?"

Burden admitted, "That's the truth of the matter right there. I *do* get courage from a gin. A gin blurs my entire conception of every problem. A gin protects me from dealing with evils in my life."

"We know all about how great booze is, Nigel," said Terranova. "But what evils are you talking about? We want hard cold facts."

Exasperated, Burden turned on the playwright. "All right! My son's a transvestite. He dresses like a woman!"

"And you can't deal with that?"

"No. I cannot." Nigel snapped.

"But somebody found out about your son cross-dressing so you had to deal with a blackmailer."

"Precisely." Burden considered the fact. "Except now that the London paper has printed an item about Cyril in a column, it's no longer a secret."

"Then you're off the hook, Nigel," said Biddlehof. "Why so glum?"

Terranova replied, "No, he's not off the hook. Not entirely. He still has to stop drinking."

"That's correct, young man," Burden said to Terranova. He faced the rest of the group. "Now I am trying to convince myself that Diana and I—that's my wife, Diana—that we have our own life to live. That Cyril and Trisha—that's *his* wife—can do what they damned well please."

"It sounds simple enough," said Marianne Turnbull, "but are you willing to see it through even if the going gets tough?"

"That is why I'm staying here at Tanglewood a little bit longer. Because my wife and I are as important as our children."

Peabo Washington had stared blankly at Nigel Burden talking about how he drank because his son wore dresses. Peabo elbowed Karen, whispering "Why are we wasting our time listening to this shit?"

Karen sat forward on the couch. "Excuse me, everybody, but my husband thinks we're wasting our time here."

Peabo dropped his head. "Jesus. Did you really have to say that?"

She ignored him and continued. "If my husband thinks he's wasting his time here, shouldn't he be telling you that and not whispering it to me?"

Biddlehof asked, "Is that true, Peabo? Do you think Nigel and the rest of us are wasting your time?"

"Yes, I do." Peabo had been in a foul mood since arising this morning. "What does this shit have to do with me?"

"And what does your shit have to do with us?" David Terranova demanded.

"Have I been laying anything on you, man?" Peabo asked.

"Yes. Your shitty attitude."

"I didn't ask to come to this Cub Scout meeting today. This is all her doing." Peabo tilted his head at Karen.

Marianne smiled at Karen. "You're here at Tanglewood helping your husband, aren't you, Mrs. Washington?"

Karen politely but firmly corrected her. "I'm here to help both of us. I've learned that if somebody in the family is involved with drugs, then most likely there's a problem at home. I want to find out what the problem is."

Peabo gibed, "You tell them, baby. You've got all the answers."

Terranova said, "No. She obviously doesn't have all the answers or she wouldn't be sitting next to you, letting you insult her like you're doing."

"What's it to you, sucker?" Peabo asked angrily.

Karen interrupted, "Thank you, David, but you don't have to defend me. I can take care of myself."

" 'David'?" Peabo turned to her. "What's this 'David' shit? You don't even know the guy!"

"I don't know you, either," Karen retorted. "The kids don't know you. You've been a stranger to all of us for the past two years."

"That's right, woman. Tell everybody our business."

Terranova asked, "What are you hiding, Peabo? We all know who you are. Where you live. How much money you make. We've seen you fly through the air on those commercials."

"Faggot," Peabo muttered.

"Where's this sense of humor you're so famous for?" Terranova asked. "Is that the best you can come up with? 'Faggot'?"

"The only thing funny around here is you, creep."

Terranova turned to Karen. "Did he *ever* have a sense of humor? Or was that all part of the press hype? Trying to create some kind of cut-rate Mohammed Ali?"

"No, Peabo *is* funny," defended Karen, sliding her hand through the crook of his arm. "The first time I ever met him, he told me a joke."

She looked around the group and asked, "Why does an alligator have more teeth than a bumble bee?"

All eyes turned to Peabo.

Ignoring them, he looked at Karen. "You still remember *that*?"

"Well?" insisted David Terranova.

"I love corny jokes," said Skip.

"Me, too," added Marianne. "But I'm awful at guessing the answers. What is it?"

But Peabo was not listening to the group. He repeated to Karen, "You still remember that old joke?"

"It was the first joke you ever told me," she murmured. "We were eight years old."

Very softly, he said, "You *do* love me, don't you?"

"Of course I do," she said, kissing her fingertip and planting it on the end of his nose.

"Hey, stop your smooching," Skip insisted, "and tell us the answer."

Marianne said, "Maybe they want to keep it to themselves. Maybe it's very personal and sentimental."

Behind the group, Roger Cooper came in the drawing room. "What's all the excitement about? What am I disturbing?"

Terranova turned toward Roger. "Why does an alligator have more teeth than a bumblebee?"

"Easy," Roger said, moving toward Betty Lassiter. Leaning down over her chair, he said, "Because an alligator doesn't have"—he playfully pinched Betty's arm—"a stinger."

Peabo jumped to his feet, shaking his fist at Roger. "After all these years you gave away the answer to my best joke."

Laughter filled the drawing room as Peabo sank alongside Karen on the couch, hamming his disappointment by leaning his head on her shoulder, shaking it woefully, and moaning "He told my best joke."

Karen joined the fun, patting his head. "You'll think of a new one, baby. You'll think of a new one."

79 ROGER LEFT THE ENCOUNTER SESSION AFTER PEABO HAD BEGUN EXPLAINING how he had started shooting speed when business pressures had become more demanding than his prize-fighting schedule. All humor had disappeared from his voice as he spoke to the group, but Roger was certain that today's breakthrough had come from tapping into Peabo's old sense of play, from doggedly trying to revitalize his good humor and foolery. Roger felt that Karen deserved as much credit as he did for the achievement.

As he hurried from the drawing room, he saw that he was ten minutes late for his three-thirty meeting with Dunstan Bell.

As he rushed into his outer office, Caroline pointed to the inner office door and said his visitor was waiting.

She called as he rushed past, "Also, Jackie wants to speak to you *urgently.*"

"Tell her I'll call when I get a minute." He closed the door behind him.

"I'm astounded by the news about you and Adrian." Bell sat rigidly in the chair facing Roger's desk. "But I suppose after Adrian's recent actions I shouldn't be surprised by anything."

It had crossed Roger's mind that Dunstan Bell might be the doctor Adrian had in mind to replace him as medical director. But he began questioning Bell as if he had no suspicions.

He inquired, "Has Adrian been in touch with you since he's been in California? For any clinical matter whatsoever?"

"Adrian? In touch with me? Good heavens, no. Adrian and I aren't close. In fact, I consider Adrian Lyell—"

Bell checked his personal opinion.

Roger decided to speak openly. "You wouldn't serve as medical director for Adrian if he purchased my half of Tanglewood?"

"Me? Be in cahoots with Adrian? Never. I wouldn't be medical director for Adrian, or anybody for that matter. I know my limitations. The Lord made me a number-two man." Bell smiled. "Possibly even third, fourth, or fifth on the ladder."

"So Adrian didn't approach you to replace me if I decide to leave?"

"No."

"Then why have you been so hostile toward me recently, Dunstan? So challenging?"

"Hostile?" Bell's pale face turned a spectrum of colors. "Oh, Roger. I think there's been a very serious misunderstanding. How do I begin? Oh, dear me. . . ."

Roger waited. Could he have been wrong?

Befuddled, Bell commenced. "The truth is, I believe you've been too dependent on Adrian. On the financial community."

"We can't exist on air, Dunstan."

"No. But—let me continue, please."

"Sorry."

"You know, I'm friendly with Dr. Tweed. Ephram Tweed."

Roger nodded. The dreaded ethics committee.

Bell explained, "Apart from presiding as the head of our ethics committee, Ephram is a board member for the Sunnydale Foundation for Rehabilitation and Research. Perhaps I was a bit presumptuous in my actions but, well, considering how busy you are with running the clinic and all, I thought perhaps you hadn't noticed in the press that Sunnydale has decided to make bequests to private clinics across the country. In fact, I put a flea in Dr. Tweed's ear this week about considering Tanglewood as a possible object for a grant."

Roger couldn't resist a loud belly laugh.

Dunstan Bell stared at him, blushing more deeply. "I know we seem to have no apparent shortage of money. But I thought that if you were less dependent on Adrian Lyell, had more freedom to pursue charitable pursuits—"

The intercom buzzed on Roger's desk; Caroline announced, "Elizabeth Kravetz is here."

"Tell her I'll be right out," he said and turned back to Bell. "I think I owe you an apology."

"No, no, no," Bell exclaimed. "Nothing's come of my word with Ephram."

"That's not what I mean. I think I owe you an apology for suspecting you were after my job."

Bell removed his wire-framed glasses. Unable to control a grin as he wiped the round lenses, he said, "Medical director? No. I'm afraid not. At best I consider myself to be a watchdog. And perhaps sometimes a too aggressive one."

Roger rose from the chair and crossed to open the door for Bell.

He said, "Watchdogs are precisely what we need. A doctor's best friend."

They shook hands.

80 CAT POWERS'S MOOD REMAINED ER-
RATIC THROUGHOUT THE MORNING,
swinging from docile to hyperactive. Her appetite was as
unpredictable as her behavior. For a midday meal, she asked
for a slice of pound cake, an extra-thick vanilla milkshake,
and a fresh peach, peeled and quartered. On the lunch tray
also came a tube of yogurt, along with her vitamins and
medication, including Crysticillin for syphilis.

Cat knew she was taking refuge in sulkiness, but she nevertheless wanted to be alone. She was pleased when Nurse
Kravetz announced that she was going to the Hub for her
own meal.

Left alone, though, Cat sank into gloom again, ashamed
of the mess she had gotten herself into. She loathed actresses
who played the prima donna or tried to wring sympathy out
of everybody around them. But she couldn't seem to pull
herself out of this miserable rut. How could she get back on
her feet?

It was three-twenty when the attendant collected Cat's
lunch tray. She had drifted back to sleep, and the movement
disturbed her. Stirring on the pillows, she heard voices in the
adjoining room. She listened more closely and recognized
that the voices were coming from a television set.

"Who's watching TV?" she asked the attendant.

"Your nurse," the young man answered from the doorway. "She's watching old movies on the VCR."

Cat lay in bed after the attendant had departed with the

tray. Wasn't it odd for a nurse to be watching video movies on duty? Oh, well. Maybe Mrs. Kravetz had come back from lunch early and didn't want to disturb my nap, Cat told herself.

A familiar voice caught her attention.

"I'll burn that dress before I let you wear it to the country club with Jim."

That's my line! Cat realized with a start. I said that line in *Triangle*. I'm hearing my voice!

Cat threw back the sheet and slipped on her slippers. She moved toward the door, grabbing a Tanglewood robe thrown across a nearby chair.

In the sitting room, Cat saw the back of Elizabeth Kravetz's head. The elderly nurse sat on the couch watching the television screen built into the far wall.

Standing behind the couch, Cat looked from Kravetz to the flickering screen. The movie's action had reached the point where Cat's character, Julie, was squabbling with her sister over a man who was also Julie's boss in an insurance office.

"But Jim's your boss, Julie."

"And he's not going to be your boy friend."

"There's room for two women in Jim's life."

"Not when I'm one of them, you little sneak."

Nurse Kravetz said without turning on the couch, "I love the determination in your eyes, Miss Powers."

"I was strong in that scene, wasn't I?" Cat laughed before she realized that the nurse had known she was in the room without turning to see her.

"You were strong in all the movies of that era. They flowed naturally into your *Jocasta* period."

Cat was impressed. "It sounds like you're a real authority on the films of Catharine Powers."

"Oh, I am," said the silver-haired nurse. "Catharine Powers was my inspiration for courage. Even in films like this one where she is a rather naughty girl. Catharine Powers is always ready to fight against all odds. And she always wins."

"But I lost the man in this film," Cat reminded her. "That mealy-mouthed sister of mine got Jim."

"She got Jim. But you got a better job in a bigger office. You were promoted out of Cleveland to the insurance head-quarters in New York. You became independent. That's what you *really* wanted."

"Hey, you remember the story better than I do."

Elizabeth admitted, "I've seen all your pictures at least three or four times."

"You have?"

"Yes, and, oh, how I've admired Catharine Powers. You've been able to pick yourself up from all kinds of scrapes. Brush off the dust and get on with life. What a survivor."

Cat admitted, "A lot of my films had a survival theme. Even into the eighties."

"A beautiful woman set upon."

Cat laughed. "Not so beautiful anymore. But certainly still set upon."

Elizabeth Kravetz froze the video's picture. Turning on the couch, she faced Cat. "Remember *The Heart Is My Keeper?* Remember how the orphanage said you couldn't raise little Cassie because you weren't married? But you kept the little angel and she became the top of the class?"

Cat smiled nostalgically. "That was a cute picture."

"My favorite, though, was *Home Fires Burning*. When your husband died and you had to change his will illegally to keep his family from taking away your home. That was strength. That was real fight."

"You're right. I was a fighter, wasn't I?"

Elizabeth reached for the video control, saying resignedly "Oh, well. They were just Hollywood stories, I guess."

Cat moved around the edge of the couch, feeling a little annoyed to hear the nurse give "Hollywood" all the credit for her screen charisma. "You might find it interesting to know, Mrs. Kravetz, that a lot of the spunk I showed in those films came from my private life. When I was making *Home*

Fires, I was battling Monogram Pictures over my contract. During *Triangle,* I was going through a humiliating divorce. I had battles on screen and off."

"You were a trooper."

"I still am," Cat said. "I'm still battling."

Elizabeth looked at her. "How do you mean?"

Cat insisted, "Here? Tanglewood? Don't you think this is a battle for me?"

The nurse's eyes dropped to Cat's figure, making her feel dumpy and fat and very ordinary.

Cat pulled the robe protectively around her throat. "I may be a little older now. Not as slim as"—she glanced at the television screen—"as I used to be. But I can still go to war."

The nurse said "I'm sure you can, Miss Powers. I'm sure you can."

"I *know* I can." Cat pointed at the small screen. "I still can do anything *she* can."

A twinkle appeared in Nurse Kravetz's eye. "Does this mean that Catharine Powers is going to win again in the last reel?"

"You better believe it." Cat nodded with determination. "As another tough old girl once said, 'Fasten your safety belts!' "

Fifteen minutes later, Elizabeth Kravetz stood with Roger beside Rita Zambetti at the switchboard, watching the lights flicker as Cat Powers called for the masseuse, the dietician, the hairdresser, the manicurist . . .

Elizabeth confessed, "I felt so disrespectful talking to Miss Powers like that. I'm such a fan of hers."

"You were doing her a favor, Elizabeth," Roger reminded her. "I think my hunch was right to make you do it. Cat Powers is a professional. She just had to be reminded what the audience expects from her."

81 AT FIVE-TWENTY, MARGIE CLARK STOPPED BY STONEBRIDGE GENERAL after work to see Lillian Weiss. Since Ray Esposito had attacked Lillian, Margie could not stop thinking that, perhaps, Lillian might have remembered seeing her take the card keys from the hall cabinet and, later, used one to let herself into Esposito's suite.

The swelling had gone down on Lillian's eyes but she was unable to speak through her wired jaws, and her taped ribs impaired movement. There were small pads of scratch paper dotted around the hospital bed, which she used to write messages to doctors and nurses.

Pulling a chair alongside the bed, Margie said, "I've got to get home and cook supper for my kids. But I couldn't pass the hospital without popping in to see how you're doing, honey."

Lillian nodded her thanks. She liked the cheery nurse. Also, she was grateful for company. Lillian was unable to talk on the telephone, but even if she were able to make calls, there was nobody to talk to anyway. Her mother and two sisters certainly wouldn't take the time to commiserate with her, let alone come see her.

"The girls at the front desk say you're doing terrific," Margie said.

Lillian made an effort to shrug. No big deal.

Margie went on cheerfully, "They also tell me you've made a very important decision about your future."

Lillian's eyes became steely.

"The girls tell me," Margie said, "that you've decided to keep your jaws wired even after they mend. That you're going to stay on a liquid diet until you lose three hundred pounds."

Lillian closed her eyes.

"Hey, I think it's a fantastic idea!" Margie exclaimed, touching Lillian's shoulder. "I'm going to keep checking in on you here and give you all the support that you need."

Lillian smiled, pleasure again in her eyes.

"I'm also going to find out for you about surgery. You know, cosmetic surgery to cut away those tummy sags you'll have after losing so much weight."

Lillian's eyes widened; she nodded as if she had been thinking about the same thing.

"See. All this is playing right into your hands." Margie smiled. "Every cloud has a silver lining, right?"

Lillian turned away her head. She didn't want to talk about what had happened to land her in the hospital.

Margie became serious. "I know you can't talk now but you'll have to at some time, honey, if you're going to press charges against him."

Lillian shook her head.

"You're not going to press charges?"

Head shake: No.

"Not against Esposito?"

No.

"Not against Tanglewood?"

No.

This convinced Margie that Lillian most likely had approached Esposito for some personal reason. Possibly even sex. She had always enjoyed talking about men and fucking and big dicks. And she had become very excited by the stories of Esposito masturbating. So she must have decided not to press charges because she didn't want Esposito telling his side of the story in court. It would forever be her secret.

Springing forward to kiss her on the forehead, Margie said, "You're my kind of girl, you know that?"

Scraps of paper from Lillian's scratch pads were on the blanket. Lillian grabbed for the small pieces of paper. They were very personal.

But she reached for them too late. Margie held one in her hand, seeing a crude drawing of a woman with large breasts, tiny waist, and curvacious hips. Pencil circles for bracelets and hoop earrings told Margie that Lillian Weiss had been lying in the hospital bed, drawing pictures of how sexy she was going to look after losing three hundred pounds.

What a survivor!

As she left Lillian's room, Margie was pleased that she had taken a few minutes to drop by the hospital. Not only was Lillian a very lonely lady, but now Margie's worries about Lillian pressing criminal charges were put to rest.

Margie stopped in the hospital corridor. Something had caught her eye.

Moving toward the nurses' station, Margie asked, "Who's that?" She nodded at a woman down on her hands and knees, with a nylon brush and plastic bucket, busily scrubbing the floor in wide, circular movements.

The nurse looked at the cleaner then glanced back to Margie. "You work at Tanglewood, don't you?"

Margie nodded. "That's Little Milly Wheeler's mother, isn't it?" she said, indicating the scrubwoman. "Gladys Wheeler? From Nashville?"

The nurse nodded. "Sad, isn't it? They don't expect Little Milly to last much longer. That's how her poor mother's coping."

The distant light grew brighter in the clouds, a blinding whiteness like car headlights drawing nearer and nearer through thick white smoke. The air was warm and everything was still, until a voice that said it was God speaking but sounded more like Daddy singing "The Old Rugged Cross" called "You've been on the road long enough and it's time to come home, Little Milly. . . . Come home, Little Milly. . . . Come home, Little Milly. . . ." Then the blinding headlights became so fierce that she had to close her eyes and, feeling a hand grip her heart and hold it motionless inside her chest, she tasted a thick sweetness that she knew was the first gulp of death. Her last thought was: Oh, Mama's going to be so mad at me if I slop any of this blood on my sheets.

82 IN DOWNTOWN STONEBRIDGE, ROGER DROVE WITH THE EVENING TRAFFIC along Division Street. Shirley Higgins sat alongside him in the Mercedes. Turning off Division, he headed toward the less commercial west side of town. He said to the head nurse, "Shirley, I appreciate you coming with me tonight. Not only do I need a witness, but past experiences have taught me that sometimes it's not wise to be alone with a female." He did not explain further, but added, "As you know, Adrian and I are having professional differences at the moment. I have reason to believe he might have involved Dr. Stone in some rather nasty business."

"You always have my support," Shirley assured him crisply, her eyes on the street numbers along Laurel Street.

Jackie's revelation a few hours ago that a private detective had followed Adrian to a small hotel in New York where Gene Stone was registered still baffled Roger. Apart from being surprised that Jackie had put a detective agency onto Adrian's trail, he could not understand why Adrian would be visiting Stone. He was certain the two men did not know one another. Furthermore, the fact that Stone had tried to get Delia Pomeroy's number yesterday was too much of a coincidence for him not to suspect that some skulduggery was afoot.

"There," Shirley said, pointing at a three-story brick building. "That's it."

Parking in front, Roger escorted Shirley up the cracked cement walkway and rang bell 2G. There was no answer. Roger tried the lobby's outer door. It was unlocked. He opened it and stood back for Shirley to enter in front of him.

Delia's apartment was at the back of the second floor; Shirley pressed the bell button, then rapped firmly on the varnished door.

"Yes," answered a woman's voice from within. "Who is it?"

"Shirley Higgins, dear," announced Shirley. "From Tanglewood."

The sound of a safety chain rattled inside the door, and the door opened.

Wearing a flowered bathrobe, no shoes, and her hair rolled into pink rubber curlers, Delia Pomeroy looked from Shirley to Roger, her face turning red as she asked, "What's the matter?"

"Can we talk to you, dear?" Shirley said.

"Talk? Talk about what?" Delia asked, her voice quavering.

Roger said, "Delia, I believe Dr. Gene Stone contacted you yesterday."

The young nurse began to tremble. Gathering her robe at the neck, she shook her head back and forth. She said, "Whatever he told you I said about you, Dr. Cooper, it isn't true. I haven't said anything to anybody yet. Not to him. Not to Mr. Lyell. Not to any lawyer like they want me to."

Shirley and Roger exchanged glances; Roger nodded, and she stepped across the threshold, saying more forcefully

"Calm down, dear. I think you'd better invite us inside and tell us what this is all about."

Roger knew he had a long night ahead of him when Delia Pomeroy buried her face in her hands, beginning to cry in loud gulps.

83 IT WAS 8:30 P.M. AND THE KNOCKING PERSISTED ON THE DOOR OF THE twelfth-floor room of New York's fashionable Park Regent Hotel.

Adrian Lyell whispered from the bed, "Did you put out the 'Do Not Disturb' sign?"

"Of course," Evelyn Palmer answered in the semidarkness. "It's the maid."

"Can't the bitch read?"

Evelyn said quietly, "The poor thing probably wants to turn down our bed and leave chocolates on the pillow."

Adrian was uneasy about being tied to the bed, but Evelyn had insisted on swapping sex roles. It was long past her turn to play the top partner in their bondage and domination games.

He asked, "Did you chain the door?"

Evelyn did not reply; she stood alongside the bed, studying the used towels heaped on the floor. Among them lay an opened jar of Elbow Grease, a half-empty bottle of Johnson and Johnson Baby Oil, a can of Crisco, along with newly purchased tit clamps, two sizes of rubber dildos, leather paddles, a piss gag, condoms—all paraphernalia she had purchased that afternoon from the Manhattan specialty sex shop, The Deep End, to use during her turn as dominant partner.

The knocking on the door became louder.

After grabbing a towel from the floor, Evelyn wrapped it around her, sarong-style, and swayed across the carpet on her black spike-heeled shoes.

"For Christ's sake," Adrian hissed, "where are you going?"

Evelyn whispered, "To get fresh towels. We'll need to shower before we go out to supper."

"No," insisted Adrian. "Don't open that door."

Ignoring him, Evelyn leaned her head against the door, calling sweetly to the maid "Dear, can you please pass me a couple of fresh bath towels?"

Behind Evelyn, Adrian lay naked, spread-eagled across the mattress on his back, wrists and ankles tied by leather thongs to the four corners of the bed. A black leather harness was strapped around his chest, a studded restrictor snapped to his penis and scrotum, a riveted dog collar encircled his neck, trailing a long stainless-steel chain.

"I better have a couple hand towels, too," Evelyn added as she unlocked the door, opening it slightly to slide out her hand and take the towels from the maid.

From the hallway, a man's voice asked, "Mrs. Lyell?"

Adrian jerked his head at the mention of the name, the sound of a man's voice instead of a chambermaid's.

Who besides his lawyer knew he was at the Park Regent? Had Bill Ruben sent round a message? Or maybe Gene Stone was sending a note concerning Delia Pomeroy? The telephone had rung in the past hour but Adrian had told Evelyn to ignore it; he didn't want to talk to anybody while they were involved in their sex games.

At the door, he heard Evelyn answer hesitantly, "Yes, I'm Mrs. Lyell . . ."

The door burst open, and when Adrian looked at the intruder, a camera's flash blinded him.

Turning, Adrian tried to hide his face. But the photographer stepped round the bed, flashing more angles of Adrian as well as the S/M equipment scattered around the floor.

Evelyn screamed at the photographer, kicking and hitting him, grabbing for the camera.

In the struggle, her towel fell to the carpet.

The photographer, stepping back, flashed a final picture of Evelyn Palmer dressed as a dominatrix—Adrian trussed in bondage behind her—and disappeared from the hotel room.

84 ROGER FUMED AS HE DROVE THROUGH THE CHILLY NIGHT ALONG THE MERritt Parkway to New York. He had left Shirley Higgins at her home in Stonebridge. The head nurse had skillfully extracted the truth from Delia Pomeroy—that Gene Stone had tried to induce her into giving false testimony against him. Shirley would be valuable, too, in Roger's defense if Delia decided later to change her story.

Roger switched on the tape deck, trying to cool his temper, but he could not get out of his mind the scheme to smear him with a sleazy allegation.

Adrian must have been desperate to approach Stone with this plan. In tonight's meeting, Delia had not divulged how she had come to know Adrian Lyell and be recommended for the Tanglewood job, but Roger was certain their acquaintance was more than professional.

It was strange to think that a mere week ago, life had been

amicable between the two partners. But beneath Adrian's suave British facade ambition and greed had been festering. How long had he been plotting destruction? Jackie had been equally shocked—and angered—when Roger had returned to Tanglewood and reported Delia Pomeroy's tearful confession. Like Roger, Jackie believed that Stone's offer to the nurse must be part of Adrian's covert plans to gain control of the clinic. She also concurred with Roger that he should definitely *not* contact Adrian before Saturday's emergency board meeting. If he made a move toward anybody, it should be Gene Stone. Roger had next telephoned his new lawyer at home; Avery Brennan had listened to the report of the young nurse's story and agreed that it would be wise to speak to Stone before tomorrow's meeting, but on no account should Roger contact Adrian. Brennan told Roger to keep a firm hold on his temper when he approached Stone, not to give the Beverly Hills doctor any opportunity to charge him with assault or harassments.

It was a few minutes past midnight when Roger turned left on Lexington Avenue in Manhattan, pulling up to the curb across the street from Gene Stone's hotel.

Mallett's was small—three narrow brownstone townhouses joined into one—with flower boxes on all the front windows. There was no sign proclaiming it as a hotel, only an art deco–style street number on a white canvas awning and a logo etched into a pair of Lalique crystal doors. Mallett's was discreet, stylish, and, obviously, very expensive.

"I believe Dr. Gene Stone is a guest here," Roger said to the pretty Asian woman seated behind a burled wood table in a snug lobby decorated with original Erté watercolors.

"Dr. Stone's out for the evening," the woman replied.

"What time does he usually come back?"

"That depends on the nightlife, doesn't it?" Pushing a pad and pen across the table toward Roger, she said, "If you'll leave a message, I'll see Dr. Stone gets it."

"Thanks, but"—Roger shrugged—"I think I'll kick around the neighborhood and try again later. Bye."

Slumped behind the steering wheel across the street from the hotel, Roger settled in for a long wait. On the seat behind him sat his gym bag packed with shaving gear, as well as a hanging bag with a dark suit, fresh Oxford cloth shirt, and tie. He wanted to be prepared in case there wasn't time to get back to Tanglewood to change before the morning meeting at the Burlingame Club.

Telling himself for the hundredth time to keep cool, Roger tried not to dwell on how many years he had been waiting to settle a long-overdue score with Gene Stone. The damaging California deposition had seemed like the last straw. But, now, years later, Stone was ready to spread more lies against him.

What hatred that guy must have for me, Roger thought. Is it really all about money? Just because he sees me as nothing but a rich kid?

Trying to shake Stone from his thoughts, Roger turned his attention to the street, appraising the well-kept neighborhood. At this late hour a few local residents were taking their dogs for a walk; now and then someone hurried along the sidewalk with a brown paper bag of groceries from a corner delicatessen.

Noticing the delicatessen's distant light, Roger remembered that he hadn't eaten anything since lunch with Jackie. Why not make a dash for a sandwich and a cup of coffee? He could keep his eye on the hotel's entrance from the deli.

Resettling himself, a few minutes later, behind the steering wheel with a jumbo ham, cheese, and tomato sandwich, along with a large container of steaming black coffee, Roger thought of the day's more professional events. Jackie had reported to him this evening that Stonebridge General had telephoned with the bad news that Milly Wheeler had died; the Wheeler family was already making plans to fly the body home to Nashville. Jackie wanted to open an investigation into the cause of death. Roger would welcome such a move. He wanted to know how the young singer had been strapped into the makeshift straitjacket and deprived of her medication.

At least there had been some good news today, too. Roger pictured Peabo Washington in the Sweat Room, smiling as he remembered the alligator–bumblebee joke. And Cat Powers might be on the way to recovery, with some help from Elizabeth Kravetz. Hopefully, the arrival of Cat's secretary tomorrow with possible scripts and a few good reviews would help her farther along on the road to recovery.

Some late-night sanitation workers moved down the street, one worker handing the other what was obviously a marijuana joint. It made Roger think of his gratis patients, particularly Ray Esposito. He remembered from Esposito's records that the construction worker was currently unemployed. He recalled from admissions interviews that Esposito's biggest fear was of becoming homeless, turning into a "bag man."

Roger brooded on a scheme that could transplant Esposito—and other needy patients—into a new city, into a new home and a new job when he left Tanglewood. A change of environment was often as important as a satisfactory outpatient program when a patient was trying to make a fresh start. Roger made a mental note to telephone an ex-patient now working at the Massachusetts State Employment Office in Boston and see if he could start the ball rolling for Esposito's future.

It was 2:30 A.M.; Roger held his empty coffee container, considering his own future. He thought pleasurably about Jackie; he had decided that his strong feelings toward her were not rash. It was now very clear to him that it was her mixture of maturity and vivaciousness which he found so damned attractive. Her dogged dedication to work this week—coupled with her genuine humility—made him respect as well as desire her. Would she divorce Adrian? Perhaps she would not want to become involved with another man so soon after a bitter separation. A screech of tires interrupted his thoughts. Across the street, a yellow taxicab had stopped in front of the small hotel.

"Gene?"

Gene Stone sat half out of the cab's curbside door, digging in a pocket to find money for the driver.

Roger called louder as he crossed the empty street. "Hey, Gene!"

Stone stood from the cab door, looking around him.

"What a coincidence," Roger called, forcing his bonhomie.

Stone blinked his eyes, trying to recognize who was speaking to him from the darkness. Roger instantly saw that Stone had been drinking heavily—and the alcohol was probably mixed with a couple of other drugs.

"It's me." Roger held out his hand, forcing the greeting. "Your old buddy . . . Roger Cooper."

"Roger!" Stone held out both hands. "What you doing here, Roger?"

Grabbing Stone before he stepped in front of the cab as it pulled away from the curb, Roger said, "I know where a party is. Want to go to a big party, Gene?"

"Party?"

"A very big party. My car's just across the street. Let me give you a ride."

After helping Stone across the street, Roger opened the door on the passenger side and patiently settled him inside.

By the time Roger turned left off Third Avenue onto 42nd Street, Stone was slumped against the side window, snoring, saliva drooling from his mouth.

Good, Roger thought. Stone's passing out saved him a lot of trouble. He knew exactly what he was going to do with him now.

Stone's unconsciousness also gave Roger time to make one last stop in Manhattan before heading back up Interstate 95.

Driving through Times Square, Roger was relieved to see the all-night shop he had remembered on Broadway, its neon light blazing: T-SHIRTS—WE PRINT ANYTHING—ANYTIME.

PART SEVEN

SATURDAY MORNING

85 JACKIE STARED AT THE EIGHT-BY-TEN PHOTOGRAPHS SPREAD ACROSS THE

op of the desk. They left little to the imagination except for some of the strange gear Adrian was wearing—for instance, what was that black sock jutting out from his crotch? And why was *he* tied to the bed? Wasn't Adrian supposedly a sadist? Didn't sadists do the tying up?

Jackie's initial reaction on seeing the photographs had been total outrage that Adrian had allowed himself to be caught in such a seamy manner. Couldn't he have been more careful? But she reminded herself that she had hired a very expensive detective agency to produce evidence of adultery and they had done a good job. Frighteningly good.

As she wrote a personal check for the private investigator, Brian Kelly, she thanked the brawny man again for his prompt service, then accompanied him to the front door.

She said, "I'll be in touch with the agency if I want you to proceed with the investigation."

Hurrying back to Administration, she locked the door, poured herself a fresh cup of coffee, and stacked the photographs in front of her on the desk to study them one by one by one.

The grainy texture added to their sordidness. Looking at them, Jackie thought of London's Soho porno district. Times Square in New York. A world she knew little or nothing about. Nor did it hold any attraction whatsoever for her.

The anger she had originally felt changed to curiosity as she studied the photographs in detail. What attracted Adrian to leather and whips and chains? Was it an element of danger? Or was he intrinsically an evil man?

Taking a magnifying glass from the desk, she scrutinized his facial expressions in different shots—surprise, horror, anger. She saw the tension in his hands, the way his bare feet pulled at the leather thongs tied around his ankles.

Examining the black socklike object on his crotch, she decided it must be some kind of medieval-style chastity belt for males. Or was she being her usual naive self? Was it gear available in every sex shop around the world?

And what was that criss-cross piece of leather equipment strapped around his chest? It looked like a larger version of those trainer harnesses mothers fasten on toddlers.

The most distressing object in the photographs was the dog collar. Adrian was always such a proud man. Such a dignified man. But a dog collar was so debasing. So symbolic of humiliation.

Thinking of humiliation, Jackie remembered how Adrian had begun criticizing her in public, drawing attention to her mistakes and shortcomings. She could easily imagine him buckling a dog collar around her neck, leading her behind him like a corgi.

Studying the woman in the shiny black leather corset, she decided that it did not matter if she was Evelyn Palmer. Jackie felt no jealousy. She remembered the love she and Roger had made two nights ago—on this very desk. In no way had it resembled the aberrant experience shared by the two people in these photographs.

Jackie hurriedly stuffed the photographs into a manila envelope. She was glad to have them out of sight. They had nothing to do with her—except to help her obtain a speedy and, she hoped, not-too-sensational divorce.

One of the desk telephones buzzed.

Jackie snatched for the receiver. The board meeting was

only an hour away and she still had not heard from Roger since he had driven off to New York last night.

Rita Zambetti said from the switchboard, "The Country Mouse is on the line, Mrs. Lyell."

"You're joking."

"No. It's Len Gibbs, the owner," Rita explained. "He says it's urgent that he speak to someone in charge."

If the Country Mouse was calling to apologize for the shocking way they had treated Karen Washington, it was too late, Jackie decided. The damage was done. They could take their apology and shove it.

"Put him through," she said, bristling.

Len Gibbs's voice was soft, ingratiating. "Thank you for taking my call, Mrs. Lyell. I know you're very busy over there at Tanglewood so I'll cut through all the rigmarole and ask straight out if I can pop round and talk about my wife's drinking problem."

"Are you seeking treatment here at Tanglewood, Mr. Gibbs?" Jackie asked, astounded by the request.

"That was my idea."

She forced herself to remain cordial. "Your wife runs the inn, doesn't she, Mr. Gibbs?"

"Yes." His voice brightened. "I run the restaurant. But the inn is Emma's domain. You know her?"

"Well enough to know she has more than a drinking problem."

Pause. "What do you mean?"

Jackie explained, "Earlier this week, Mr. Gibbs, your wife turned away four people I sent to your hotel."

Gibbs laughed weakly. "Oh, you must be referring to that unpleasant little incident with that boxer guy's family. I think that's all blown over by now, don't you?"

Jackie fought for composure. "Mr. Gibbs, hear me out. Please.

"First of all, I want to say it's very brave of your wife to face her drinking problem. It's difficult to do. Believe me. We see it every day here at the clinic. It's also extremely

loyal of you to stand by her. But before we continue, I am
obliged to tell you that I feel your wife might be very uncomfortable in—shall we say—the 'integrated' surroundings
here at Tanglewood."

"But that colored guy will be gone soon, won't he?" asked
Gibbs.

"Perhaps," Jackie said, controlling her anger. "But the
gentleman will not be our only black patient, Mr. Gibbs."

She continued. "Comfort is necessary in treatment. Your
wife might not be comfortable in our mixed atmosphere.
Or—for the sake of discussion—she might make life uncomfortable for other patients. I suggest you think about that
detail, Mr. Gibbs. Think about it very, very carefully."

When Jackie put down the phone, she wondered if she
had been unfair, even unethical, by not encouraging Gibbs
to send his wife to the clinic.

But why should Emma Gibbs be welcomed with open
arms after Karen Washington had had to run around the
countryside, looking frantically for a motel room, having her
private life smeared across television screens and newspapers?

Infuriated, Jackie was prepared to go into the Huddle and
explain her convictions to the department heads.

Thinking of the Huddle, she glanced at the desk clock and
saw that it was almost ten-fifteen. An hour to go before the
meeting at the Burlingame Club.

She wondered if Adrian had come to Stonebridge for the
meeting as promised. She would be ready for him. Late
yesterday afternoon she had succeeded in obtaining a restraining order barring Adrian from Tanglewood for the
duration of their divorce proceedings. The gatehouse had
already been notified.

86 CAT POWERS SAT IN A STRAIGHTBACK
CHAIR IN THE MIDDLE OF THE SITTING
room of her Orchard Pavilion suite, a pink smock tied
around her neck. Michele the hairdresser stood alongside the
chair with scissors and comb; on the floor in front of her
chair knelt the pedicurist, Carlotta, painting Cat's toenails a
pale-purple gloss.

Across from Cat, Linda, the secretary, sat on the couch,
film and television scripts piled in front of her on the coffee
table, a folder of reviews in her lap.

"Miss Powers, I don't think you saw what the *Newark
Herald* said about you in *Streetcar*," said Linda, producing
a small clipping.

Cat waved it away. "That's history. Let's talk about the
future."

Alongside the chair, Michele insisted, "Miss Powers,
you're going to have to sit still."

"Sorry." Cat straightened rigidly in the chair, then continued more enthusiastically to her secretary. "Tommy
called me from Miami last night. He thinks I should consider
opening *Streetcar* in Florida. Play Miami for a week. Maybe
New Orleans. Atlanta. Dallas. Lead slowly out to L.A. to
open at the Ahmanson. That way I could whet people's
appetite. Build up publicity."

"Terrific, Miss Powers," Linda said, then cautiously
added, "But it sounds like a lot of hard work. Do you think
you have the energy?"

"Tommy asked the same thing. He doesn't want me over-commiting myself."

Powder-blue eyes shining, Cat said, "You know, I think he really still loves me, in spite of everything."

"It sounds like he does, Miss Powers."

"Tommy deserves some kind of medal for what he's been through with me over the past weeks. We started out great. But the show threw me for a loop. I lost my nerve. I started depending too much on that crummy Gene Stone. That was mistake number one." Deciding not to mention syphilis, she laughed, adding "And let's face it. I haven't exactly been looking like a glamour puss."

Raising one hand toward Michele, she said, "But we're changing all that, aren't we, dear? Tell Linda what we've decided to do."

Michele, tucking the ends of Cat's damp hair under her neck, explained as if lecturing students, "First, we're taking off a couple inches all over. Then we're going to lighten it a few shades—"

"Ranch mink," Cat said excitedly.

Michele added, "Then put in highlights and lowlights all over—"

"Frost it in gold," Cat interpreted.

Looking at Linda, she said, "Knowing I've got Tommy to keep happy, I can do anything, Linda. Anything. Go back to *Streetcar*. Tour in it. Face audiences. Have critics roast me. See, I've got somebody to work for. Plus I have fans to keep happy."

Wiggling her fingers, she said, "Talking about work, let me see that movie-of-the-week script about the older woman who steals the husband away from the younger woman. The one set in Chicago. I'd like to film more in Chicago—be near Tommy's work as much as I can."

Linda quickly produced the slim red binder, surprised at Cat's enthusiasm for new projects.

"Also I want you to call Chatwyn for me," Cat continued.

"Have him send up some decent-looking clothes. Something loose I can cinch in later when I lose weight."

Behind the chair, Michele insisted, "Miss Powers, *please*. You're going to have to sit still."

The morning sun was breaking through the hazy October clouds as Skip Ryan strolled over the fallen leaves with Crandall Benedict in the garden behind Tanglewood's main house. Skip said to the good family friend, "Remember me telling you this week that David Terranova was in my therapy group and he was razzing me for wanting to be a writer?"

"Indeed I do," said the chubby novelist. He'd approached Terranova during the week about that very matter.

"Well, yesterday in our session," Skip continued, "Terranova complimented me. He said he really liked what I said about PCP and thought that I should think about putting it down onto paper."

"What a constructive idea," said Benedict. "And have you taken his advice?"

"You bet. I've been working on something all night."

"See," Crandall Benedict said as he kicked through the dried leaves. "Sometimes it just takes a little praise to get a writer going."

Listening to Skip excitedly explain how he was turning his drug experience into a short story, Benedict wondered if he could glean something from the young man's enthusiasm. If an aspiring young author could teach him how to get to work without drinking, then it would be more than a fair trade for having—indirectly—helped him.

In Security, Leo Kemp sat at his desk, aviator glasses pushed to his forehead as he dictated ideas onto his cassette recorder for the speech Roger Cooper had asked him to deliver next week to all clinic employees.

The ideas came quickly: staff security education . . . monthly refresher courses on surveillance equipment up-

dates . . . closer cooperation among everybody on the pay-
roll . . .

Kemp already had a title for the speech on improved
security: The People Factor.

87 IN THE EMBASSY SUITE AT THE BUR-
LINGAME CLUB, COFFEE CUPS RESTED
on silver placemats dotted around the conference table. Tanglewood's board meeting was in progress.

The late-morning gathering was informal; a fire crackled
in the red brick fireplace; the six board members were
dressed in tweed jackets and cardigan sweaters. Their attention was directed toward Adrian Lyell addressing them from
his chair at the table; to Adrian's right sat the New York
lawyer, William Ruben; across the table sat Roger Cooper
with Avery Brennan.

Adrian looked dapper in a gray flannel suit, a yellow silk
foulard square tucked into the chest pocket. As he spoke, he
moved his eyes from face to face to face, from Senator William Baird, to realtor Dorothy McCall, to newspaper publisher Warren Tolan.

"When I originally proposed the idea of Tanglewood to
Roger Cooper," Adrian said in his most impressive British
accent, "I foresaw a venture that would benefit both patients
and community."

The board members nodded their approval around the
table.

"Tanglewood surpassed even my wildest dreams,"

Adrian said proudly. "Our recovery rate was ninety percent. Patients clamored to check in for treatment. By the end of the first year, we were in the black."

A satisfied expression on his suntanned face, he continued in a strong voice. "With our initial success, we were able to hire more staff. To improve equipment. We even developed a fledgling charity program."

Across the table, Roger dipped his head to hide a frown. Adrian had always scoffed at his gratis patient scheme.

Full of self-assurance, Adrian continued. "We were attaining the goals we set out to achieve and all the while our accountants kept saying expand, reinvest, diversify."

He looked at the banker, Carlton Frazer. "I do not have to tell any of you here this morning how important it is for a business to progress with the times."

He moved his eyes from Frazer, to Clive Gower, administrator of Stonebridge General, to Sharon Gizer of the County Clerk's Office. "As we prospered, I envisioned us widening our scope. Encompassing new horizons. Taking on greater challenges. But, alas, my partner was of a different mind. Roger Cooper saw us remaining small. His idea for expansion was to charge patients less for treatment."

Adrian held the table's attention. "But I believed Roger Cooper and I could mend our differences. Why should we not be able to arrive at a suitable agreement for Tanglewood's future? After all, together we had nurtured the clinic from infancy."

He paused. "At least, that was my opinion."

Looking at the six board members, he added, "That is, until I heard the bad news."

He lengthened his second pause for dramatic effect, then resumed in a confidential tone, "A man is seldom thanked for digging up hurtful memories from the past. But I must do precisely that because a problem has arisen which has roots in the past.

"I'm speaking about a malpractice suit brought against

Roger Cooper in Santa Barbara, California. By a female patient."

Tapping a buff folder in front of him on the table, he said, "I want to take this moment to draw your attention to our partnership contract. Particularly to paragraph seventeen. Clause three. Which is also referred to as our morals clause."

The chairman, Carlton Frazer, interrupted from the head of the table. "Adrian, we're all familiar with the terms of the contract. Please come to the point."

Adrian said, "I have concluded, Mr. Chairman. That is, except to call in the witness who has verified my worst suspicions about Roger Cooper. I speak about a matter far graver than his unwillingness to go along with expansions. Namely, sexual harassment and abuse of the staff."

There was a stunned pause in the wood-paneled room; the board members exchanged glances.

Carlton Frazer looked bewildered. "These are serious charges, Adrian. You have a witness who confirms them?"

Adrian nodded. "Someone who can speak at first hand of Roger Cooper's professional misconduct."

For the first time in the meeting, Adrian looked directly across the table at Roger.

With all eyes on him, Roger pushed back his chair and said, "I guess this is as good a time as any for me to say my little piece before Adrian brings in the dancing girls."

Rising from his chair, Roger gave a brief account of how he had met Adrian Lyell when he had been working at the Mandrell Clinic, how they had first laid plans for Tanglewood.

"We had very good years together. Not only did we develop a sound recovery ratio but we made a little history. As the board knows, we also made money.

"Over the past five years, I've also pursued the charity scheme that Adrian mentioned. To many it might seem like a Robin Hood situation, taking money from the rich to help the less fortunate. I won't waste your time now explaining how I would like to develop a nonprofit scheme at Tanglewood. I will only say that I would like to see us become more involved in top-quality care that wouldn't be compromised by financial temptation. As we all know, there are profits at Tanglewood. I personally believe that profits are better spent on further rehabilitation than put into condominiums and golf courses that have nothing to do with a medical program."

Roger met Adrian's challenging stare across the table. "So, yes, it is true. Adrian Lyell and I do have opposing views about Tanglewood's future. But I had no idea that Adrian had gone so far in preparing his vision for the future, until a few months ago, when he showed me blueprints for a real estate complex. Nor did I have any idea that he had gone to Los Angeles to raise money for his new vision of the future until Tuesday, when I saw him on a television show. The next day I received his formal offer to buy my half of the clinic. But it was not until yesterday that I got my biggest shock."

Roger paused for his own dramatic effect. "Adrian Lyell had set about to smear me."

The accusation did not appear to surprise Adrian; he shook his head in a confident denial.

Roger looked at Carlton Frazer. "I think I should take this opportunity, Mr. Chairman, to say that the witness whom Adrian is planning to produce this morning is not able to attend our meeting."

To Adrian, he said, "You did invite Delia Pomeroy here to give testimony against me, didn't you?"

Adrian's face went white. He said nothing.

To the table, Roger explained, "Delia Pomeroy is a licensed practical nurse employed at Tanglewood. She gave a written statement to my lawyer this morning and will not be making an appearance at this meeting. The contents of that deposition are available to this board."

"You're bluffing!" Adrian hissed.

Roger replied directly to Carlton Frazer. "Perhaps Adrian

Lyell will see if I'm bluffing when I introduce the person *I* have invited to address this morning's meeting."

He asked, "Do I have the board's permission to invite that person into the room?"

Carlton Frazer looked at the other five members; they nodded their agreement.

Roger moved toward the double doors.

A few moments later he returned with Gene Stone. Stone was unshaven, looking crumpled in last night's clothes.

Adrian leapt from his chair; Ruben grabbed him by the arm, pulling him back down alongside him.

"This is Dr. Gene Stone," said Roger. "Dr. Stone arrived at Tanglewood last Sunday as a private physician to one of our patients. The day before yesterday, Dr. Stone left Tanglewood and met Adrian Lyell in New York."

"It's a lie," Adrian shouted.

William Ruben put his hand on Adrian to quiet him.

Roger asked Gene Stone, "How many times have you met Adrian Lyell?"

Stone dropped his head. "Once."

"When?"

"This week."

"Where?"

"In New York. At a hotel called Mallett's."

Roger asked, "How well do you know me?"

"You were an intern at California Health when I was a resident there," Stone answered.

"Is that our total history?" Roger asked.

Stone stared bitterly at Roger.

Roger persisted, "Our paths never crossed between California Health and now?"

Stone still did not reply.

Carlton Frazer called, "Dr. Stone, if you don't answer the question, we might think you have something to hide."

Stone admitted, "I gave testimony in a malpractice suit against Cooper."

"What happened to that suit?" pursued Roger.

"You know damn well what happened," Stone raged.

"Tell the board," Roger said calmly.

Stone dropped his head. "It was thrown out of court."

"We can't hear you," Roger said. "You're mumbling."

Stone repeated more loudly, "It was thrown out of court. Your name was cleared."

Satisfied, Roger continued. "Perhaps now, Dr. Stone, you can tell the board how you came to meet Adrian Lyell in New York yesterday, and what you discussed at that meeting."

Stone reluctantly proceeded to explain how Adrian had telephoned him at Tanglewood to approach Delia Pomeroy.

Roger breathed more easily as he listened to Gene Stone's confession. Earlier this morning in the Stonebridge motel room, Stone had awakened from his drunken sleep in a rage and had threatened to have Roger arrested for kidnapping, coercion, and taking him illegally across a state line. Roger, in turn, had vowed to bring legal action against Stone for trying to suborn false testimony if he didn't appear at this morning's meeting and tell the true story to the board. In another wing of the Downtowner Motel, Roger's lawyer had been taking a written statement from Delia Pomeroy.

When Stone finished addressing the board, Frazer asked, "Adrian, how do you respond to all this?"

The New York lawyer answered for Adrian. "I have advised my client to remain silent until we have assembled all the facts."

"Mr. Ruben," Frazer said, "Over the past five years you have acted for both Mr. Lyell and Dr. Cooper in Tanglewood's affairs. Such a history could place you in the position of having a conflict of interest if you advise Mr. Lyell individually against Dr. Cooper. Of course, if you don't agree with my view of the matter, we can always refer it to the Bar Association."

Rebuffed, Ruben sank back to his chair.

Again, Frazer asked, "Adrian, do you have anything to state at this moment?"

Adrian's voice was low as he glared across the table at Roger. "You think you've been clever, but you won't get away with this."

He removed a document from his suit pocket and, waving it at Roger, said, "This restraining order might keep me away from Tanglewood. But only temporarily. I'll break it. Believe me, I'll break it."

The statement surprised Roger. What restraining order?

From the far end of the table, Frazer asked, "Roger, do you know about such a document?"

Roger shook his head. "No, sir."

Ignoring the other people at the table, Adrian continued to Roger. "You and she are in this together. I know what's going on. But you won't get away with it."

She! Roger struggled to hold back a grin. The restraining order must be part of Jackie's divorce action against Adrian.

Frazer asked, "Does this restraining order pertain to your personal or professional life, Adrian?"

Adrian fixed a cold, hateful glare on Roger. "I'm beginning to suspect there's little difference."

"Be specific," Frazer insisted. "Does the document arise from a personal or professional area of your life?"

"Personal," answered Adrian. "My wife has filed for divorce."

Frazer nodded. "Then let us proceed with the business at hand."

He addressed the board. "We're here this morning to vote to keep Tanglewood working as the institution that it's licensed to be by the State of Connecticut. It's with surprise that we now must also consider the possibility of criminal charges and the blare of undesirable publicity such actions could involve."

To Roger, he said "I don't think I'm speaking hastily by advising you, Roger Cooper, not to press charges of perjury—if for no other reason than to protect the clinic's good name, which everyone has worked hard to build up over the past five years."

Looking at Adrian, he said, "For such leniency, I would advise Adrian Lyell to sell his shares—at the fair market value—to Roger Cooper, or to any other party acceptable by the board."

Adrian sprang to his feet. "Never! I'll battle Roger Cooper to the bitter end. To the bloody bitter end."

Frazer remarked calmly, "I'm sure that Mr. Ruben and Mr. Brennan—or any other lawyer you may ask, Adrian— will tell you that Roger can press for criminal charges against you, and with the evidence he apparently has from Dr. Stone and the young lady, you could never get a license to operate Tanglewood as any form of enterprise."

Adrian stood alongside the table, staring down at Roger. "Don't get too cozy out there," he threatened. "You haven't heard the last of me."

Turning from the table, he stalked toward the door.

A hush fell over the room as Adrian slammed the door behind him.

Frazer broke the silence. "Now may I call for a vote? Resolved that Adrian Lyell shall sell along the lines I suggested?"

At the conclusion of the voting, Roger stood and received congratulatory handshakes for his victory. Feeling slightly dazed, he forced a smile for each board member. It seemed sad that a very good period of his life had ended with Adrian's attempt to ruin him. Still, he thought with a wry smile, the good guys had won.

88 IT WAS 11:45 A.M. WHEN JACKIE TELE-
PHONED HEAD BOOKKEEPER, RENEE
Newby, in Accounts. The phone was answered on the
fourth buzz.

"Morning, Renee. Jackie here," she said cheerily into the
receiver. "I thought I recognized your car coming down the
drive a few minutes ago."

"I just dashed into the office for a few minutes. To do
some work I didn't get to yesterday." Impatience in her
voice, Renee added, "If you have more questions to ask me
about insurance, Jackie, please save them for next week
. . . or ask somebody else."

"Oh, no, darling," Jackie continued pleasantly. "I'm not
calling to trouble you with questions. It's the matter of Accounts double-paying some employees."

Pause. "Excuse me?"

Jackie proceeded. "I first caught an overpayment on the
electricity bill, Renee. Then when a masseur's wife telephoned me this week, asking what she should do with the
overpayment on her husband's check, I began to do a little
checking. It seems that your office has been overpaying
everyone in physical therapy. I had two more telephone calls
this morning reporting it."

Renee's voice became less testy. "Are you . . . sure?"

"Absolutely," Jackie said with total confidence. "But
you're in a hurry now, Renee. This can keep until Monday.

What does your calendar look like for us to get together and discuss this?"

"W-why . . ." she stammered. "I'll come in and see you first thing Monday morning."

"Good," Jackie said. She was certain there was no fraud involved in the matter, only a rather serious mistake. "Shall we meet at, say, nine o'clock Monday?"

As she put down the receiver, Jackie felt her first moment of triumph. Renee Newby had been ready to dismiss her for being a pest. It was nice, then, to be able to stick to her guns and stand up to a seasoned employee like the head book-keeper.

Jackie was just reaching for the telephone to buzz for her lunch tray when she heard a knock on the door.

"Yes?" she called.

The knocking repeated.

"Come in," Jackie invited.

The door opened; she saw a smiling face peek around the door.

"Roger!" she jumped from her chair and raced across the office. Pulling open the door, she exclaimed, "How did the meeting go? What happened?"

Roger stepped into the room and closed the door behind him. "The board voted for me."

"You did it!" She threw her arms around him. "You did it."

"I didn't do it alone."

"I'm so proud of you," Jackie said happily, kissing his cheek.

"If it hadn't been for your news that Adrian had met Gene Stone in New York, I wouldn't have got to first base."

She pulled back. "Did you find Stone last night?"

"Yep. It took a little arm-twisting to get him to cooperate. But I got everything out of him."

"Clever you."

With more concern, she asked, "What about Adrian?"

"Adrian made his appearance at the meeting. He was very impressive, for a while. Until he got nasty."

"That will be Adrian's ultimate undoing. That bitchy tongue of his."

Roger wrapped his arm around her. "Do we have to talk about all this now? There are more important things to discuss. Such as, how do you feel?"

"Everything has been happening so fast in my life that I only know I've never felt better."

"Honest?"

"Honest. And I'm thrilled and relieved and proud to hear your good news."

Roger glanced at the desk. "How's everything going in here?"

"Fine." She admitted, "Work's so much easier since you gave me some confidence. But stop all this about me. I want to know about you. How do you feel? Don't forget I haven't seen you since you set off for New York last night."

"I'm better now that I've seen you."

"You are so sweet," she murmured.

He kissed her gently on the lips. "Of all that's been happening this past week, the best was finding you. In my own backyard."

She blushed. "That's exactly what I was thinking. About you."

"Oh, wait." He stood back. "I forgot the most important thing."

He brought a hand from behind his back, holding a green piece of clothing. "Remember? I promised to buy you a present when I saw you leaving your exercise class."

"For Christmas!" Jackie laughed, recalling how Roger had stared at her workout clothes and how self-conscious she had felt. They had come a long way since then.

"It's a little early for Christmas," he said, holding out a green T-shirt with a message printed on it.

Jackie held the bottom of the T-shirt and read:

TANGLEWOOD
ADMINISTRATOR.

"Do you accept?" Roger asked.

Grabbing the shirt, she said, "I do . . . I do . . . I do."

Wrapping her in his arms, he said, "I might want you to say that again. In front of a couple of witnesses."

Jackie answered with a kiss; their embrace continued as the telephones began flashing and buzzing on the big desk.

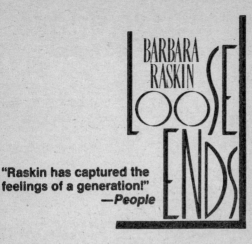

BARBARA
RASKIN
LOOSE
ENDS

"Raskin has captured the
feelings of a generation!"
—*People*

By the author of the million-copy *New York Times* Bestseller *Hot Flashes* BARBARA RASKIN

LOOSE ENDS
_____ 91348-6 $4.95 U.S.   _____ 91349-4 $5.95 Can.

BESTSELLING BOOKS
to Read and Read Again!

HOT FLASHES
Barbara Raskin
_____ 91051-7 $4.95 U.S.   _____ 91052-5 $5.95 Can.

LOOSE ENDS
Barbara Raskin
_____ 91348-6 $4.95 U.S.   _____ 91349-4 $5.95 Can.

BEAUTY
Lewin Joel
_____ 90935-7 $4.50 U.S.   _____ 90936-5 $5.50 Can.

THE FIERCE DISPUTE
Helen Hooven Santmyer
_____ 91028-2 $4.50 U.S.   _____ 91029-0 $5.50 Can.

HERBS AND APPLES
Helen Hooven Santmyer
_____ 90601-3 $4.95 U.S.   _____ 90602-1 $5.95 Can.

AMERICAN EDEN
Marilyn Harris
_____ 91001-0 $4.50 U.S.   _____ 91002-9 $5.50 Can.

JAMES HERRIOT'S DOG STORIES
James Herriot
_____ 90143-7 $4.95 U.S.